18mm
BLUES

GERALD A. BROWNE

18mm
BLUES

WARNER BOOKS

A Time Warner Company

R00233 34842

Warner Books, Inc., 1271 Avenue of the Americas, New York, NY 10020

W A Time Warner Company

Printed in the United States of America
First Printing: March 1993
10 9 8 7 6 5 4 3 2 1

Library of Congress Cataloging-in-Publication Data

Browne, Gerald A.
    18mm blues / Gerald A. Browne.
        p.   cm.
    ISBN 0-446-51661-9
    I. Title. II. Title: 18 millimeter blues.
PS3552.R746A614   1993
813′.54—dc20   92-54098
                                                               CIP

Book design by Giorgetta Bell McRee

For my grandmother, Emma,
who was so generous with her love.

Know you, perchance, how that formless wretch—
The oyster—gems his shallow moonlit chalice?
Where the shell irks him, or the sea-sand frets,
He sheds this lovely lustre on his grief.

—Sir Edwin Arnold

18mm
BLUES

HOW IT BEGAN

Pearling.

The boat wasn't good for much else. It had only a two-foot draft, which enabled it to clear the sharp reaches of most reefs and get into the kind of comfortable lagoons that pearl oysters prefer. On open sea, however, this advantage was more than paid for. Even relatively mild chop could cause the boat to toss around so roughly that Bertin would have all he could do to keep it just about on course.

Besides, Bertin wasn't much of a sailor, disliked being out on spacious water. Three jacks had won him half the boat. Four months ago in a game of seven card upstairs over the Pink Secret, a snack bar and storefront whorehouse on Soi Chia Yot.

The fellow who'd wagered half the boat was someone who most times went by the name of Miller or Millard, although, when necessary, he was good at saying he was someone else. He and Bertin were in the same league, both knock-around foreigners (or *farangers,* as the Thais called them) with no allegiance except to self, the sort who plied all Southeast Asia, turning up wherever

their instincts told them their chances at doing anything to get
more might be better.

Miller, oddly enough, hadn't carried on badly after losing half
his boat. Just shrugged his face, made an ugly mouth at the three
nines that had misled him, and taken it as merely another unfortunate
nick in the way fate was whittling away at him.

Bertin had expected a lot more reaction. He felt deprived. To
him, being able to gloat and poke at the soreness of a loser were
also pleasures of winning. He was small like that, small of heart
while physically large. Well over six feet, thick boned and, in his
prime at thirty-seven, as strong as he looked. His mere presence
seemed to dare anyone to find fault with him. His huge hands
were intimidating, as were his coarse features and askew teeth.
There wasn't a single elegant thing about him. He knew that, but
he'd also learned there was no scarcity of the sort of self-deprecating
women who needed to find that appealing.

Only with the hope of rubbing it in, Bertin had immediately
demanded that Miller show him what he now owned half of. For
all he knew, he said, there might not even be a boat.

Miller had obliged. After hitting Bertin up for a double Mekhong
cane whiskey downstairs at the whorehouse bar, he led the way
out into the neon-tinged Bangkok night. Around the near corner
and up Ruam Chai Street, over the tipped here and sunken there
sections of narrow sidewalk, all the way to the Klong Sen Seb,
where the boat was. Bertin couldn't make it out very well because
of the dark and because there were so many other lesser vessels
around it. Off-duty water taxis, empty vending boats and such tied
up for the night. What he could see of it didn't impress him.
About thirty-five, maybe forty feet long, he estimated, with a hull
painted shiny black, which made more obvious all the many places
where it had been scraped and gashed. It sat too high in the water,
was fat looking and its mast seemed an afterthought, stuck too far
forward, contributing to the impression that it was bow heavy.

It had occurred to Bertin then that he'd put up and could have
lost good money for this ugly, bastard boat—actually for only half
of it—and now that it was an actual boat there before his eyes and
not merely the word *boat*, a sleek and valuable thing the way
Miller had said it when he extended it to the pot, Bertin felt it
unfair that he should have to be disappointed. He had also

realized at that moment that a boat, even one like this, or, especially
one like this, couldn't be half owned. He followed Miller aboard,
stepped over the gunnel, experienced the unsubstantialness of the
vessel beneath him, how it shifted slightly, its hull slippery in the
water, so easily disturbed. Miller lighted a lantern to show the way
into the pilot house and down through a hatch into the cabin,
where the air was so compressed with Miller's personal odors and
the fumes from the boat's engine that it seemed about to combust.
Bertin glanced at the bunk on the left, evidently where Miller
slept. The bare ticking of a punished mattress, a single uncased
pillow, the coil and twist of a sheet of faded batik. The bunk
opposite by less than two feet was burdened with layers of Miller's
personal belongings, including a moldy, rigored high-top shoe
that chose that moment to fall to the gangway, causing a sound
like a single thump on a bass drum.

Miller set about hurriedly to clear his things from the second
bunk, to make equal room, relinquishing a half.

Bertin told him not to bother.

It wasn't a week later that the anonymous body of Miller or
Millard or whoever was found bobbing in the Klong Phadung
among the pilings beneath the place of business of a poultry
merchant. It appeared at first that Miller had drowned, however
closer examination disclosed he'd been stabbed, only once but very
accurately.

Which was how Leon-Charles Bertin became the owner of the
whole boat.

And, in the chain of circumstances, how, on that early March
morning in 1974, he happened to be at the helm of it five miles off
the western coast of Thailand, headed north-northeast.

Bertin had only an approximate idea of where he was. The
creased and faded chart that he looked at every once in a while
wasn't really much help and he didn't know how to use the sextant
that had been among Miller's things. In Penang he'd come close to
asking a fishing boat captain to show him how to determine
position from the sun and stars with the sextant, but he'd already
drunk a couple of hours with the man and had bragged and lied a
lot about experiences and couldn't get himself to admit he didn't
know something like that.

So as he had all the way down the eastern coast of Thailand and

Malaysia and through the Singapore Straits and on up, he was now going by the sight of the shore, keeping the gray-green line of it constant as possible, never out of view. At six knots an hour, which was the full speed of the boat's single-diesel seventy-horse-power engine, along with knowing he'd been under way since five that morning, he was able to place on his mental map of the Thailand Malay Peninsula just about where he was. How far he yet had to go was something he was less certain of. Because he had no definite destination, was bound for merely an area.

The idea of it had first come to him about two months after he'd moved aboard the boat, thrown and given away the worst part of Miller's stuff and stored his own in. For a while the choice got down to either the Sulu Archipelago around Tapul and Tawitawi in the southern Philippines or the French Polynesian Islands, of Tuamotu. He was familiar with the Tuamotus having at one time spent over a year in Papeete, so, naturally, he favored going there, but at the same time he reminded himself of the various reasons why it would be better if he never showed up in those parts again. What's more, getting to the Tuamotus would mean having to be at least a month of days on the open sea, even if he hopped and hugged from land to land all the way to Fiji. He doubted he could handle that.

So, it was going to be Sulu. That was settled in Bertin's plan until one hot night at the Girlie Girlie Bar on that iniquitous Bangkok alley called Soi Cowboy when he got to talking with a pearl dealer, an educated Chinese who wasn't sweating even though he was wearing a fairly heavy suit and a tight knotted tie.

They started on the subject of the possible talents of a particular whore who was phlegmatically offering herself from behind the glass-partitioned part of the establishment. She was number forty-five, according to the tag pinned to her inadequate brassiere. Bertin and the Chinese man agreed she had a lot of Western in her and that it was most likely American black. When number forty-five disappeared to go to work on someone, the conversation between Bertin and the Chinese man stopped and, after a half a drink, started again, hitting lightly upon a couple of topics before getting snagged and staying on pearls.

Bertin enjoyed fibbing that he was a full-time professional pearler, was doing extremely well at it. He had in truth worked for various oyster shell dealers during his time in and around Tahiti. As a cleaner or grader or bagger of those large shells with the most iridescent, highest-grade mother-of-pearl from which cheap souvenirs and crosses and such are shaped. But he'd never been a pearler. Not to say he'd never had a valuable pearl in his hand. It would be impossible for anyone with Bertin's shifty ways to be in Tahiti for any length of time and not come into pearls one way or the other. Bertin also told the Chinese man that he'd been cheated out of the rights to a black pearl bed in Marutea, that otherwise he'd be a millionaire many times over by now.

"One hears all sorts of stories," the Chinese man said, at least not pointedly doubting Bertin.

"I'll soon be off to Sulu," Bertin told him casually.

"So you're a pearler."

"Yes."

"Not many of you left."

"Makes it all the better."

"At one time, years ago, naturals of a fair enough quality came out of Sulu. Mostly creams and not large. On the average only about five millimeters, but well formed as I remember."

"Nothing wrong with some nice creams," Bertin contended.

"Not at all."

"I'll take a hatful any day."

"But white is more desirable now. And pinkish white. Although Latin people, people with swarthy skin, still prefer creams."

"You're not telling me anything I don't already know."

The Chinese man made an apologetic face. "In my business there is a tendency to recite," he explained.

"What I'm getting is you don't think I should try Sulu."

"That's your business, you're the pearler."

"Just out of curiosity, where if not Sulu?"

"Any number of better places from what I hear. How many divers do you have?"

"Three. Polynesians. They're good but not dependable." Bertin mentally commended himself on how truthful he sounded.

"The amas are most dependable if you can get them."

"Amas?"

"Japanese women pearl divers."

Bertin nodded, as though he'd misunderstood. "I've been meaning to give them a try."

They talked on. For several drinks. By the time the Chinese man went around the bar to the whorehouse part to choose number forty-five, Bertin had profited much more from him. Sulu was out as the place where he'd pearl and the west coast of Thailand up as close as possible to Burmese waters was settled on. Also, Bertin got the name and number of a man in Phetchaburi who would most likely be able to arrange for some Japanese women divers, as long as the deal that was offered was fair.

Bertin made sure the compensation he promised the amas was generous. Fifty dollars a day each or a third of the worth of whatever pearls were found, whichever was more. Nothing in advance, pay when the diving was over. They were to meet him in Ban Pakbara.

For a while yesterday he'd thought they weren't going to show up or were lost. He waited at the boat all day and was beginning to speculate on how he might arrange for other divers when, around dusk, they arrived. The two women, and the boy. Carrying black canvas suitcases. No mention had been made about there being a boy and no explanation was offered. He was an obvious Amerasian, nine or ten years old, his bright blue eyes incongruous with his heavy black Japanese hair. For some reason Bertin had expected the amas would be younger, probably energetic girls in their late teens, however these were adult women. At least in their midtwenties or more was Bertin's guess. They were physical opposites. One taller, about five foot nine and slimmer and not very strong looking. The stockier, thicker-chested one, Bertin believed, would be doing the deeper, more strenuous diving.

Bertin had decided in advance that the forward part of the boat would be theirs. He didn't want them wandering around, coming into the wheelhouse and going down into the cabin, getting into his things. He'd made those terms clear right off and they'd politely accepted, had spent the night on the foredeck, and now that the boat was under way, they were still there. He couldn't see them from the wheelhouse because the superstructure of the cabin was in the way, so it was like he was alone out there on the boat. He wished there were someone to talk to, someone with a few things in common to trade lies with, only to pass the time. Not these Japs. He'd had no use for what few Japs he'd ever had anything to do with, the way they never said much and acted superior. It was as though they always knew what was coming next and had the ability to see into him all the way to his bones.

Bertin looped a line over the wheel to keep it steady on course. Went down into the cabin and gathered up his dirty laundry, adding to it the very soiled shirt and trousers he had on. Took them up to the stern, tied the bunch of them with a light nylon line and tossed them overboard. Fed out enough line so his laundry was dragging about fifty feet behind, skipping and skimming the water and being pulled through the peaks of waves. He reminded himself not to leave it out there too long. The last time after only twenty minutes all he'd got back was shreds.

He took notice of the distant southern horizon. Big explosive-looking clumps of clouds, gray as lead. That was no squall, he thought, but a really angry storm. He went into the wheelhouse and checked the barometer. Saw it was normal, holding steady. That far-off storm would stay far off, he told himself. It was probably on an east-to-west course across the Andaman, would miss him by miles. Still, he'd keep his eyes on it.

He glanced eastward and was reassured that the shoreline was still the same.

A sharp repetitious sound finally succeeded in making him aware that an inner shroud was loose and whipping against the mast, and when he looked up to it he saw also that one of the ties on the boom had ripped apart. He'd avoided considering the condition of the boat, but it was reminding him. No telling what was happening to the teak hull beneath the waterline. Worms had gotten to it in places, no doubt. He'd heard it said more than once that wooden-hulled boats had a lot of worm troubles in tropical waters such as these. Then there was the sail. He'd never had it up because he wouldn't know how to handle it, hadn't even hoisted it to air it or dry it out. Folded and lashed so tight to the boom, by now it was probably rotted. As for the engine, he was entirely dependent on it. That bothered him. Every time it coughed or one of its cylinders missed or it decided to change its sound the way boat engines seem to do arbitrarily, he got more worried.

He stood at the stern, reached down and found himself by way of the loose leg of his undershorts. Urinated into the wake. Two weeks ago he'd passed a couple of kidney stones that felt like shards of glass all the way out. He thought there had to be more of the same up in him, so ever since, every time he urinated, he expected such pain. But there wasn't any now. Only relief. He pulled in the line and his laundry, didn't spread it out, just tossed it in a bunch on the aft deck to dry.

The day was going. Bertin headed the boat for shore and put in at the first port he came to, which happened to be Khok Kloi. Finding the place on the chart gave him a fix on where he was. He refueled that night and got under way again the next dawn.

North along the coast until, in keeping with the chart, a group of islands came into sight. Various size islands. Some miles large but most were much smaller, no more than five hundred feet around. Craggy steep humps covered by the cling of tropical growths. No wash up or beaches around them. They looked as though the sea had thrust them upward, and perhaps at one time ages ago it had. The chart gave some of the larger ones names: Ko Phra Thong, Go Ra, Khao Pram. Bertin bypassed those because they were inhabited and the waters around them were probably already overworked. He'd have better luck in places more remote, he believed. Soon he came to a cluster of small islands occupied only by gulls. He ran between them, chose what looked to be a promising channel. Cut the engine and threw out the drogue, the conical-shaped device that more efficiently than the anchor would minimize the boat's drift.

He was excited.

About actually to become a pearler. Enormous wealth awaited on the floors of these waters and he intended to get a share of it, his share, plenty.

No need to tell the amas it was here that he wanted them to dive. They were already preparing. The taller, slender one named Setsu leaned over the side, peered down into the water, appraising its current, searching for anywhere the sun might be penetrating enough to reveal the bottom. She knew from experience that often such innocent-looking channels such as this turned out to be deep troughs. But the water there told her nothing. She gave up on it, stepped back, and with a total lack of self-consciousness removed her clothes. Folded them neatly, placed them just so next to her canvas bag. She contained her hair within the stretch of a white rubber swim cap and put on a pair of diving goggles, situating them, for the time being, on her forehead. Next a soft, woven cotton belt with a loop located at the hip to accommodate a twelve-inch flat steel bar with a bent tip, much like an ordinary pry bar but sharply pointed. The end of a hundred-foot length of cotton line was attached to her belt in back by Michiko, the other ama. She was Setsu's sister, at twenty-four younger by two years. She would remain on board to tend the lines and to teach the boy more about how that should be done.

Setsu dropped over the side into the water.

Michiko tossed her a woven hemp basket, then threw in the descending weight, keeping it well within Setsu's reach. The ten-pound weight was made of cast iron, shaped like an inverted mushroom, had an eye on its stem for a line to be tied to it.

Setsu lowered her goggles into position. Placed her feet on the flanges of the weight and began her breathing. Took a rapid series of deep-as-possible breaths that she blew out with such force they were whistles. Her nod signaled Michiko to play out the lifeline and, at a rate exactly fast enough, the weight line. Time of descent would cost breath.

Setsu rode the weight all the way down, felt, as usual, the temperature of the water become increasingly cooler. At bottom she estimated the depth was seven fathoms, slightly more than forty feet. Reflection had prevented her from seeing this far down, but now visibility was good, the bottom struck with adequate sunlight. She glanced up at the black underside of the boat, thought it ominous. Gave the weight line a signaling tug and swam from it.

It was second nature for her to be in an underwater realm such as this. She wasn't at all intimidated, swam about easily, using little effort, relying mainly on the propelling motions of her legs and feet. Quite a few amas had taken to wearing flippers and some had even resorted to using scuba gear. She'd tried both, and, although such assistance gave her more speed and allowed her to cover more area, it was wrong, reduced her freedom, spoiled it for her. She preferred not to be fettered, to rely purely on the specialness of her own given ama strengths and abilities.

She quickly surveyed the sea floor all around. Saw that this channel was divided into three sections: an abundance of mustard-colored sunward-reaching ropes of weed on the left and the same on the right. Between, a cleared swath thirty to forty feet wide ran down the channel. The bottom of that swath consisted of no pebbles that she could see and very little sand. It was mainly pale, bared granite, resembled an unpaved road of humps and dips, the sort formed only by much use.

She guessed the reason.

Swam from the edge of the swath toward the middle of it and there allowed herself completely to relax. At once, the current claimed her and began carrying her, supporting her. Face up as she was, deep away from the world and so comfortable, for an instant some part of her suggested she go along with it for as long as it would take her to be breathing water.

The current was deceitful, hidden from the surface. Its force had swept and created the swath. Its flow was too violent for there to be any oysters, she thought. With several strong kicks and a maneuvering twist she defeated the current and paused at the lesser agitated edge of it close to the seaweed.

She'd been under only about a minute, still had breath. But not enough for what she had in mind. She sighted upward for the hull of the boat, found it, swam diagonally up to it. Surfaced, for more deep, whistling breaths while Michiko again threw her the weight, and the boy threw her a smile with some relief in it and she took that with her as she rode the weight again the forty or so feet to the bottom.

The place to look, she thought, was along the sides among the kelp. She swam into the kelp, felt the familiar, friendly brush of its slick foliage. Saw the sinuous dancing of its shoots. There hadn't been a sign of a fish before but now here they were. Some brilliant yellow show-offs, a school of blue-brown others, more modest.

The bottom here was right, composed of sand, with bits of shell and fragments of coral in it. Her practiced eyes scanned the bottom and caught upon the proper sort of protrusion. An oyster with only the rounded, scalloped edges of its paired upper and lower shells exposed, the rest of it buried in the soft sand. The oyster was open about an inch, trying to feed and at the same time remain mostly hidden from predators such as starfish, octopi, skates and snails. Careful not to have the oyster snap shut on her fingers (how early she'd learned the pain of such a pinch), Setsu

dug close around it with both hands and removed it from its
refuge. It was, indeed, a pearl oyster, the sort pearlers call a silver
lip, and scientists call *Pinctada margaritifera*. It was about eight
inches in diameter with a rough brown exterior comprised of
numerous radial ridges that showed a hint of white and a few pale
yellow spots. A prize that might contain a prize. Setsu deposited it
into her woven hemp basket.

She knew, according to the gregarious nature of oysters, where
there was one there'd most surely be others. Perhaps she'd come
upon a plentiful family also pretending to be asleep in their bed.
She swam around among the gray coral and sponges and masses
of weeds, found four more silver lips before surfacing again.

The moment Bertin saw those five oysters come up in Setsu's
basket he just did manage to hold back shouting for joy. He took
them to the stern and transferred them to a large tub, one of two
he had placed there to receive the abundant catch he anticipated.
At once he set about to open one of the oysters. Using an old
Burmese knife designed especially for that purpose that had been
among Miller's things, the sort of knife Burmans call a *dah-she*. Its
long, somewhat curved blade was honed extremely sharp and
attached, as though grafted, to a whalebone handle carved crudely
with the saying *Buddha is generous*.

Bertin placed the oyster with its hinging part up on a wooden
block. He forced the blade of the knife through the elastic ligament
with which it held itself and its tough adductor muscle, causing it
abruptly to surrender its determination to remain shut. The oyster
sprang open.

Bertin immediately saw the pearl.

Plucked it out.

It was only about five millimeters in size, Bertin estimated, no
larger than a baby pea. But a nice creamy pink and perfectly
round. He held it up between his fingers to give its luster the
benefit of the afternoon sun. Had it been double its size it would
have been worth easily ten thousand dollars, perhaps twenty,
wholesale. He was encouraged. Felt all around the squishy insides
of that first oyster on the chance that it might contain another
pearl. It didn't. He tossed it overboard and eagerly opened one of
the others.

It had a twice larger pearl in it.

But badly misshapen, an asymmetrical lump. It was the sort that for the sake of selling was made to sound more desirable by calling it *baroque*. This one was even lamentable in that category, had many welts and pits and inconsistent luster. Why, Bertin thought, would an oyster with the wherewithal to produce a pearl of beauty create one as unsightly as this. Oh well, it would be worth something. He kept the *baroque*, placing it along with the first small perfect pearl in the nearby black lacquer bowl that he intended to fill.

Meanwhile, Setsu was diving, thoroughly searching the most likely sandy areas of the bottom. Over that afternoon she made thirty dives, stopping only once for a quarter-hour rest. She felt early on that this wouldn't be a really good place, however she gave it every possible opportunity to prove her wrong. Altogether she came up with only thirty-seven oysters. On her final dive she swam closer to the underwater wall of the nearest little island and found three awabi (abalone). These single-shelled creatures had clamped themselves steadfast to a rock. She pried them loose with the iron bar and put them in the basket. They were quite large, would do nicely for supper.

Surfacing with the awabi she handed the basket up to the boy.

Bertin rushed down the side deck and yanked the basket roughly from the boy. Probed for pearls in the exposed flesh of each of the awabi. None. By then Setsu had climbed aboard, and, as Bertin was about to discard the awabi into the sea, her hands took firm hold of the basket while her huge dark eyes took hard hold of Bertin's eyes. After a long moment he relinquished the basket and returned to the stern.

The black lacquered bowl contained the reason for Bertin's irritation. Only six pearls, including the *baroque*, and the baby pea-size one was the best of the meager lot. The other four were of better size but marred with pocks and pimplelike protrusions. Certainly a far cry from the fortune he'd anticipated. At this rate he wouldn't make enough to offset the cost of fuel. He busied away that thought by pulling in the drogue, starting the engine and moving the boat up and out of the channel to the protective leeward side of an island. Got close up as possible, dropped anchor.

He sat in a folding chair on the aft deck, drinking red wine from a tin cup, gnawing at a hunk of hard strong cheese and longing for some proper bread. The wine wasn't a good burgundy so the tinny taste from the cup didn't matter all that much. And the cheese, he wasn't even supposed to be eating cheese. A doctor had told him cheese would cause his kidneys to make stones. Hell, his stones were probably as good as those, he thought, glancing at the contents of the black lacquered bowl. Perversely, a lighter mood suddenly poured into him and he almost laughed aloud at where he was and what he was hoping for.

On the foredeck Setsu was being tended to by Michiko and the boy. Michiko had poured two pails of fresh water over Setsu to rinse the saltwater residue from her. Then, before the air could dry her, Setsu lay on the deck while apricot oil was massaged into her skin, the molecules of the oil taking the moisture of the water with it as it penetrated. Special, longer attention was paid her legs and feet, for they had done most of the diving work. Michiko tended to the left and, simultaneously, the boy to the right. The boy had become good at this and enjoyed doing it and there was just as much care and love in his hands as there were in those of Michiko, who let him continue on Setsu's ankles and insteps and toes while she prepared the raw supper. She washed the awabi more thoroughly before slicing them because Bertin's fingers had been into them.

By the time supper was over the long twilight was waning. Setsu sat with her back against the cabin trunk, Michiko, beside her, had eyeglasses on and was writing postcards that she'd picked up in an everything store in Ban Pakbara. The boy was restless, getting up and down, wandering the foredeck but minding Setsu by keeping to it. He had her patience, she thought, and that caused her to catch upon an instance when she'd been about his age and showing her patience, as for perhaps the hundredth time she listened to her grandmother Hideko Yoshida recite family history and pridefully tell of her great-grandmother Amira's exploits as an ama.

For twenty generations or more, as far back as could be remembered of anyone being told by anyone, the women of the Yoshida family had been amas. An honorable profession, romantic in the way it demanded female courage. How mystical and practical the gathering up of the offerings of the great mother sea!

Originally the family had lived on the island of Tsushima out in the Korean Straits. In the early 1800s all the Yoshidas, including even most distant cousins, migrated to the village of Wajima in Noto prefecture. There were many amas living in Wajima, an entire society of amas, so the Yoshidas felt comfortably in place and before long had earned a respected standing.

It was customary for most of the amas of Wajima to spend the diving season (from late spring to early fall) working the more generous waters out around the island of Hegurajima, thirty miles from the mainland. In the eyes of the Yoshida amas of that time no place could have been more beautiful, and eventually they'd grown so attached to it that throughout each off-season their spirits longed for Hegurajima. They heeded the longing, gave in to it, moved one and all out to that island and settled on its northernmost tip close by the lighthouse. From then on Hegurajima was where they thought of as truly home.

And it was where, shortly before the turn of the century, the West discovered these Japanese women who dove. It was thought and expressed then how contrary they were to Victorian convention. So actively brave and, scantily clad in revealing wet white (if at all), they plunged into the sea time and time again in search of pearls. Incredible how deep they went and how long they remained under. They were able to better stand the coldness of the water because of something special about their female bodies, it was said. By all means worthy of curiosity, an attraction one would never regret going that far out of one's way to see: the amas of Hegurajima.

That was during the time of great-grandmother Amira, whom Setsu had always been told about so much. Very early on it got so Setsu would enjoy reciting aloud to herself practically word for word those stories about the great ama, the great-grandmother, Amira Yoshida.

For example, the account of how Amira had taken part in the 1905 pearl fishing season of Ceylon. Never had there been another to equal it. Forty thousand persons from almost every direction assembled on what had only a week before been a desolate stretch of beach on the Gulf of Manaar. All sorts. Picture them. Delicate-featured Singhalese, muscular Moormen, thick-limbed Kandyans, Weddahs, Chinese, Jews, Dutchmen, half-castes and outcasts. There were boat repairers, mechanics, provision dealers, cooks, clerks, coolies, servants, priests and pawnbrokers. Even jugglers, acrobats, fakirs, gamblers, beggars and, of course, many women on hand to sell themselves. Such a babble of languages! What a confusion of activity! Everyone intent on what might be gained from the pearls that ironically were mere irritations to the oysters that contained them.

Five thousand divers! Imagine such a number, five thousand. Most were Ceylonese Moorman and Lubais from Kilakari, also many Tamils from Tuticorin, Malayans, Arabs, Burmans. Not many Japanese and only a few amas, however those few were by far the best divers and the most industrious. On days when the seas were considered by others to be too rough to dive safely, the amas, Amira among them, defied the undertows and worked the bottom as usual.

The boat from which Amira dove was an oversize dhow that had come there from Bahrain. It was painted bright orange except for its figurehead, a crudely carved interpretation of a serpent, that for some reason was painted blue. The boat had one large square sail of hand-woven cloth and riggings made of twisted date fiber. The captain or master or *sammatti,* as he was called, was a bearded and dishonest Persian, who had an uncanny talent for picking out which of the oysters brought aboard by the divers contained the choicest pearls. Defying anyone to object, either the divers, line tenders, the boiler or the pilot, he would open those certain oysters, remove their pearls and store them in his jaws. No matter that it was prohibited, that every oyster was supposed to be contributed unopened to an aggregate that would at the end of each day be divided among all. Great-grandmother Amira would glare at this Persian, silently but explicitly, to convey her mind. Despite numerous opportunities not once did she ever secret a pearl anywhere upon or within her body.

The usual depth she was required to dive was ten fathoms (about sixty feet), which was no strain on her, as she had been down twice as deep. During each dive she gathered as few as fifteen or as many as fifty oysters.

By midafternoon when the boat headed for shore it was often bringing in twenty thousand.

Those were divided daily, unopened, with the divers of each boat receiving a one-third share, of which a third went to their rope tenders. The question then for Amira was whether she should open her oysters and have her compensation be the value of whatever pearls, if any, they might contain. Or to sell her unopened oysters on the spot to one of the many pearl merchants. Amira seldom gave it a second thought and when she did she only had to picture herself sitting forlornly amidst a pile of empty shells.

She sold to a shrewd Indian, a Chettie from Madura, who dressed quite fashionably in semi-European attire, carried a walking stick and wore patent leather boots, which, as the days passed, were being abraded and dulled by the beach sand. To ensure that she continued to sell her unopened oysters to him, he always forlornly reported that those he'd bought from her the day before had been entirely without pearls—or had contained only a few nearly worthless seeds. Amira knew, of course, that he was exaggerating, to put it politely, and she would have preferred it if he'd admitted that they were accommodating each other.

By decree of the Ceylonese government, the season of 1905 ran from February twentieth to April twenty-first. Sixty days were scheduled but only forty-seven were worked because of holy days and storms. The total number of oysters taken was 81,580,716. (It was estimated that 20,000,000 more were illicitly opened.) The catch yielded pearls that brought at local worth 5,021,453 rupees ($2,000,000). In 1905 money it was an enormous amount.

Right after that Ceylon season Amira returned home to Hegurajima. The sum she brought with her was not a fortune but far more than any Yoshida ama had ever earned. With it she paid to have a small but sufficient house built for her sister and to have rooms added to three other of the Yoshida houses situated closely together there on the point near Hegurajima light.

Although great-grandmother Amira died many years before Setsu was born, from this manner of hearing history and elaborating with imagination, Setsu felt she knew Amira well. In fact, one of those rooms that Amira had added on eventually became Setsu's bedroom, so Setsu thought of Amira as a benefactor as well as an ama that she should live up to.

There was never any doubt that Setsu would be an ama. She believed, as did others, that she'd had the secrets of the profession passed on to her while still in the womb. Hadn't her mother continued to dive for months after Setsu had begun kicking and rolling within her? Hadn't Setsu been born early, in a *hiba*, one of those meager stone houses along the Japanese coast meant to be where an ama might take temporary refuge?

Even before Setsu was old enough for deep water she would go out in the boat and help while Harimi, her mother, dove. The boat was a wide, high, fat-bellied rowboat, and Setsu enjoyed the dry thumping sounds it made whenever she or her father moved about in it or something struck its sides. Father would often have her tend the line that was attached to mother's waist, and she'd feel the tugs and tensions of it as mother, like a large fish, moved along the bottom ten or so fathoms below. (It occurred to Setsu years later how umbilicallike it was, but with the dependency reversed.)

At age twelve she officially became an apprentice ama. Required to practice diving by retrieving speckled pebbles in the shallows. Forbidden to go out to the sea. It was boring for her. She was already too advanced an underwater swimmer, knew how to hyperventilate before going under and how to preserve the oxygen she took down with her by relaxing and never expending unnecessary effort.

She was tall for her age, taller by a head and thinner than any of the other apprentice amas. Such a long, slender neck that her contemporaries called her *jotu*, crane. She was self-conscious of her slimness until Harimi told her it was something that had been held back two generations for her, that great-grandmother Amira had been similarly constructed.

It indeed did seem that her slenderness made her a better swimmer, allowed her to slice through the water with more speed and surely more grace.

She became a full-fledged ama at age fourteen. Began accompanying mother down the steeps of deep water, sharing those special regions with her. They swam along the bottom nearly within reach of each other, pointing things out, signaling. Mother would indicate an abalone and swim on, leaving it for Setsu to pry at its cling and take up to the boat to father. Pleasing father, allowing him to brag at night in the tavern about how many Setsu had brought up.

Pearls.

When Setsu was seventeen she found an oyster that had done its best to hide from her in an inconspicuous underwater crevice. The pearl in it was like its soul, she thought, a lustrous twelve millimeters round. She was reluctant to sell it, kept it for a while wrapped in a square of silk in a tiny white lacquered box. She thought possibly it was the part of her spirit that was great-grandmother Amira that convinced her to let it go to a dealer in Kanazawa. She put the money away.

By then, as expected, sister Michiko had also become an ama. And sister Yukie, the youngest, had begun apprenticing. Michiko was never a consistently good diver. One day she'd dive acceptably, the next she'd use any excuse to get out of having to go down. She confided to Setsu that when she was only thirty feet under she felt as though she were being crushed, and at sixty feet she often was overcome with panic. Yukie apparently would be even less of an ama because she really didn't want to be one, was merely tolerating the path of tradition.

Father died.

And Hegurajima was not the same. The presence of his absence was everywhere. His ashes were kept in a porcelain jar within a blue brocaded silk box. Placed on a widened window ledge from which the sea could be seen. One afternoon at dusk, mother took the urn out a hundred yards from shore. Removed its lid rather ceremoniously. Scattered the ashes. They were momentarily a gray, unwilling wisp on the surface, then the vigor of the sea took them.

That didn't help enough. A few weeks later mother decided on more drastic action: they'd move. All the way across the southern midsection of Japan to the prefecture of Mie. A hamlet there called Wago was almost entirely inhabited by amas.

As soon as they were halfway settled in a small rented house nearly sides against sides with two other similar Wago houses, they began diving. Not from a boat as they were accustomed, but from the shore. It wasn't a lenient, sandy shore. There were jagged rocks all the way to the waterline, even when the tide was out, and the surf was intent on pounding belligerently against them. Setsu tried to locate a spot where the suck and pull was not so strong, where she and Harimi and Michiko could safely enter the water. Finally, an ama who was familiar with those shores showed Setsu a nearly concealed narrow inlet, little more than a slot really but protected so it offered easy enough access.

Numerous amas were working these waters, and although in a sense they were competitive, they weren't territorial. The mother sea and its offerings, according to ama code, were there for them all.

Some days, but only some, Yukie also dove. Long before then she'd completed her apprenticeship and was a capable diver. Unlike Michiko, being underwater didn't disturb Yukie, except that it wasn't where she ever wanted to be. Harimi didn't take her to task for having such an attitude, didn't call her lazy or any of that. Neither did Setsu. Setsu felt that this phase of Yukie's would eventually be dispelled by the ama spirit that, surely as her heart, was in her. For the time being, however, while they dove Yukie would usually watch from the perch of a rock high enough so not even her feet could get wet.

Harimi was diving differently. Setsu noticed. For one thing Harimi wasn't resting frequently enough. Nor was she coming up from being deep slow enough to compensate for the changes in pressure. Several times after she'd surfaced Setsu saw trickles of blood from Harimi's nostrils. Worst of all Harimi was taking greater chances, swimming down into treacherous places that in the past she'd have avoided, such as chasms created by piles of boulders that very well might at that moment choose to be disturbed, cave in and bury her.

It got so that when they were diving, Setsu had to be so mindful of Harimi she was unable to give adequate attention to what she herself was doing. She had a long talk with Harimi, during which, without being disrespectful, she more than merely mentioned Harimi's foolhardy behavior.

Harimi didn't deny it. With caring eyes into caring eyes, Setsu suggested that Harimi stop diving, at least for a while. Not a word of resistance from Harimi. She admitted that her self-endangering ways had been deliberate. She promised to stay out of the water. Anyway, she said, diving was no longer as gratifying for her as it had been, probably never would be again.

So, then it was up to Setsu and Michiko to earn the money that was needed. Each day they sold their catch to the men who waited onshore, wholesalers who in turn sold to other wholesalers at the seafood market in Nagoya. Setsu learned early that it didn't pay to bargain too hard with the dealers. Whenever she had, they'd left her standing there with her catch and no one to sell it to except a local dealer, who, aware of the circumstances, paid her even less.

September came to Wago, and quite suddenly the sea turned cold. The diving season was over. For something to do many of the amas went to work at the tuna cannery in Suzaka.

During the third week of that month an unpredicted typhoon blew up from the East China Sea. The cultured pearl farms located in Ago Bay were especially hard hit. Many of their wooden slatted rafts out in the bay were demolished or extensively damaged. The underwater netting attached to those rafts was ripped every which way, and from the pocketlike containers of those nets hundreds of thousands of pearl oysters were strewn over the bottom of the bay—oysters that had been implanted with nuclei and were well along in the lengthy process of developing pearls.

The pearl farmers were distraught, stood to lose everything. They knew all too well that oysters were temperamental creatures. Oysters disliked being disturbed and might demonstrate that by dying. Their only recourse was to retrieve as many as they could as gently as possible.

Everything would depend on the amas of Wago.

The pearl farmers struck a liberal deal with them: so much for each live oyster each diver retrieved, nothing for the dead ones. It would be costly, but such incentive was needed—the water was cold and getting colder by the day.

The amas went to work.

For warmth most of them waited until the sun was well up before beginning. A few, including Setsu, Michiko and Yukie, started at first light. Skimmed along the bottom filling their baskets, oyster after oyster increasing their earnings. Fortunately the bay wasn't very deep, at the most about seven fathoms in some areas, on the average about four, so Setsu, Michiko and Yukie were each able to make ten or twelve consecutive dives before having to climb up onto one of the rafts and sit within a blanket until their skin regained color and their teeth stopped chattering. To chase their shivers they drank hot sake from a thermos and swigged cups of plum brandy.

Yukie was being extremely helpful, not a peep of complaint

from her. She worked as arduously as either Setsu or Michiko, matched them dive for dive. Setsu was proud of her, told her so.

They dove for five days straight and would have kept on if it hadn't been for a dispute among the pearl farmers. The oysters all looked alike. They were all of the species *Pinctada martensii* or, as they were called, *akoyas*. Not large, only about four inches in diameter. How then could the pearl farmers determine which oysters and how many belonged to whom? Three days bickering before equitable portions were settled upon.

Setsu, Michiko and Yukie returned to work. The water seemed much colder. No matter, they dove determinedly. Twenty out of every hundred oysters they retrieved were dead, adding to the increasing dead piles located at various points along the shore. Ago was an irregular bay with a great many coves and islands and small inlets. When Setsu, Michiko and Yukie had gleaned one place they moved to the next. After twenty-three days, well into October, the bottom of Ago had been mostly picked clean and the rafts and holding nets repaired and all the surviving oysters placed back into their peaceful pockets.

The Yoshida amas celebrated their windfall by taking the train to Nagoya for a day of shopping. New shoes, some tortoise-looking barrettes and some ribbons for their hair. Setsu bought Harimi a new dress mostly made of silk, a green dress of such a lively shade and pattern that Harimi had to be persuaded into it. They had a noon meal at a modest restaurant off Sukara-dori, then went to the Tokugawa Museum of Art, where they marveled at all forty-three parts of the Genji-monogatariemaki scroll by Fujiwara Tahayoshi.

The following spring.

Harimi stopped blaming Hegurajima and began expressing her longing for it. She decided to return there, but only for a visit, with her brother and his wife, she said, a short stay.

Setsu knew better.

No sooner was Harimi gone than Yukie left for Tokyo. No amount of reasoning from Setsu could talk her out of it. She was meant to be a city girl, she contended, could take care of herself. For a start she had nearly enough money from her Ago Bay earnings.

Setsu realized then why Yukie had dived so earnestly at Ago.

She knew approximately how much money Yukie had and how swiftly and dispassionately Tokyo would eat it up. It was painful for her to imagine Yukie at the mercy of Tokyo. At the train station along with her good-bye Setsu stuffed into Yukie's purse what remained from her own Ago earnings and, as well, some from her pearl savings. Instead of crying when the train pulled out she bit on the knuckle of her thumb.

That same spring was the one of William.

William from San Francisco.

He occurred the day Setsu was diving alone from the rocks a few miles from Toba. Observing her from an impersonal distance. By now Setsu was used to such watching by foreign tourists. Normally after ten minutes, when they hadn't seen as much as they expected (perhaps a flash of bare breast or bottom every so often but all else happening underwater out of sight), they went away.

Not he. An hour from the time when she'd first noticed him he was still there. Wasn't that in a way a tribute? she thought.

She'd taken three catches ashore to transfer them to her larger basket and still he kept his distance. So, on the fourth time it was somewhat forgivable that he came closer. Not intrusively close but close enough for his raised voice to be heard by her.

"I would like to take photographs of you," were his first words. He had two serious cameras slung around his neck. "I'm a professional photographer. I want to photograph you."

Setsu returned to the water but she didn't stay in as long as before. Brought back only a single small awabi for her main basket.

He'd come closer so there was no need for him to shout and, keeping his eyes fixed on her face, not once scanning her nudity, he told her his name and what he was and verified by presenting her a card.

"I'll pay to photograph you," he told her.

"Why?"

"Because you're beautiful."

Setsu concealed that she was flattered. "How much will you pay?"

He told her.

She thought it too much, more than she'd earn over three weeks of diving. She kept that to herself, consented with one stoic nod.

It wasn't until near the end of the second roll of film that he asked her to smile, just the trace of a smile, calm, gentle. It went well with the fragility of her face, didn't disturb the composure of her cheeks and eyes.

She was naturally graceful, her wrists and hands never without tone. Perhaps that was due to all the stretch and length that had been required of her body underwater. He said, this William, that it was impossible to take a bad picture of her.

She was surprised how susceptible she was to compliments.

The whirr-cluck after whirr-cluck of the shutters. The intervals as he dug into his jacket pockets for more film to reload. Those were opportunities for her discreetly to study him, to see how tall he was and to like his brown hair and intensely blue eyes. She decided he had a kind American face and very competent fingers. She wasn't sure of how she felt about the chest hair that showed at the V of his unbuttoned shirt.

They were by then calling each other by name, occasionally sharing laughter, relating and responding as two people usually do when caught up in a mutual endeavor. And when, after two, nearly three hours, the photographing was done and Setsu dressed and took up her baskets and she and this William American walked together in the direction of Toba, they both felt regret that it was over.

And so it wasn't.

He had rented a car. Drove her to her house in Wago. She dropped off her baskets of catch and went on with him to where he was staying: a *ryokan*-type hotel called the Toba Seaside.

He never once hurried her, and that was good.

She never once pretended coyness, and that was good.

He didn't believe in the original sin and in her Shinto beliefs there hadn't ever been one.

She felt for the first time in her life that she was as beautiful as she truly was. He caused her to feel it all the more with his considerate lovemaking.

She stayed the night, and in the morning slept beyond his quiet departure. On the floor next to the sleeping mat she found a slip of hotel notepaper bearing in his neat printing his full name and his San Francisco address and telephone number along with the words *please write or call.*

During the next few weeks Setsu looked at that slip of paper numerous times. It helped her see William again. However, she did not look at it so much after she'd missed her period and was told she was pregnant. She folded it three times and carried it in her pocket with other things awhile. It became so soiled and frayed that ultimately she discarded it.

She legally named the child Ayako after her maternal great-grandfather. The boy was now eight years and eight months old, and there he was, barefoot, bareheaded, nothing on but a pair of white cotton twill shorts hanging from the studs of his hipbones, his innocent skin deeply sunned, so the whites of his Asian-shaped eyes appeared all the more white. There he was, evidently feeling confined by this boat but not being a trouble, standing opposite her in the prow, unaware that he was being lovingly studied, preoccupied with wondering the sky as the night was beginning to bring out stars.

His middle name, out of respect, was William, and she preferred to call him that, or *Chi'sa sakana* (little fish), her pet name for him because he was such an excellent swimmer.

Setsu both loved and liked him. Never in her eyes was he regretted, never a mistake but a blessing. And he was devoted to her. She had kept him close, with her wherever, and whether or not that was good for his psychology it kept him out of range of the ridicule most part-East part-West children are subjected to.

Night now.

Michiko rolled out the three sleeping mats, placed them, as usual, side by side on the deck. The three lay upon them within touch of one another but not yet touching. Setsu allowed her warm friend tiredness to overcome her. Her last thoughts before sleep were a premonition and a promise: despite today's lack of success this pearling trip was going to be very profitable. And when it was over they would go home to Hegurajima and to Harimi there, who now enjoyed diving only every so often for memories.

THE NEXT MORNING

As soon as there was definition to go by, Bertin got the boat under way. In and out between the islands for a half hour before shutting down and throwing out the drogue. There was no special reason for stopping there off the tip of that island. Bertin merely had a hunch that was where they should try the bottom.

He was wrong. Although he didn't give Michiko, who would be diving today, much chance to explore the area. When she went down twice and came up with nothing, Bertin started the engine and signaled her to come aboard.

All day it went like that. Bertin didn't give any one place enough time, impatiently hopped around, from here to there, listening to his hunches, and no doubt that was the reason why, as the sun was going, all they had to show for the effort were three small pearls of a quality worth no more than a drink at some bar.

Bertin again anchored the boat leeward of one of the islands and well into the night sat on the aft deck gulping from a bottle of cheap brandy. Cursing everything, the entire situation all the way back to Miller and his *fucking three nines*. Should have listened to people he'd met who'd once been involved in pearling, Bertin thought. Evident now that they were right about all the pearl oyster beds having been picked clean and all the places where pearl oysters had been so abundant being now polluted. All this effort was just another of his asshole tries for the big money, Bertin told himself—constantly in his head but never in his hand.

Double gulps from the bottle didn't quench his bitterness.

Fuck pearling, he thought, he wasn't going to chase oysters that weren't anywhere. What he'd do tomorrow was put in at the nearest Thai port and kick these Jap divers off. No matter that according to his agreement with them so far he owed each a hundred and fifty dollars. To pay them would be like infecting the wound. With them gone he'd sail down to Penang and find a buyer for the boat, wouldn't even paint it up to make it look better or anything, just get rid of it and get into something else. That's what he'd do.

He finished most of the bottle and it finished him for the night. He slumped, his head dropped, then all of him dropped to the aft deck.

He didn't feel the sudden lurch of the boat as the anchor line snapped, nor was he conscious of any of the various motions as the current got to it.

The current seemed to enjoy having its way with the boat, took it down that channel to another, spun it twice around where there was a sort of basin and, helping it to just barely avoid collision with sharp rocks, carried it through a narrow outlet. To the sea proper. There it relinquished the plaything to the night wind.

The night wind was not a violent wind but one made up of a steady stir and frequent firm gusts. More than forceful enough, however, to catch the excessive freeboard of the boat and blow it farther and farther out.

When, well into the next morning, Bertin opened his sticky eyelids he was looking straight up to sky. He didn't realize what had happened until he sat up and looked to starboard and port and saw only ocean. He stood quickly, his head suddenly cleared. Rushed forward and pulled in the weightless anchor line, as though proving what had happened would help.

How long had they been drifting? Bertin wondered. Evidently quite a while for there not to be any land in sight. So, where the hell was he? West of those islands of yesterday, sure, had to be, but how about north or south? North would be bad. Those islands of yesterday must have been only a few miles within Thailand jurisdiction, so it was possible these waters now were Burmese. Burma had a nasty political disposition, an attitude of belligerent isolation. No trespassing. Anyone who violated its borders, went in by land to find rubies or sapphires or for any other reason, such as pearls in Burmese waters, stood a good chance of being killed. Burmese army patrols were thick along the border, shot intruders on sight. It would be the same out here. Any moment a Burmese patrol boat or maybe even a destroyer could come bearing down and, without even asking or warning, start firing on them.

Bertin glowered at Setsu, Michiko and the boy. Fucking Japs, he thought, they probably knew when the anchor broke loose. Why hadn't they awakened him? It was typical, their abiding so steadfast to his rule that limited them to the foredeck. Inflexible bastards. And look at them now, standing there absolutely expressionless, no help at all, not even sharing his distress.

He went aft and started the engine. Because it was yet morning the sun told him which direction was east. He swung the boat around, lashed the wheel to hold course. Got out Miller's binoculars and scanned the horizon. Saw nothing on the hazed line of it, however the glare off the water prevented him from being certain. He scanned again, all around, more slowly, his pessimism expecting to come across something that would turn out to be a Burmese patrol.

And there it was.

An interruption of the horizon. A darker thing, not large.

He was headed straight for it or it was coming straight at him. He strained to make it out. Useless to try to run from it, he thought. That might make matters worse when it caught up. Maybe he'd be able to bluff his way out. It wouldn't be the first time he'd lied for his life. Sweat was trickling down his rib cage.

He kept the binoculars focused on that dark object.

And not until he was only a couple of miles from it, did he accept that it was something fixed in place, a piece of land, an island way out there by itself. From his perspective at that moment its horizontal profile was wedge-shaped, higher by fifty feet or so on one end. A grove of palms on the lower end seemed to be providing balance. As the boat drew closer Bertin realized how small an island it was. Less than a half mile long.

Anyway, Bertin thought, thank God or whoever for it. He'd use it for cover, remain with it until nightfall. The prospect of sailing at night made him uneasy, but it was the safer of his choices.

He circled the island to determine where the boat would be less likely seen. The island's opposite side turned out to be proportionately wide because it included a crescent-shaped lagoon that had been created by a reef of coral. The demarcation between the roil of the sea and the calmer, contained water was easily visible.

Bertin decided on the lagoon and sailed back and forth along the reef, searching for a break in it that would allow access. Four times back and forth. The reef was like a continuous rampart, the forbidding spires of its coral growths and the more solid built-up sections of it reached within inches of the surface and, in some places, above. Apparently there was no way in.

He ran the boat back to the side of the island he'd initially approached. Hurriedly attached the spare anchor and let it drop. The boat was then only about thirty feet off the higher end of the island, holding parallel with it, black against dark, fairly well blended. Bertin cut the engine and made coffee, which he laced with some from another bottle of brandy in case the adrenaline wore off and the hangover he was supposed to have had got to him.

At that moment the boy, William, was lying front down on the foredeck with his head extended over the side. Peering down into the calmer water between the boat and the island. He remained like that for a while, then sat up and from a small cloth bag that had once contained salt he removed an ample pinch of roasted rose leaves.

He moistened the leaves with saliva and formed them with his palms into a ball and, after he'd made sure that it wasn't too wet by testing it against his forehead, he used it to rub the lenses of Setsu's diving mask. It was an old ama method of preventing the lenses from fogging, and it had been his given responsibility for two years.

Finished with Setsu's mask he took up his own and gave it the same thorough treatment.

Setsu knew it was his botherless way of asking could he go for a swim. With the long bus trip to Ban Pakbara and the past several days of diving, William hadn't been in the water in a week. She waited for him to bring his look around to her with the request in his eyes. No reason to deny it. It wouldn't be an annoyance to the man Bertin and the water appeared agreeable.

A single nod from her.

Within seconds William had jumped in.

The sound of the splash he'd made as he entered the water touched off in Setsu the suggestion that she share the swim. Seldom these days did she get to swim merely for the fun of it and with him. Hurriedly, she put on her mask and dropped overboard. Submerged, she found him about twenty feet from her, headed away. She caught him unaware, grasped his ankle and enjoyed seeing his expression change from alarm to delight.

They went to the surface for air, then swam underwater together along the coral-studded base of the island. Giving in to the spirit of the moment, they playfully pursued a wayward clown fish that darted away but soon returned for more play. They also pantomimed, performed silly posturing for each other's amusement, and when William did riding a bicycle, Setsu did applause. They swam close beneath the boat, pretended to beat upon its slime-coated hull, were tempted not to pretend, which they knew would have aggravated the sour-tempered Bertin. Laughed, which caused them to lose their air. Surfaced for more.

Resuming the swim, William suddenly made for the bottom. Setsu wasn't concerned. The depth there was no more than six fathoms, she estimated (thirty-six feet). William had been deeper a number of times. She kept him in sight as, leisurely, she followed him down. Approaching the bottom, she saw it consisted of a dark sand with an unusual indigo cast to it. The indigo became more pronounced as she drew closer. She grabbed up a fistful of the sand, released it and appreciated its iridescence as the dappling sun caught upon its particles.

She noticed that William had taken up an object from the bottom. He pivoted to show her. Just then, a lemon yellow something claimed the water between them with swift, lively swerves. After about fifteen seconds, as though satisfied that it had sufficiently startled, it swam up in the direction of the surface.

Setsu recognized its precise motions.

A sea snake.

Wide flat tail, distended, venom-storing jaws.

She had encountered sea snakes at various times but never one such as this. Not this color nor this large. Six feet long, at least, with a girth equal to her upper arm. She'd heard it said rather too lightheartedly that sea snakes were often shy, at times friendly and always unpredictable. They required air, protruded their heads above water every so often to fill their lung, which ran the entire length of their body. They were, of course, extremely poisonous.

Setsu couldn't get William up to the boat and out of the water quickly enough. She explained the danger to him in two solemn, pointed sentences and then gave attention to what he'd found on the bottom and brought up.

An oyster. As big around as a dinner plate. It was thick, convex, weighed ten pounds, was mainly gray to black with radial ridges delicately tipped a flashing blue. It was, Setsu presumed from its size and all, the type of oyster pearlers speak of as a *max* and marine biologists call *Pinctada maxima*.

Bertin noticed and came forward. Compared to how incited he'd been by oysters just two days ago he was now almost indifferent. Surely he'd never again get so worked up over them. He demanded the oyster without saying a word and William, concealing reluctance, handed it over. Bertin took it to the aft deck, placed it on the wooden block.

Left it there while he relighted a half-smoked Gauloise and took off his canvas shoes to air his huge feet, which told him his toenails needed clipping. They'd told him that a month ago and if the clippers had been right there he'd have seen to it, however...

He took up the *dah-she*, the Burmese knife, and went at the oyster. Because of its size he had difficulty keeping it up on edge long enough to allow him to sever the ligament at its hinge. Finally he managed, cut through its adductor muscle as well, so the oyster lay flat. He lifted off the top shell as though he were uncovering a serving dish.

The pearl stunned him.

To such an extent that he didn't believe it was a pearl, nor did he trust his eyes. He was afraid to touch it, for it might be merely an illusion and his fingers would come away with nothing between them. He closed his eyes and pinched his upper eyelids sharply left and right, inflicting pain to reassure reality. And yes, there it was, within the iridescent nacre of the interior of the shell, lying comfortably in the variegated black-and-dun-colored mantle, that slick and soft but gristly-looking skirt of flesh around the oyster's body.

It was huge, this pearl, about three-quarters of an inch in diameter (later it would measure eighteen millimeters or .7079 inches with a weight of 153.14 grains), and it required the coordination of two fingers and a thumb for Bertin to pluck it out. As he held it up to examine it he moved well away from the side of the boat for fear that his excitement might cause him to fumble it overboard.

How round it was, appeared perfectly spherical! And flawless, not a bump or pit or any other kind of spoiling blemish on its complexion. Its orient or luster was so deep and rich Bertin could see in it his image distinctly, mirrored and surrounded by a luminous aura.

All those attributes, however, were secondary to its color.

It was blue.

Not just a hint of that shade to be seen if held a certain way in a particular light, but an intense outright blue. The blue of a fine Burmese sapphire, or that of a cornflower at its summer peak. Flashes of cobalt came from it, as though it were transmitting beautiful, innermost secrets.

Bertin hadn't ever even heard anyone tell of such a pearl. Was he perhaps the first ever to see one? Whatever, he knew what he had in hand was a rare and extraordinarily precious gem.

He'd keep it to himself, not let the Japs in on it, was his immediate thought, But then, a far more lucrative possibility occurred to him.

He went forward to them, showed the pearl to them. They gathered around and gazed at it with wide-eyed wonderment. Didn't comment or question or reach to touch it, as it lay there in the depression of Bertin's upturned palm. He flexed his hand slightly, activating the pearl's luster, which provoked vowel sounds of awe from Setsu, Michiko and the boy.

Bertin was amiable now, and collaborative. He reminded them that they were his one-third partners. Possibly, he remarked, the bottom here was covered with such oysters containing such pearls. Think of it. Think of having a handful.

Setsu didn't really need such persuasion. In her mind's eye she was already diving and finding.

Michiko and William would tend the lines.

Setsu dropped into the water, adjusted her mask, took a dozen hyperventilating breaths and with her gathering sack rode the attached weight to the bottom. The bottom of indigo-colored sand and sea snakes. Perhaps, Setsu thought, as she took a quick look all around, that sea snake had been a solitary one. And the same might be the case of that blue-pearled oyster. She didn't put stock in either presumption.

She searched the bottom swiftly but thoroughly in one direction and then another, her whereabouts guided by the underwater base of the island. Her lungs were just commencing to burn when she came to where the bottom dropped abruptly and became much deeper, a sort of trough that ran perpendicular with the island. From the looks of it she guessed the depth of the trough was about thirteen fathoms. A swarm of shrimp came streaming by, a translucent cloud, just as she went up for air alongside the boat.

The first thing she saw as she broke the surface was Bertin's face, avarice and anticipation in it. He was kneeling on the deck, leaning over the side, awaiting her. No doubt expecting her to hand him up an oyster or two. She chided herself mildly for the pleasure she felt from disappointing him.

She remained in the water while Michiko attached the catskin bag to the right side of her face mask strap. Two rubber tubes ran from the bag. One tube was inserted in underneath the edge of the mask; the other, the longer, went to Setsu's mouth. She blew into that second tube, thereby inflating the bag to its limit. It was a flesh-colored balloon half as large as her head. Again, she rode the weighted line all the way down.

At once she swam to the trough, continued over the edge and down into it. Wasting no time, for time was breath. Sought the bottom. Reached it at a depth of fourteen fathoms (eighty-four feet). The pressure down there was thirty-six pounds to the square inch, so it wasn't so easy for Setsu to move about. She felt the thumping of her heartbeat; the pace of it well over a hundred to the minute. Her insides were intimidated while outwardly she remained in calm, confident control.

By now the catskin bag had deflated, the air in it having been forced by the pressure through the tube and into the space of Setsu's mask. That offset somewhat the effect her eyes would have suffered because of the pressure. They would have bulged grotesquely, near to the point of popping from their sockets. There would have been searing pain as the muscles that held her eyes in normal place were strained. As it was, with the catskin bag arrangement, a makeshift ama device, what eye pain she felt was endurable.

She investigated the trough. A strange aspect of it she immediately noticed was the good visibility. At that depth it should have been murky, sombrous. However, shapes and shadows were sharp, and she could even make out the consistent texture of the sandy bottom, those same bluish grains. What wasn't to be seen were oysters. Not a one.

She followed the trough in to the base wall of the island, and not until she'd turned and looked back and up did she realize she'd passed beneath a sizeable overhang. More unexpected was the formation directly overhead: a vertical shaft made up of irregular layers of stones and the clings of various corals. It was as though she were at the bottom of a deep crudely constructed well looking up to its surface—an oblong patch of calm, which was intensifying the sunlight that struck upon it.

How long had she been down? How far to air? Her sense of fractional time was keenly developed, like a stopwatch in her head. She trusted its accuracy. It told her she'd been under a minute and a half. Two and a half was her limit. In keeping with her usual caution, she'd play it safe, allow ample margin rather than put off surfacing until the last seconds.

She was about to swim back out the trough and go up when it occurred to her that it would require less breath time and effort to go up right there, up the shaft. As well, that would be continuing on, not disappointing anyone, including herself, by surfacing empty-handed again.

She undid the lifeline from the back of her belt, tied two knots at the end of it. Her way of letting Michiko know she was all right, merely exploring someplace where the line would be a

34 GERALD A. BROWNE

hindrance. She jerked the line sharply three times and saw it being pulled away.

A glance up to the patch of surface that she was now committed to. She flexed her knees a bit. The sand beneath her feet gave a little, then held for an upward push, much less than a full-out spring, which started her upward. That, along with the buoying air in her lungs, made rising nearly effortless for her. With respect for the decrease of pressure and the effect that could have on her, she'd go up slowly. She had plenty of breath time, she thought.

As she ascended she considered the shaft. It was about twelve to fifteen feet in diameter with the rocks of its sides stacked haphazardly, some flat and some on end, some protruding and others creating recesses. They were for the most part a dull, dunnish brown color, and it was that characteristic which, when she was about a quarter of the way up, allowed her to make out the snake so well.

It was lying on a ledge in a neat, tight serpentine arrangement. About five feet from her. Partly in soft shadow, partly in the strike of the sun. At first sight its head was only slightly extended, its chin resting on the flat of that rock, rather coylike or perhaps insouciantly waiting to see what might come along. When it caught sight of Setsu, its head, and that section of it that could be thought of as neck, alerted, stiffened abruptly and crooked up. It was bright lemon yellow, possibly the same snake that had made such a surprising appearance earlier. Was just as large.

Setsu's insides leaped. All her internal organs felt as though they were cowering against her rib cage and spine. Nevertheless she managed to keep her limbs in control, maintained her upward progress, which out of another necessity now was practically a slow float. She was close enough to see the scales of the snake, their symmetry, and to some extent, its eyes, small and black. Unreadable eyes because of their blackness, however Setsu was certain they were on her, and that she was at the mercy of those eyes, depending on what messages it was at that moment transmitting to the snake's brain, hostility, apathy or who knew what.

Within seconds she was up past that ledge and the snake. Except for her feet and lower legs. Her feet and lower legs seemed like laggards, vulnerable, inviting attack. But then they caught up and were also above the snake's immediate close range.

More snakes about halfway up.

They were all around, folded into niches, fitted into cracks, swagged over outcroppings. There were lemon-yellows but also some that were as green as an unripe apple and others a pinkish, feminine color.

Any moment Setsu expected one to shoot out at her with its lethal bite. If one did, all might. One would get them started.

From a seemingly unoccupied horizontal crevice, one did emerge. But sinuously, slowly, came right at her, directly to the space between her upper arm and her side. A pink snake. With a swift purposeful spin it wound itself three turns around her upper arm. Brought its head up so its eyes were level with hers. Stared curiously into her fright. Opened its jaws as wide as the hinges would allow, displaying its long, curved fangs.

More like a yawn, though, than a threat, the way it closed its mouth. More like a parting embrace than an antagonistic squeeze the way it tightened a degree around her arm before gracefully unwinding from it.

She continued upward, glanced down. Saw that a swarm of tiny shrimp, a translucent, pastel cloud of creatures, was directly below her. The snakes began feeding upon the shrimp, whipping up the water as they gorged. A frenzy with swift slashes of lemon-yellow, sudden bolts of brilliant green, muscular belly-up roils of pink. The snakes no longer had interest of any sort in her.

However, a lot of her breath time had been spent. She didn't know how much. The danger had disoriented her sense of time, that stopwatch in her head, and now she'd have to go by what her body told her. Especially her lungs. Already they were signaling her with some burning. At fourteen fathoms, the depth from which she'd started up, her lungs were contracted to about a third of their normal size—an involuntary reaction to the pressure. Now they were still only about half the size of what they should be. They were demanding that she hurry and let out the breath she was holding.

She couldn't. Not and survive. If she expelled her breath her buoyancy would be lost. And there'd be nothing in her with which to fight against sinking. She'd known of amas, the best of swimmers, who, for one reason or another, had given up their breath while still deep down. If someone hadn't gone down

quickly and brought them up they would have drowned. But here,
there was no one above to help her. She still had six or seven
fathoms to go.

Her legs were also complaining, some of their strength leaving
her. Better she should use them while she still had them, she
thought, and did four successive propelling kicks. Made her arms
help, kept her fingers tight together, her hands cupped to get all
she could out of them. She knew she shouldn't go up so quickly,
but the pain across her chest was intense now, the breath crowding
her windpipe, some of it coming up into her mouth, swelling her
cheeks. She clamped her hand over her mouth and pinched her
nostrils to keep it from escaping.

Her head broke through the patch of calm surface as though
shattering it, the old, used breath exploded from her and a deep
fresh one relieved. She floated in place a long moment to allow the
replenishment to reach all of her. She had an intense headache
from having ascended too rapidly, but that was a common ailment
with amas, and she knew an ama way of dealing with it. Merely
dipped down, held her head underwater for a minute.

She was inside the lagoon. It was about three-quarters of a mile
at its widest point, otherwise a little less.

The water there was disturbed only enough to cause geometric
reflections on the sandy bottom. Not deep. At the edge Setsu
could stand and walk. The deepest area was along the reef, just
inside it. As much as five to six fathoms there.

Setsu swam out a ways on the surface, then dove and investigated the bottom. After only a dozen or so strokes she came upon
an oyster. The same sort William had found, a *max*, with a thick
shell large as a dinner plate, blue-flecked radial ridges. It shut its
shell abruptly as she reached for it. She put it in her sack and
searched around for others.

Came upon them.

An entire bed of them. So many she didn't try to count. Large
as they were, her sack couldn't hold more than five, and after
gathering that many she placed her sack down and swam over the
bed, allowing the possibilities of what she'd found to register.
From now on, she thought, she would be a notable ama, one
whom others spoke about often and admiringly. They would, no
doubt, exaggerate her exploits. Exaggeration always flavored such

devotion. They would tell of the snakes and put in bizarre underwater dragons, whirlpools and masses of tiny voracious sharks. She would become the venerated name Setsu as her great-grandmother had become the name Amira, a legend to be recited. It would be told how she returned home to Hegurajima with great wealth to build her mother an elegant house, one of several she would pay to have built within a walled compound to be occupied by Yoshidas. There would be enough money for generations. Silk on their bodies, television sets and visits to foreign places for their eyes. William, in beautiful shoes, would go with her to San Francisco.

To confirm such wonderful prospects, Setsu looked for an oyster that had, so to speak, gotten out of bed, one apart from the rest. She located such a loner and approached it more stealthily, stayed close as possible to the bottom while almost imperceptibly moving toward it. The oyster was feeding, had its shells open about two inches. Setsu cocked her head and hardly disturbed a grain as she pressed her cheek to the sand within three feet of the oyster. Peered into it and saw the sphere of brilliant blue it contained.

Oh *hai*! The numbers of this day would be long remembered.

She retrieved her sack. Instead of returning the perilous way she'd come, the snake way, she swam to the reef and over it to the open sea. Swam against the wind, through the sudden drops of swells and hoisting crests, all the way around the point to finally reach the boat.

Bertin was pleased to see the oysters and elated when he'd opened them. The five yielded four pearls: two of about eighteen millimeters, two only a couple of millimeters smaller. All of remarkable perfection and all blue. Bertin invited Setsu, Michiko and William to the stern and allowed a quick pot of tea and nibbles of sweet rice cookies. Setsu related what she'd gone through. Bertin did sympathetic clucks and he made his eyes wide when he thought amazement was called for. When Setsu said where the oysters were, he was sincerely interested. She told him it would be better, easier if he moved the boat around the point and anchored close to the reef.

He agreed. The danger of being seen by a Burmese patrol still existed, however an exceptional pearler such as he had to take chances, Bertin told himself.

The boat's new position allowed both Setsu and Michiko to work the lagoon. They slid over the reef and gathered into their sacks. Swam back and handed their catches up to William, who dragged them to the stern. Bertin had repealed his territorial restriction and was also demonstrating his better nature to the boy, sharing with him the very first sight of another pearl and exaggerating disappointment when an oyster was barren. There was even some encouraging back patting and a couple of covert swigs of wine from a bottle, and William, susceptible to such camaraderie, truly enjoyed doing his part, handling the sixty-pound sacks.

As quickly as the oysters were brought aboard, Bertin opened them. The black lacquer bowl, now a more worthy repository, held only the larger pearls, those of superb quality and eighteen-millimeter dimension. Others of lesser size and of a quality that Bertin would have been overjoyed with just yesterday were relegated to a glass tumbler that hadn't been washed since Miller.

Bertin was so caught up with accumulating pearls and the certain wealth that followed that he forgot about the barometer, and when about midafternoon he went in to look at it he loathed what it indicated. His plan had been to pearl until dark, remain anchored there and pearl the entire following day. Clean out the lagoon, even if it took a week. However, the barometer had fallen one and a half degrees since he'd noticed it near a reassuring 29.50 that morning.

He sighted through the binoculars at those clouds to the south. They were definitely closer and, it appeared to him, coming on fast. What kind of storm was that? The clouds of it were huge and dark on the bottom, flat on top. All the way across the southern horizon. Now he was able to make out the way they were churning, getting worked up. He lowered his binoculars, listened intently. Heard a distant deviating rumble followed by a sharp clap. It was trying to talk to him, this storm, he thought, telling him *watch out, asshole, here I come*. And hear the wind? It had picked up, playing the part of precursor, whistling around the mast.

He went back to opening oysters and getting pearls.

But couldn't keep his eyes off those clouds.

Possibly they were a baby tropical cyclone, he thought, and perhaps not so much of a baby. It would be just his luck, now that he had so much, never to live to enjoy it because of the boat getting swamped and he drowned or bashed to death up against the reef.

Fuck that, he said aloud.

He went forward as Setsu and Michiko were arriving again, each with another sackful of oysters. They had been working the lagoon simultaneously, going and coming together, enjoying the task more because of that. This time as Bertin and William lifted the sacks aboard, Bertin complained with an agreeable grin that they were too efficient for him, were bringing too many at a time, so the unopened oysters were piling up on him. It was a compliment the way he said it. He suggested they stagger their trips, coordinate so when one was returning the other would be going.

Michiko climbed aboard to rest on the foredeck while Setsu swam back over the reef to the lagoon. William dragged one of the full sacks to the stern. Bertin lugged the other.

William was removing the oysters from the sacks and arranging them neatly so they could be systematically opened when Bertin struck him. William was about to look up and perhaps he had somewhat, perhaps he got a glimpse of the blow just before it landed. A snapping, back-handed blow to the side of his head, huge right-hand knuckles against boy cheekbone. Such force it lifted William off his feet, sent him flying into the wheelhouse and against the bulkhead there, transformed into a limp, contorted heap.

Bertin went to the foredeck. Michiko was sitting with her legs drawn up, hands clasped at her ankles, her head resting on her knees. She seemed unaware of Bertin there, or at least she wasn't aware of the danger of him.

He looked down upon her from behind. Saw the definition of her bowed spine, her black hair wet tendrils against the skin of the back of her neck. He thought from her position she was practically offering herself.

He grabbed her throat with both hands, hands so large and throat so small his thumbs and fingers overlapped. Gave her no chance to cry out, applied more than enough sudden pressure to prevent that, and what resistance she put up was no match for his hold, merely some futile flails and twists and kicks. He enjoyed killing by hand, had done it twice before, felt the spasms, the voice box crush, the cartilages and vital passages compact.

He didn't release until she was surely dead. He picked her up and dumped her over the outboard side.

It wasn't only that he didn't want to share the blue pearls and their worth with the Japs. Just as important, perhaps more so, he didn't want anyone else knowing the source, this island. He was confident that he'd be able to find it again, and if *he* could, certainly so could they. Typically, they'd return and load up on these blues, might bring other people as well, and before long there'd be who knew how many on it. Killing, as Bertin saw it, was justifiable, in fact, called for.

The body of Michiko floated for a few minutes alongside the boat, eerily banged against it some, then sank. At about a fathom down a current caught it, carried it beneath the boat and in the direction of the reef.

Thus, as Setsu was returning with a full sack, had swum over the reef and was proceeding to the boat, for a moment the body of Michiko was directly under her. Her kicks came within inches of hitting upon it.

Bertin awaited Setsu, extended his hand to receive the sack. He tossed it on the deck, turned away and feigned being busy with it for a long moment, then turned back.

Setsu had climbed aboard and removed her mask. As she took off her cap she looked around for Michiko.

Bertin got her by the hair, from behind. His right leg wrapped around the front of her legs to clamp her in place. It happened so swiftly she didn't have a chance to struggle. Bertin jerked her head far back, so her long neck was stretched, arched up. In practically the same motion he drew the *dah-she*, that Burmese knife, across her throat from just below her left ear to just below her right. Not even so much as half a scream from her as her carotid arteries were severed and her jugulars and facial veins. Her windpipe and esophagus sliced clear through.

At once there was a great deal of blood, a lot of it on Bertin. He didn't mind. He picked up Setsu and dropped her overboard like so much waste.

Went aft then to finish up with the boy.

The boy wasn't where he'd been in the wheelhouse. Hiding, Bertin thought, but the boat didn't offer many places for that. He searched the cabin thoroughly, even looked into the cupboards and other storage spaces obviously too small to contain anyone. The engine compartment too, which was crowded with engine. He went over the boat systematically stem to stern, searching again where he'd already searched. He concluded that the boy had come conscious and dived overboard. That had to be it, and in that case, the boy was as good as dead.

Bertin started the engine.

Hoisted the anchor and pulled in the drogue.

Glanced hard at the storm and the descending mercury in the barometer. Swung the boat around sharply to an easterly course and said a prayer on behalf of the engine.

CHAPTER ONE

Grady Bowman caught on a thought and paused about halfway through his shave. He looked out the bathroom, through the dressing room to Gayle's unmade bed. It had been unmade when he'd arrived home at three A.M., and although he'd about 98 percent expected Gayle wouldn't be there, the bed bothered him.

He'd been making the circuit for the past sixteen days. Starting with Denver, then Houston, New Orleans, Atlanta, Boston, New York, and, finally, Chicago. At least twice a year, some years three times, he traveled around and met in person with clients of the firm he worked for, the Harold Havermeyer Company. Havermeyer himself used to go on such trips, and so had the Havermeyer before him, but it had been left up to Grady since he joined the firm nearly ten years ago. Some of those trips had been successful, others not so. This one fell somewhere in between, would have been really good had Lawler in Boston been able to decide on that lot of emeralds. There'd been no way for Grady to sell him. All Grady could do was stand there and watch Lawler sell and unsell himself and finally end up unsold.

Last night's flight in from Chicago was one of those evidently destined to misfortune. It was an hour and a half late taking off, and after a half hour in the air had to return because of a mechanical problem. Then there was the hour and some wait for another plane to be readied and the problem Grady had had with his pistol. As usual when he flew with goods, he'd turned in his pistol to airport security for safekeeping in the plane's control cabin. However, with the switch of planes and crews the pistol was forgotten in the copilot's flight case, which was finally located but was locked and had to be broken into.

So, altogether, the last leg of the journey had been everything but good for Grady and a measure of amend was surely called for. Gayle's bed, however, was unmade and empty. Grady believed he was too exhausted to think about it. He let his clothes drop anywhere, vetoed a shower and got into his own bed. Eyes shut, Grady felt sinking and drifting, but then the emptiness in the bed turned his mind back on, and his mind did the same to the rest of him.

He switched on the bedstand light. How long was it that she hadn't been there? he wondered. Got up to perhaps find out. Went nude out to the landing and downstairs to see if there was a dated note from her where she usually left them whenever it occurred to her. Nothing was on the hall table nor propped against the black-and-white photograph of them framed in ornate English silver. It was an enlarged version of the submitted flash shot that had appeared seven years ago on the wedding page of *Town & Country.*

In his semisomnambulant state it was easy for Grady's attention to get held by something. Such as Gayle as she'd appeared that day, well tanned, slick lipped, haloed by a white floral headpiece, no claim of chastity in that audaciously beautiful face. He doing the mild hug, sort of smiling, certainly not his best smile, dazed really, trying to nonchalant it.

He went into the study and played back the messages on the answering machine. Days and days of them, including the six or seven long-distance that were him and his wordless disconnects. Otherwise only trivial calls such as from the pesticide service a week ago and some woman friend of Gayle's miffed because Gayle hadn't shown up for a dinner party last week, hadn't even called with excuse or apology.

The kitchen. It was clean, the sink was dry, the counters a bit dusty. The coffee left in the coffee maker had evaporated three inches and was scummed blue-white.

Grady didn't really need further indications, such as the ten days' accumulation of newspapers on and around the front entrance or the avalanche of mail beneath the slot or the total vacancy of the second right-hand built-in-dresser bottom drawer where Gayle kept her better, trickier lingerie.

Gone again, he thought, mentally sighing. This time for longer. Ten days at least.

He roamed the house. There wasn't much of him in it the way it was done. She hadn't let him contribute except when it came to some of the outside plantings. So the house was her. Every room and every area of every room and every possible surface within every room was intentionally cluttered. With tasteful and expensive things but nonetheless cluttered.

The low burled chestnut table that served the fat-armed sofas of the living room seating area, for example. There was hardly room left on it to place down a wineglass. A leather case with its lid ajar just so contained a set of nineteenth-century bone dominoes with several spilled out just so, never to be further disturbed. Packets of letters postdated early 1900s, British stamped and addressed in the very practiced hand of the time to several someones in Yorkshire and Northumberland, were tied by dainty silk ribbons, the curled strands of which invaded perfectly an antique brass spyglass positioned just so next to an antique sterling silver porringer stuffed just so with dried pink miniature roses in slight disarray. Lorgnettes, things of tortoise, a just so stack of old leather-bound books of odd sizes buffed and so patined they looked as though they'd been adored, read and reread countless times.

Highly polished pairs of used riding boots in the rear hall, floral-banded, wide-brimmed straws on brass hooks or supposedly tossed over the knob of a chair. Persian carpets, varnished woodwork, paintings of high-strung dogs, cats, horses and boats.

The arranged disarrangements overfed the eyes. But that wasn't how Gayle saw it. To her it was accomplishment worthy of not admitting she'd been assisted by one of San Francisco's most sought-after interior decorators.

To Grady the decor was paradoxical, very much like Gayle and very much unlike her. He never came right out and said it reminded him of a Ralph Lauren display.

He was up for the night now, he believed. Too tired to get to sleep, that was actually it, nothing to do with Gayle, he told himself. Went to the kitchen to warm some milk, but the half carton of it in the refrigerator had gone sour. He settled for a twenty-three-ounce-size Perrier that he twisted open with more strength than was needed and took swigs from on his way to the study. Such large, fast swigs the burst of its fizz burned his palate and the start of his throat.

He sat on the green leather Chesterfield sofa with the cold green bottle in his hand, the base of it resting on his knee. Thought a while about tomorrow, which already was, thought he'd call in at nine and say he wouldn't be in until two. Thought about how he must look from across the room, bare ass adhering to leather in the low light. Did an alone thing, brought the bottle to his crotch, between his thighs, snugged it with a squeeze. After the initial sensation, he couldn't tell which was winning, chill or warmth, the bottle or his balls. He set the bottle on the side table where its sweat might very likely leave a ring. Toppled over onto the sofa's hard arm and brought his legs up, shifted onto his side, knifed his legs to himself and, without another thought, slept for four dreamless hours.

Now it was eight-thirty and he was finishing his shave, giving his cheeks and chin some upward strokes. He splashed his face with two handfuls of hot and dried briskly with one of the fine linen hand towels Gayle had asked him never to use. No aftershave or cologne, this wasn't an aftershave or cologne day. He'd smell his true clean self.

From his suits he chose a slouchy, double-breasted brown light wool that was fresh from the cleaners. Liberated it from the plastic bag, suspendered it and got into it, along with a soft cream cotton shirt and the tidy small knot of a brown grounded tie. Didn't appraise himself in Gayle's full-length mirror. Put his pistol into the everything drawer of his dresser, put his ready cash to pocket, put at once out of mind the suggestion to himself that he make the bed, took his attaché case and went down and out.

He used the twenty-minute drive from Mill Valley to the toll bridge to make friends with the day. It was something he frequently did, left off the radio because the music would likely be either songs involving emotional situations unlike his own or abrasive hard rock stuff that would only potentiate anyone's early morning hostility. As for the news, was it ever really news? Just a carousel of public affairs with seldom a happy horse.

Anyway, this day was a pretty June day, nice sky and everything. Some clouds around but none that looked like they'd form a gang and cause rain. The tie-up at the toll was, as usual, worth it for the bridge, so cheerfully painted and strong and complicated. Since 1981, the first time Grady ever saw the bridge, he hadn't ever taken it for granted. Even on the way home after his most devastating days he was able to get out of himself enough to appreciate it, let it lift him.

As it did today.

By the time he reached Market Street and parked the Ford Taurus in the open lot opposite the Phelan Building, his spirit was boosted two, going on three notches. The old ivory and black marble lobby of the Phelan was as impeccable and deserving of appreciation as ever, and five of the seven people Grady shared elevator number two with were gingerly carrying cardboard containers of coffee and the slight steam from the tiny puncture holes in the lids of the cartons seemed playful.

Every tenant of the thirteen-story Phelan was in one way or another involved in the gem and jewelry trade. Thus the structure was, in effect, a sort of community made up of specialists dependent upon one another or in compatible and sometimes not so compatible competition. So, Grady recognized five of his fellow passengers and was acquainted well enough with the other two—a first-rate stone setter and a younger man who dealt in semi-precious goods—to exchange smiles around *good mornings*. The setter was next to last to get off. On ten. He seemed eager to get to work. Grady thought probably he'd promised some client, Shreve and Company or someone of that importance, that he'd have a particular piece of work completed first thing that morning.

Grady went to the top, which was mainly taken up by the

Harold Havermeyer Company. The designed ensignia HH was in gold on the heavy double doors (only the door on the right could be opened) and beneath the ensignia, like an explanation of it, was the firm's full name.

Grady's name wasn't on either door.

Harold Havermeyer was his father-in-law.

Now and then over the years Harold would make a point of indicating to Grady where on the door he intended to have Grady's name put. Harold's tone always inferred it was imminent and a few times he emphatically tapped the exact prominent spot with a forefinger. However, having it done seemed always to slip Harold's mind.

It got so it was embarrassing for Grady, who told himself that his name on the door wasn't a rung on his ladder.

The girl at the HH front desk was new, extremely pretty and, probably for both those reasons, overdressed. Earrings so dangling they barely cleared her outdated, padded shoulders. Grady discerned the cool *may I help you* in her eyes and beat her to it by introducing himself and asking her name.

He went on down the hall to his office, on the way glancing into the largest office, which was Harold's. Harold hadn't come in yet. His office was the only one with personality because that was how Harold wanted it. His desk was a *bureau plat,* a reproduction but nevertheless a *bureau plat*. His chairs were convincingly distressed *bergères,* the rug a high and thick piled Chinese, pale blue. The paintings were original oils, two portraits of anonymous British nobles and a Normandy landscape that featured cows by a turn-of-the-century impressionist who hadn't made E. Bénézit but who nevertheless had been a turn-of-the-century impressionist. Harold also had a private toilet. He never referred to it as that but rather as his w.c. Too, there was an impressively stocked bar, though Harold refilled a perpetual vintage '66 Graham port bottle with seven-year-old Sandeman.

The rest of the HH space, reception area, halls, other offices and even the vault room were painted a surely inoffensive dove gray in a flat finish. The woodwork a shade darker. Matching wall-to-wall nylon carpet throughout, and the only thing allowed to be hung were framed oversize examples of fairly recent HH advertisements that had appeared in trade journals and various fashion and snob publications.

Grady's office was an adequate twelve by twelve. The view from

its one window was the unattractive aspects of some nearby
shorter buildings, their undoubtedly grimed black roofs, air-
conditioning and elevator facilities, a great many standpipes. The
savers were an oblique slice of the bay on certain clear days, the
sky when it was blue or having a sunset, and that attitude Grady
came to naturally.

The office wasn't merely superficially tidy. There was no dust on
or under, and everything was in its place. Kept that way by Grady
with more than just a little help from Doris, his secretary, who
preferred to be known as his assistant. They weren't affiliated
compulsives. They just shared the belief that precious stones and
pearls, asked to be as flawless as possible, were in turn deserving
of cleanliness and order. It was something that had been impressed
on Grady the very first day he went to work in the gem business
on New York's Forty-seventh Street.

Grady removed his suit jacket, loosened his tie and collar and
rolled his shirt sleeves up two cuffs' width. Sat behind the gray
metal desk in the vinyl upholstered chair that by now his 180
pounds had broken in to his fit—the chair that was at times a
sanctuary, at other times a trap.

He was in dire need of coffee before beginning anything, and
his stomach had a right to complain of neglect. The last thing he'd
put into it was a soggy airport tuna salad sandwich at Midway
about eighteen hours ago.

As though hooked up to his thoughts, Doris came in with a cup
of steaming black and asking, "Would you like some of a bear
claw? I only got one but I'll share it. I would have gotten two but
they only had one left and everything else looked like yesterday's,
even the glazed doughnuts if you can imagine." Most work
mornings she stopped in at a bakery several doors down from the
Phelan and could tell what was stale by sight.

Grady's stomach threatened to refuse bear claw. An acidic
growl.

Doris must have heard it. "I'll send down," she said.

"Fried ham and egg."

"On what?"

"On anything. Make it fried ham and egg and cheese."

"You shouldn't ever let your blood sugar level get this low."

He shooed her away with a couple of backhand flicks.

She'd left her bear claw on a square of wax paper on his desk. He considered it, picked at it. Teasing nibbles of sugary chopped pecans. The coffee was bad, bitter, but it felt good.

He snapped open his attaché, took from it several rubber-banded batches of three-and-a-quarter by two-inch briefkes, those special papers folded five times a certain way to form an inescapable pocket for gemstones. All gem dealers used them. Each of these briefkes bore a cryptic series of letters and numbers in Grady's handprint on its upper right-hand corner, so Grady would know without opening whether the stones a certain breifke contained were rubies, emeralds, sapphires or what. The code also told him how many stones were in each lot, their size and quality. The price, top and bottom, was in his head.

He placed the briefkes on his white, tear-off desk pad, along with a printout that listed individually the goods that he'd taken on his trip. He knew precisely what lots he'd sold, to whom he'd sold them and for what price and terms. He went down the list and made appropriate notations opposite each of those lots. He hadn't yet summed up the amount of business he'd done but had an approximate idea how much it was. Found when he totaled it now he was only about twenty thousand off.

What it came to was $695,800.

On one trip last September he'd done over a million one.

Doris returned with the sandwich. Unwrapped it dutifully and placed it in front of him. "Your eyes look glazey," she commented.

"This is shitty coffee."

"Eunice made it." Inferring that anything this Eunice person touched would turn bitter. "The coffee maker needs to be scoured. She can't lower herself to do it. I've been putting it off just to see how long she'll put it off."

"Meanwhile I suffer," Grady said after a swallow. He tongued egg yolk from the corner of his mouth.

"Poor you," Doris said.

Eunice was Harold's secretary and so-called assistant. She'd been with Harold for eight, going on nine years. A short woman in her late thirties apparently not at all self-conscious about her flat chest. She dressed more than a degree too tight and too severely, avoided bright colors, overdid her eyes and had never learned the art of lipstick, just smeared it on, hit or miss straight from the

tube usually without the aid of a mirror. She often looked as
though she'd just been brutally smacked.

Eunice disliked Doris, had from the minute Doris came to work
at HH. Over the past four and a half years she'd done her best to
have Doris fired, most recently only two months ago. It seemed to
be a plot constantly on her mind, just waiting for Doris to slip up
in some way. Grady tried not to take sides, however Doris was so
likeable and loyal to him that he was tempted to pick Eunice up,
shake her and tell her to stop being so goddamn territorial.
Another thing about Eunice that vexed him was her evident
disinterest in gemstones. For all she cared she might as well have
been working in a bank.

Not so with Doris.

She had a love for gems, not to own them particularly but to
enjoy looking into them and knowing them. She'd spent nearly a
half of a week's pay on a first-rate, color-corrected ten-power loupe
that she wore every office hour on a gold chain around her neck,
the accoutrement of a professional. And when she asked Harold to
have the firm help pay for her Gemological Institute of America
courses and he didn't see any reason it should, she was determined
to save up for them. Grady discreetly gave her the tuition money
as a birthday present six months in advance.

Doris was more attractive than pretty, but she stole a few
degrees for herself by making the utmost of what she had. Legs,
for instance. She had superb legs, knew it and never hid or
handicapped them. And waist, a waist so narrow it appeared
cinched. She played it up with fashionable belts and with blouses
that had sheer midriffs. Naturally, such a slender waist complemented all adjacencies—hips, buttocks and breasts. The latter she
used as a visual revenge whenever Eunice got an accurate shot off
in their ongoing feud.

Grady liked Doris.

She loved him. And was outright about it, told him early on
and since had reminded him every time she felt the need.

Grady could have taken advantage. She wanted him to, encouraged him to. When it happened to be one of his lonely times or
when they were both riding a crest because of having pulled off an
exceptional deal, possibly Grady was within a couple of words and
a certain touch of getting into that kind of complicity. He'd kissed

her twice on the mouth, once rather lingeringly. She'd groped him once, about a year ago. Not an inadvertent brushing grope but an intentional full-handed helping that caught him so unaware he flinched. She'd laughed. He'd laughed. Her explanation for that sudden aggressive behavior was her imagination needed something substantial to go on. She hadn't helped herself to him like that since, however he expected she might, and the anticipation was rather enjoyable.

While Grady devoured the sandwich, Doris picked up the sales report from his desk. Scanned it. "No one took the pinks," she observed brightly. "I thought the pinks would be grabbed right up." The pinks, as she called them, were ten matched two-carat sapphires, round cuts of an intense pink color. Of all the gems in the HH inventory they were Doris's favorites. On her way-down days, PMS days or just whenever she came in in need of some instant emotional elevation she'd go into the vault, get out that lot of sapphires and get into their happy pink atmospheres with her ten-power loupe.

"I came close to selling them in Houston," Grady told her.

"How close?"

"Within two hundred a carat."

"Who was the cheap, Gilford?"

"Better. I didn't get to see Gilford."

Doris grinned smugly. "I think you didn't sell them on purpose, probably didn't even show them."

"You're wrong."

"Again," she sighed.

One of Grady's phone lines lighted. Doris picked it up. Covered the mouthpiece and told Grady, "It's Lawler."

"Put him on speaker. I want him self-conscious."

Doris did as told.

Grady waited a beat, then started with plenty of attitude. "Morning, Fred."

"How are you, Grady?"

"Couldn't be better."

"I gather you had a successful trip."

"Should I admit it?"

"Business is slow here."

"Sure, you only did a half million yesterday."

"I mean honestly slow."

He wants the emeralds, Grady thought. "Honestly slow" means he wants them. "Well," Grady told him, "if you called for commiseration you've got it."

"That's comforting."

"What else can I do for you besides take pity?" Grady asked lightheartedly, gauging that the conversation was about to come to its purpose.

"Those emeralds I was considering..."

"Oh, those." Grady let fall downscale, inferring the emeralds were past history.

"You've let someone else have them?"

"Not exactly."

"Don't play with me. It doesn't become you and it insults me."

"Just trying to hold my own, Fred. Just trying to hold my own."

"You been out there with Havermeyer too long."

"Maybe."

"Why don't you come back east and get hooked up with me? I'll bet we could cut a better deal than you've got."

"I'll give it thought."

"Do that. I mean it. Anyway, do you still have those emeralds in stock?"

"Yeah." While this exchange was taking place Grady had gone through the briefkes and slid the stones from that particular one onto the surface of his white, tear-off desk pad. Had drawn a circle around the stones, as though to keep them from straying. A habit of his.

The emeralds appeared special. And they were. A pair of older stones of exactly eight carats each. Like so many older stones their quality was superior, with a particular ideal green vividness that divulged their origin was Colombia. To be even more precise, out of the Muzo mine. They might very well have been part of the cache of a fifteenth-century conquistador and then counted in the riches of some Castilian duke. More recently they'd surely been the principle stones in the tiara of a Nob Hill matriarch, wife of one of San Francisco's gold rush scions. Harold had purchased them discreetly from a relative of that lady, one who needed desperately to cover some unfortunate stock margins. Harold often plucked such treasures from such family trees, believed he was only second to the late Harry Winston in that regard.

"Now, how much was it you were asking?" Lawler inquired, hoping lack of memory would convey lack of serious interest. "Twenty, wasn't it?"

"Thirty-five."

"Oh now I recall. Thirty was what you were asking. I can still hear you saying thirty and my thinking that was too much."

"You're right, thirty was the number."

"But you'll take twenty."

They were talking thousands, per carat. Grady put some silence to work. Lawler broke it with, "Anyway, at least you'll consider twenty-five. Just consider."

"They're worth more."

"Maybe. Maybe I'd agree with you if I had them here for another look, but as I remember what they were, the fair figure is twenty-five."

Grady was quite sure he could eventually get thirty a carat from someone. He could also memo the emeralds to Lawler at thirty. That was send them to him fully insured by way of Wells Fargo Armored Delivery. From the moment Lawler signed for them they'd be his responsibility. Grady decided against that because Lawler would probably get stuck in ambivalence again.

"Take into account how long we've been doing business, you and me," Lawler said. "Twelve years."

"Ten."

"Twelve with the two when you were in New York."

Lawler was right. It had been twelve years. Grady had brought him as a client to HH. The firm had done well with Lawler, who bought big and paid promptly.

"All right, Grady, I'll tell you," Lawler went on, "although I'm embarrassed to say it. These emeralds, I won't make on them. They're not for a client, they're for my wife."

Too often better goods such as these suddenly made certain dealers generous to their wives. It was, nine times or more out of ten, bullshit in order to get a lower, personal price. However, Grady couldn't recall Lawler ever resorting to it.

"Did I mention I got married again?" Lawler asked.

"No."

"Thought I did."

"I didn't even know you were divorced."

"Priscilla died a year ago last fall."

"Sorry to hear that." Grady hadn't ever met Priscilla, but Lawler had raved a lot about her, lopsided loving raves.

"My present wife, Jessica, is much younger, which, of course, is edifying for me. You know what I mean."

"Sure, edifying."

"I want to show appreciation, do something really special for her, something that'll knock her out."

Four hundred thousand worth of emeralds should do it, Grady thought cynically. Lawler, now in his midsixties, was having to buy his way, and considering these emeralds for this Jessica, there might be some matinees but no half fares. Now that he understood the circumstances, Grady was all the more certain he could get thirty thousand a carat from Lawler. Instead he said, "Tell you what, Fred, inasmuch as you have a new and, I'm sure, beautiful young wife . . ."

"She's twenty-five."

". . . and because of all the future happiness you've got coming with her, you should have the emeralds at just that . . . twenty-five. Do you need terms?"

"No. I'll overnight you a check for the full amount. Four hundred, right?"

"Four hundred, done."

When Lawler was off, Grady sat for a long moment with his gaze fixed on the gray nothing of the wall opposite his desk. Since leaving home that morning he'd managed to keep Gayle contained in a compartment back a ways from the front of his mind. But now she was rattling the gate of it furiously. If she got out she'd cause devastation.

He reinforced the gate with distraction. The briefkes, the sales report sheet. On the latter he included the four hundred thousand now forthcoming from Lawler. That increased the total to the more prideful figure $1,095,800.

Then there was his leather-bound agenda and the notes to himself he'd jotted in it. He went through them. Without looking up he said to Doris, "Among the pearls we have on hand are some ten, ten and a halfs, pinkish white. Will you get them out for me, please?"

Doris went to the vault across the hall. She returned empty-handed. "No ten, ten and a halfs."

"You sure? There were six strands. Kumuras. I noticed them myself just before I left on my trip."

"I believe Harold sold those yesterday."

An ironic grunt from Grady. "They've been lying in there six months and now that I need them they were sold yesterday."

"We've got several hanks of nice nines, nine and a halfs. Maybe some are Kumuras. Want me to check?"

"No." For years Grady had been trying to land a certain client in Atlanta. The man did a huge business throughout the South, knew his importance and was extremely demanding. Grady had promised him Kumura pearls of ten, ten and a half millimeters in a pinkish white, the current most popular shade. Expensive, but price was no problem. The man had asked how much, Grady had quoted top dollar and there'd been not a word of haggling, just the firm stipulation that the pearls be nothing less than Kumuras.

Like most dealers Grady had a favorite precious gem. He appreciated the blood red impact of Burma ruby and the ethereal blue of Kashmir sapphire and, as well, the reviviscent green of Colombian emerald. However, foremost in his heart and head were pearls.

Larkin, a New York dealer and Grady's first employer in the trade, had been an indelible influence. Pearls were Larkin's passion. He didn't merely introduce Grady to pearls, he infused Grady with a high regard for them and a great amount of knowledge. Whenever an important pearl dealer from Kyoto or Bangkok or somewhere came to show his goods, Larkin would make sure Grady was present to hear and observe, to learn.

Larkin would also take Grady along to the exhibitions of magnificent jewelry to be auctioned at Sotheby's and Christie's. Together they'd examine the various lots, paying special attention to the pearl necklaces being offered, louping pearl after pearl of each strand. Larkin would point out what made them fine or less so. The larger, white, more translucent South Sea and Australian pearls, the now extremely rare Burmese and Persian Gulf creamy naturals, the more recently fashionable cultured blacks from Marutéa.

Larkin imparted.

Grady soaked up.

They attended the auction sales, conscientiously noting next to each numbered lot in their catalogues how the bidding went, along with their opinions and comments. Most of the pearls sold at those auctions were in period jewelry, such as a necklace consisting of ninety-three Burmese cultured pearls graduating perfectly in size from ten and a half to fifteen millimeters. Once the treasure of a duchess, the bidding for the necklace spiraled swiftly to a million and was finally knocked down for a million seven. And to think that he, Grady, had had that necklace in his hands! Had run it through his fingers! Had magnified its complexion!

Frequently, after a day, Larkin and Grady would walk down to Forty-sixth and the Algonquin Bar. They'd sip Tennessee whiskey over ice while their conversation would hop, for instance, from the latest New York City controversies to baseball or boxing to the transparent greeds of politics. Inevitably it would land on the topic of pearls, and there it would remain.

Larkin was a veritable archive when it came to pearl lore, things he'd read or heard about or experienced. Grady listened enrapt as Larkin told of the Hindu custom of placing a pearl in the mouth of the dead. To symbolically exemplify the deceased person's purity in this life, thus increasing the chances of a more pleasant go at it in the next. The more perfect the pearl the greater the influence. The wealthy used valuable sea pearls for this purpose. The not nearly so wealthy used cheap placuna pearls, dull and calcined. The poor had to try to fool the gods with grains of rice.

Did Grady know that Charles VI of France was given powdered pearl with distilled water for his insanity? Did he know that Pope Adrian was never without his amulet of Oriental pearls and dried toad?

Now he did.

Not all of Larkin's pearl talk was anecdotal. On one February night while the streets and sidewalks outside were being layered with fine prevailing snow, Larkin got onto the subject of the so-called Pearl Crash of 1930. Larkin related it as though it was as important as any other history. Prior to that year, he said, the only pearls that were recognized as true pearls were the naturals, those that oysters produced entirely on their own. The culturing of pearls had come a long way since its inception in Japan around the turn of the century, however it required that a bead-shaped pellet be implanted within the oyster to irritate it and cause it to coat the pellet with a nacrous substance. No matter that the nacre was the very same that created natural pearls or even that the procedure of layers of it aggregating was an identical natural reaction. A cultured pearl was just that, cultured, and therefore had no right to be called a pearl.

The pearl dealers, who then numbered about five hundred in the world, felt strongly about this. They took their argument before an international court in France that decided in their favor. Cultured pearls, the court ruled, could not be represented as pearls, the word *pearl* couldn't be used to market them. They were beads, nothing more.

The problem that remained, however, was how to tell a pearl that was a natural from one that was cultured. No scientific method had yet been devised. The two appeared so similar that some pearl dealers began including less expensive cultureds in their lots of naturals, thus greatly increasing their profit. This practice became quite widespread, so it soon got out, and when it did, the banks that felt they'd been duped into lending on packets of pearls considerably overvalued refused to extend credit.

Simultaneously, there was the stock market crash and world depression. The purchasing power of the wealthy weakened to near impotence. In a single day the prices of natural pearls dropped 85 percent. All but a handful of pearl dealers were ruined. There'd be no recovery. The Persian Gulf countries that had been so involved in pearling realized greater riches in their oil. The legendary pearl beds such as those in the Gulf of Minar were gleaned beyond control. Those that weren't were already becoming polluted. Never again would there be a great natural pearling season.

The opportunity for cultured pearls to flourish was so obvious and easy that it seemed like destiny. Only the Arabs refused to accept pearls that had been cultured. Their belief, that only God should create such beauty, still persisted.

Larkin and Grady.

They also used to play a little game to sharpen their perceptive abilities. They'd place two pearls of only five millimeters or so on the bar, a natural and a cultured, then challenge each other to tell bare-eyed which was which. Grady became uncanny at it, in fact, far better than Larkin. Grady would study the pearls so intensely that at times they seemed magnified, and when he held them enclosed in his fist it was as though they compliantly revealed their identities to his senses.

Now, Grady was stymied. For two hours he and Doris had without success phoned around to various resources trying to come up with six strands of ten, ten and a half Kumura pinkish whites.

"Do they have to be Kumuras?"

"Yes."

"I have others."

"Thanks anyway."

Kumuras, in Grady's opinion, were the finest cultured pearls to be had. Most important, they were consistently fine. Kumura wasn't a place in Japan, as so many people believed, but a pearl-growing family with pride and high standards. The local Kumura representative, Tad Katoh, called on Grady regularly. Grady had tried to reach Katoh in this crisis, but he was somewhere in Japan on vacation. Grady also attempted to explain his problem to someone at Kumura headquarters in Shikoku but to no avail.

Now he was down to going through business cards he'd accumulated, many from the five-day Gem Trade Show he'd attended last February in Tucson. Transient encounters. The face that went with each card went unremembered. Who had been Arthur Kammerling, an amethyst and topaz carver from Idar-Oberstein, Germany? Or Hamid Naina Sally of Colombo, Sri Lanka, whose specialty was yellow, green and color-changing sapphires? Or a semiprecious dealer from Belo Horizonte, Brazil, an opal dealer named Bary from Coober Pedy, S. Australia, or for that matter a ruby dealer from, of all places, Moscow, Idaho?

Then there was Yuji Ohimi, the San Francisco representative of the Deep Sea Pearl Company, located in Otsu, Japan. Grady thought he vaguely remembered Ohimi, a tall, nearly bald, white-haired man, calm mannered and well dressed. On impulse Grady dialed the number on the card. He told the man who answered, presumably Ohimi, what he was looking for, six hanks of ten, ten and a half Kumura pearls, pinkish white.

"Do you have them?"

"Of course," Ohimi said.

"When could you show them to me?"

"Eleven o'clock."

Grady didn't see how that was possible. It was already quarter to eleven. Nevertheless, at eleven sharp Ohimi showed up at the HH reception room and was escorted into Grady's office.

Ohimi wasn't the man Grady had thought he recalled. This man was short, no more than five feet, and so stocky he was bulging his clothes. He had on a dark blue gabardine suit shiny from too many consecutive wearings and pressings, and his abundant black hair banged down over his forehead and ears. He was also wearing a fixed Japanese grin. He bowed perfunctorily and placed his black, scarred case on the seat of one of the chairs across the desk from Grady.

From the looks of the man Grady thought he wouldn't know much, if any, English, but as it turned out, he spoke it so well Grady suspected he might be more Los Angeles than Otsu.

"Please, show me," Grady said.

Ohimi had difficulty with one of the snaps on his case. Grady recognized the man's embarrassment, felt sorry for him, told him, "Take your time."

After considerably more pushing and pressing at the sticking snap it sprung open. From his case Ohimi removed an imitation chamois necklace folder, white but very soiled from being handled. He peeled away its Velcro closure and placed the floppy folder on the desk. Stepped back.

Apparently Grady was supposed to open the folder further. Anticipating that he was about to be pleased he lifted its overlapped flaps aside, left and right.

There were the pearls.

Eight hanks strung on acrylic line, each tied off with an elaborate royal purple tassel made up of slippery silk thread. Grady knew instantly and bare-eyed that before him lay a perfect example of everything that could be wrong with cultured pearls. He took up one of the hanks. It was much too heavy. A giveaway that in the culturing process the shell beads that were implanted in the oysters had been inordinately large, in order to produce more swiftly a pearl of larger size. Too swiftly for Grady, who without trying could make out the shadowy shape of the bead beneath hardly more than a couple of layers of nacre. He'd be willing to bet these pearls hadn't been allowed even six months to develop. What luster they possessed was superficial, would wear away in practically no time, and the unknowing owner, seeing her precious necklace becoming dull, would wonder what had happened, probably blame herself.

Hell, these pearls weren't even drilled well, Grady noted as he sighted them through his Nikon ten-power magnifying loupe. The edges around many of the drill holes were flaked, and the solution of Merthiolate that had been used to give these pearls a pinkish cast had concentrated in those places.

All in all these pearls were the antithesis of Kumuras. Grady told Ohimi that, bluntly.

Ohimi wasn't fazed. "Kumura quality," he contended.

Grady put the hank back into place and closed the folder.

Ohimi reached across and flipped the folder open. "Kumura quality," he insisted.

Grady had the urge to sweep the whole mess off his desk and into his wastebasket. Instead he stood, towered over Ohimi, sent down an unmistakable, dismissive glare.

Ohimi surrendered his smile, kept his head lowered but his eyes up and was mumbling gripes in Japanese as he took up his goods, dropped them negligently into his case and, without performing the obligatory bow, did his exit.

Some morning, Grady complained to himself. He turned and looked out the window for a long moment, as though something out there would be offered as a palliative. It occurred to him that he'd set and kept his own borders. How long had it been since he'd given serious thought to expanding his existence, to annexing another's? Not just a momentary impulse, squelched as swiftly as it came to mind, but serious thought.

"Mister Havermeyer won't be in today."

"Oh?" Grady didn't need to turn, knew that haughty affected voice belonged to Eunice.

"But he wants you to join him for lunch at two."

"Where?"

Eunice told him, and at half past one Grady was on his way to Harold's house across the bridge in Belvedere. One of the Bay Area's choicest residential roosts. Houses there went for millions even though only a few were situated on what might qualify as estate-size acreage. The large houses right on the water were especially side-by-side close, which, in a way, attested to the class-bonded sociability of their occupants.

Harold's house was one of those. A ten-thousand-square-foot contemporary whose backyard included frontage on Richardson Bay. Previously Harold had owned a house of traditional style in nearby Tiburon. It had eventually cramped Harold, not provided adequate blank wall for his collection of art nor free space enough for his sculptings and precious *objets*. In that regard this present house was most conducive, stark symmetry, all white and glass. Like a personal museum.

Grady pulled the Taurus into the fine graveled drive. The car was extremely dirty from having been parked in the airport lot for two weeks. It looked out of place in front of the clean, sleek structure. He got out and went up to the oversize entrance door. There wasn't a doorbell or knocker. Merely Grady's weight on an inset portion of the entranceway would activate a chime inside.

He stood in place three minutes that seemed longer before deciding the fact that he was early was the reason Harold wasn't home. Harold was always precisely on time or very late. Earliness exposed eagerness, he contended.

Grady went around to the side of the house, past impeccably lidded garbage bins to a gate. He reached over, slid the bolt aside and proceeded to the rear terrace. There was a square-shaped swimming pool like an island of ideal colored water surrounded by a sea of ideal green grass. White tubular loungers, chairs and tables arranged just so. A bright blue Italian marketplace umbrella and a painted white steel flagpole, a real tall one. Harold had a collection of flags, even some that hardly anyone could identify, such as those of Madagascar, Suriname and Tibet. Most frequently for the implied impression he flew the tricolor or the Union Jack. At the moment nothing had been hoisted, Grady noticed, although right then there was a breeze that could have caused a lot of nice furling and fluttering.

Grady's hope half expected he'd find lunch all laid out on one of the terrace tables. He'd looked forward to a leisurely couple of hours of sterling, crystal, linen and a bottle of one of Harold's show-off wines. But only a half a plastic bowl of cashews, probably stale.

Grady looked to the house. No discernable movement inside. Where was the Balinese houseboy? Normally he'd be hurrying out to ask was there anything Grady wanted.

Grady took off his suit jacket and moved a lounger around so he could sit facing the bay. The water was choppy and the sun striking upon it exaggerated its pointilistic impression. White bloated triangles of boats were running and tacking. The highrises of San Francisco a more definite backdrop than usual and, nearer, the protruding, dun-colored lump of Alcatraz, which caused Grady to consider there were all kinds of detention.

Harold got there forty minutes late. By then Grady was dozy. Harold told him not to bother getting up, pulled a lounger around for himself. Grady would have welcomed going inside, had had enough of sunning in his business clothes.

"Want a drink?" Harold asked as he sat.

"Yeah."

"Tall or short?"

"Tall, thank you."

Harold didn't look in the direction of the house, merely held two fingers high. In less than thirty seconds the houseboy arrived with the drinks. Harold must have told him to have both tall and short ready. The drinks were a Mezcal and pineapple juice concoction topped with a half-inch kicker of 180-proof rum. To not have to gulp his way through the rum Grady requested straws.

"How did the trip go?" Harold asked.

"Not bad." Grady had brought along the sales report, believing it would please his employer and father-in-law. He got it from his jacket pocket, handed it across.

Harold pushed his Gianfranco Ferré sunglasses up onto his forehead so he'd have a clear, untinted view of the report. He just squinted at the bottom line.

Grady was awaiting a smile or some praising reaction.

Only a faint uninterpretable grunt from Harold. He allowed the sales report to drop to the grass. At once the breeze stole it away through a bed of birds of paradise to get caught up in an oleander hedge.

Grady told himself he wouldn't retrieve it, not even had it accidentally slipped from Harold's fingers.

Harold repositioned his sunglasses, took a sip and crossed his feet. He was wearing a pair of elevator high-top sneakers. Had those and all his shoes custom made in Italy so they'd give him two inches more height. Not because he was so short. He just wanted to be taller than five eight in stocking feet, believed that at five ten to eleven he could get away with claiming and feeling he was close to six feet, which, as he saw it, was the masculine summit.

Harold admitted to fifty, would be sixty-two come October. He'd had his eyes done, lids and all, eight years ago and needed to have them done again. His hair had gone gray and white and its front line was well in retreat, but he hadn't done battle with that. The exposed skull skin was thoroughly freckled. For some reason his eyebrows had remained dark, and the contrast of them bushy and unkempt as they were along with his surprisingly deep voice gave him a paradoxical attractiveness. He smiled a lot. Not because he was well humored but because his number five tooth, the right upper bicuspid, was crowned with gold and a certain degree of smile would flash it. Harold had practiced before mirrors and was able to gauge by the tension he asked of his cheek muscles precisely the measure of smile required.

As for style, Harold had little of his own and was ambivalent about from where he should borrow. At times he dressed the WASP, at other times the Bijan. He had the most professional-looking golfing outfits and the best set of sticks a lot of money could buy. Belonged to the Belvedere Country Club, where his claim of severely torn ligaments in his right shoulder that would never properly heal was believed with sympathy. How unbearable, his not being able to play!

Then there was trout fishing. He owned the proper, impressive tackle. He'd talk streams and flies with anyone anytime, had elaborate opinions of the Beaverkill, the Frying Pan, the San Juan, the Middle Fork of the Salmon, said the Upper Yellowstone around Livingston was his favorite water. As though he'd fished them all. As though.

Harold held his arm up, fist clenched.

The houseboy came within seconds with a silver dish of macadamia nuts.

Grady wondered when they were really going to eat.

"Did a shipment arrive from Sri Lanka this morning?" Harold asked.

"Not that I know of."

"Probably still in customs. Juja is sending some yellow sapphires they say are the finest they've found in years."

"Cooked goods?"

"They say not but I hear Juja is hurting, so they could be cutting back on reliability. Look into it."

"Sure."

"The whole fucking market is hurting," Harold grumbled, as though the thought was more lenient let out. He munched and asked, "Heard from Gayle?"

"No."

"I spoke to her last night early."

"Where is she?"

"With her Aunt Miriam in Rancho Santa Fe, but she doesn't want you running down there."

Grady tried to recall anyone ever mentioning an Aunt Miriam. "When's she coming back?"

"As soon as everything's settled. It would only be confusing and painful for her if she came back now."

"What's not settled?"

"Gayle wants a divorce."

Grady allowed the words to sink in. They didn't have the impact they should have. "Shouldn't *she* be telling me?"

Harold sat up so his words would be right at Grady. "Look, Bowman"—What happened to Grady? Grady thought—"I didn't have you over here today to get tangled up in your emotional attitudes. It just happens that Gayle says she wants a divorce and I'm not the one to talk her out of it. Hell, divorce is no big deal, just an evolutionary paragraph, so to speak, a kind of healthful hitch that breaks up the tedium. Know what I mean?"

Grady knew. He'd heard it from Harold a number of times before, nearly syllable for syllable, Harold's condensed rationale for his four failed marriages. Once at a dinner gathering someone had pressed Harold to explain those words, and all Harold could do was repeat them.

"No," Harold continued, "I very definitely don't want my life sullied by your resentments and despondency."

Why presume I'm despondent? Grady thought.

"Naturally my favor falls on Gayle's side," Harold said, "and I'll be looking out for her interests."

"Very definitely and naturally."

"Are you ridiculing me?"

Grady looked away.

"Anyway, Bowman, what you and I have to straighten out has to do with business."

"Like what?"

"To get right to the bone of it, considering the deterioration of your and Gayle's relationship, I don't see how you'll be able to function comfortably in the firm."

He's right, Grady thought.

"Neither of us wants to suffer that kind of aggravation, do we?"

Grady thought he sure didn't, said so.

Harold flashed his gold crown. "Good. I've always had faith in your business sense."

Always isn't forever, Grady thought. Always is as long as there isn't a hitch, no need for an evolutionary paragraph. He didn't know whether he should laugh or be bitter.

"Of course, I'll help you get resituated any way I can." Another gold flash. "Actually it's been a pretty good ride, ten years, hasn't it?"

What shit, Grady thought.

Harold's face tightened again. "The other matter we have to set right is the house," he said.

Grady gathered Harold meant the house in Mill Valley. When he and Gayle were first married they'd lived in a leased apartment on Russian Hill. Gayle seemed to be satisfied with it for a while, less than a year, really, but then insisted on the house. Harold insisted on financing it, as though his holding the mortgage was a gift. "In case there's ever a sudden need to have it free and clear," he'd said. It was all drawn up tightly, the 30 percent down, the monthly payments including interest. A fifteen-year mortgage with balloons. Not a payment had been missed.

"Gayle wants the house," Harold said. "You know how much it means to her, the time she's spent on it. That's all she wants. No alimony or any of that, just the house. That's fair enough, isn't it?"

"No."

Grady stood, took up his suit jacket by the crook of a forefinger, didn't give Havermeyer even another glance. Went over to where the sales report was caught in the oleander hedge. Wounded a few birds of paradise getting to it. He decided against going out by way of the garbage side of the house, went up the steps and into and through it, on the way taking what he was certain would be a last look at the large painting he especially liked in the entrance hall. An Elizabeth Bouguereau. So long painting, he thought, you're too good for him.

CHAPTER TWO

A half hour later Grady was sitting on Muir Beach. Up on the shoulder ridge of sand the tide had built. His shoes and socks off, trouser legs rolled to his knees, shirt unbuttoned and its tails pulled out.

Thinking of other places he'd rather be.

Cozumel, Mexico, came to mind. In a world out of the ordinary, seventy feet down in the Tormentos Reefs, among the huge coral pinnacles and heads, being merely one of the swimming creatures along with eagle rays and schools of angelfish. His favorite dive, Tormentos. Did the black, big-eyed, at least two-hundred-pound grouper he'd had such lengthy communion with there eleven years ago still claim that sandy valley? Groupers probably didn't have such a life span. But he hoped so.

Even more where he'd rather be was Litchfield, Connecticut. Home. The three-story Federal-style house. Not purely, severely Federal because of its Victorian revisions, but in its heart and bones recalling the year 1785. Painted white, of course, with black wooden shutters, and like most of the other houses there along North Street set back the distance of a large lawn. Wrapped in front and along nearly all of one side by a wide, railed porch. A glider on the porch, an old standing one of metal with springs that refused to be silenced and striped canvas-colored cushions, kept up for the sake of memories. Wicker chairs and tables that were brought from the garret of the barn every year about the time when the dogwood petals fell. Returned to the barn soon after yellowed maple leaves began accumulating in their seats.

He could go back. Would. Not phone and have younger brother Jeff meet him at Kennedy or Bradley. Hurry the surprise of himself up the uneven brick walk and up the five steps of the porch and on in to his father, Fred, and his mother, Ruth, and perhaps even his older sister Janet and perhaps even his grandmother Wilma. They would be at the supper table passing portions or eating from trays while watching television. They'd maul him with hugs, pepper him with kisses, and after things had settled he would sit and exchange updates with them and he would notice that his mother and father, as ever, couldn't be within reach of each other without in some way touching.

His mother would love readying his room on the top floor, the one where the apple tree tips scratched eerily across the window screen when there was wind. Just below where the wasps squeezed in and built combs. He'd lie in that bed and reacquaint himself with that certain darkness. He'd delight in regression.

He would be eighteen again, no, fifteen. It would be the June when he'd begun at the White Flower Farm. There'd be the early morning two-mile bike ride to work along the black-topped road, passing the piled and nearly continuous rock walls and the jostling patches of wild lilies with that particular day's blossoms enjoying their turn. He'd do whatever tasks the people at White Flower wanted, proud of being able to work, whether it was helping customers load purchased plants into their cars or dividing seedlings into separate containers or edging the display beds or merely deadheading petunias. It seemed the harder the work, the more he liked it, shoveling, hauling topsoil, stacking fifty-pound bags of mulch. He'd pedal home with his jeans caked and his fingernails jammed with soil, some days almost too exhausted to smile.

He loved plants, the astounding intricacy of ferns. The acquired strength of trees, all that. Irises. During their season he'd seldom pass their bed without giving way to appreciation for their tongues and beards and the perfect arrangement in their fragrant throats.

He had learned land, learned growing. His interest surpassed his White Flower Farm chores, was intensified by books dealing with famous gardens. Versailles, of course, Hampton Court, Blenheim Palace and other grand ones, and many just as grand to him in their own way such as Barnsley House, Old Westbury, Villandry, Cranborne Manor, Sissinghurst. There were texts to help affiliate him with André Lenôtre, William Kent, Inigo Jones, Henry Wise, and Capability Brown. And in some instances there would be examples of their plans, showing in scale and detail intersecting paths and *allées*, positions of trees and gates, statuary and fountains, walls and arbors, *parterres* and hedges.

On quite a few Saturdays he would take the bus down the length of Connecticut for the purpose of the main reading room of the New York Public Library, on Fifth Avenue. He pored over articles published by the Royal Horticultural Society and such otherwise unattainable volumes as *The Formal Garden in England and Scotland, 1906*. And then he would take the long bus ride home with his head full of the future.

The University of Connecticut at Storrs. A landscape architect was what he'd be.

But at midterm of his fourth year at the university he'd been invited to spend the vacation at the home of his classmate Wendell Larkin, in Manhattan on East Seventy-fifth Street. Wendell's father, Matthew, was a gem merchant specializing in colored stones and pearls with offices in the trade district on West Forty-seventh.

Matthew Larkin asked Grady about landscape architecture. Grady explained some things and, in polite turn, asked Larkin about gems. Larkin had shown him, taken Grady to the office one morning and instructed him on how to use a loupe and let him look into a twenty-carat sapphire, a top-grade bright Ceylon. Grady wasn't merely interested, he was captivated by that intense blue inner atmosphere.

It was as though the vibrations from the crystal structure of the blue had shot into Grady's eye and instantaneously appropriated his brain. He held the stone away but returned it to his eye, again and again.

Larkin realized Grady's fascination at once and was stimulated by
it. He took other gemstones from his safe and introduced Grady
to the interior realms of emeralds and rubies and the lustrous
complexion of pearls. Larkin was the shower, Grady, the looker.
What was supposed to have been a half hour of satisfying curiosity
turned out to be three hours of engrossment. Grady was so
dazzled, so taken, that he'd hardly tasted the pastrami sandwich
lunch that Larkin had had sent up from the deli.

Grady and gemstones.

Coup de foudre! Love at first sight.

He'd told himself perhaps he'd had such a reaction because of
the kindredness of flowers and gems—their color, their mutual
requirement of earth. Just as the beauty of flowers had to be
grown, so did that of gems, crystal by crystal.

Grady gave a great deal of thought to that affinity and decided
to use it. After he graduated and had his degree, he put off
pursuing his landscaping profession, went to New York City and
took the courses offered by the Gemological Institute of America.
He wanted to be a certified gemologist. Larkin hired him full-
time. Salary and commission, office and access to the safe.

He'd remained with Larkin four years.

Until Larkin took ill and had to close down.

Larkin had helped him get the job as a stone buyer for that
most prestigious retail jeweler, Shreve and Company in San
Francisco. Grady had gotten along well right from the start with
the people at Shreve. He'd impressed them with his knowledge of
gems and his business sense.

It was through Shreve that he'd become acquainted with Harold
Havermeyer. The worst he'd heard of the man was that he was a
shrewd deal-maker, in the gem trade a high compliment.

Harold cultivated Grady, gradually. Over a two-year period
there'd been lunches and dinners and outings on his boat. Harold
had allowed Grady to see only a degree more than his public face,
enough to make Grady feel the privileged confidant. Grady hadn't
been naive, not taken in. There just wasn't any reason to suspect
Harold of self-serving motives. Their relationship was well within
the normal business-social overlay, and it hadn't come as a surprise
to Grady when Harold began dropping into the cracks of certain
moments the hints of the possibility of Grady becoming affiliated

with the Harold Havermeyer Company. Harold accelerated Grady's ambition, dilated it and shaped it to suit his own uses.

Grady was well aware of the direction he was headed and, when Harold had come right out and propositioned him with a bit more than a promise but less than an inevitability that a partnership of some kind would be down the road, Grady had joined HH and felt he was on the right course.

Meanwhile there'd been Gayle.

Brown-eyed, honey-haired Gayle, probably the most beautiful woman Grady had ever been around, and surely the most unrepressed. She was usually there when Grady got together with Harold, sometimes expensively dressed at lunch, often barely dressed at the pool or on the boat. Grady had plenty of opportunities to steal looks at her body, and frequently she caught him at it and sentenced him to solitary with a defiant stare.

The first time they were alone together at night was after a supper following the symphony. It was raining and she had volunteered to give him a lift home. They were in evening clothes, and she'd had her dress pulled way up to free her legs for driving. Grady had kept about half his attention straight ahead. They were going up Geary, the cadence of the wipers contrary to the tempo of Luther Vandross singing "She Doesn't Mind." Gayle wasn't teasing. He doubted that she ever had been, when, late going through an amber light, she reached over and got his hand and led it to her, to the in between that she swung open for him.

Loose leg holes. Just a strip of silk, no impediment.

She told him later, and it was only half a fib and a commending one at that, that within the twenty blocks to his place she'd come twice. Because the touch had been his, she'd said.

For the following two months Grady had felt off-register, altered by so much sexual wallowing. The power she admitted he had over her body was flattering. Whenever he'd said he was burned out, one way or another, she'd ignite him. Had his system always had the potential to produce so much semen? Wasn't too much of anything toxic?

"We needn't get married but we should," she'd told him one night when she was on top and they'd both just come and he was softening.

He'd known from the start she was clever. Had taken pride in that aspect of her, witnessed it often in the way she maneuvered, charmed out of uncomfortable situations, white lied so credibly. However, it wasn't until the fifth married year that he'd learned she was and had been most clever with him.

The ninth floor of the St. Francis Hotel.

Suite 908, where Grady had kept an appointment to show goods to George Keller, a client from St. Louis. Nothing unusual about that; quite a few clients preferred the courtesy. He'd come out of 908 at the very moment when the door to 909 across the way opened and a dark-haired middle-aged man wearing a hotel towel pushed a room service cart out into the hall.

Grady had caught at most a five-second glimpse of Gayle in 909, nude in an armchair. She was unaware that he'd seen her and denied it when he'd confronted her but only stood her ground for a half hour. Then she'd shifted her tack to confession and tears. It was, she contended between choking sobs and a lot of nose blowing, a first-time slip, a dumb dalliance. She pleaded forgiveness. Reasoned for it. Wasn't she deserving of one carnal error? (Her exact words.)

That her passion with him hadn't ever waned was in her favor. Was it possible she could come home from all those specious shoppings at Neiman Marcus, girlfriend luncheons at Fleur de Lys, browsings of Chinatown and so on, and still be able that same night to make such responsive love with him?

He thought so.

But he gave her the benefit of the doubt. Let her squirm off the hook for the St. Francis stray. Even if he couldn't forget it, he wouldn't ever bring it up.

Gayle was disappointed.

As though she felt he hadn't been adequately provoked by the chink in her that she'd exposed. She was determined that he should be. Increased her shoppings and browsings, made guesswork out of them and thinned her excuses until they were thoroughly transparent. It had been a sort of perverse campaign during which she taught him to decipher her lies the moment she was telling them.

And now this—the inevitable divorce from Gayle and the sudden severance from Harold Havermeyer.

Fuck them. And fuck Aunt Miriam in Rancho Santa Fe, who

was most likely a dark-haired, middle-aged man or lead guitarist on tour with some heavy metal group currently playing Milwaukee.

Sand fleas were excited around his bare toes.

A gull swooped to see if he might leave a scrap.

He wasn't bilious bitter, but he did feel a seven-year chunk had been taken out of him, one out of every five of his days. Gayle wanted the house? Well, she couldn't have it, at least, not all of it. He had four hundred thousand equity in the house. Gayle could have what she was legally, if not morally, entitled to. Half. She could also have all her catgut-strung wooden tennis rackets, old framed photos of Yale rowing crews and other crap. If he had to, he'd fight and fight dirty for his two hundred thousand share. He was going to need that money and more . . . to get the Grady Bowman Company on the door and off the ground.

CHAPTER THREE

During the cognac and coffee phase of a sit-down dinner for ten last November, the conversation had somehow gotten onto the subject of wills, the legal kind, and Julia Elkins, with nothing to contribute, not even mild interest, had tuned out.

Now she sort of wished she'd listened. Not that she felt it vital at age thirty-four to know more about wills than she'd managed to glean from certain books over the past couple of weeks, but perhaps, she thought, she'd missed something that would have put her on surer ground. She had to trust that this lawyer, Martin Browderbank, in whose reception room she was now seated, would understand the simple kind of will she wanted. It wouldn't do if he complicated and took weeks to draw up the papers for her signature. In fact it wouldn't do if he took days.

Tomorrow was Thursday, the eighteenth of June, the deadline she'd set on her mind's calendar. An arbitrary date, yes, but procrastination wouldn't become an adversary as long as she didn't let it get started.

Having a will was an afterthought, really. From her point of view what she could leave anyone wasn't much. Her collection of her own paintings were the most valuable and would be more so afterward. Then, there was her Jeep Cherokee, and a few minor pieces of jewelry such as the strand of pearls she now wore. She wanted Royce to have the paintings. For six years he'd been the steadiest, most dependable person in her life. Her next-door neighbor Royce, who couldn't help but lilt and be light of foot and drop the famous names he claimed he'd *been with,* which was how he put it. It didn't matter to Julia that Royce's homosexual escapades were figments. They were entertaining and amusing and, she believed, according to her extended way of believing, they were true. Kind, thoughtful, gentle-minded Royce, who looked after her cat, Maxx, and had surprised her several times when she'd returned from trips to find he'd put her studio in impeccable order. Royce, who really did know how to make the best *crème brûlée* she'd tasted since her days in France. He loved her in the way that had become acceptable to her. Their relationship was complex only in its simplicity. He was the only genuinely asexual person she'd ever known.

It was he who'd insisted she wear this hat today. (He was often around to be involved in her getting dressed.) This insouciant construction of felt touched with a few small feathers. She'd bought it at I. Magnin last year on an afternoon when she'd had some frivolous energy. Had tried on twenty hats and decided on this one only because she'd already tried on twenty. Ever since then it had been kept from dust in a tied tight plastic bag up on the second shelf of her bedroom closet.

The giving in to wearing it today had set off a chain reaction. The hat had demanded that her natural blonde hair be not so relaxed and more attention be given to her makeup. The slacks and sweater she'd planned on wearing were not at all right, but a short-sleeved afternoon dress of sleek, somewhat animate rayon was, in a rich blue shade that complemented both the hat and her eyes. Then required were compatible shoes, a pair of medium-heeled pumps only a year out of style and hose that unobviously idealized the complexion of her legs.

Although it wasn't how she'd intended to look, she was now rather glad she'd been influenced. There'd been a time in her life when fashion had been important to her, however not lately. It didn't matter that with her height and slender figure she looked well in clothes, nor that she had the taste required to exceed safe, repetitive choices. Fashion, like most other things of that nature, had become degree by degree, season by season, irrelevant. Anyway, the image of the artist was better served by inelegance, she rationalized.

As though prompted by those thoughts, Julia took up from the reception room side table the June edition of *Vogue*. Paged through it mindlessly until it occurred to her that the women of the photographs, they with their put-on ennui or predation, exemplified detachment. Who could touch them? How could they possibly be anything other than misunderstood? There, in those crowded challenging eyes and impatient mouths and insubordinate stances, was insularity most blatant. They knew, these lanky sisters mired in vanity, perhaps temporarily medicated by vanity. They knew even if they weren't yet aware that they knew.

Julia came to a perfumed page, sniffed it obediently, then, for a respite, lowered the magazine. Enough so her eyes overlooked the crease of its binding and focused upon the man seated across the room.

She'd noticed him before, of course, but now, she had the opportunity to more than merely notice. He seemed to be napping. At least his eyes were genuinely closed. Perhaps he was resting his eyes. What was she doing? Just something to pass time, Julia told herself. She wasn't studying him because he was a man and an attractive one at that. Had the person with whom she was occupying this waiting space been an older woman or a child she'd have done the same. It was a practice she'd come to rely on, the observing of others in detail, the mental painting of them, so to speak. Often it had helped cool down the buildup within her subjective furnace.

The first thing she contemplated were his shoes. Shoes usually betrayed the person. His weren't new, nor were they cheap. Black, cap-toed, probably self-shined. Italian made, according to their better leather and more delicate soles. How neatly he'd tied his shoelaces, she noticed. His plain dark gray socks revealed by the seated hitch-up of his trousers said nothing except that they were plain dark gray, appropriate for his suit, a conservative, subtly striped gray on gray worsted that fit him well. He had ample shoulders for the slouchy cut of the unpadded jacket and his white shirt appeared soft, not at all punishing to his neck. However, that tie, the bow tie, spoiled everything. It was wine colored with a small gray geometric pattern. Looked like some rare species of butterfly about to take flight.

Julia despised the tie but forgave him for it. At least it wasn't a clip-on sort. Perhaps he'd been in need of a rebellious note that morning or perhaps he believed bows provided jauntiness to his cachet and he was phobic when it came to mirrors.

Except for the bow, she approved. He was, she guessed, in his midthirties, no gray yet at his temples and nothing contrived about his hairstyle. Dark brown hair combed straight back. Tended eyebrows but not overtended. A good honest nose and some extra strength in his chin. His hands weren't relaxed; they were half clenched, only a swift reflex from becoming fists. What was he ready to fight? Julia wondered.

He stirred, opened his eyes.

Julia brought the *Vogue* up. A stockbroker, a marketing or publishing person or something of that sort, she thought. Married to his college sweetheart and wishing they hadn't had so many kids so soon. Such was life. And hardly a moment to consider what it was until there weren't many moments left. Distractions, including the unpleasant ones, were a blessing while they lasted. Fortunate were those who could make them last all the way from oblivion to oblivion.

She placed *Vogue* back on the table, decided not to look into the edition of *People* that was there. Glanced across at the man, and because his attention happened to be upon her, she smiled. A mere acknowledging smile. He responded with a smile, more of a smile than hers. She liked his smile, so she couldn't take too much of it, looked aside, not really seeing the fox-hunting print on the wall, looked down at the Persian area rug on the walnut-stained hardwood floor, then at her watch, which told her it was already ten minutes past her ten o'clock appointment. And the man over there might be scheduled ahead of her. She had things she needed to accomplish, mainly the painting she'd promised the gallery, a commission from her last show. She'd gotten up at dawn and done some work on it in order to be able to finish it on time. Anyway, she didn't want to spend a good part of this day of all days in this legal box.

She asked the man, "Are you waiting for Mister Browderbank?"

"No," he replied, "Mister McGuin." McGuin was the other half of this law firm.

"Is he running late?"

"Yeah."

"Seems to be the nature of the beast."

A resigned shrug by the man.

A concurring sigh from Julia.

Silence entered the exchange. Julia recrossed her legs. Her hose caused a frictional sound, much like a sizzle. She was arranging the skirt of her dress when the pearls happened.

For no apparent reason, the thread between the sixth and seventh pearls down from the clasp of Julia's twenty-eight-inch-length necklace chose that instant to give way. A surprised oops from Julia as, like some living thing, the necklace slid down her front and out of her lap. Proper knots prevented some of the pearls from coming loose, however a great many rolled free, scattered individually in every direction, as though delighted with the prospect of escape.

Julia began retrieving them.

The man helped.

At first they bent over and picked up from the surface of the Persian rug those most obvious. Next they were down on their hands and knees, searching and finding the creamy white spheres. The more evasive ones had rolled all the way to the baseboard and to corners. Some necessitated reaching way in under the couch.

"I didn't realize they were so small," Julia commented as she found one of four millimeter size trying to be overlooked behind the back leg of a chair. She deposited it into the man's cupped hand. For some reason Julia now felt the necklace was safer with him.

"Do you think we've found them all?" she asked.

"Probably not, but nearly. When did you last have them restrung?" he asked.

"I never have," she replied. "Oh, how embarrassing!"

"Happens to people all the time."

"Really?" Nervous laugh. "How do you know that?"

He didn't answer.

"Do you go around helping people pick up their pearls?" she asked lightly. "Is that what you do?"

He was examining the pearls, tossing them respectfully back and forth from hand to hand, causing clicks, holding up those that had remained stranded. "Hair spray, perfume and such gets to the thread and eventually rots it. Pearls should be cared for and restrung twice a year, anyway at least once." He continued to look at them, saw they were only fair quality but nice enough. Four to eight millimeter graduated. Twelve hundred retail. "These weren't properly strung to begin with," he told Julia.

"They should have been," she said. She'd bought the necklace from a New York jeweler, on Fifth Avenue at that.

"There weren't proper knots between each pearl," the man explained. He seemed about to hand the pearls over to her when, as though on second thought, he said, "I could have these restrung right for you. On silk."

"Don't bother."

"No bother, really." He gave her a business card.

She saw that the Harold Havermeyer Company and its address and telephone number had been neatly crossed out but not Precious Gems and Grady Bowman. A telephone number was hand-printed near the name. "My new ones are being printed," he told her and read her ambivalence. "No need to worry. I won't make off with your pearls." He smiled her an even better smile. "If you want I'll write you a receipt for them."

"That won't be necessary."

"Okay then, I'll have them for you within a week. How can I get in touch with you?"

CHAPTER FOUR

A t half past noon that day Julia arrived home from attorney Browderbank.

Found that two birds, common sparrows, had gotten into her studio by way of a broken pane of the skylight. The week before some boys and perhaps a girl or two higher up on Potrero Hill hadn't been able to resist that expanse of panes and had flung some heavy hexagonal-headed bolts at it. Evidently it was mischief they'd needed to get out of their systems as they hadn't been throwing since. Julia, instead of driving up and complaining to parents and all that, had decided what the hell, let them have this fling.

But now the sparrows. Were they lovers come in searching for a softer more private place to nest? Or a couple of buddies on an expedition for better quality crumbs? Well, they had regrets now. Way up there, two stories up, out of help's reach, panicking, beating hysterically against one pane and then the next, fooled by the clarity, believing what looked to be sky was sky.

The sparrows had Maxx crazed. Julia's Russian Blue cat. He was up on the tallest possible thing, which happened to be the top of a seven-foot-high metal storage cabinet. Up there despising his futility but keeping his eyes so fixed on the birds he seemed to be trying to will them into the fatal error of giving up their twelve feet of protective altitude.

Julia called Maxx down but he ignored her, ordered him down but he still wouldn't mind, was entirely removed, heeding only primeval genes, absorbed in a kill. Julia gave up on him.

She went to the front hall and up to her bedroom on the second floor. Having been away for hours she was able to realize how strongly the odors of painting permeated the place. Her intention when she'd renovated the house was to keep her work and living spaces separate. To create the studio she'd knocked down the walls and eliminated the ceilings of the rooms situated in the north half. Then created double-doored passageways to serve as buffer chambers between the studio and the rest of the house. The arrangement would have been more effective had she been less lax about the doors. More often than not they were left wide open, the purpose of those intermediate spaces lost to the synaptic relativity of artistry and ordinary existence. Too, there was the sort of negligence that Julia came upon now as she opened her closet door.

She saw four pairs of sneakers, so thoroughly and thickly splattered they appeared to be made of paint. Their eyelets caked, laces saturated and so rigid they couldn't be untied. (She had to shoe-horn her feet in.) Several pairs of jeans and a pair of overalls in the same condition, like stiff tunnels into which she inserted her legs. Time and again she'd reminded herself to leave her messy smelly things in the studio, however, she forgot so regularly the rule no longer had any force.

She unpinned and removed her hat. Disregarded the plastic bag it had been kept in, tossed the hat up onto the second shelf. It tumbled back down as though protesting. She let it lie where it fell.

Took off her clothes, everything, hurriedly as though she were removing shackles. Hung up the dress but left shoes, hose, underthings batched on the closet floor. She decided against the old jeans and overalls, even the old sneakers. They'd been faithful and she owed them consideration, but her skin told her it wouldn't tolerate them today. For the past year she'd often painted while nude. In fact nudity had been growing into one of her conditions for painting. She didn't entirely believe it had elicited the something extra from her that had resulted in what many regarded as her best work, however neither did she entirely believe in coincidence.

After scrubbing off her makeup, she contained her hair in a cheap blue cowboy bandanna.

Went down to the studio. The sparrows were still nervous and chirping but had found a high perch. Maxx, by then resigned to quandary, had reverted to his normal superior forbearance and was sitting by the rear door, gazing up at its knob. Julia let him out.

The studio was, as usual, a mess. A comfortable, familiar mess. It astounded people, especially the magazine and newspaper interviewers who came there, that Julia was able to compose such impeccably ordered paintings while besieged by such rampant disorder. When asked about that her stock reply was presumptuous but too flip to be taken seriously. "Hasn't that always been the neat trick?" she'd say, no doubt referring to God's and her own accomplishments.

Had she only picked up the newspapers and the plastic bowls it would have made a difference. When she spilled or dripped paint, varnish, thinner or whatever on the enameled hardwood floor, to avoid stepping in it she covered it with a sheet of newspaper. When paint fell on that sheet of newspaper she simply covered it with another. The paint dried, the newspapers stuck. The plastic bowls, shallow, one-quart size, she'd paid less than a reasonable price for at a liquidation sale south of Market Street. Bought a thousand, so she used them indiscriminately to mix in. Colors exacted to her vision canvases ago, so precious then, evaporated, hardened, crackled in those bowls that were everywhere, hundreds of bowls. And nearby just as many mayonnaise and pickle jars and paint cans, gone dry with stirring sticks and forsaken brushes upright in them. Brushes that had been favorites were abandoned or lost in the chaos, their bristles rigored, turned ugly, curled. There were used rags, sponges, silvery gallon containers of varnish and linseed oil, thinner and turpentine, the screw tops of them somewhere.

The expanse of a permanently placed trestle-type table off to one side was beneath a section of soft, raw pine boards nailed to the wall upon which she stuck-pinned sketched ideas, inspirations, photos, reminders of things she wanted not to forget that she'd forgotten. That table and her larger ten-foot easel were the dominant things. She preferred to work on the large easel, felt it contributed more than functional support with its substantialness and heft, served rather like a steadfast anchor while she floated about in rarer realms. The surface of a smaller table was her palette. It could be rolled about, a willing thing to be nudged this way or that, pushed aside or brought closer. And, when it became too coated and uneven with daubs, swirls and mixes, all that was required to give it a fresh top were a rectangle of wood and a few nails. She often thought of it as her devoted collaborator, and if she were ever being dispossessed and allowed to carry away only one thing that little table would be it.

She wasn't sure whether or not she wanted music this afternoon, nevertheless she chose some compact discs and put them into the player, not in any particular order this time. Normally she began with something that had a lot of energy, like a Roxette. What came up first today was some Bach that was entirely wrong, too processional, solemn. She cut it before it could get to her and then it was Van Morrison doing "I'm Not Feeling It Anymore" causing Julia to bob her head and dance her arms and shoulders almost involuntarily as she made her way to the easel.

She took a good, long critical look at the canvas that was on it.

Was the background complementary enough? Did it look like a Rothko trying too much to look like a Gaugun trying to look Derain? No, she thought, this landscape of the southern Oregon coast was her looking like no one else. Her friend the little table née palette agreed. And that was prime enough to start her squeezing cobalt violet from a fresh tube, and from another equally fresh, cobalt rose. She also decided this final go warranted fresh brushes, got them from the cabinet.

And began.

She worked practically nonstop for four hours, not even aware that she'd run out of music. She would have continued had the light not been deserting her. Then she put a Wynton Marsalis on the player, switched on the daylight fluorescents and went right back at it, working until close to nine, to finish satisfied.

As always after such a long, intense stint she felt let down, was all at once clearly conscious of the time, the conditions of where she was and her fatigue. She shoved the sticky-handled brushes into a jar and poured in some cleaner. Used some of the cleaner to remove much of the paint on her hands and, as well, the drips and dribbles that had fallen onto her bare feet.

She padded into the kitchen and decided against instant coffee, brewed a whole pot of fresh ground Colombian in the automatic maker. She was hungry, so sliced apart nearly half the length of a loaf of Italian bread, upon which she put a slab of Ghirardelli bittersweet chocolate. Placed that in the microwave on convection and watched the melt through the little window.

She took a mug of the coffee and the enormous chocolate sandwich into the adjacent room, which she called her parlor. Turned on a lamp and sat on the edge of the French daybed that was overpillowed and situated beneath the front windows. The chocolate had cooked to a crust and the bread had become crustier and combined they tasted especially delicious. She took big, jaw-straining bites, and after the first few chewed them longer. Counted aloud in a whisper fifty chews each mouthful.

"Don't wolf your food, Julia."

"I'm not."

"For proper digestion it takes at least fifty chews. I want to see you do fifty."

"Supper will take all night if I have to do fifty."

"I'll be watching, young lady."

That hadn't really happened to her, Julia thought. None of her before time seemed as though it had happened. She was only connected to it, or it to her by some extremely tensile fiber. Anyway, it shouldn't have happened and if it had to it should have happened differently. Mother should have been capable of more than sporadic fits of cherishing. The cherishing times stood out, held the keys to the locks on their gates in her memory.

Berry picking was one. Berry picking in that patch of whiplike brambles at the edge of that certain field partway down the road between Amenia and Sharon. Some farmer's field of wild oats and hay grass with a lot of red-winged blackbirds in it. The NO TRESPASSING signs didn't apply because unless picked the berries would go to waste. Surely there were more than the birds could eat, mother had remarked. She, Julia at seven years, hadn't been tall enough to reach the upper brambles where the berries were thickest, so mother had interrupted her own anxious picking to bend down to her. They ended up crawling into the domain at the base of the stalks. Enduring scratch and snag to get to the berries that had so ripened they'd fallen. Sweetest of all. "Not as sweet as you," mother had said, up close, nearly nose to nose with her in that little prickly jungle. From the crawl and crush the knees and bottoms of their jeans were stained magenta. Full baskets, a full afternoon, one fuller heart and jam making together tomorrow.

Rare occasion.

Mother hoarded her words, her smiles and demonstrations of affection, as though she'd been allotted just so many. She expended even fewer on father. He was a malleable sort, who'd shaped his persona to fit, who crept back into the silent remove of himself and could only appear to prefer it.

At times he was talkative and at times demonstrative. It was as if he'd suddenly spill over. He was a sign painter by trade. A thin man with sparse exceptionally controlled hands. There'd been afternoons and some early nights when Julia was permitted into his workroom and up onto a high stool at his long table. To be with him while he blocked out the letters of a sign on a sheet of metal, or a strip of oilcloth or piece of cardboard. She hardly dared breathe as she watched him fill in the outlines, usually with red or black, amazed at how straight he was able to flow the paint on at the edges. Hers had to be wordless appreciation or she'd be banished.

Father never made much money. Enough for rented places to live in was all. Even less when FOR SALE and GOING OUT OF BUSINESS and KEEP OUT and other signs began to be mass produced and sold in hardware stores and such. He gold-leafed the names and titles of many far more successful men on office doors for not much per letter. And when times got even slacker he painted names and address numbers on rural mailboxes.

Julia believed that was as intimate as she'd ever been with him, the closest to sharing. Her with him in the secondhand, ten-year-old Dodge pickup going over the lesser roads of northwestern Connecticut, up into Massachusetts and around Columbia County in New York. Soliciting mailbox work. She wasn't bashful about going up to a farmhouse front door and asking. And when she returned to the car bringing him an order, what triumph!

"You're some girl," he'd say, "some girl."

The both of them were gone now, twelve years gone when an instant on New York State Route 44, a mile out of Millertown, took them. The instant sooner or the instant later wouldn't have instantly killed them head-on.

A psychic, a woman in Paris with hair like a mass of rusted steel wool, told Julia that her parents' deaths were more intended than accidental, the conclusion of the lessons they were supposed to learn in these lifetimes. Julia thought that was bunk, but she regretted having seen the psychic because ever since, that premise had been like a rock in her shoe.

"Gone is gone forever, over is over forever," she now said aloud with conviction, and then mumbled, "whatever *forever* is."

She left the daybed and got a bottle of wine from the hivelike rack in the pantry. The bottle of vintage '84 Chateau Margaux she'd bought over a year ago for now. She uncorked the wine, wiped its upper neck and lip clean, got a delicate crystal goblet from her almost genuine-looking Empire breakfront and went upstairs. To her bedroom and the bedside drawer where she kept her death.

Actually, she didn't think she was keeping it as much as it was awaiting her.

The four amber vials were right there where they'd been for those many months, ready to facilitate, forbearing her ambivalence. By now she felt there was only one vial she could absolutely count on. She'd been meaning to call and ask Dr. Fremont how old sodium pentobarbital could be and still be good, and once a couple of months back she'd gone into a pharmacy to ask that, but there'd been others waiting before her at the dispensing counter so she'd put it off.

One of the prescriptions went back to when she'd lived outside of Cody, nearly four years ago. Two were around a year old. The certainly potent one was dated April fifteenth last. Those several times when she'd opened the vials to examine the capsules and reflect on their adequacy, she'd been careful they didn't get mixed. She would dump the capsules from one of the vials into the palm of her hand. How identical they were! Absolute equality! And such a vibrant color, a cadmium yellow, the shade of buttercups, as pretty as candy. They seemed to be promising their effect would be sweet.

There'd be none of that tonight, no mere flirting with it.

She poured some wine, took more of a gulp than a sip. That was one regret, that she hadn't drunk more wine when she'd had the chance in Burgundy and the Rhône and places. Well, maybe next time, she told herself facetiously and ridiculed the thought with a little laugh aloud.

The promised canvas was done. The will had been willed. Her organs pledged, her request not to be put on a life-support system legally made. Maxx would be cared for. There was no reason in the world to put it off.

She ascertained that the vial she opened was the recent one. Dumped the thirty capsules it contained into the footed candy dish that was on the nightstand. Brilliant yellow intermixed with the aubergine of Caswell black currant cough lozenges. The yellows outstanding. No way to miss them. Each capsule contained a hundred milligrams. Ten capsules added up to a gram, so three grams altogether. *Death commonly occurs after the ingestion of two grams or more of sodium pentobarbital* were the words she'd read in the *Physician's Desk Reference* the day she was browsing Waldenbooks.

So three grams should surely do it.

Especially when potentiated by the grand *vin* Margaux.

She wouldn't, however, stuff all thirty capsules into her mouth at once like just so much popcorn. No, she'd relish the doing, prolong it, experience as much as she could of the transition, so to speak. Like this!

With a slight flourish and the dilatoriness of ceremony she placed four of the capsules on her extended tongue, and washed them down with the wine that remained in the goblet.

She wasn't being dramatic, she told herself. There was no one to be dramatic for. Drama requires audience and she had audience of none. She was on her way to doing it, she was really going to. Her disposition tonight matched her inclination, she thought.

Emptiness.

And no outlook, nor trust in the prospect, of fulfilling.

She downed another ten capsules quickly.

Fixed her pillows, plumped and arranged them, got beneath the covers, neatened the top edges over and around her. Lay on her back in a corpselike symmetrical position, waiting for the first sensation, which she would accept as the signal to swallow more of the yellows, and rapidly.

Meanwhile she would enjoy while it was under way the experience of the release from that which so long had plagued her. How long? When had it first overcome her?

She'd been born with it, everyone was.

All right, granted, but when had she first become aware of it? Through and through.

She knew, thought back to then, to that day she arrived in the small town of Dinard on the coast of Brittany. She'd had the final falling-out with Jean Luc after telling him her opinion of his paintings, those huge white square on white and blue square on blue monstrosities that qualified him as a minimalist. He'd slap on a layer of white, contemplate it for a month, then, as though inspired to decision, paint on a slightly whiter or less white square. His sycophantic friends at the Ecole des Beaux-Arts would rave, and when their *éclat* diminished he'd restore it by simply painting another variation, a gray gray or a beige beige.

Honest admission, the reason she'd stayed with Jean Luc for the second of their two years was the sex. Friction and fantasy, that's all it was. The fantasy part finally came up blank, and the friction of it desensitized when, in front of everyone at a gathering, Jean Luc used her modest but sincere work as an example of (his words) a so-called artist being victimized by self-deceit. She wasn't about to take ridicule lying down.

"Fucking fake!" she retaliated.

"*Con Américaine*," he spat. American cunt.

Good-bye sex. Better she should do without.

From Jean Luc she went west into Normandy. Loaded down with nearly all that belonged to her, she stayed in affordable, inconvenient hotels. A few days here, a few there, floating, watercoloring, enjoying being aimless, eventually despising the oppression of her several pieces of luggage.

The towns where she spent time became smaller and smaller, the accommodations cheaper and cheaper. Crocy, Desertine, La Tricherie. Dinard was not a destination. It just happened to be where she reached the coast. By then she'd shucked off most of her carry, just left things behind. Felt lighter in spirit, more the part of the vagabond artist without a suitcase on the end of her arm. Instead, a blue nylon backpack containing three changes of underthings and socks, one change of all else and her box of watercolors. Her fold-up easel was secured to its straps, a table of watercolor paper under her arm.

Dinard. In mid-January it seemed to be a town in coma. Still breathing but not animate. The purveying shops and restaurants so dependent on summer were closed. Even the places that didn't appear closed were closed. The streets of the town had lost their purpose with hardly a car or person moving along them. On the other side of the year they'd be bustling, money would be changing hands, the English would be there, nine hours by ferry out of Portsmouth.

Julia wandered Dinard's lesser streets, believing it was there she'd most likely find a place to stay. Dreary old unwelcoming streets. She gave up on them for Avenue George V, the wider main way that ran along and above the beach. The afternoon was turning to dusk. The sun that should have been in the western sky was clouded out. Dampness was invading, the grit of errant beach sand was beneath her steps. It appeared that she'd have to settle for some deep doorway.

She continued down the avenue, thinking the beach on her left wasn't at all Boudin. Even a single striped umbrella would have done it a world of good. Up ahead across the avenue on the right was the largest hotel, Le Grand. A gray structure of nine stories, lonelier looking because of its size. All its many windows shuttered, hundreds of windows. Julia wondered whose responsibility it had been to close them. Out of curiosity she went up to the hotel's front entrance, peered in through the glass of one of its formidable doors.

She saw a light inside, and a man.

The man noticed her, came to the door and for a long moment, separated by the glass of it, which was like nothing, looked her over. She would never really know what he saw, of course, but what she saw was a hulk of a man with a mass of gray hair that met a mass of gray beard that hid his mouth. He had clear young eyes and a kind right hand because it unbolted the door so that she could enter.

His name was Monsieur Varen. He volunteered that he was the off-season concierge, caretaker, janitor, hotel minder or whatever. They sat opposite each other in two of the hard upholstered chairs of the lobby. No one else was in the hotel, not a soul, then again, he said, perhaps a soul or two. He smiled at that and his mouth, Julia thought, was like a sea urchin in a bed of weed revealing itself, glistening slick pink.

He took for granted she was an artist and she liked that. He asked to see some of her watercolors and especially cared for one she'd done in Vernon of a field speckled with poppies. It was the most expressionistic thing she'd attempted, bordered on abstract, but he recognized what it was immediately, held the watercolor at arm's length and said, "*Coquelicot!*" as though enjoying the word.

She made him a gift of the painting.

He gave her a place to sleep. And more.

She would have considered one of the sofas in the lobby a luxury, but Monsieur Varen wouldn't hear of it. She was, after all, in a manner of speaking, his guest. He left her seated there, and after about a quarter hour returned for her, took her up in the cage of the main elevator to the ninth, the top floor. To one of the choice front rooms. The bed had been freshly made and was turned down, the tall windows opened, their shutters swung aside. On a tray on the main table was a bottle of Vichy, a half bottle of local cider, two baguettes, a slice of ham and a jar of *confiture de framboise*. Julia guessed the Vichy water and the preserves had come from the hotel kitchen, the cider, ham and bread from Varen's supper. She was touched by his thoughtfulness.

"There is no running water nor electricity," he informed apologetically. "But there are candles." He indicated several on the dresser.

"I prefer candles."

"I'll draw some kitchen water and leave it outside your door."

"Thank you."

"*Ça ne fait rien,*" Varen said and was gone before Julia could thank him again.

She got acquainted with the room. It, everything in it, had that odor usually assimilated from being so near the sea. Not unpleasant really, just distinctive and not how one would preferably have chairs and drapes and bed linens smell. The nap of the wall-to-wall carpet was clotted from being usually damp and trampled. The sheets and pillowcases overstarched. There were two rather identical darker areas on the upholstered headboard where the backs of heads had been placed, causing hair oils to be transferred.

These were observations, not complaints.

What remarkable luck! One minute she's out in the street believing she'll have to use a doorstep for a pillow, the next she's all comfy in a room that probably cost five hundred a day high season. Monsieur Varen had certainly restored her faith in the French male. Was it possible she'd be able to stay there a few days? To do some seascapes. She'd ask the kind Monsieur but in a way that surely conveyed she wasn't trying to take unfair advantage.

She heard him now outside the door, expected his knock. But when, after a long moment, she opened the door, he was headed down the darkened hall to the elevator, his back to her, bidding her, "*Bonne nuit, mademoiselle.*"

"*Bonne nuit, monsieur,*" she called out and brought in the two pails of water he'd left.

Oncoming night was swiftly taking color from everything. Julia looked out the open double window and could hardly distinguish the demarcation of shore and sea. The avenue below was an undisturbed gray stream. The room had also turned gray. She closed and latched the window. Lighted three candles and stood them in their own melt in hotel ashtrays, to revive the rose beige of the tall walls, the deep burgundy of the carpet, the floral pattern of the bedspread and drapes, her own flesh and clothes.

She ate at the main table by candlelight and afterward pushed the chair back and put her feet up. The cider was more toward hard than soft, had a slight warm kick to it, sweet and acidic to the tongue and throat. It reminded Julia of the autumns not many years ago when she'd worked in the apple orchards around home and up in places like Ancram and Austerlitz. Picking for so much a bushel and sometimes helping at the cider press for so much an hour. Saving every dime, eager to work in order to save and thinking of her savings as her *someday leaving money*. And look where it had taken her, beyond Jean Luc and all the way to the top floor of a hotel on the Côte d'Emeraude.

A contented sigh came from her, then a feeling of well-being so pervasive it caused a smile. She was thoroughly pleased with herself and with having encountered the kindness of fellow human being Monsieur Varen.

It was at that moment her outlook inverted. Her optimism drained. Why just then, when she was feeling so at one with the world, had she been struck by such severe reality? Perhaps her breaking off from Jean Luc had brought it on. Or was it prompted by her being the lone occupant of that large hotel? The proximity of all those separate forsaken rooms, the infection of so much emptiness? Or had it been what had occurred at the entrance of the hotel, the instant when she and Monsieur Varen had been separated by the clear glass door panel and through it had tried to decipher each other? Whatever, no doubt it had been all the while within her just below the surface, waiting to be revealed with the most possible impact.

She felt her isolation.

Julia Elkins alone all the way with Julia Elkins. No one else, not really.

She'd known, of course, that was how life was, but she'd never dwelled upon it. Throughout her emotionally detached childhood she'd looked forward to the adult time when she'd be out on her own. That would be when her sense of solitariness would dissipate, countered by her exposure to others, relationships, the back and forth trading of experiences. She would be permitted to be demonstrative and be the reason for demonstration. There'd be no end to such exchanges, she had thought. There was so much to share.

However, she had just come to realize that sharing, absolute open-hearted sharing, which seemed such a natural human necessity, was actually an illusion. Every word, touch, smile, even pain, would be limited to interpretation. There'd be no connections adequate enough to disprove the insularity, only a lifelong series of futile attempts to connect and time after time of deluding one's self.

Blessed were the entirely self-involved, perhaps. And the totally ignorant, possibly.

It wasn't a matter of believing or not, of having faith or not. Apartness, literal apartness, was the bitter, irremediable fact of life. And the more sensitive the person the more exasperating it would be.

That had certainly been the case with Julia, who now, twelve years after Dinard, had had enough of it, was giving up. She and her apartness in her bed in her house on Portrero Hill in San Francisco with over a thousand milligrams of sodium pentobarbital in her system and more at the ready.

Lord knows she'd tried to endure, had sought ease through all sorts of things, from prodigal passion to penitential psychotherapy. None of her love affairs had exceeded a one-month stand, and after hearing her out during the first forty-five-minute session, the psychiatrist she'd gone to in Manhattan diagnosed her as a depressive with recurrent melancholia and obsessive thoughts. She went along with him for three months. The antidepressant medication he prescribed didn't do her any good because, contrary to his theory, she wasn't chemically unbalanced; her brain was using a normal amount of the normal kinds of neurotransmitters that were normally firing across the normal synaptic gaps of her brain cells. Evidently, depression wasn't her problem. Desolation due to perceptivity was more like it. Her self-diagnosis was the Nathanael West-Sylvia Plath-Jules Pascin syndrome. When she told that to the psychiatrist he'd laughed. When he'd laughed she never went back.

Then began her Cody, Wyoming, phase and painting in earnest. No use reviewing that. Instead, a gulp of Margaux, accompanied by the bellowing of a distant harbor horn. San Francisco night language.

There was heaviness now in her hips and legs. Her buttocks weighed a ton. The small of her back felt as though it was collapsing and her fingers didn't want the responsibility of holding the wine goblet. How could she be so heavy and yet feel so floaty? A deep breath was impossible. Her insides just below and behind her breastbone were being softly crowded. She'd have to be swift about it now.

Her hand seemed detached, a creature acting on its own as it slowly reached for oblivion.

CHAPTER FIVE

I t definitely wasn't white light.

Nor a tunnellike arrangement of the sort people who've had near-death experiences describe.

Instead it was an undimensional dark crimson, caused by the rhomboidal-shaped slash of sunshine on Julia's face. Her eyelids went up slowly like a lazy theatrical curtain, and there, in the chintz-covered overstuffed chair across from the bed, sat Royce.

His eyes opened wider as he noticed hers open. "Oh, back from the dead," he said with a too abrupt smile, meant to inspire.

"That I am." Her voice was strong and clear, as though it had been impatiently waiting again to be used. And her mind was sharp. It wasn't like her, even in normal conditions, to come so immediately awake.

"I've fed Maxx and brought in the mail. You left your coffee maker on and the pot went dry. It may or may not be cracked," Royce reported.

Julia was wondering why she was so thoroughly oriented. She remembered everything, her every action and thought, right up until she'd gone to black. That she'd tried suicide now seemed ridiculous. Anyway, she'd botched it and was glad she'd botched it. She looked to the side table. Only purple lozenges in the candy dish, no yellow capsules. The drawer to the stand was closed and no wine bottle or goblet in sight. Evidently Royce knew or at least suspected what she'd tried. She liked him for not mentioning it, although his *back from the dead* remark hadn't been too far off.

"Next time warn me when you're going to take a sleep cure," Royce said, letting her know he was letting her completely off the hook.

"You're a dear," she said.

"A universal opinion."

"And I've got to pee."

He stood and turned his back and she bounded nude out of bed for the bathroom. A long, loud pee. She flushed when only halfway through to override the sounds. Tried to ignore the mirrors but a glance told her she looked none the worse, in fact, better, more vibrant. She attributed that to all the sleep she'd gotten, was even more convinced of that when, after putting on a robe and returning to the bedroom and Royce, she noticed what he had on. His pale blue velour jogging outfit with royal blue piping. He jogged around the Portrero Hill playground three afternoons each week, Monday, Wednesday and Friday, was obsessed with routine, so much so that at times he'd referred to himself as an undeviating deviate.

That would make today Friday, Julia thought. It would mean she'd been out thirty-six hours straight. Perhaps she'd come closer to dying than she realized. She didn't recall a thing for the whole thirty-six, not a toss or turn or even a fragment of dream. Normally she dreamed so vividly she was able to play back every scenario and nuance. But not this time. Strange. Probably an effect of the barbiturate.

Royce took in and exhaled a noisy rather feminine breath, his habitual punctuation for concluding. "Well," he said, "got to run and I can't, just absolutely can't be late for work. They let three poor souls go yesterday and I have a feeling they only missed me by one." He was an afternoon to midnight clerk at the reception desk of the Stanford Court Hotel. One of the reasons he liked the job was it required that he be highly presentable, which provided him with an excuse for his overmeticulousness and extensive wardrobe.

He went to Julia, conveyed with his eyes that she shouldn't repeat her attempt, told her with his smile he was assured. "Ta, hon," he said, gave her an upper body hug and left.

Julia took a shower, and while the nearly unbearably hot water was beating upon her skull, it occurred to her that there was something urgent she should do. But she didn't know exactly what. It was more a strong sense than anything specific. Something she'd forgotten because of the drama of the past few days? If it was important it would come to her, she decided.

She dressed, was too ravenous to cook anything. So she drove down the hill to an eating place on Carolina Street and had a four-egg tomato and cheese omelet, rye toast and coffee. Wolfed it down, cleaned her plate. Returned home with that same sense of urgency foremost in her mind.

She took a critical look at the canvas on the easel that was supposed to have been her final work. She could do better, she thought, would. She stood in the midst of the mess of her studio and was revolted by it. An entirely new reaction. Perhaps that was what needed doing, she thought.

She threw out a lot of stuff, three trash bins full and some loads in cardboard cartons. Got rid of all the used plastic bowls and the opened quart and gallon cans scummed with paint from as far back as two years. Gathered up the layers of newspapers from the floor, using thinner and a scrubber on those that were stuck. She spent an entire day on brushes. Cleaned and treated those that were salvageable, felt guilty about those with bristles beyond saving. They had, she thought, served her well and were not deserving of such abuse. She bunched and bound them with string, wrapped them in a shroud of fresh brown paper and put them in a clean, substantial carton. Sealed the carton with masking tape and, before placing it out with the other trash, said a silent thanks and thought a ritual.

At the late end of the third day the studio was cleaned and reorganized to Julia's satisfaction. The place seemed happier with the new orderliness, especially the storage cabinet where the brushes were now all lined up on their own shelf above the shelf where tubes of medium were arranged according to color. Julia vowed to everything that she wouldn't ever again allow such a mess. Probably.

Still, that sense of there being something she absolutely should tend to was pressing her. What the hell was it? Could it be something inconsequential to which she'd given a thought and it hadn't receded to its proper place in her mind as it should have, something of no great matter such as having her hair trimmed or the car washed? Minds could be tricky like that when they wanted to be, she believed.

Four days went by. During that time, just in case, she subjected her Jeep Cherokee to a torturous-looking automatic wash and got herself a trim at Transitions. While she was downtown she browsed some stores, including Gumps, where she especially appreciated a display of exquisitely detailed Suzuribako, lacquer writing boxes, and various pieces of carved lavender jade. Perhaps it was viewing those things that put her in a shopping mode.

At Saks she intended just to try on but ended up buying a simply stunning black Issey Miyake for more than she'd ever before paid for a dress. Just had to have it for some reason, and of course new shoes as well, a pair of Bruno Magli's that perhaps didn't look the price but felt it when she had them on.

She thought she'd shopped herself out until she came onto the place that had just opened on O'Farrell. A shop offering all sorts of tasteful, unusual *petites choses*, little things. Objects d'art and just *objets*, like a private collection. There, she was drawn to a shagreen and ivory military hairbrush and comb set, a silver art nouveau shoe horn and an antique business card presentation case of alligator with 18k gold corner trim. She settled on the case, yes definitely the case.

"Shall I gift wrap it?" Julia was asked.

"Oh...yes," Julia replied.

And while that was being done Julia questioned her sanity. A business card case for five hundred and seventy-five plus tax? My god, why? She didn't even have a business card.

Anyway, it was done. She went home, got nude and sat upon a high stool at the large table in the studio. Munching three different varieties of Pepperidge Farm cookies.

She ought to stretch and prepare some canvases, she thought. Not yet, she decided.

Then the owner of the gallery on Octavia Street phoned to say he'd sold two more of her works and it might be beneficial for all concerned if he had two others to hang in their place.

While on the phone with him, half hearing his words, she contemplated the dendritic cracks in the white plaster surface of the near wall. Her eyes ran from those to the raw pinewood bulletin board, her mind tagging along. Passed the pinned-up articles and scribbled notes to herself to the far left edge and a small white rectangle, upon which her entire attention abruptly focused. She hung up the phone with an interruptive good-bye. Liberated Grady's business card from the stab of a red-headed push pin and as she examined it realized it was the reason for all the recent nudging.

But what was she supposed to do, call this Grady Bowman person? He'd said he'd call her when her pearls were ready. Best to wait. Why? To hell with that. She dialed his number. After the fourth ring his answering machine activated. She hung up as soon as she heard his recorded voice.

That night she called again, twice. Got his machine, didn't leave a message. It occurred to her that perhaps he was there, screening his calls, so the next morning when she phoned and his machine answered she said her name, her number, the day and the time, somewhat expecting he'd pick up, but he didn't.

This went on for a week. She'd begun painting and, although she was able to lose herself in that, every so often she'd stop, go over to the phone and dial his number, which by then was as indelible in her memory as a mantra. Sometimes she'd listen to his entire twenty-second recorded message, visualizing him along with it. Twice she awoke at three in the morning with the urge to phone running repetitively across the mental apparatus behind her forehead, like on that building in Times Square. Wouldn't it be terribly audacious of her to phone at that hour? Supposing he answered, what would she say? Fuck it, her expression countered. So she heard the touch tones, the rings, him recorded, and had an awful time getting back to sleep.

By the next Saturday morning, Julia stepped back from herself and realized how irrational she was being. Almost as if her life depended on her reaching this person. She'd heard of fixations but never thought she'd include such behavior in her repertoire.

Actually, she had only a vague, and probably incorrect, recollection of what this Grady Bowman looked like. He hadn't been anything special, anyway not a seismic six, she told herself, just somewhat more attractive than average. Anyway, thank heavens she'd come to her senses. If need be, she'd unplug the phone for a day or two.

She got her soiled laundry from the hamper and took it down to the service area adjacent to the kitchen. Then she started filling the automatic washer with hot, and was separating colors from whites and dainties from tough stuff when the phone rang.

It was he, saying he'd gotten the message that she'd called.

She came close to demanding where the hell he'd been.

He apologized for not having gotten back to her sooner, had been out of town. The genuine way he said it eliminated most of her steam. "Your pearls are ready," he told her. "Shall I have them delivered to you, or what?"

"What would *or what* be?"

"I could hold them for you until..."

"Any other alternative?"

"I suppose that depends on how urgently you need them."

"Let's say quite urgently."

"In that case I could bring them to you myself, today. Where are you located?"

That wasn't how she wanted it. "I'll be coming into town. I could meet you somewhere."

"When?"

"Today, at noon. I could meet you at say... the Sheraton Palace in the Garden Court. Would that be inconvenient?"

"Not at all. See you there," he promised and clicked off.

Julia bathed, did her daytime makeup and her hair and spent most of the next two hours determining what she would wear. Not the new Issey Miyake, she figured, anyway, not yet. She finally settled on an effortless-looking two-piece rayon and cotton in what Royce had several times said was by far her most conspiratorial color. Pale, slightly warm green. The blouse was little more than a superior T-shirt, simply effective. The skirt, above the knee short, was cut on the bias and ample, so it had a hint of flounce. Her exceptional legs did it justice. A pair of t-strapped medium-heeled sandals, enormous faux stone ear clips the exact color of her eyes, her better gold wristwatch, a veto of gloves and then a veto of the veto on the basis that she wouldn't put them on, merely have them in hand as though she'd had them on...

She arrived at the Sheraton Palace and the Garden Court at twelve-fifteen, just tardy enough to have him there before her. She paused, stood on the landing above the immense place and its sea of widely spaced, white-linened tables, about two-thirds of which were occupied. She surveyed the thirty tables on the right, and the thirty on the left. Didn't see him, or, she thought, perhaps she didn't recognize him. She surveyed again before the maître d' came to her aid and led her over the deep red and gold patterned carpet to Mr. Bowman's table. Just the table, not him.

No great matter, she told herself as she was being seated, possibly there'd be other opportunities for this Grady to be smited by a full-length view of her walk. Besides, his impression of her wasn't important. She'd just get back her pearls, have a brief lunch, and adieu.

"Did madame wish something to drink?"

She thought vodka gimlet, said Perrier and fresh lime.

Eight slow minutes passed.

She spotted Grady coming down the center aisle, fifty feet away. Diverted her eyes to not have him know she'd been watching him. Acted surprised when he reached the table. He simultaneously sat and apologized.

"I was held up," he explained.

"And evidently you valued your life more than your money," she said, smiling.

After a beat he got it. "You're fast," he said. He asked what she was drinking and after she told him ordered a Glenfiddich neat.

"Make that two," she said.

He did. "You come here often?"

"Occasionally."

His eyes ran up one of the nearest fat marble columns and across the expanse of glass panes sixty feet above. "Not exactly cozy," he commented.

"That's why I suggested it."

A blank nod from him.

She liked him without the bow tie, approved of his unbuttoned shirt collar. And his softly shouldered double-breasted gray blazer. She wondered if he was wearing suspenders or a belt. She'd bet suspenders. He was, she decided, a great deal more attractive than she recalled from the week before or perhaps she was now seeing him through different more appreciative eyes. That was how it seemed. "You were away?"

"In Nevada for a week."

"Where in Nevada?"

"Tahoe and Reno."

"I take it you like to gamble."

"You might say that, I was up there filing for a divorce. My attorney, Tom McGuin, has a place in Tahoe on the Nevada side, a condo. He let me use it to establish residency."

"Then you're divorced."

"I go back up in six weeks for the decree."

He spoke of it so indifferently it occurred to Julia that he might be one of those compulsive marry-ers with six or seven divorces to his debit. After a brief, assaying look she decided his weren't the eyes of a man of that sort, much too much sensibility in them. Anyway, his divorce and all was his personal territory and she shouldn't yet be nosing around in it. She veered the subject abruptly, got on to a film she had seen recently, one that in her opinion didn't deserve the raves it was getting.

Grady had seen the film and thought the same of it. On his last selling trip for HH he'd had nights to kill and gone alone to see that one and quite a few others.

They ordered lunch, made as little as possible of it, just a couple of crab salads. Ate and talked. Julia found it difficult to keep the conversation in neutral. Something in her seemed to be pushing her to get to know him swiftly. They skipped and skimmed along on such diverse topics as the global warming trend, overpriced arugula, the charlatanry of spiritual channeling.

"These days it seems practically everyone is in touch with some long-departed, talkative soul," Julia said.

"Are you?"

"Hell no. It's absurd, don't you think?"

"Probably."

"They used to put away people who heard voices. Now they let them set up shop. I for one suspect there isn't an *other side*, as they call it."

"There might be something to it."

"You really believe that?"

"Let's just say I don't have any reason not to."

"Do you believe you've lived before?"

"Once in a while I feel as though I might have. Haven't you ever experienced that feeling?"

"Yes, but I don't think anything as important as that should be based on vague once-in-a-while hints."

Grady was willing to bet that beneath her pragmatic surface was a wondering, imaginative Julia who perceived mystical meaning in most everything. He himself had never been literal minded or handicapped by deduction. Whenever he considered his outlook he gave a lot of the credit to the flowers of his youth, especially the irises. "You haven't always lived in San Francisco, have you?"

"No, I was raised in upstate New York."

"Whereabouts?"

"Ever heard of Amenia?"

"Sure, I used to call it anemia."

"Everyone does. You've been there?"

"Around there." That caused Grady to go once over the memory of a long-ago night in the grass of an apple orchard on the outskirts of Sharon with a girl from there who so craved sensation that she was oblivious to the deep, wet grass and the rot of the windfalls it concealed, which her back crushed to sour and stain her dress.

Julia noticed the recall in Grady's eyes. "I just triggered something?"

"Yeah."

"Nothing bad, I hope."

"Quite the contrary," he admitted with an appropriate smile.

His wife must have been blind and paralyzed from the waist down, Julia thought. "How long have you been married," she asked, not intending to. It just came out of her, as though the words had their own will.

Grady didn't mind telling her. He hadn't spoken to anyone about it other than his attorney and a bartender in Tahoe. Spilling it to another woman might be therapeutic.

"You don't appear to be hurt or bitter," Julia said.

"I'm not, just bristling."

"Bristling's only a first-degree reaction. You'll soon be over it."

"You're an expert, huh?"

"I've never been divorced but I've been bristled, any number of times," she grinned.

"How many is any number?"

"I don't know, really. I don't count some that I used to count. In fact the grand total is constantly decreasing. What was she like, this wife who's given up on you?"

"Complex."

That was kind enough of him for him to still be in love with her, Julia thought. She asked if he was and believed his *no*. "What was her name?"

"She's still alive."

"I prefer to speak of her in the past tense, do you mind?"

"I guess not. Her name was Gayle."

"Was she pretty?"

A shrug and then a conceding nod from Grady.

"Gorgeous?"

"Gorgeous."

"Not just in your eyes?"

"That's for sure." He hoped she didn't press him for any more. He didn't want to go into the lying and the fucking around because there wouldn't be any way for it not to come out sounding as though he felt victimized and sorry for himself. Neither of which was the case. Gayle had been Gayle, the daughter of Harold, and he'd come down an altogether different road with a more fortunate bundle of values. As he saw it, the worst thing about the marriage had been the waste of years. He wondered if he told Julia that would she understand. He sort of thought she might. He watched her catch the waiter and convey without a word that she wanted a refill of coffee. A negligible but giveaway indication of her larger self-sufficiency. It occurred to him that on first impression she was unlike any of the women he'd known, been with.

She brought her attention around and on him again, like a boat resuming its tack. "Let me ask you something just out of female curiosity. And you don't have to answer if it purges up something too sordid or messy." She waited a long beat to allow him to refuse. "What was the one thing that Gayle did that you disliked the most?"

"Big or little thing?"

"Let's stick with little."

Grady laughed, a private, self-amused laugh as he ran down that inventory. "It's a toss-up," he said, "between buying luggage and posturing."

"Buying luggage?"

"Yeah. She refused to take a trip anywhere, even for just a weekend, unless she had new luggage, brand-new whole sets, from Mark Cross, Fendi, Hermès..."

"Morabito?"

"Probably. We had closets and a basement storage area crammed with once-used luggage."

"Strange."

"It was phobic, I think. She wouldn't discuss it and I eventually gave up asking her about it."

"What about the posturing?"

"That wasn't as odd. I've seen women do it but not so obviously and to the extent that Gayle did it. We'd be sitting talking, and all of a sudden without a lapse in attention she'd slip herself into a pose, turn a shoulder this way or that, suspend an arm, tilt her chin, look at me over her cheekbones."

"She did it when you were out someplace?"

"Even more when we were home alone."

"That griped you?"

"Christ yes, why couldn't she just be herself?"

"Maybe she didn't think herself was enough."

Grady wanted to get off Gayle.

With perfect timing Julia excused herself and went to the ladies' room. Grady watched her walk, believed she had legs equal to Doris's. Some woman, he thought. She was evidently bright, possibly very intelligent. Spunky, perhaps strong willed. Although she wasn't a raving beauty she was above average attractive and, in her favor, not straining to make too much of her looks. Yes, he liked Julia Elkins. Yes, he'd like to know her better.

When she returned to the table he sensed she'd prefer silence for a while. She looked around and at him. He looked around and at her. They were eyes-to-eyes for a long moment. Without breaking the look she told him, "I read somewhere that whenever a woman is looking at something she wants her pupils dilate."

"At the moment yours appear normal."

"Then it's not true," she quipped, too late to reach out and recapture the words and have them unsaid. What had gotten into her? Only rarely in her life had she been aggressively vampy and never on such short acquaintance. Now that she thought of it she hadn't been the same in quite a few ways since her recent death-defying sleep.

"Regarding your pearls..."

"Oh...yes, my pearls," she muttered, a bit embarrassed that what was supposed to have been foremost in her mind was last.

"I don't have them for you."

"That's not what you told me."

"I know. They were being restrung by a Hungarian woman I've used before. Dependable and by far the best stringer around. She was supposed to have them ready by Wednesday. When I stopped by her place this morning she wasn't there."

Thank you, Hungarian pearl stringer, Julia thought, for guaranteeing this wouldn't be a first and only meeting. Now she could slow down. Her second thought was how delightful it would be if Grady was fabricating the Hungarian woman's inaccessibility and actually had her pearls in his pocket.

CHAPTER SIX

That was the start of Grady and Julia.

They remained at that table in the Garden Court of the Sheraton Palace long after the other Saturday lunchers were gone, long after Grady thoughtfully settled the check so the waiter wouldn't have to be attending. The table for four, round and really large enough to accommodate six, turned into a white-covered horizontal barrier, which Grady overcame by moving his chair around next to Julia's. Not just to facilitate their talk but to also put them in range of touching. They didn't touch, didn't even clasp hands, however the possibility was there and the imminence and the anticipation.

The following day was Sunday, and they spent it together, learning each other as they walked some of San Francisco, climbed steps and had espresso and dipped chocolate biscotti at Caffe Puccini on Columbus Avenue in North Beach. They sat with legs dangling over the sea wall of the Marina to watch windsurfers. Ended up on the grass of Golden State Park sharing the Sunday *Chronicle* while around them islands of families and lovers sprang up or disappeared.

For Julia the day was like a canvas that she was preparing, layering it with background so that soon it could take detail and color more vibrant.

For Grady the day was like preparing a garden, enhancing the soil of it with acquaintance, getting it comfortable for planting.

Julia told him about some of her days in France, didn't omit Jean Luc but didn't elaborate on him either. She assumed Grady guessed there'd been involvement. She recalled how, when she'd first arrived in Paris, she'd taken an apartment in Montparnasse, a seventh-floor walk-up hardly more than a closet. Because the concierge had confided that it had once been occupied by Kiki Prin, better known as Kiki of Montparnasse, the celebrated intimate of numerous accomplished artists during the twenties and thirties. Julia related how she'd suffered the climb and cramp in order to imagine the incorporeal visits of Pascin and Dubuffet, Soutine, Foujita, Léger, Man Ray and others. Before too long she found out that nearly all the concierges of the area misled with that Kiki fib, that Kiki had actually lived in more generous quarters at 5 rue Delambre and later at 1 rue Brea.

She'd told the concierge off.

No, actually she was obliged to him for having inadvertently supplied so much inspiration.

What about Cody, Wyoming? Why had she chosen to live in Cody?

It wasn't something she'd planned, she'd decided on it after she was all packed and ready to move. Someone had circled it on a map of the western states that she'd bought for a dime at Goodwill, so her eyes had been drawn to it and in that instant she'd made it her destination. At times when she looked back to finding that circle on that map she thought it providential, because Cody had been so right for her, right from the start.

She'd found an ideal situation on a thousand-acre spread in the valley of the Upper South Fork on the Shoshone River. The people who owned it were from St. Louis and usually only came there during the warm months. They needed someone on the property year-round, just to be there and oversee, not really to caretake. Her place would be the four-room plank-sided structure with all the conveniences situated three hundred yards from the main ranch house. They worried that it would be too isolated for her.

Not at all. She indulged in the solitude, got carried away with it, became annoyed whenever the pickup of the caretaker came rooster-tailing up the road or came thinking he was doing her a service by snowplowing her an access.

Her talent took hard hold while she was in Cody. One autumn she must have painted the Absaroka Mountains fifty times.

She saw nature in finer detail and expressed it in masses. Masses that surely weren't or barely weren't adjacent. The mountains not adjacent to the sky or the tree line not adjacent to the meadow the way she saw them. And the vitality of everything almost hiding. In her renderings an underlain mass of brilliance usually peeked around the edges of a sullen mass of overlay, the components of reality contributed to the appearance of illusion. She would never be able to paint any other way.

"I really like your paintings," Grady told her.

She doubted he'd even seen one.

"A business acquaintance in New York has one of your works hung on the prime wall in his office. I coveted it and told him so, but he wouldn't part with it. I've also seen your work in a gallery downtown, on Octavia Street I believe it was."

Another point in his favor, Julia thought. Was he ever piling them up!

In turn Grady told her some about himself, what it had been like growing up in Litchfield. Described his family one by one, told her how his father, a pharmacist, had owned the only drugstore in town and from the prescriptions he filled knew the diagnosed ailments of everyone in the vicinity. The store had had a luncheon counter for toasted cheese sandwiches, milkshakes and fizzed-up, cloud-topped ice cream sodas. His father was retired, sold the store to a chain that had taken out the soda fountain and counter and otherwise modernized the place with too much fluorescent light, Formica shelving and pegboard.

Grady and Julia got together a lot during the next week. Went across the Bay Bridge for some jazz at Yoshi's and stayed for only one set because they wanted to talk, not listen. Went to the "Stick" to see the Giants blank the Dodgers. Went out thirty miles to Woodside to the estate called Filoli to marvel at its formal gardens and allow Grady to impress with his knowledge of plants and trees, the Chilean myrtles, the New Zealand beeches. Went to a movie. Grady suggested a newly released comedy that was playing at the Northpoint but didn't insist when Julia was for a Japanese film at the Gateway called *Heaven and Earth*, a samurai epic directed by Haruki Kadokawa. Slashing of swords, decapitations and struttings, subtitles that seemed contradictory to the overemphatic dialogue. Grady found the film colorful, tried to get a hold on the plot. Julia, on the other hand, seemed as though she understood every word and nuance, sat enrapt throughout.

Friday night Grady purposely stayed away from her. He hadn't said he'd see her or promised to phone. He grabbed a slice and a Pepsi at a pizza place on Pacific and drifted downhill to Geary. At Pat O'Shea's Mad Hatter he stood at the bar with a double Glenfiddich. Eyes aimed up at the baseball on television but not much registering. He was getting into Julia Elkins way too deep and too fast, he told himself. No matter that he didn't feel as though he was being irrational, there was no denying that he was on the emotional ricochet and prone to making another huge mistake.

He hadn't given Gayle a thought all week. Julia had chased Gayle, swept out the remnants of her. To that extent Julia had been good, but it didn't mean he needed Julia. Need was a big admission. Anyway, he thought, being out alone tonight was a way of gauging what was what. He felt fine in his space. If he were to lop the last week or so out of his life, have amnesia about it or whatever, it wouldn't be that big a deal; he wouldn't have missed much, just Julia.

Fuck you, just.

At eleven he was all out of resistance, went to the pay phone. Her voice went into his ear and down to his knees and got to everything else along the way.

"How late is it?"

He told her.

"I was getting ready for bed," she said. "Where are you? Are you all right?"

No one except his mother had ever asked caring like that. "I just thought I'd say good night. I'm fine."

"What did you do today?"

"Leased an office for one thing."

"I know you mentioned you'd been looking. Is it what you want?"

"It'll do. Can we get together tomorrow?"

"I was planning on painting tomorrow. If I don't paint I'll get stiff."

"Can I come watch you paint?"

"I've never painted for an audience. Probably it's something better done alone."

"Seems like it would be." There she was, he thought, not a lot of miles away but near enough to walk to. So, why couldn't he be with her? Too late tonight, too busy tomorrow. He'd heard of and known women who enjoyed the getting but not the having. Was she one of those? Should he risk asking her about the day after tomorrow?

"Do you really want to come watch me paint?"

"Yeah."

"You'll get bored."

"What time shall I be there?"

"Whenever you want, just come."

Much happier, he had another drink and went home, which was now the week by week affordable hotel room on Fillmore Street. Didn't sleep solidly, kept waking and seeing if it was tomorrow. Got up at three and watched Gleason reruns until four. Got up for good at six-thirty. He had in mind waiting until ten. Parked down the hill from Julia's and read the morning paper as long as he could. Shortly after nine he drove up and parked in her driveway. Thinking he was early and his eagerness obvious. He went around the side to the studio entrance. The door was open and she was at the easel.

She stopped work and got him some coffee. He'd already had four strong cups, two more than usual, and was sure another would give him the rattles. She sat him on one of the high stools at the big table and went back at it. He thought it proper not to make conversation, although he had a lot he wanted to say to her, told himself not to abuse this privilege of sharing what normally was a private time for her. His attention was ambivalent, interested in the paint colors mixed and applied as though they were her internal garden, and taken with her, her intensity as she focused or contemplated, stepped back and appraised. He didn't realize how much tone her body had built up until she took a momentary break and he saw the letdown, a minor collapse.

"I usually paint in the nude," she said lightly. "And until recently I've been quite sloppy. I don't know what's gotten into me. All at once I seem compelled to be neat. Look, not a dribble or even a drop."

She was barefoot, had on a gauzy white cotton skirt that wasn't quite opaque and a blue-and-white striped cotton boy's shirt with its sleeves rolled up to the elbow and its front unbuttoned four down. She came over to the table with a brush in hand, reached for a Pepperidge Farm oatmeal raisin.

It was as if Grady had promised his arms that the next time she was within range they could have their way. One of his arms pulled her to him, the other went around and surely captured. For an instant Grady was eyes-to-eyes with her, able, it seemed, to hear her eyes. Her pupils were dilated with want, declaring it.

That first kiss was not all crush and feeding. There was adequate sureness in it to allow prelusion, lips reaching on their own to achieve the slightest touch, brushing as lightly as possible, back and forth, while tongues remained contained, pink, slick animals poised in their lairs.

The kiss lasted even when it hesitated, even when it was not a touching kiss it was bound by anticipation and with breaths mixing. Julia hadn't ever felt so strong and yet weak. For Grady the same. Aroused and in the darkness of their kissing, in the parrying of tongues, the sucking exchanges, Grady was told by everything within him, like the voice of his blood and all his organs and fibers, that this was not merely sex.

"Let's go upstairs," she whispered and led him up to her bedroom, where she threw off the covers completely and transformed the bed into a plain, sheeted tract for loving. He paid no attention to his own undressing, did not deny himself the part of it that was the observing of her removing what little she had on, the arming out of the boy's shirt, the undoing and dropping of her skirt and her stepping from the circle of it. Her fingers were his allies. He was surprised but grateful that she wasn't inhibited.

Actually, Julia had never been so entirely shameless. It was as though some membranous constraint had been removed, leaving her exempt of guilt, released to range the entire realm of sensation, whatever pleased. Exercising such total latitude, she reached down and felt herself, felt how gorged were the exterior lips down there, puffed apart to create between them a wettened crease, reigned over by her clitoris, usually reticent but now erect, demanding to protrude, insisting to be touched.

He came to her, his erection unwieldy, like an antenna determining the way, and it was then between them, embraced against the skin of his stomach and the skin of hers, and she slid both her hands into that vise from the left and the right to claim it.

He resisted the extreme hurry he felt, asked his awareness to register surely the surroundings, the fragrance of her, the faint apathetic sounds of the city in motion, the form of her shoulder blades, the small of her back, the ladder of her spine. As though he was supplying a private time capsule before he was beyond the point of any such objectivity.

The slash of sunlight upon the sheet was upon them. They lay against each other full length, gently pressured. Both were grateful that this first time was in the bright time of day, allowing eyes their due participation.

She kneeled up beside him so her eyes could travel him, his various planes, and transitions, neck to shoulder to chest to abdomen. It seemed she could hear the speed of his blood, the high-pitched, sustained note of his passion. Watched his chest heave bellowlike, his abdomen go concave with tension, his effort to keep his eyes open as her fingers traced his erection, length and breadth, and especially the taut, finest skin of all.

CHAPTER SEVEN

They were, all that day and night, lost in the loving land.

The following day, Sunday, they tacitly agreed on replenishment but were constantly reassuring each other with spontaneous touches, arms around, smiles. They refrained from declarations of love, kept those words nearly said in their throats while they were being surely said in their eyes. Time would tell, they felt. In fact, time was telling.

They drove down to Market Street for Julia to see the office Grady had leased. Two rooms on the second floor of 760, the Phelan Building, the same where Harold Havermeyer so extensively occupied the top. Grady's new office was in the rear, its windows shadowed by the heights of close-by structures. The previous tenants had been two Armenian brothers, specialists in cutting and polishing. One could see the scars of their labor on the bare floor, where their workbenches had been anchored and where oil had too often dripped and permeated. One plaster wall was thoroughly splattered with oil. And in another place there were crumbling gapes where the supports of a heavy shelf had been torn out.

Seeing the space now for the second time and with Julia along, Grady had misgivings. It wasn't only that it diminished his feelings of self-importance, the space also presented less than ideal conditions under which to evaluate precious gems. He'd known that he probably could have done better elsewhere, however he'd thought it best that he be located there in the Phelan, where the trade was centered.

Julia looked thoroughly about both rooms, considered them for a long moment. "Don't fret, love," she told Grady, "paint will do wonders, just wait and see."

His office became her project. She didn't exclude him from it but neither did she always consult him either. She chose the paint, a bright but somewhat kind white. And the carpeting, an industrial sort but not entirely tech, gray with a small geometric black and white for the impression of texture. She saw to it that the plastering was done and that more than an adequate number of fluorescent lighting fixtures were installed, the same as she had in her studio, the kind that simulated daylight. Instead of settling for merely Levolor blinds on the two windows she added a major touch of elegance with some amply swagged portieres, edged with tassels and held back with wide matching braids. She also arranged for the leasing of office furniture, chose pieces as understated and as indestructible as possible.

Grady was overwhelmed by her enthusiastic interest. He thought it a bit strange that she should get so caught up in it. Not just involved but avidly so, to the point of appearing driven. It was as though she personally had a great deal at stake. He didn't dwell upon it or find fault but heeded his heart and easily convinced himself it was just her way of demonstrating her caring feelings for him.

Meanwhile he was buying some of the equipment he'd need, such as a Mettler PL 1000C electronic scale, a 10x to 90x Bausch & Lomb microscope and, most important, a really safe safe, an SLS12, insurance rated AAA.

The day when the office was being painted Grady arrived shortly before noon to find Doris as well as Julia up on ladders rolling it on. Doris greeted him with a warm smile but indicting eyes.

"I quit Havermeyer," she told him.

Julia had on jeans. Doris had on a skirt, and, up on the ladder as she was, her slender, ideal legs were hardly ignorable. Grady tried to refrain from looking up as he asked, "Why? Why'd you quit?"

"I couldn't take another second of queen titless," Doris replied, "and I figured you'd be needing someone. As a matter of fact," she said pointedly, "I thought you'd be needing someone a lot more than you evidently do."

Julia shot Grady a glance and a grin.

Grady told Doris, "I can't afford you."

"That's okay, you will be able to down the road a ways and I'm willing to chance the trip. I've saved up for just this sort of opportunity."

"You mean emergency."

"I mean what I said," Doris contended.

Julia liked Doris for that.

"On one condition," Doris added for Julia's benefit, "no sexual harassment." Feigning all business, she dipped the roller into the tray and slathered a swath onto the ceiling. Later, however, when she had the chance, she told Grady, "Some sidekick you are. I wait years for a go at you and before I can say either yes or please, you go and let someone else have her way with you."

Grady shrugged.

"You in love with her?"

"Quite possibly."

"I can understand why. She's nifty. But if it goes sour all I ask is you give my sugar a try. Deal?"

"Deal," Grady said, sure it would never come to that.

So, the office was completed, all the way to the softening of corners with plants and Grady's name on the door, which Julia watched a professional sign painter do with critical interest. Still lacking were paintings for the walls and an inventory of gems.

Julia remedied the bare walls with several paintings on loan from her personal collection. All but the prime wall to the right of his desk. That was reserved, she said, for a work in progress.

As for the inventory, Grady could hardly do business without it. The most he could do was "middle" some deals, that is, find out what someone was in the market for, then, through contacts, find it, have it memoed out, put an acceptable higher price on it, and thus earn a margin.

Grady called around to people he knew in the trade. A few

responded as they should have, promised to help supply Grady with some goods. Most, however, had been contacted by Harold Havermeyer, who, in his slick way, had sown the rumor that Grady had been let go because of an impropriety too despicable to mention, one so flagrant, in fact, that daughter Gayle could no longer tolerate him and had resorted to divorce. Thievery was insinuated. The most serious breach of code. "Trust him at your own risk," were Harold's words.

As trustful as people in the gem trade tended to be it didn't take much to make them distrust. It was the nature of the business.

One morning Grady and Harold were the only passengers in an elevator at 760 Market. Harold chinned up aloofly, fixed his eyes straight ahead.

Grady couldn't resist. "Harold," he asked, "isn't that shit on the corner of your mouth?"

Harold flushed and gritted.

Grady made fists in his pockets and got out on two.

He needed capital. Having been merely an employee of HH all those years, he had no commercial credit. He went to several banks and filled out their applications, which made him realize how unqualified he was for any sizeable loan. No collateral, no previous similar loan history, insurmountable sins according to their way of looking at it. A couple of banks, including the branch of one where he'd kept his account, were willing to extend him a high-interest, short-term personal loan of twenty thousand, but that was all.

While at his bank he removed whatever was of value from his safety-deposit box. His sunny day things was how he'd always thought of them, a little eclectic horde that he'd acquired over the years from estate sales and other opportunities. Including a set of English art nouveau gold and sapphire buttons, a ruby pendant signed by Vever, another signed by Manboussin, and still another rare and very good one signed by René Lalique, a gold coin struck by Septimius Severus to commemorate the games held in Rome in A.D. 206, a 1921 Cartier bedside clock in lavender *guilloche* enamel, an Audemars Piquet pocket watch and a circa 1850 Carlo Giuliano bracelet comprised of red and green garnets.

Grady estimated the lot was worth at least a hundred and fifty thousand. He took the pieces first to a retail dealer on Grant

Avenue who specialized in such merchandise. The dealer put on the usual buying face, straight and dubious, and acted as though he was doing Grady a favor by merely looking at the things. Actually, he looked at them very carefully and his appreciation was apparent. He sternly offered seventy-five thousand, take it or leave it.

Grady surprised the man by leaving it. Walked six blocks to Pine Street and another retail dealer, a tall, snooty woman who said right off and too quickly that she liked some things and not others and was probably interested only in the Giuliano bracelet. She kept mumbling that she doubted the authenticity of most of the hallmarks and signatures although, she admitted, the Cartier clock was definitely Cartier. When she thought she'd sufficiently disparaged the goods she offered ninety thousand, and, when Grady packed up and headed out, she capitulated with a hundred and twenty-five.

Which Grady accepted.

It was a start, a good start, but more was needed, and Grady was confident that more was forthcoming.

The next Tuesday he flew to Reno and got his divorce decree. Flew back that same day and, with papers in hand, was in attorney McGuin's office early Wednesday morning. McGuin phoned Gayle's attorney and by immediate messenger provided him with a copy of the decree. The messenger returned with Harold's certified check in the amount of two hundred thousand. Grady's rightful community property, half of the equity in the Mill Valley house.

There was more than the satisfaction of money in the way Grady had caused Harold to cave in on that matter. It had to do with something Harold had pulled off seven years ago and boasted about to Grady.

Harold was a compulsive collector of fine things or at least things that appeared to be authentically fine. Sculptings, paintings, antiquities, precious *objets* and the like. As with most collectors Harold got as much enjoyment from the act of acquiring as he did from owning. Either quite soon or eventually he tired of things, be they authentic or fake.

Harold had a great many convincing fakes. First-century Grecian statues with members and noses broken off that were actually no more than twenty years old if that. Egyptian pieces that hadn't seen a tomb. Antique Mayan figures well done in Yucatán by a family of eight to provide them with enough money for a flight to Disneyland. Stuff like that. Harold acquired these at fake prices but with invoices testifying to their authenticity and showing that he'd paid a proper high price. Thus he was able to insure the things for a lot more, often ten to twenty times more, than he'd put out for them.

Seven years ago Harold arranged with a fence in Los Angeles named Harry Fox to have everything stolen. In Harry's parlance it was a *gimmie*, a no-risk kind of burglary. According to Harold and Harry's agreement, Harold was in Palm Springs the weekend the break-in occurred. The alarm system was purposefully on the blink, wouldn't be fixed until Monday. The thieves simply backed up a van to the door and cleaned house. Ninety days later Harold collected the insurance. Six million dollars. And went on a fresh acquisitioning spree.

Harold's mistake was made one day out on the boat when he was bored and feeling ego starved and spouted on to Grady about how he'd pulled off the *gimmie*. In detail. So, recently when it came to this confrontation over the Mill Valley house, all Grady had to do was phone Harold and ask him if he'd heard from Harry Fox from Los Angeles lately.

Anyway, that two hundred brought Grady's capital up to a comfortable enough level for him to do some serious business. He was in high spirits, divorced from Gayle, wanted to celebrate. He wrangled reservations for dinner that night at Donatello, set his mind on the elegant Donatello atmosphere and his appetite on a lot of great Northern Italian food.

Julia wasn't for Donatello. She suggested Yoshida-Ya, a Japanese restaurant on Webster Street. Japanese food was about as contrary as possible to the *orecchie-d'elefante* and other such dishes Grady had looked forward to, however, he went along with it.

When they were shoeless and settled cross-legged at a low table at the restaurant Julia ordered sake, but not just sake and for certain not a California one. She specified Harushika, a fine very dry type brewed in Nara, Japan, claimed she preferred it and promised so would Grady after a taste. When the sake was brought she did the pouring, gracefully handling the small, pinch-necked ceramic bottle. Poured into his cup first and waited until he'd drunk before pouring into her own.

"It has a bit of a tail," she commented after savoring a sip. The word *shiripin* came to mind for no apparent reason. She didn't realize that in Japanese it meant *having a tail*, thought it was merely some nonsense syllables.

Grady assumed by tail she meant aftertaste. Evidently Julia knew sake, he thought. There was so much he had to learn about her.

When she asked his permission to order dinner, he was glad to be relieved of the responsibility. According to his experience with women and Japanese food he was quite sure she'd give the raw stuff a wide berth and stick to such things as tempura or shabu shabu.

Julia, however, ordered a wide variety of sashimi, raw giant clam, raw yellowtail, raw tuna, both dark and light, raw sea urchin and double helpings of awabi, raw abalone. When her selections were brought she inspected them thoroughly before she allowed the waitress to place them on the table. She wasn't entirely satisfied with the way the sea urchin was arranged, sent it back for tidier embellishments. Grady enjoyed that, and the way she'd taken over and tended to his needs. She inquired whether or not he approved of everything and mixed the soy sauce and wasabi, the fiery green horseradish, into a paste for him to slather on his raw stuff. He was fascinated by her dexterity with chopsticks, the way with no trouble at all she was able to pincer up just about anything with them, rice or whatever.

Julia, meanwhile, was somewhat confounded by herself. For one thing, she hadn't ever particularly cared for Japanese food. The mere idea of eating fish raw had been enough to bring her close to the point of gagging. And here she was now relishing every morsel and telling herself she didn't know what she'd been missing. The awabi she found particularly delicious. As for chopsticks, she'd tried them a few times in Chinese places here and there and gotten fairly competent with them, but she'd never achieved this much efficiency. Maybe, she thought, that was because she'd tried too hard before and it had actually been easy all along. To prove her new, minor accomplishment she scooped up passion fruit sorbet with her sticks and, without a drip, carried the swift-melting lump to Grady's mouth.

Then came tea and talk. Julia steered the conversation onto what might be Grady's next business move.

"I'm going to Burma," he told her.

"Why there?"

"Each February right after the Chinese New Year the Burmese government holds an important sale of gems in Rangoon, sapphires, rubies, pearls. I should be able to pick up some nice goods at a favorable price."

"February you say?"

"Yeah."

"I know I'm a good reason for you to lose track of time, but not monthly hunks of it. This is June, not February."

"For some political reason they called off the last February sale," Grady explained. "Now they've called it on for the week after next."

"Okay, I've got nothing against Burma. When do we leave?"

He shot her a *we question mark* look.

"I'll pay my own way," she said.

"I'm just going to hop over and back."

"How long will hopping over and back cause you to be away?"

"Five, ten days at most," he replied, trying to nonchalant it.

"Five, maybe ten? Well then, how about if I also pay *your* way? I won't be a bother, promise, except in bed, of course. The rest of the time I'll sketch and get some fresh ideas. From what I gather, Burma must be colorful."

Grady had intended to invite her along, had had doubts she'd want to go. Five to ten days away from her would be torture. He thought it might be a point won if he admitted that.

He did. And it was.

Within the minute she also scored by making him a gift of the alligator leather business card case she'd bought weeks ago. Earlier that evening when she was getting ready something or other had reminded her of the case and then made her realize why she'd bought it. For him. Even before she'd become aware of her interest, for him.

Grady was delighted with the case, admired its patine and its

18k gold corners and couldn't wait; right then and there put some of his new business cards in it.

Thanked her with a kiss.

And another, longer and more intensive, when they were in the car on the way to 760 and the office. He'd first headed for her place, was eager to get there, but she'd casually suggested they stop by the office for a moment. His passion hadn't wanted to. She insisted. And when they got there he saw why.

Now hung on the wall to the right of his desk was the painting she'd been working on. Signed and dedicated to him in its bottom left corner. It was a complex painting, consisted of numerous underlays and overlays, was both subtle and vivid, distinct and obscure. The most dominant shape in its composition was a dark irregular triangle, a sort of high-topped shoe shape. Below that in one spot within a mass of vivid blue were numerous yellow, pink and green swirls.

"Like it?" Julia wanted to know.

"Very much," he told her and, after another long moment of study, half-guessed, "it's a seascape."

"Isn't it though?" she grinned.

"Someplace you've been I suppose."

"Not that I recall. Actually, I think it's purely a product of my imagination."

CHAPTER EIGHT

It was supposed to have been only an hour layover in Bangkok, a welcome hyphen during which they would recover their ground legs, stretch, walk their circulation back to normal and, without hurry, make their Thai Airline connection on to Rangoon. However, because there'd not been any of the usual countering headwinds at thirty-seven thousand feet all the way across the Pacific, they'd been put down in Bangkok an hour ahead of schedule. Then, as though deliberately to nullify such accommodation a computer monitor in the main terminal told them the takeoff of their connecting flight was delayed an hour.

So, three hours. Hardly a hardship, but much of the good anticipation and endurance they'd had when they'd boarded in San Francisco had already been thinned down by the penalties of such a long-range air trip, and now to be unexpectedly detained, confined like prisoners by the airport and forced to serve three limbo hours, seemed unreasonable.

Julia was handling this extra waiting better than Grady. Taking it rather in stride and feeling pleased with her patience. The patience demanded by public waiting of this sort had always been one of her shorter suits. B.G. (before Grady) she'd always been sigh prone and jittered when asked to tolerate such a waste of her time. Her reaction now was definitely an improvement, she thought, another, she thought, that had come along with her radically better outlook since Grady had entered her life. What could she attribute it to other than passionate contentment, a filling on the way to being fulfilled? A change among the numerous changes she was experiencing, to be able to sit there in a hard plastic seat at Bangkok airport gate number 14 without fidget, squirm or pace, limbs exact and still, breathing so tranquilly that even her inside hearing couldn't hear it. What could explain this difference in her, allowing time to flow through her like a silken stream? The reason had to be him.

He, on the other hand, was obviously uncomfortable, unable to conceal his impatience with the situation. Every so often mumbling little sibilant curses that he probably didn't even realize were coming out. He was never at his best when subjected to such trips. Wished he could be, wished he could be like those many dealers he knew who could, with hardly a weary eye or spine, fly from New York to Tel Aviv to Geneva and back and without the need for repair time, be ready to be off again.

Not he.

He had the handicap of an extremely sensitive circadian clock, that cerebral device of everyone that to varying degrees reacts adversely to deviations from routine. Lag got to him so easily, causing his legs to resent the load they supported and the sealed-over sutures of his cranium to feel as though they were straining and just might come apart to allow his gray matter more room.

Once, on a buying trip for Larkin, Grady had arrived in Ouro Prêto, Brazil, in such a condition. His reputedly good eyes were so impaired that he turned down a lot of sacrificially priced emerald half-caraters. Regretted having done so when the lag left him and his faculties sharpened and the competitor who'd bought the lot showed it to him and Grady realized how fine, really, those emeralds and their price were. That he'd lost out on a profitable deal hadn't bothered him as much as why he'd lost out on it. Lag, fucking lag. He'd never told Larkin about his battle with it, nor anyone else. Kept the encumbrance to himself to keep it from ever being used in business against him. Besides, it wasn't an easy thing to admit man to man.

He'd hoped having Julia along on this twenty-four-hour flight would make a difference. It didn't, not essentially. His lag was beyond her presence. In fact his trying to conceal it from her created an extra degree of strain that he had to cope with. Still, when he summed it all he knew if she hadn't been along in other numerous ways he'd have been worse off. Worse off without her various smiles and their honesties. Worse off without the entertainment of the private mysteries conveyed by her eyes. And the collaborative caring she so often demonstrated. Made him feel she was decidedly with him. Did so, for instance, with spontaneous touches, the claiming of him with her hands, the sign language said by her mouth and its instruments tongue and teeth, by such aggressive things as having the attendant remove the armrest so she could snuggle and press. Every several hundred miles she massaged the back of his neck, if not subduing, at least with care competing with the tension that accumulated there. He was made to feel he was her man. At the same time he was made to realize how desirable it was to feel in her debt.

She was, in his opinion, an excellent traveler. The antithesis of Gayle. She allowed him to stow her principal carryon bag in the overhead compartment, but then when she wanted something from it, got it down and back up again by herself. Asked the flight attendant for two pillows right off rather than one and then another. Didn't complain about her ears being stuffed up or spill anything or remark a half dozen times that she should have worn a roomier pair of shoes. She actually read the books she'd brought along: a paperback version of a biography of Cecil Beaton and a copy of Alice A. Bailey's *The Soul and its Mechanism*. Napped when Grady felt like napping, talked when he wanted to and evidently sensed when he was talked out. Didn't hum or la de da along with whatever music she was listening to on her Walkman. Nor did she whip out an array of utensils and repair or redo her makeup every hour. Truly an ideal traveling companion, Grady thought, so much unlike Gayle, who would have let it be known with clenched teeth hisses and intruding demands that she was feeling neglected when he struck up a conversation with the man seated across the aisle.

That man was obviously a businessman. In his late fifties and dressed the part in a vested gray suit of hard finished wool. Wearing black lace-up, cap-toed shoes, one of which was marred cruelly by a scuff. No doubt, he could have paled down his florid complexion considerably by forsaking image, loosening his tight knotted tie and unbuttoning his collar.

The man introduced himself as Clifton, Lawrence Clifton from Chicago. As happenchance would have it he too was a gem dealer, by preference did business mainly in sapphires. That established, both he and Grady submitted a string of names to determine mutual acquaintances in the trade. There were several, including Larkin, Grady's first and unforgettable employer. Clifton had for years done business off and on with Larkin, knew about him well enough to say, "Last I heard he'd had another stroke. In Florida."

"Fort Lauderdale."

"Damn shame. No one had better eyes. In his time Larkin could grade a mixed lot of sapphires in less time and more accurately than anyone I've ever known, and that includes those chinks in Bangkok who've always been magical at it. Phenomenal eyes." It was the ultimate compliment one gem dealer could pay another. The ability to sight into a precious stone and know practically everything about it, not just its quality and value, but, as well, its place of origin—continent, country, area, often even the very mine that had yielded it.

"Larkin loved pearls," Grady said reminiscently.

"Didn't he though."

"Taught me plenty."

"How long were you with him?"

Grady told him.

"Now that I think of it I believe I remember him speaking of you, favorably. Tell me your name again."

Grady said it while his mind went back to the bar of the Algonquin with Larkin and that favorite topic, pearls. He returned to take notice of Clifton's professionally manicured nails and passé dental work, caps that no longer convinced because they didn't fit the gums. Grady wasn't being critical as much as observant. "Where are you headed?" he asked.

Clifton enjoyed replying. "Hong Kong first, then on to Colombo for a day before Rangoon. What about you?"

"Rangoon."

"For the Emporium?"

"Yes."

"Ever been before?"

Grady disliked having to admit this would be his first Emporium. He'd heard so much about the event, mainly from older dealers such as this Clifton and from Larkin and others, that it seemed attendance was prerequisite to being thought of as thoroughly experienced. Grady had been particularly impressed by the accounts of profitable, fine goods that had been purchased at the Emporium of one year or another. He had, of course, dealt a fair number of Burmese stones over the years, knew them well enough. No sapphires were more valued, except perhaps those rarer lazy ones out of Kashmir. And Burmese rubies, the true pigeon bloods. One such ruby of four carats had sold at auction only a few years ago for five hundred thousand a carat. Burmese pearls and jade were also considered superior.

Such riches.

Grady was looking forward to having a chance at them on the Emporium level, just one step out of the ground and therefore far less expensive. He knew it probably wasn't going to be absolutely easy. Fine goods weren't going to just pop into his pocket. However, it wasn't beyond possibility that he'd make some better than merely good deals, and he imagined himself returning to San Francisco and the Phelan Building, causing a stir of envy as word got around that he was starting up his business with a spectacular inventory.

Have you seen Grady Bowman's goods?

I've heard.

You've got to see. Burmese beauties. The buyer at Shreve took only a quick look and wanted the lot.

Couldn't happen to a nicer guy.

Oh, how it would hurt Harold's ears.

Clifton now asked, "Are you going to be looking to buy for someone or for yourself?"

Grady gladly told him.

"Well, I hope you won't be disappointed. In fact, I hope the same for myself. The last Emporium I went to was hardly worth the trip. That was in '82. Year by year before that it had gone downhill. The lots that were offered, anyway all but a few, were made up of second-rate goods with a first-quality head of about ten percent."

Grady had heard as much but he continued being attentive to hear Clifton's version. Clifton paused to blow his nose into the fluff of an ordinary white handkerchief, examined with a mixture of curiosity and distaste what he'd discharged, enclosed it with a bunchy fold and inserted the handkerchief into his inside jacket pocket. "Damn dry air they pump around in these jets. Always raises hell with my sinuses. I'm no good for a week or two after a long flight."

Grady's misery enjoyed the company.

Clifton went on. "Every year the Burmese government gave one excuse or another for the decline in desirable goods offered for bidding at the Emporium. Blamed the heavier rains, the depletion of certain mines, trouble with rebels such as the Karens and the Mons, just about anything that sounded reasonable."

"One would think they'd be eager to sell their goods to the West."

"They are eager and they do sell, only not as straight and aboveboard as one would imagine. The Burmese government is military. It runs everything and takes its whack up and down the line. The lower ranks circumspectfully pocket their nibbles, the top of the brass, of course, help themselves to the flagrant big bites. Thus it stands that for a soldier, especially an officer, say a lieutenant or captain, to be assigned to one of the rich gem-mining districts such as Mogok is thought of as a privilege, the next best thing to being given outright instant wealth."

Grady imagined while Clifton verbally drew it for him.

"Doesn't matter that those mining areas for the most part are chronic war zones occupied by rebels. And not just a few insurgents here and there but thousands of real angry, well-armed Karens, Mons, Hachins and the like. Plenty dangerous, but for the Burmese army officer well worth the risk. Between firefights he goes around to the numerous ruby and sapphire pits, which, as you may know...I'm sorry, stop me if you're knowledgeable about these things..."

"No, please, go on."

Clifton obliged. Told how the pits weren't large, on the average measured about thirty feet in diameter and half that deep. So the army officer from his vantage up on the edge was able to see everything that went on. Told how the men worked in muddy water up to their crotches, water that had seeped or rained in. It was all quite primitive. They dredged the bottom with flat pans of tightly woven bamboo, brought up dirt and gravel from the mucky bottom. The army officer kept a sharp eye on what they brought up, what they emptied onto the sievelike screen situated at the edge of the pit. The silt and grit got hosed away leaving the gravel. No one, certainly not the mine operator, was allowed to touch that until the army officer had looked through it, spread it, rolled it over, picked the most promising rough rubies and sapphires from it. If he was new at this he was probably fooled by the dull material that adhered to the surface of some of the stones, often to some of the much finer ones, disguising them so they appeared to be no more than ordinary gravel. But he, like the fortunate army officers before him, soon learned what he shouldn't overlook. He and his greed became sure-eyed, able to recognize the better stuff no matter how thick and ugly its skin.

Grady imagined it. A diminutive Burmese army officer with a pocket or two of his fatigues bulging with what he, Grady, would happily settle for a mere few of. "What then?" Grady asked Clifton. "Where does that rough get sold?"

"Across the Thai border," Clifton replied and went on, telling how the Chinese dealers from Bangkok were the main buyers, how they usually situated themselves on the Thai side, not in a village but out along one of the remote, nearly indiscernible paths that crisscross in and out of Burmese territory. Paths known and used by locals but hardly anyone else. Most of the transactions were carried out at night, the darker the better. The buyer would prop a strong flashlight upright, aiming its beam through an opening in the jungle growth overhead. The large amount of cash he'd brought along would already be shallowly buried somewhere close by. He'd sit and wait, hoping a Burmese officer with ruby and sapphire rough to sell would notice the beam and come to him. He might wait all night in vain. If so, he'd move to another spot along the path. Sometimes it would take a week of such nights. It was dangerous business. There was always the chance that soldiers of one rebel faction or another might spot the beam and get to him. The rebels knew about this regular trade in contraband gems. They roamed the border areas at night searching for those vertical beams of light. When they spotted one they hurried to it, killed the buyer right off and located his money. The Bangkok buyers paid a fat price for the rough, but, of course, when the rough reached Bangkok and was cut into finished goods it was worth a great deal more.

Clifton was a frustrated storyteller, Grady decided, but he allowed himself to go along with it, mentally placing himself some night along the Burmese-Thai border, waiting awhile and then doing swift business with a Burmese officer, trading the dollars he now had in his money belt for a chamois sack of precious stones, a veritable fortune in fine Burma rough. He could hear the contained stones clicking against one another, fine ruby against fine sapphire as he shoved the sack into the largest pocket of whatever he was wearing. But then came the realization of the peril involved in such an undertaking. It shot a shudder through him and he snapped back to Clifton's face across the aisle. "Anyway," Clifton was saying, "that's why the last ten to fifteen Emporiums have been so paltry. Seems the government high-ups have conducted them merely for show, to keep their personally profitable traffic in contraband from being altogether obvious."

Grady thought about how he'd hate having made this long trip merely to look at mediocre goods. "What about this year?" he asked. "What are the expectations?"

"Word is the government will offer up a considerable amount of fine grade. That would be in keeping with its recent change of heart in regard to doing more trade with the West. I tend to believe it. Otherwise I wouldn't be here."

A flight attendant came down the aisle, causing Grady and Clifton to have to draw back from their outward leaning and momentarily eclipsing their views of each other. It more or less concluded the subject.

"Where in Rangoon will you be staying?" Clifton inquired.

"The Inye Lake Hotel," Grady replied.

Clifton evidently disapproved.

"Something wrong with the place?" Grady wanted to know.

"It's not the hotel I would have recommended," Clifton told him, "but at least you won't be staying at the Strand."

"Someone suggested the Strand, said it was colorful."

"It's been trading on that description ever since the British left in '48. Anyway, if you do nothing else, beware of the generals. They'll be swarming around the Inye Lake."

Grady thought he meant high-level army types. Clifton set him straight: "Guys who present themselves as retired generals and look in every way as though they might be. They all use more or less the same approach and they're really good at it, have it down pat. First that sort strikes up an amiable conversation into which he slips the fact that he was once in charge of one of the outlying mining districts such as Magok. After a little bullshit about that he'll turn hush hush and confide that he still has a connection at the mines, someone who regularly supplies him with gems. He might be willing to part with a few, he says. For a price. Which will be a high enough price to make it more convincing. What he's selling, actually, are, of course, synthetic stones, cubic zirconium ruby-looking reds, sapphire-looking blues with silk and all the other right kind of flaws in them to make them credible."

"Thanks for the tip," Grady said politely, though not believing for an instant that anyone could fake out his eyes.

Clifton took a loud heaving breath and let his eyelids close. "I'm going to doze," he said and tugged with a finger at his shirt collar, as though imploring it not to choke him while he was unconscious.

Grady sat back in his reclined business class seat and looked to Julia on his right. When he'd last given her his total attention she'd been engrossed in the Alice A. Bailey book having to do with souls. Had she overheard any of his conversation with Clifton? It seemed she hadn't. She let the book drop to her lap so her then liberated hands could claim Grady's upper arm. Her head used his shoulder. After a long moment of silence that was like an allotment to the auguring of the future Julia had said in a tone part encouraging and part the assuming of responsibility for her words: "Don't worry, hon, you're going to do even better than you hope. I just know it."

That had been during the flight.

Now, here they were short of destination, having been deposited in Bangkok at Don Muang International Airport. They had an hour of the time waste yet to go. Grady couldn't stay for more than ten consecutive minutes in the seat there in the proximity of gate 14. One of the seats in a row of rows, identical, hard, indestructible plastic molded to fit the cheeks of the universal ass. He'd get up and walk anywhere until reminded of his weariness, then come back to sit and feel afflicted. Whenever his look caught upon Julia's he'd try for what he believed was a smile close enough to his true, relaxed one or he'd say something light. He was almost certain she was unaware of the strain in him, the terrible lag sensations. He reasoned that had she been aware she probably would have brought it up, tried to talk or even love him out of it, maybe. Best that she was as she was, okay, collected, taking care of herself, he thought.

She got up, told him she was going to the ladies' room. She was gone for longer than should have been required and Grady got to glancing uneasily every so often in the direction of the ladies' room, down the long straight corridor of that arm of the terminal. Then he kept looking steadily for her, concerned for her until he caught sight of her returning. He appreciated the confident stride of her, the sensuality in its strength as her thighs lefted and righted beneath the ample cotton skirt she had on. And it occurred to him that during his concern for her he'd not felt lagged and that made him wonder if it might not be entirely or at least mostly psychological. He hoped so and he hoped not.

He didn't realize she was miffed until she was close, sat down hard in the next seat.

"Why is it," she said to the situation as much as to Grady, "that ordinary things cost like the devil in an airport? Do you know how much I had to pay for this?" She held up a pack of Wrigley's Doublemint gum and didn't give him time to guess. "Thirty bahts," she said. "Can you imagine? Thirty bahts."

"How much is that?"

"About a dollar and a quarter. When in your life have you ever paid a dollar and a quarter for a pack of gum, except maybe in an airport? They figure when they've got you they should take you. What an outrage!" She blew out a funnel of invisible chafe. Grady had never seen her so annoyed, and over such a minor thing. It made him wonder what other furies she was capable of.

Would she, for instance, be this aggravated if he ever forgot to raise the toilet seat? He thought so. Decided after hardly a few moments of consideration it was in her favor that she was so volatilely stoked. It gave her tone. He wouldn't want her predictably agreeable. As a matter of fact, he told himself, he was rather looking forward to their first vigorous difference and, of course, the intense loving that would follow. Not that he wanted theirs to be one of those fight and fuck relationships. He'd never let it get to that.

While these were Grady's thoughts he watched Julia rip open the pack of gum to reveal the silver foil-wrapped ends of the five sticks it contained. His lagged eyes, fixed on this inconsequential procedure, seemed to magnify each step of it. The coordination of her thumb and the nail of her second finger pulling out the top stick, tearing away its green paper wrapper (outer garments) to show its foil covering (flashy underthings), then inserting a thumbnail beneath the helpful serrated edge to peel off the foil and have the thing...nude.

She folded the length of the gum twice, put it in her mouth.

She hadn't yet told him she loved him, Grady thought, at least, not verbally. She did a stick of the gum for him and he opened his mouth to receive it.

Nor, for that matter, had he in words told her he loved her, he thought.

Another stick for herself, another for him. That left the last.

He refused it but believed she'd insist he have it, but she didn't, just denuded it and added it to her chew and resumed where she'd left off on a page of Alice A. Bailey, a paragraph having to deal with the reasons certain souls might be reluctant, even refuse, to make the transition into the afterlife.

CHAPTER NINE

Close to three hours and precisely 374 air miles later Grady and Julia were being processed by a customs official at Mingaladon Airport in Rangoon. The official was an unattractive fellow with such a severe and irregular overbite that the tip of his left incisor was visible when his mouth was closed. That, along with the deep downward creases from each corner of his mouth and the obdurate glare of his dark eyes, caused the immediate impression that he was unfriendly.

However, in return for a look through Grady's and Julia's passports the official activated such a smile that it seemed he might have found something amusing on the pages. There in magenta and green ink were the seven-day visa stamps and, inserted for examination in the back of Grady's passport, were the applied for and issued Union of Burma credentials that identified him as a qualified gem dealer approved to attend the Emporium. Also there, the required currency form Grady had filled out in duplicate just prior to landing. It not only required that he declare how much money he was bringing in but that during his stay he also keep a written account of every exchange and expenditure he made. The whole thing would have to balance out precisely upon departure. Grady considered declaring only a hundred of the hundred and fifty thousand he had on him. There had been instances in his pursuit of gems in various other foreign places when being able to come up with some unexpected cash had worked wonders. Thus, his hand had wanted to write a hundred thousand on the currency form. His better judgment, however, owned up to the whole hundred and fifty.

Passport, credentials, forms, all were in order. The official, as though expressing personal joy, raised his stamping device high and slammed it down on a vacant passport page. Noting date and time of entry. Then came the first words he'd spoken: "*Hkunni*," he said, "seven, seven days, no more." He held up seven fingers and wiggled them for emphasis. Grady, in boning up on the dos and don'ts of Burma, had read how strict the government was about visitors adhering to the length of their visas. Seven days meant not an hour more. Overstayers would be punished. Punished?

Grady and Julia proceeded to the next area, where their baggage would be inspected. The inspector they got was no less good-natured, although Julia thought it intentionally perverse the way he made a shambles of the contents of each bag as he searched. She prided herself in being an excellent, extremely organized packer, and now there were her silkies and flimsies and, as well, her everyday, practical cotton underthings topping the peak of a haphazard pile. Grady noticed how the inspector kept coming back to those and riffling through them.

"What nerve," Julia remarked.

Grady hoped she wouldn't cause a scene, thought she was bound to as without waiting for the inspector's consent she flipped down the lid of that particular bag and zipped it up. Then all four bags were closed and zipped and the inspector wielded a chalky, yellow crayon to slash his validating mark across the face of each. They proceeded then through an outward opening door to where, most prominent, was the teller's window of an official money exchange. Grady converted a hundred dollars into a sheaf of kyats. Gave half to Julia for her possible needs.

Neither Grady nor Julia felt as though they'd finally arrived in Burma until they were out of the terminal, in the awful humidity and being ulteriorly welcomed by what must have been twenty hustling taxi drivers.

The taxi they chose was a 1957 Chevrolet Bel Air, red and cream with its original paint miraculously surviving. It had a whiplike radio antenna, no hubcaps and one of its tires was a vintage-type whitewall, no doubt weary of being time and time again recapped. The driver and owner of this vehicle was a typical slightly built Burman with a contradicting moon face and a stringy mass of jet black hair. He smiled and kept smiling as rather victoriously he loaded the bags into the trunk. One of his upper front teeth, Grady noticed, was completely gold capped and inset with a heart-shaped piece of lavender jade.

The driver got behind the wheel, started up, but wouldn't pull out until the fare was negotiated. He began with a straight face at fifty kyats (approximately seven dollars), which was tantamount to thievery. Grady, on principle, didn't let him get away with it, nor with a reduction to thirty kyats. Grady knew from his pretrip reading what was fair, and twenty-five kyats was settled upon. The driver pulled the taxi out abruptly and soon had it beyond the airport complex and headed at its old-age full speed south in the direction of Rangoon City.

It was late afternoon. There had been the usual brief but drenching daily rain and the air was still steamy from it, more redolent than fresh with the pervasive scent of some sort of spice. All the windows of the car were down (no handles to roll them up), and, despite the humidity, it felt pleasant to Grady and Julia to have the fifty-mile-per-hour turbulence striking their faces and whipping their hair. Meanwhile, the driver was offsetting his tedium by making the playful most of the depressions in the highway where rainwater was pooled. He splashed every possible puddle, swerved sharply several times to splash some he would have otherwise missed.

All the way down Prome Road to where it intersected with Yard Road. A turn onto Yard and then after a short ways the view about a quarter mile off to the left was enriched with the stupa of a major pagoda, a single, sharp, bell-shaped spire coated with gold. A little farther on the stark white multi-tiered base of the pagoda could be seen. This sight was erased by a right turn onto Kaba Aye Road, followed within the minute by another right for the long hooking drive of the hotel.

The surrounding grounds of it were extensive. The shrubbery, azaleas, camellias and the like, and the trees, various palms and other tropicals, were nicely trimmed and shaped. Julia, but especially Grady, was encouraged by how verdant, well nourished and tended were the large areas of lawn and the many ample beds of flowers.

Then there was the huge hotel.

A five-story chunk of concrete. Built by the Soviets in 1960, its architectural personality was unmistakably Khrushchev—a close cousin or perhaps even an identical blueprint twin of one of those make-do structures put up about that same time around Moscow to house the common comrades. Flat sided, no such thing as a balcony or a setback, small, repetitious windows. The only embellishment, and that no doubt an afterthought, was a red canvas canopy from curb to front entrance. Four soldiers stood precisely spaced to the left of the entrance. Four more to the right. Staunch look-alikes, identically uniformed, bandoliered, automatic rifles slung, they appeared ready to take on trouble or cause it. Except, Grady noticed, none of them had on shoes. Didn't being shoeless make them not so intimidating? Grady told himself to ignore them or consider them a sort of honor guard.

He and Julia entered and crossed the spacious lobby. It was moderately bustling, and other soldiers were standing here and there. At reception the clerk turned to the varnished teak counter to serve them. He would have been a nondescript Burman had it not been for his mouth. It was naturally pursed, crimped all around, looked as though it would be painful, or, at the very least, difficult for him to open it.

He didn't. His greeting was a single nod.

Grady produced his and Julia's passports and his Emporium credentials.

The clerk didn't look at the passports, just took them. He glanced at the Emporium credentials, consulted a reservation list, ran down it several times until he had Grady concerned.

"Bowman," the clerk discovered aloud, mispronouncing the first syllable.

To Grady it seemed that he'd only just heard his name but, as well, seen it come from that mouth.

"Three-thirty-seven," the clerk said as from somewhere beneath the counter he came up with a key attached to a clear disc the size of a Ping-Pong paddle.

"We wish to be shown the room first," Julia said firmly.

"Yeah, we'd like to see it," Grady seconded. Actually, he and his lag were ready to settle for any space that would allow him to get horizontal for a while.

The clerk summoned a porter who took the key and led the way to one of the elevators and on up to the third floor. Three-thirty-seven was two-thirds of the way down the excessively wide corridor. The porter unlocked the door, swung it open and waited outside while Grady and Julia went in.

The room had a high ceiling but was small. Crowded by its furnishings, which were only the essentials: a double bed, night-stands, dresser drawers, an armchair. All of a lesser quality than even average guest-proof motel room furniture. It was veneered blond, a half-century outdated with the brass plating of its cast iron pulls and knobs worn off. Beige wall-to-wall carpet that had been given up on, stained upon stain and with little or no nap left along bedside and in other most-used areas. The place was so permeated with cigarette and cigar smoke that Julia held her breath as she gave it the once-over.

Hurrying out she remarked, "I've stayed in better than this years ago in Lam Pam." As though that was unlikely but the most suitable comparison she could think of.

"Where?" Grady asked, glancing back longingly at the bed.

"Where what?"

"Where's that, Lam whatever?"

"I've no idea what you're talking about."

"I must be hearing things."

"Must be."

"Or you must be saying things."

"All I said was I've stayed in better."

"I sure as hell hope so." Grady let it go at that, and within a minute or so they were back down in the lobby facing the clerk with the pursed mouth. Who was impassive to the fact that they didn't like the room, merely stated that it was a *deluxe* accommodation.

"The best you've got?" Grady asked incredulously.

"Our superior deluxe rooms are all taken," the clerk informed, and, after a beat, added, "I believe."

The *I believe* wasn't missed by Grady. He realized the clerk's
cash register eyes, should have earlier on and saved all this bother,
he thought, and went into his pocket for a hundred kyat note
(about fifteen dollars). While his fingers were at it he decided for
sure measure they should double that. He slipped the two hundred kyats to the clerk.

Evidently discretion was unnecessary. The clerk examined the
money in plain sight, tucked it into his jacket pocket, sucked his
lips tighter in triumph, and came up with the key to 543,
presumably a superior deluxe.

This time the baggage went up with Grady and Julia. To 543,
which promised to be better because it was located at the very
end, facing the corridor. It really wasn't more of a room. It was
just as small, just as badly furnished, just as used, just as smelling
of smoke. Neither Grady nor Julia commented on it aloud, even
after the porter was tipped and gone. Grady felt that he'd been
tricked, taken, and Julia, sensitive to that, held back expressing her
fault findings, as valid and obvious and numerous as they were.
Instead, first thing, she removed the coverlet from the bed, turned
down the sheet and plumped the pillows. Hummed as she unpacked
hers and his.

"I'm hungry but sleepier than hungry," she said as she lay down
nude beside him.

"Order something up," he mumbled. Tomorrow was the first
day of the Emporium, he thought. He'd have to have his best eyes
and his head straight by tomorrow. He doubted he'd be able to
get to sleep. His mind was racing so. But within a couple of
minutes it went over the cliff and plunged into sweet black.

CHAPTER TEN

The Emporium.

It was held in an area of the hotel situated off the main lobby, a large facility perhaps most adequately described as a convention room or auditorium. The room was more than just adequately lighted, brightly so, with numerous fixtures extended from the twenty-foot-high ceiling. Beneath the lights were counters joined end to end to form rows. The surfaces of these were covered with a black fabric and they were similarly skirted. Situated as they were, the rows of counters created wide aisles. A wider, perpendicular center aisle helped circulation. Barefoot but armed soldiers were positioned around.

Upon the counters, offered in individual lots, were the gemstones. Contained in unfolded paper briefkes like doilies placed on shallow glass dishes. Each lot was identified by an assigned number. There was no possible way for anyone to miss or mistake any of these corresponding numbers inasmuch as they were so largely and prevalently displayed. From behind the counters an attendant was assigned to watch over each lot and answer any inquiry.

Evidently the government had given considerable thought to the arrangement of everything. And to how to its best advantage the selling was to be conducted.

None of the lots of gemstones could be purchased outright. They'd be auctioned. Not in the customary verbal way whereby one bidder might top another and in turn be topped. There'd be no open bidding such as that. Rather, as each lot came up for sale in numerical order, buyers would be allowed to submit a single bid by noting upon a small printed form the amount they were willing to pay along with a number that had been assigned to identify each buyer. Then the form was to be fed into the slot of a large stainless steel receptacle located in the center aisle.

To let the buyers know when a particular lot was up for bidding a color slide of it and its number would be projected upon a screen fixed high above the front of the room.

Five minutes exactly was allowed for the bidding on each lot. When time had expired, the officials in charge would open the receptacle and go through the bids. Purportedly the buyer who bid highest would acquire the lot. His number would be announced and displayed on a second, smaller screen. Meanwhile bidding would be under way on the next lot.

At the moment, early on the first morning of the Emporium, being presented for sale on the screen was a lot consisting of a hundred pieces of ten-carat moonstones. These were several degrees bluer and therefore more desirable than the usual skim milk blue sort. The German dealers in particular were interested in the lot while others gave it hardly any attention.

About two hundred dealers were there. From just about every European country, and from India and Australia, Japan and Israel. Chinese dealers from Hong Kong and Taipei who'd come for Burma jade. Dealer-agents for the Saudis and Kuwaitis and for the sultan of Brunei, who if the mood struck could overpay merely for the satisfaction of financial bullying. The dealers from the United States were considered prime buyers. They numbered about fifty and were mainly from New York City and Chicago, men who were well acquainted and whose camaraderie was heightened by their being together in a place so far from home and so foreign.

The dealer Clifton from Chicago was one of these. Grady ran into him and they conversed briefly, but somehow the flavor of their exchange was different from the one they'd had on the flight, not nearly so outspoken, strained by the atmosphere. Grady also encountered a couple of Forty-seventh Street dealers he'd known fairly well from his Larkin days, but he didn't hook up with them and they didn't seem to want him to, just suggested vaguely getting together for drinks when it was convenient.

So, Grady was a loner. He didn't mind.

After all, he wasn't there to socialize, and besides, he told himself, he really wouldn't enjoy talking trade. He went around to the various lots alone, also telling himself as he examined them that he really didn't need anyone else's opinion.

His eyes were at their all-time best, his mind sharp. He'd slept close to twelve hours, without a toss or a change of position that he could remember. The most beneficial sleep he'd had in his adult life, it was as though some concerned spirit had overtaken and sedated him. Less fanciful, he thought, the reason he'd slept such a good necessary sleep was Julia. Her and her arms around, knee contacts, various ways of keeping in touch.

Anyway, when he'd awakened at dawn his lag symptoms were gone. He didn't have even a remnant of those, and the clock of his system seemed reset. He'd showered and all that and enjoyed a sense of well-being throughout his shave and while getting dressed in his sincere blue suit. He and Julia had an omelet breakfast in the hotel's main dining room. Then, after several parting-temporarily-type kisses and assuring him a half dozen times not to worry she could look after herself, she'd taken off in a taxi with a pad, charcoal sticks and other sketching necessities, and he'd headed for the Emporium armed with his trusty ten-power loupe and optimism.

Pink sapphires.

A lot of ten matching stones totalling in weight twenty carats on the nose. Two French dealers were examining them and Grady had to wait to have his look. He pushed them slightly about with his special tweezers, disturbed them and caused them to respond with scintillations. They were eye clean, he decided, but badly cut. He picked them up with the tweezers, all ten, one after another. Did so with the sure deftness of a professional, swiftly without fumble or drop. Sighted into each with his magnifying loupe and proved to himself these were not "Burma-like" but Burma top-grade. They were, without question, the finest pink sapphires he'd ever experienced. Hot pink, a real punchy pink, feminine. They brought Doris to mind. Doris, his assistant, who was back in San Francisco tending the office and who'd always been so taken with that lot of pinks in Harold's inventory. Harold's pinks were watery and weak by comparison.

Grady imagined himself returning to San Francisco with these Burmas among his buys. Doris would orgasm. He thought he might bid on the lot. According to its number, it wouldn't come up for bidding for a while yet, but he'd watch for its turn.

He continued down along that row and around to another row, getting a feel for the scope of the offerings, stopping here and there to examine certain lots that caught his interest. The peridots, amethysts, tourmalines, garnets and the like were excellent semiprecious goods, however they obviously were being used as fillers to make the event seem more extensive. The rubies and sapphires, emeralds and alexandrite, pearls and jade were what nearly everyone was there for.

There was much jade and much interest in it from the Chinese. Grady was amused at overhearing a group of Chinese dealers discussing the merits of a rough boulder that was the Emporium's jade centerpiece. The boulder was a good five feet high and three in diameter and had a small window polished on its surface for a clear view into its interior. The Chinese were taking turns looking into the window and from their rapid high decibels, one would have thought they were having a heated argument. Another such cluster of Chinese dealers, these from Hong Kong, were vociferously boiling over a lot of imperial jade beads, those of the finest quality and green (the green of Prell shampoo).

Grady knew very little about jade. He was aware that the far better was found in Burma, had been for centuries, but that was about it. Maybe he ought to learn jade, he thought as he bypassed jade lot after jade lot, but then, he told himself, never in his lifetime would he catch up with the Oriental expertise.

The lot of pink sapphires was coming up for bidding. The slide on the overhead screen changed, and there they were, suffering considerably in reproduction. Grady wrote his assigned dealer number in the proper space on a bidding slip, then figured how much he'd bid. Total weight, twenty carats. He'd have to recut them and lose about 20 percent, or four carats. He'd probably be able to get $6,000 a carat, $96,000 for the lot, $56,000 profit if he now paid $40,000 for it ($2,000 a carat). Those figures set in his mind. He printed $40,000 in the proper space on the bidding slip and dropped it into the stainless steel receptacle.

Well, he thought, I've gotten my feet wet.

He stood around, waited for the result of the bidding for the pinks, and when after it came up on the screen and the dealer number shown wasn't his, he felt a little drop in his spirit. He lifted that away with the thought that there were many other lots of fine goods here, plenty for everyone and he'd get his.

He roamed around a while longer and by then it was early afternoon. Went to the adjacent covered terrace where lunch was being served, chose a table off to one side next to an abundant growth of apricot-colored hibiscus. Ordered a Dewar's and water but on second thought a beer, a local brand called Mandalay, that turned out to taste better than Grady had expected. He drank one, ordered another.

As it turned out, the beer provided an entrée for the man seated at the next table. "You like our Mandalay," he observed cordially in Grady's direction.

"It's quite good," Grady said.

The man didn't need more than that to move in. He dragged his chair around so he was at Grady's table, more next to rather than across from Grady. "We also make a good gin. You should try our gin," he suggested and in the same breath asked if he was intruding.

"Not so far," Grady told him.

The man wasn't fazed. He was bronze-skinned, obviously Burmese. His short-cropped grayed hair and brush mustache were distinguishing, as was the Western way he was dressed, in a well-tailored vested suit, neat shirt, understated tie. Chipped, soil-occupied fingernails, however. He lighted a 555 brand cigarette and within the smoke introduced himself as General U Daw Tun, emphasis on general.

Grady had suspected as much and what he next anticipated wasn't long coming. After some brief neutral chat, General Tun got into his pitch. He was retired. During his later service years he'd been in charge of certain military efforts in the province of Shan. Many insurgents in Shan. Also many sapphire and ruby mines. And so on until he took a briefke from his shirt pocket, inserted it among the packets of sugar in the sugar bowl and pushed the bowl to Grady.

Grady louped the two six-carat oval-cut rubies contained in the briefke. He had to admit they looked good, had all the characteristics of fine Burma, even some minor convincing flaws. Indeed, first-rate pretenders.

General U Daw Tun was only asking sixty-five thousand for them. That was if Grady bought both. Otherwise thirty-five for either.

Grady passed, politely.

The general strained a smile, put the refolded briefke back into his shirt pocket, got up and went looking for easier prey.

Grady finished his beer and returned to the Emporium. He submitted an unsuccessful bid on a lot of blue oval-cut sapphires and he also got topped when he bid on some fairly fine blue cabochons.

The next day went just about the same for him. After making three bids he was still empty-handed. Was it because his bids were too low? He thought not. Then was it because other dealers were overpaying, the deep-pocketed Japs for instance? Maybe not. Maybe the auction was rigged. Maybe when those who were running the thing didn't receive a bid high enough to suit them they put up one of their own numbers. Grady's discouragement wouldn't put it past them.

On the third day he came across *the* pearls, lot 341. He'd looked at some other pearl lots but hadn't seen any that measured up to these. Rare not only in size (twelve millimeters) but, as well, in every aspect of desirability: luster, roundness, complexion, iridescence, rich white color. There were four twenty-inch hanks. Grady took his time, examined each pearl of each hank carefully. The longer he looked the more he felt that these were what he must have. If he went home with only one buy it would have to be lot 341.

Which was up for bidding.

Grady had to hurry to fill out his bid.

A hundred thousand dollars.

He crossed out that amount. Shot the works. A hundred fifty thousand. Done! He dropped the slip into the receptacle. Waited, watched the officials open the receptacle and remove the bids. There were quite a few, fifty or so it appeared. Grady didn't care how many there were. For him it was like after a horse race, waiting for the win number to be displayed when he'd just seen his horse finish lengths ahead. Sure thing. Put it up there, baby.

His dealer number was 112.

The number displayed was 92.

A mistake?

Fuck no.

The dealer numbered 92 was standing nearby. Grady heard him blurt victoriously, "Got it!" He was a Bond Street–attired Englishman with diamonds, two caraters linking his shirt cuffs.

Grady felt foolish, diminished. He went up to the room, changed into lightweight casual clothes, sneakers and no socks, and went out for a walk, down the grassy slope to an inlet of Lake Inye, where, with effort, he was able to appreciate some lemon-colored water lilies.

He didn't notice the young Burmese girl right off. Perhaps she'd been there and he'd been too preoccupied to notice her, or possibly she'd followed him down. She was seated on her haunches about thirty feet away at the edge of the inlet, distant enough for privacy, yet close enough to make out facial expressions. From the way she was dressed Grady took her to be a peasant girl, anyway someone poor. The plain short-sleeved green blouse she had on was faded, and she was wearing what in Burma is called a *longyi*, simply a couple of yards of cotton cloth (hers a blood red shade) wrapped and tucked at the waist to form an ankle-length skirt.

The girl's gaze was evidently fixed on the slicing courses of three windsurfers far out on the lake, although Grady once caught the turn of her head and got the feeling that even if it had been only a glance she'd taken all of him in.

What mostly intrigued Grady was the cheroot she was smoking. Twice as fat as the fattest cigar he'd ever seen and about ten inches long. A roll of dried white corn husk bound by a red thread. It seemed to contain a mixture of ingredients, including tobacco. It looked as though the jumbo cheroot would be too much for her to handle, diminutive as she was, but she was its boss, brought it to the center of her lips, holding it from below in the European manner, dragged on it so strongly that her cheeks went concave and her face was like a bellows being worked as she took puff after puff without inhaling, creating a minor cumulus around her head.

Grady watched deliberately, as though she were a permissible tourist attraction. The ash on the burning end of the cheroot became so great it dropped off. Grady decided to let that signify the end of the episode, went back up the slope to the hotel and the room.

Julia hadn't yet returned from sketching. There was still an hour of that day's Emporium left and Grady thought about getting properly dressed again for another try. Instead, might as well make himself useful. He stood up on the bed and tried to eliminate the noise of the wobbly ceiling fan by taping Burmese fifty pyas coins to the upper surface of its blades. However, that surface was so coated with dust and lint he couldn't get Band-Aids to stick to it. He wiped off the blades with a damp hotel towel, waited for them to dry, then after a half hour of trial and error managed to get the coins taped in place so their weight brought the blades into balance. The fan showed its gratitude for the attention by rotating with only a steady, much less intrusive hum.

Julia arrived shortly thereafter, her hands coated with charcoal and chalk, a dark smudge in the center of her forehead above the bridge of her nose, Ash Wednesday looking.

"How'd the sketching go?" Grady inquired.

"Great," she replied from the bathroom and over the run of the faucet as she washed up. "I've got enough for a whole show and then some. Such colors! Everything is so much more vivid, even the ordinary."

Grady was ambivalent about wanting her to ask how the day had gone for him. When she didn't ask he was rather relieved. Probably she could sense his discouragement, he thought. A part of him wanted to complain, especially about not getting those twelve-millimeter pearls, but he wouldn't allow it.

She came from the bathroom saying brightly, "Well, now I'm fit for kissing," and went directly to him for that purpose, offered her lips. When he took them, hers began taking.

Neither had anticipated lovemaking, but now spontaneously they were bound for it. And during it this time, merely to gauge how much of herself she'd given up to Grady, she tried to put off her coming, to anesthetize with willpower. However, it was him within her and enclosing him and, as it had all the many previous times they'd loved, the maelstrom, so much more than just a stir of sensation, reached and caught her, sucked her into its current and she couldn't help but swirl with its slick wet and contribute her own rotations around his thrusts. And after her first coming, when she'd recaptured her mind, she thought no amount of sense of power could equal the pleasure of such submission. She would wallow in it.

Later, still in the afterward, with their brains, but what felt like their hearts, saturated with natural pacifying chemicals, they lay faceup on the bed, listening to the mosquitos and a ball game. Julia had repaired the canopy of netting that enclosed the bed by gathering the fabric and tieing a knot with it wherever there was a hole. Grady wondered how the mosquitos managed to get into the room. The windows were not the openable sort, but there the insects were, smelling blood and buzzing round trying to get to it. Like gem dealers, Grady thought.

The ball game was coming from the radio built into the face of the nightstand. A tinny sounding radio that crackled and faded every now and then, as though reminding it should be appreciated. Grady appreciated it. The Pirates against the Padres, no score, bottom of the sixth half a world away. When he'd turned the radio on and searched back and forth on the dial for anything familiar or even understandable, he'd come across what was no more than a blip until he'd fine-tuned it like a safecracker. He doubted the Burmese cared for baseball, guessed what he was receiving was stray waves. Bouncing off some satellite?

He turned onto his side toward a Taco Bell commercial. In the going daylight he again noticed the numerous cigarette burns on the edge of the nightstand, some had burned all the way through the blond veneer, caused charred grooves. What sort of person would do that? He imagined and fought off the thought that they were related to him by having once occupied this space, particularly this bed. He tried not to visualize the condition of the mattress beneath the sheet beneath him and Julia.

Raps on the door.

Most likely the chambermaid disregarding the PRIVACY PLEASE sign Grady had hung on the exterior knob.

He got up, put on that day's undershorts and opened the door slightly. No one was there. Stepped partway out into the corridor, looked both ways. No one. Puzzled, he returned to the bed and Julia. "Hungry?" he asked her.

She said she was and got up and while slipping on a robe said she hoped they could find a more suitable restaurant than the one they'd tried to eat at the night before in downtown Rangoon near the Sule Pagado. Every dish they'd ordered except dessert had been laced with tiny, angry, tongue-searing red peppers. She said she'd inquired and there was a Japanese restaurant on Maha Bandoala Street. Couldn't they go there for some *abura-age*?

"What's that?"

"Fried bean curd. Lately, I've had such a craving for some *abura-age*." Again raps on the door.

This time Grady was quick to it, swung the door open.

There stood the young Burmese girl Grady had observed at the shore of the lake. Only now that he saw her up close he realized she wasn't all that young. In fact she was a mature woman. He'd been misled by her slight build and delicate features. It occurred to him that she might be an employee of the hotel, however there was a furtiveness about her, the dark pupils of her eyes were shifting peripherally. Grady asked what it was she wanted.

She didn't reply, slid past him to be in the room, and, when Grady didn't immediately close the door, she bowed a beg pardon and shouldered it closed.

She was too small and fragile-looking to be intimidating. Grady again asked her what she wanted.

The woman replied this time but not with words. Rather by extending her fisted hand to Grady and uncurling her fingers to reveal something wrapped in a soiled patch of ordinary white cloth. An insistent thrust of her hand conveyed to Grady that he should take whatever it was.

He complied, undid the cloth. It contained an oblong piece of gem rough. A six-sided crystal about an inch and a quarter long, a third that in diameter at its widest point, with water-worn rounded edges. It didn't look like much, almost entirely crusted as it was with a coarse, variegated black and rust-colored material.

Grady took the piece of rough to one of the bedside lamps, looked at it under the light. Visible here and there through its coating was a pink to reddish tinge. He held it up to the lamp bulb and a redder red was discernable. Impetus enough for him to examine it with his loupe.

When he had it magnified for his right eye he turned it over and over until he found a less-crusted spot on its end, and a tiny natural window. He sighted into it, saw the fluorescence, the cherry red glow of its interior atmosphere. Was caught up in it for a long moment, then came back to objectivity. He assumed the woman wanted to sell the piece. He tilted his head sharply, silently asking how much.

"Four hundred fifty thousand," the woman told him and added, "kyats. But I do not want kyats. I want dollars."

Grady figured it into dollars. Seventy-five thousand. He shook his head no.

"Too much?" the woman asked.

A more definite nod from Grady. Because he had just advised himself to be sensible. Good eyes or not he wasn't experienced when it came to judging colored rough. For all he knew and with what little he was able to see, this could be merely semiprecious, an extraordinary spinel crystal or a fine garnet. And even if it was a ruby, even a Burma, it could be a bad one, zoned and included. And what about this woman? Mightn't she be the female of the species *retired general*?

"Three hundred thousand kyats," the woman reasoned.

A part of Grady shoved his prudence aside, told him that was more like it, fifty thousand dollars. Still he hesitated.

The woman sagged.

Julia gave her a therapeutic drink of water.

There was a fifth of Dewar's on the dresser. The woman looked longingly at it.

Julia poured three fingers of the whiskey into a hotel glass.

The woman downed that in three consecutive gulps and without a grimace, as though it were no more than tepid tea. Then, evidently primed, she explained that she was a Mon from the village of Kyunchaung near the Three Pagodas Pass. Did they know the Three Pagodas Pass? They didn't? (That was incredible.) Then did they know the Khwae Noi? No? Otherwise known as the River Kwai (the same as the bridge)? Ah, good! The headwaters of that river are only a walk from Kyunchaung.

The woman was satisfied with having established that much common ground. She went on.

Her husband's brother had been a member of the Mon Way to Freedom guerrilla group, which was part of the National Democratic Front but only like a little finger of it. And, because he was her husband's brother, government troops came and hung her husband to death and said it was a suicide, which she knew was a lie because it is a Buddhist belief that anyone doing suicide would be punished by having to suffer five hundred and five more lifetimes and deaths by suicide. They wanted to hang her too but she did not let them find her. She got away with only the piece of ruby, which she had found at the foot of a small mountain near Thaybre a year ago and kept hidden for when trouble came. Only one other person had laid eyes on it. Her good cousin, who had off and on been a ruby miner. He told her its value or she wouldn't have known. She needed the money, much money to buy herself a new identity there in Rangoon, all the proper papers so that she might be allowed on an airplane to Singapore. She had two relatives in Singapore, rice dealers, the woman said.

"The pour soul," Julia sympathized.

The woman smiled and lifted her blouse to reveal a pistol shoved in the waistband of her *longyi*.

Done for effect, Grady thought dubiously. He took another lengthier look at the piece of rough, heard through his concentration Julia telling him, "Buy it, darling." He told himself not to listen to her. His right eye was watering up from its focus being so fixed and intense. Fifty thousand wasn't all the money in the world, he thought. If only he'd gotten those twelve-millimeter pearls today this would be no decision. No money left, no decision. He hated the idea of going home empty-handed or merely with a couple of average lots of sapphire melee. He went into the bathroom, where his money belt was hung on the inside of the door. He had sixty thousand in cash, all brand-new hundreds, and two Wells Fargo cashier's checks of forty-five thousand each. He counted out five hundred of the hundreds and returned to the bedroom. Julia was fortifying the woman with another stiff hooker of scotch.

The dealer in Grady told him forty thousand would do it, probably even thirty-five, but then the circumstances found a chink in his harder side. He slipped the sheaf of hundreds into the woman's calloused palms.

And the piece of rough was his.

Next morning Grady tried to put the day before out of his mind. After a roll and coffee breakfast in the room he got dressed for business and went down to the Emporium.

Julia, just for the change, she said, went along, despite his telling her that he doubted he could get her in because it was for dealers only, strictly. At the admittance table at the entrance Julia presented herself as a dealer, in fact, Grady's partner (an ever so slight insinuative inflection on *partner*). Who could turn her away? Certainly not the stern, little official there whom she sprayed with smile. He wrote out and embossed a special pass for her, and she was in.

Grady thought she'd want to stay close to him, go around with him as he looked at the various lots, want him to show her a few things. However, she wandered off on her own, and he looked to the bidding. What was up for sale at that moment and the next several lots to be offered were jade. The Chinese dealers were worked up. They both amused and irked Grady. They'd get what they came for, he thought, contrary to his own prospects. He'd decided to be there today only because he wasn't entirely out of hope and not a quitter.

He was looking at a fairly good ten-carat padparadscha when Julia came and appropriated his loupe. Left him bare-eyed, unable accurately to appraise anything. After a while he went in search of her, found her two rows down examining some blue sapphires in an amateurish way: without tweezers, bent over to them so she was shielding the needed light, and moving the loupe erratically trying to focus. Several dealers of different nationalities had stopped and stepped back, clogging traffic somewhat as they admired her position from the rear.

She told Grady, "We must buy these."

"Oh?"

"Definitely." She was quite taken.

"It's not just a matter of buying," Grady said, "not that easy." He explained the Emporium's required procedure.

She grunted knowingly. "Anything that complicated has to be full of conniving. Anyway, at least we ought to try to buy them."

"Why?"

"They're pretty."

They'd have to be more than that, Grady thought. Rather indulgently he louped the sapphires. And saw Julia was right. These were clean blue bright number ones, as they were referred to in the trade. Extremely clean. If bought right they'd sell very right. He didn't mind telling Julia that. "Good eyes," he complimented. She exaggerated modesty with a big shrug.

Grady continued looking into the stones. Sixty carats in the lot. Ten round cuts. Round cuts this good were a bit unusual. He felt his want activate, like someone had just thrown a switch.

An hour later that lot, numbered 593, came up for bidding. Grady was about to fill out his bidding slip.

"How much do you think?" Julia asked.

Grady's decision was being tossed back and forth between eighty thousand and ninety thousand.

"Better to pay a bit more and get them than scrimp and not," was Julia's advice.

Grady wrote in ninety thousand.

"They'll go for a hundred and twenty," Julia thought aloud.

"I don't have a hundred and twenty." Grady regretted having bought that piece of rough.

"Then forget it."

He made out a new slip, bid all he had, the hundred.

It wasn't enough.

To make it worse he ran into Clifton, who was happy to relate he'd just gotten lot 593, those nice number one rounds, for a hundred fifteen. Grady didn't let Clifton know he'd bid on them, just told him *nice going*, exchanged a few more words and drifted away.

Julia was disappointed and perturbed. Saying *shits* under her breath. Grady asked if leaving appealed to her.

"Anytime," she replied.

"I mean Burma."

"I'm with you."

She went up to the room to pack. Grady, meanwhile, had a taxi take him downtown. There was one important loose end he had to tend to. He was let off on the corner of Merchant Street and Barr in the heart of old British Colonial Rangoon. Walked along Merchant, cut up Thirty-sixth and around to Pansodan Road. Found on Pansodan the sort of shop he was looking for, a small, second-rate place trying to appear to be a jewelry store while also offering an array of way overpriced Burmese mementos.

Grady came right to the point, asked to see some synthetic rubies. Was told that the shop handled only genuine rubies. How about genuine synthetic rubies? Grady pressed. The shop owner decided that when a large fraudulent sale wasn't possible a small legitimate one would have to do. He brought out a dozen or so briefkes containing synthetics of various cuts and sizes. The same sort of convincing Burma-looking goods that retired General Tun had tried to pass off on Grady the day before yesterday. Grady bought a cushion cut of six carats for a hundred dollars a carat.

He taxied back to the hotel. Julia was in the lobby with the baggage. They checked out and a half hour later were at Mingaladon Airport trying to get through customs.

Their bags were thoroughly searched again, disheveled again. Including their carryons. The customs inspector took particular interest in Julia's sketches, apparently approved of them, was fascinated with her charcoal, chalks and all that. Perhaps he had aspirations.

The crucial thing was Grady's currency form. He'd gathered from conversations with various dealers that the Burmese government, arbitrary as it was, was deadly serious about visitors accounting for every penny brought in, spent and taken out of its country. Hardline Burmese bookkeeping intended to discourage currency smuggling and other contraband activities (such as attempting to depart with precious stones that hadn't been purchased from a government-connected source).

Upon arrival three days before, Grady had declared a hundred and fifty thousand in his possession. Now, upon leaving, he had about a hundred and would have to account for the difference. If he revealed he'd bought the piece of rough from that cheroot-smoking woman rebel it would probably be confiscated.

What to do? To start, he listed every currency exchange he'd made, exactly what he'd put out for the hotel, meals, gratuities and all. Then there was the ruby he'd bought from retired General Tun, fifty thousand for that.

The customs official considered that item, asked to have a look at the stone. He unfolded the briefke containing it, examined the scintillating cushion-cut red.

As far as Grady was concerned it wouldn't matter whether or not the official had eye enough to know synthetic from genuine. Either way fifty thousand would be accounted for. Grady watched the man's expression change to amused knowing and then to smug spite. Read the man's sentiments: *good! another fucked-over American.*

Within the hour Grady and Julia were airborne. Julia waited for the seat belt sign to be dinged off before going into her smaller carryon.

For the eraser.

Gray, malleable charcoal eraser that from her use during sketching had become an unsightly, variegated lump about the size of a large prune.

She dug at it with her fingernails, peeled the eraser stuff away from the piece of rough.

A conspiratorial grin.

She dropped the stone into Grady's hand. He bare-eyed it with the help of the afternoon sun that was striking that side of the plane. He hoped to God what he was looking at was what he hoped it was.

CHAPTER ELEVEN

Mahesak Road.

In what is now referred to as the old *farang* (foreign) quarter of Bangkok. To all appearances, Mahesak is unremarkable, just another side street. On its three short, straight blocks there is no *wat* (Buddhist temple), no new high-rise or ancient landmark, not even the offerings of some girlie bars. What's there is only a tight line of similar, older buildings of one or two stories that have changed little other than their faces over the past hundred years.

How dependent they seem, these squat buildings pressed side against side, as though jostling for inches, squeezing and being squeezed, giving off the impression that they must be suffering what might be called architectural pain.

Squeeze and pain. Suitable for the type of commerce conducted daily on Mahesak. For it is here that most of Bangkok's gem dealers do their business. Dealers, mind you, not jewelers. Although there's a bit of jeweler in nearly every dealer as there's some dealer in most jewelers, the distinction is made. The jewelers of Bangkok are scattered throughout the city. They have public concerns, retail mentalities. The Mahesak dealers, on the other hand, are a concentrated community closer to the earth, that is, closer to the treacheries that go on along the violent borders Thailand shares with Burma and Cambodia.

Any Mahesak dealer of consequence has his line of supply from those providing but perilous areas. A networking team, perhaps, to cover simultaneously various points. Or a partner with whom he takes turns being the carrier. Or his connection might be as tenuous as someone he's hired by the trip who he hopes will prove trustworthy.

The carrier goes out with money, buys and brings. Comes back when he's accumulated a satisfactory number of stones. Rubies and/or sapphires, some faceted, some in the rough. Occasionally he returns with a single stone, one that is especially large and too promising to put off being bought.

Such *brings*, as they're called, are never apparent. The arrival of the carrier is never even a minor event. It just blends in with the everyday comings and goings of Mahesak, an unhurried pace blamed on the steamy weather though more likely it is a habitual, intentional cover-up of the anxieties that go along with the surreptitious acquiring. (Millions' worth brought sewn within a trouser cuff or tucked where a molar had been between cheek and gum.) Millions are all the more reason not to rush. The prudent attitude is serious nonchalance, as though every moment is no different from the one before or the one ahead, while underneath, in the underbelly of each transaction, dwells a venal quickness, the swift reflexes of the mind needed not only to profit but also to not get taken (the ultimate embarrassment).

The gem dealers of Mahesak. Strangely, there are few Thais among them. Perhaps Thais just don't have the personality for it, they with their tendency to smile first and if at all possible sidestep friction. Their absence is filled by a stew of nationalities. Self-eminent Germans, umbilicated to the cutting factories of Idar-Oberstein; shrewd, and friendly, coal-eyed Armenians; some excessively patient Arabs. Many caste-conscious East Indians, especially from New Delhi and Darjeeling, who never seem to have the desire to go home even when there is next to no profit to be made, who'd rather stay and make a penny than leave and not. The majority of dealers are Chinese. They're the most successful, the more industrious ones with the wherewithal to exploit. They owe their financial edge to their day-by-day, deal-by-deal tight fists and their instinct to know precisely when circumstances are right to risk everything.

This, then, on that Thursday morning in early June, was the sphere and milieu Grady and Julia entered when they rounded the corner of wide, bustling Silom Road and walked north up Mahesak. Grady's stride was a little heavy in the heel. He still had remnant misgivings about staying over in Bangkok, and it was occurring to him that by now, if they'd been able to connect right away with a flight, they'd be only a couple of hours out of San Francisco. He told himself he wouldn't have minded terribly being layed over for seven hours and catching Northwest's non-stop night flight, which had the first available space. He'd been perfectly willing to make the most of that layover, to taxi into Bangkok proper, see some of it and have a good meal. Julia, however, believed that Bangkok was deserving of more than a few hours. At first that was just an opinion she impassively expressed. Next it came out as a pointed remark. Then a rather adamant preference.

Grady was swayed by the way Julia had endured without complaint the room at the Lake Inye Hotel, put up with that awful furniture screwed to the wall or floor as though anyone in the world would ever want to steal it, and the wall-to-wall carpet so stained and contaminated-looking that to expose bare feet to it had seemed a health risk. As much as Grady wanted to get the next long leg of inevitable lag over with, get back home and give his all to his new business, he more or less persuaded himself that he owed Julia a portion of comfort. In fact his debt was greater than that; he owed her luxury.

So, with carryons and baggage they proceeded by taxi to the Hotel Oriental where, when asked by the registration clerk how long they'd be staying, Grady, in a moment of romantic magnanimity, had replied, "At least several days." Shortly thereafter they were unpacking and stowing and hanging their belongings in the drawers and closets of the five-hundred-dollar-a-day suite on the twelfth floor, overlooking the river. Julia going about arranging her cosmetics and other personals on the shelf over the counter in the elegant marble bathroom and humming and dah-dah-dahing to herself a song that was decidedly, stridently Oriental. Grady thought she was getting into the spirit of the place.

Now, next day, here they were on Mahesak, putting off any sight-seeing until they'd satisfied their questions about the piece of red rough bought in Rangoon. Whether it was a crystal or spinel or ruby or what. And if a ruby as claimed, how good a ruby? Fifty thousand good?

Grady hoped to find out by finding Alfred Reese, a Bangkok dealer who'd called upon him years ago when he'd been buying for Shreve and Company. They'd had a long pleasant lunch and gotten along well and Grady had bought a lot of nice lavender sapphires. Sapphires and rubies were Reese's métier. He truly knew them. Grady hadn't seen Reese since that day, but there'd been some long-distance transactions, numerous phone calls, quite a bit of nonbusiness conversation. Reese, as Grady recalled him, was a tall man, six five or so, with a stoop. He wasn't merely round-shouldered but had a stoop so extreme that a drip of water from the tip of his nose would have missed his toes by six inches. By now he would be in his late fifties. He'd been born and raised in Pawhuska, Oklahoma, gone to school in Stillwater and gotten into the gem business in Tulsa. Buying trips to Dallas, Chicago and New York preceded the trip to Bangkok that changed his direction. The only reason he returned to Tulsa was to settle some legal loose ends including a pending divorce and to turn every-thing that was surely his into cash.

The thing about Bangkok that got Reese was something that wasn't there. The concept of original sin, the yoke of it. Reese hadn't realized how restrained he'd been by it, libidinously suffo-cated, until the Thai women, those little beauties, unknotted him and caused him to take deep, totally responsive breaths. They and their ways stripped him of the Methodist Sunday school cupjock and converted him into a happier-to-be-bareass Okie cowboy Buddhist.

So that was Reese, the dealer Grady and Julia were looking for on Mahesak. It had been years since Grady had spoken to Reese and there hadn't been an answer that morning when Grady had tried phoning him. The address Grady had for him, 531 Mahesak, would be along there somewhere. The sidewalk was insufficient for two-way foot traffic. Grady and Julia had to go single file to make room for those walking in the opposite direction. None of the businesses appeared hospitable, they noticed. Not one open door. Most had steel gates across their entrances, and electronic locks. Some were numbered in Thai, some in Arabic, others had no numbers at all.

Grady and Julia walked the entire length of Mahesak without coming upon 531. They doubled back and inquired. The third person they asked pointed it out. A narrow place looking bullied by its adjoining buildings. No windows. A steel-faced door. The entire front from street level to roofline was painted a high-gloss dark green enamel that emphasized here and there the buildup and flaked-away patches of numerous previous coats. Grady thought back to the times he and Reese had talked long-distance. He'd never pictured Reese talking from a place such as this.

Julia found a buzzer button inset on the door frame, gave it a jab. Nothing. She gave it another, more insistent. After a long moment the door clicked open, allowing entrance to a short, narrow landing at the bottom of a flight of stairs. Nowhere to go but up. Gritty, metal-edged stairs. At the top was a similar landing and another equally formidable door with a peephole in it at eye level. Being peeped at made Julia uncomfortable. She repressed an impulse to make a face. Grady doubted, considering how long it had been, that the door would be opened by Reese.

But it was.

Glad to see Grady, glad to meet Julia. An unexpected pleasure, Reese said with more Oklahoma twang than Grady remembered him having. Reese led them to an area not partitioned off from the rest of the second floor but which he good-naturedly and some-what apologetically called his office. There was a formidable late-model safe in the corner and a refrigerator of about the same size next to it.

Reese didn't look an hour older, Grady thought. Whatever he was getting out of life apparently agreed with him. It caused Grady to give his own ways and means a moment of comparative consideration and in the next moment reach the conclusion that a long term with Julia was going to make the same world of difference for him.

Reese offered drinks, cold Polaris mineral water was settled upon for all. Grady and Reese spent the next ten minutes reacquainting, touching upon, almost as though reciting résumés, high points and some of the lows of their recent years. Julia just sat there and tried to appear interested, contributed nothing, held back making the wry quips that came to mind. Why didn't they just get to the reason for being there? she thought. After all, it wasn't as if Reese was a long-lost genuinely missed relative. She was relieved when finally Reese said he presumed Grady was there on a buying trip, and Grady told him he'd been to the Emporium, was on his way home.

"How'd it go?" Reese asked.

"Not all that great." Grady understated and allowed some silence while he omitted telling Reese how he'd been outbid every time.

"They're such bullshit, the Burmese," Reese said. "Mean little fuckers too." He looked to Julia and begged pardon for his language.

A blasé shrug from Julia.

"Did you get to buy anything?" Reese asked Grady.

"Just this." Grady brought out the piece of rough.

Reese took it and took a look at it. Shifted his eyes aside, then brought them back to the crystal. Grady believed he saw Reese's interest intensify. No doubt Reese knew ruby rough, had seen a lot of it. "What do you think?" Grady asked offhand.

"Looks okay."

"Just okay?"

"Can't say more than that for sure until we get some crud off it. That all right with you?"

"Sure."

It was precisely what Grady had hoped for, had come for, and he liked that he hadn't had to ask the favor. He followed Reese across the room to a workbench. Reese flipped a switch that started the spin of a grinding wheel. He gave the piece of rough some deciding inspection before applying one of its surfaces to the wheel. Did it cautiously with practiced fingers and just enough gentle pressure.

The stone sounded mortal, tortured, screeching the way it did as the diamond-coated wheel abraded its worthless skin. Reese gave the same attention to its five other surfaces and its ends. Then treated it to another kinder wheel to polish it some.

He spat on it. Held it up to the daylight fluorescent light. Louped it from various angles for a couple of minutes. Next pincered it with a pair of locking tweezers and mounted the tweezers in place on the nearby microscope so the now cleaner crystal was held below the lens. He clicked on the microscope's attached light and sighted into its binocular eyepieces. Adjusted the tweezers, adjusted the focus and looked and looked. Without comment or even some little sound like a grunt that Grady might interpret. Finally, still silent and expressionless, he backed off and gestured that Grady should take a look.

The magnification was forty times.

The realm that Grady viewed was rich deep red, entirely, except for...

"See the silk?" Reese asked.

As though Grady could possibly miss it. An arrangement of rutile needles. They intersected one another at an angle of about sixty degrees, were interwoven densely, glittering. Silk. To Grady's eyes it was like seeing a vast number of headlights transformed into four-armed stars by a red rainy San Francisco night.

"Notice how fine woven the silk is?"

"Uh-huh."

"That's what's telling us it's Burma goods. Not Ceylon. If it was Ceylon goods the needles would be a lot more slender, with a coarser weave. If it was Thai or African goods there'd be no silk at all. It's Burma, all right."

Grady knew most of what Reese had just said. It was elementary geminological textbook stuff, but he let Reese say it. The important thing he'd just learned was what Reese had taken for granted. It was ruby. How good a ruby was yet to be determined, but surely, considering the carat weight, it was worth more than the fifty he'd paid for it. "Want to sell this piece?" Reese asked.

Grady didn't reply immediately. He was enjoying looking at profit. Finally, he gave his eyes a rest. "You want to buy it?"

"Maybe, maybe not."

"If maybe, what would you offer?"

"A fast deal, a right-now deal, I might go two hundred thousand."

Grady didn't say two hundred was an insult, didn't want to

bother with that old obvious routine. Instead, he refused with just a shake of his head.

Reese removed the ruby crystal from the microscope. Bare-eyed it again. "I myself don't have the kind of money you probably want, but I know someone here who does."

"How much would that be?"

"You tell me."

"I don't have a figure in mind."

"Think about four hundred thousand."

Grady enjoyed thinking about it. A chance to pick up a fast three-fifty, if Reese was serious, and he seemed to be. A certain sort of gem dealer reasoning told Grady that if the ruby crystal was worth four hundred here it would be worth perhaps half again as much on the market back in the States. And even more when it was cut. "I'm going to have it cut," he decided aloud.

Reese accepted that Grady's mind was made up, wouldn't press further. Cutting the piece was what he'd do if the piece of ruby was his. "Who'll you have cut it?"

"Merzbacker, probably," Grady replied, wishing that could be. "Or at least someone of that level." Merzbacker had the reputation of being the best cutter of colored goods in New York City and one of the best in the world. He was said to be temperamental and extremely slow but seldom got less than the most out of a stone.

"You want to put yourself through all that?" Reese said.

"Be worth it."

"Merzbacker'll take six months to let you know whether or not he wants to do the stone, and just as long as that to get to it. Fucking prima donna. In my opinion there are plenty of cutters as good as Merzbacker."

A dubious grunt from Grady.

"Maybe not plenty," Reese retracted, "but shit, there are four hundred thousand cutters in this country. Most of them have been cutting gems since they cut their teeth. Some are so good at it they'd be stars on Forty-seventh Street. William Shigota and a few others I know of. That's what I'd do, let Shigota cut it. At the least you ought to let him take a look at it, long as you're here."

"Will you call him for me?"

"No problem." Reese went to his desk, rifled through the center drawer and found Shigota's business card for Grady.

During all this, Julia had kept to herself, wandered about the room, overhearing what was said but not seeming interested. Grady had thought, considering her involvement with the piece of ruby up to that point, that she'd be right there at his side, anxious to have a turn at the microscope. It was as though she knew the outcome, had already been told the ruby was a ruby, believed that, and all this proving wasn't necessary.

Now she was standing at a counter off to the right giving her attention to some loose pearls that she'd found lying there. Evidently Reese had been grading and matching them when Grady and Julia arrived.

Grady went to her, realized how caught up she was in the pearls. They weren't all that special, nice enough ten-millimeter creams mostly but not worthy of her. He'd had in mind for quite a while improving on the ones he'd substituted for her strand, that the stringer had made off with. Perhaps this was a good time to do that. He asked Reese, "Can you show me some pearls for Julia?"

His words seemed to snap Julia back to there and then. She smiled, the sort of pleased smile usually meant to convey everything was going well.

"You're in luck," Reese said and went to his safe. "It just so happens that I got these last week from a Safartic dealer who's been trying for ten years to get out of the business." He brought a dozen large self-sealing clear plastic bags to the counter. He opened them and laid the cultured pearls they contained out upon a white velour cloth. Lined the pearls up neatly hank next to hank according to gradations of color. They ran from white to creamy white to pinkish white.

Grady's eye told him they were eight to eight and a half to nine millimeters, except for those subtle pinkish ones second from the right, which were nine and a half to ten millimeters. Those, he decided, were best of all, what he'd try to buy, although he'd go at them by way of the eight millimeter whites on the opposite end.

His approach was thwarted by Julia's going right for those best pinkish ones. That hank consisted of four eighteen-inch strands, tied together by numerous winds of purple silk embroidery thread and a tassel of the same. The strands clicked against one another as she picked them up, held them up high with her right hand, appreciated them with her eyes and her free hand, ran her fingers down their lengths, a caress.

Grady was surprised that she was so enamored with pearls. She'd never indicated as much. Her giveaway eagerness toward these pinks was going to cost him, but he forgave her for that. He took out his loupe and examined their complexion, found it was much better than merely acceptable. He guessed around thirty thousand when he asked Reese how much.

Reese didn't have a chance to say because from Julia came: "They're not what I had in mind."

"Oh?"

"Not at all," she said, "they're perfectly lovely but..."

"They're the perfect shade for your coloring," Reese told her.

Which was also Grady's opinion.

"That may be, however..." She hesitated, returned the hank to its place on the velour, went reflective for a moment, then asked, "By chance do you have any blue pearls?"

"Blue?"

"Pearls don't, as a rule, come in blue," Grady told her.

"Never?"

"Not that I know of. How about you, Reese, blue pearls?"

"Nope."

"The Japanese pearl farmers have been tinting pearls for years," Grady said, "because most of what they grow comes yellowish. To make them white they soak them for a while in bleach. To give them a pink cast they use a solution of Merthiolate. The longer they soak and the stronger the solution, the pinker. So I guess blue-looking pearls would be possible with blue ink or something." Grady looked to Reese for support.

Reese did a stoop-shouldered *why not* shrug.

"I wouldn't want them if they were dyed like that," Julia said. "They wouldn't be authentically blue."

Grady challenged her. "When have you ever seen or heard of natural blue pearls?"

Julia was suddenly confused, couldn't reply. She went over to where she'd left her carryon, looked into it for no reason other than to hyphenate the moment, slung it over her shoulder and conveyed to Grady with a glance that she was ready to go.

He thought the thing about natural blue pearls was something she might have read about in some work of fiction, or perhaps it should be chalked up to her artistic bent. He hoped he hadn't embarrassed her. Anyway, he was sorry she hadn't let him buy those pinkish tens. He could have gotten them at a nice price, and someday down the line she was going to look back and wish he had.

He thanked and hand-shook Reese. So did Julia. They went out the upper door and down.

When Reese was sure they'd gone he made a long-distance call. First he asked the man on the other end if the promise of the substantial sum that had been made quite a while back was still in effect. He was told that it was. He pressed for additional rewards, such as profitable, sure-thing business deals. He was assured they would be forthcoming. Did he have the man's word? He had it.

Satisfied, delighted that he would benefit so largely from such slight effort, Reese informed the man that at long last someone had made an inquiry about natural blue pearls.

Then told him who.

CHAPTER TWELVE

At that moment on the corner of Mahesak Road and Silom, Grady and Julia had paused to discuss options. It was only a five-block walk back to the hotel, Grady said, so shouldn't they go there and have a proper lunch? Julia wasn't for that, said they could get something to eat along the way. Along the way to where? Grady wanted to know. To the ruby cutters, Julia told him, that William Swaboda. Shigota, Grady corrected and said that could wait until after lunch or even until tomorrow. Julia gave it much greater priority, said so. And before Grady could say another word, before he could contend that he'd had an extremely early breakfast and nothing since, Julia hailed a taxi.

What came swerving to the curb was something that looked like an oversize golf cart. It had only one front wheel, was bright blue and yellow, open on both sides and the rear, with a roll bar and a canvas top. The driver, if one could call him that, was all smile, ready to roll. He had a two-week black and gray mustache and a month of beard, some of which appeared to have been plucked. Had on a red baseball-type cap with a huge visor.

Grady walked away in the direction of the hotel. Julia confidently watched him going, counted his strides, mentally wagering on eleven. She was one short. He turned, did a pleading expression, said, "To hell with you, Julia," to save some pride, returned to the taxi and handed the Shigota business card to the driver, who studied it for a long moment and claimed, "I know."

"Is it near or far?" Grady asked.

"I know," the driver assured.

"Short ride or long ride?"

The driver nodded twice, made a face to express that the question was absurd and said another, "I know."

At that point Grady noticed the driver was wearing two stainless steel digital watches on each wrist, had the snarling cartoonlike, wide-jawed face of a deity tattooed on the back of his left hand and three lines of Thai lettering tattooed lengthwise on his arm from his watches to his biceps, evidently some wise and protective Buddhist quotation. "Who could mistrust such a man," Grady quipped as he and Julia climbed in.

Before they'd had a chance to get settled the driver lurched the three-wheeler under way and cut across the pack of the traffic on Silom. Got into a left lane for a right turn on Krung Road, a major way that became New Road, which became Songwat Road, which became Chakraphet Road, which took them close by a couple of major gold-spired *wats* and also the group of attractive structures that form the Great Palace. The traffic was near to coagulating all the way. Although they were bound for a destination where possibly Grady would do some business, it was rather like a sight-seeing trip.

But not a comfortable one by any means.

Hard plastic seat, exhaust fumes, noise enough to accumulate a headache because of the vehicle's two-stroke engine.

Grady also disliked that he had no idea how long a trip this would be. As they crossed the river by way of the Phrapinklao Bridge he told himself it had to be over soon. He looked to Julia. She mimed nausea. He felt guilty and responsible for having given in to this inconvenience. He told Julia, "Serves you right."

About a quarter mile past the bridge the driver picked up Charon Sanitwong Road and headed north for three loud, full-speed miles. That put them in the northwest section of Bangkok's sprawl, an area called Bang Phat. It wasn't as built up. Houses were only here and there and so were what appeared to be small factories. There were numerous narrow *klongs* (canals) and thick, green, overgrown stretches. The driver turned off with authority onto a lesser unmarked road and an even lesser one, as though certain of direction. Finally he pulled over.

Had they arrived?

The driver grinned back over his shoulder at them. He kissed the brass standing Buddha amulet he had on a cord around his neck to demonstrate that neither he nor they need worry about being lost, however he appeared perplexed as he again looked at the address on the Shigota business card.

"I know," Grady mocked.

"Try not to be so stingy with belief, darling," was Julia's advice. She was beyond being merely thirsty, her face was wind burned, the humidity had her perspiring so that the soaked elastic band of her panties was chafing her hips and a few of her favorite worst swear words were crouched in her throat. She'd been a punished but uncomplaining passenger for over an hour. Could she at least get out and stretch?

The driver got under way again with renewed certitude, and perhaps his amulet did have powers of a sort, for after they'd gone only another two hundred or so feet and taken another sharp short left there it was: the Lady So Remembered Gem-Cutting Factory.

That was what the sign attached high up on the side of the building said in crisp red professionally painted letters on a white background. In both Thai and English. A long sign on a long, tall one-story building situated at the end of a narrow *klong*, right on the water, relating to it with a slatted dock and pilings.

As remote as it was it wasn't alone. There were several houses close by, a settlement of twenty to thirty across from it and others within sight down the *klong*. All similar and typical, modest teakwood Thai houses, raised and amiably open.

About fifteen feet from the entrance to the factory was its spirit house, permanently at eye level upon a solid pedestal. A seriously built little house, as architecturally correct as it could be. Its various sections of roof precisely pitched, its windows and doors in scale and properly placed. It had carefully finished eaves, porches, balconies and railings and at every possibility, wherever there was an edge or corner or peak, it was elaborately trimmed with motifs, such as repetitive lotuses and six-pointed stars. The interior of it was a powder blue, its outside coated with a dark red madder to better show off the many places where it had been given gold leaf upon gold leaf.

As amusing and decorative as it appeared its purpose was considered practical. It was hoped that this fancy little abode was so attractive the resident spirit would prefer it over the main structure, be content to watch over the welfare of the main structure, not feel the need to enter there and cause such mischiefs as sudden quarrels or mysterious accidents or fires. Additionally the resident spirit had to be kept pleased with offerings, tidbits of food, flowers and other necessities.

At the moment the resident spirit in the spirit house of the Lady So Remembered Gem-Cutting Factory was possibly appeased by the bouquet of white lilies that had been placed on its pedestal along with four joss sticks. The edges of the petals of the lilies weren't discolored and wisps of smoke were rising from the joss sticks, so, evidently, these offerings had been made only a short while ago.

Spirit within the spirit house or not, in Grady's opinion this cutting factory way out here wasn't where it should be, nor from the looks of it could it be much. He was thoroughly skeptical as he and Julia entered the place, and no less surprised once he was inside.

The interior was clean and organized. One room about fifty feet by twenty-five with two office spaces partitioned off at one end. The walls and concrete floor were painted white, as were the steel beams overhead and the roof they supported. Workbenches were arranged in exact rows, about sixty of them, surfaced with white plastic laminate. Each bench was equipped with a motorized electric grinding wheel.

The cutters seated at the benches were Thais. They had on identical pale blue short-sleeved shirts. Slight of build as they were and with their cropped black hair it was difficult to tell the men from the women. They all had the same intentness, were entirely focused on their tasks, apparently immune to tedium, not at this time in need of interplay or even music. The impression was one of conscientious precision, reassuring to anyone hoping, as Grady was, to have a valuable precious stone transformed into a much more valuable faceted beauty.

William Shigota was at his desk in his office. He glanced up, saw Grady and Julia and came out to them. Bringing a business smile and a *wai* (palms together, fingers pointed upward, a bow of head).

Grady presented his business card and introduced Julia.

The screeches and whines of the faceting wheels made it impossible for discussion there. William led them to his office. Before getting settled Julia requested something to drink. William offered either cold tea, lemonade or beer. Without hesitation Julia chose beer. Grady would have the same. William didn't summon someone to fetch it, went for it himself. Julia used the short while he was gone to blot her face with a tissue and redo her lips. Her hair was a mess, blown stringy and tangled, but she didn't have time to do much with it other than give it a few comb throughs with her fingers. Grady wondered why she was bothering at all.

William came back with a tray bearing three mercifully cold bottles of Sapporo and chilled glasses. He poured perfect heads, distributed. "How did you get here?" he asked.

"Alfred Reese recommended you," Grady replied.

"Yes, he phoned to say you might be coming by, but what I meant was did you come by taxi or what?"

"I wouldn't call it a taxi."

"Don't tell me you came by *tuk-tuk*?"

"That sounds right," Julia said. "I'm dreading the return trip."

"You have it waiting?"

"Rather than get stranded out here wherever we are," Grady said.

William took it upon himself to go out, pay the proper fare and dismiss the *tuk-tuk*. The driver was resentful, complained with a scowl. While waiting he'd been trying to settle on how much he'd overcharge these *farangers*. William knew that was the case and for the sake of inverse fairness gave the man a few extra five baht and two baht coins, which came nowhere near the anticipated amount but expressed understanding enough to satisfy.

"*Tuk-tuks* are fine for a short haul," William said when he returned to the office, "a few blocks but not farther. What a ride you must have had."

"An adventure," Julia said, making light of it, "during which I was the death by splat of a vast variety of bugs."

"If ever you have the need to come here again best to hire a water taxi," William advised. "Faster and much more pleasant. When you want I'll call for one to take you back to your hotel."

Julia had already drunk most of her beer. It hadn't really slaked her thirst. Beer never did. Should she ask for another? Another would make her feel bloated and get her a little high. She'd have to pee a lot. She could already feel a pee coming on. She should have gone for the lemonade. Now she needed to belch. She had the impulse to open her mouth and let it erupt. Instead, she turned her head aside, kept her mouth closed and shielded with her hand. The restrained discharge momentarily punished her nasal tissues. She thought, When I get back to the hotel, and am I ever looking forward to that, I'll take an up-to-the-chin, duck-down-under cool bath and then a twenty-minute nap. Order up a heap of cold fruits, maybe some gorgonzola and crackers. Hurry and get this over with, she mentally told Grady.

Her silent entreaty was like a starting gun.

William sat forward on his desk chair.

Grady placed his emptied glass on the tray.

The rough ruby was introduced.

William inspected it with a ten-power loupe and then with a forty-power microscope. "Nice piece," was his conclusion.

"How nice?" Grady wanted to know.

"Not pigeon blood Burma but closer to it than most goods I see." He turned the crystal this way and that, bare-eyeing its various aspects. "You might have noticed there's some zoning here." He indicated an area of the stone where its red appeared diluted, was fainter. "That will influence the cut," he said.

"To what extent?"

"Depends. The tempting, easy way would be to saw it here and here, amputate the zoning so to speak."

"You wouldn't do that?"

"Not even if you insisted."

"Why not?"

"Once the zoning got sliced out you'd be committed to going for weight rather than best color. What you'd end up with would have a purplish character, looking more like Thai than Burma. Know what I mean?"

"If you're asking do I know how to tell Thai from Burma goods..."

"I didn't mean to infer that. I apologize. At times I tend to be too elemental."

A forgiving shrug from Grady.

"Anyway, if I were to take that approach to the cut you'd be disappointed."

"That's how you see it?"

"Yes."

"Of course that's only your opinion," Grady challenged.

"Which is what you've come for," William parried a bit sharply.

Grady absorbed that, liked it. He about half-decided he liked William and would continue liking him as long as his supply of such principles held up. Principles, Grady often felt, were much rarer in the trade than gems.

William, on the other hand, sensed that the first level of caution had been overcome, a measure of trust established. It was to Grady's credit that they had reached this point so quickly, something that, as a rule, was possible only with the naive or fools or a person with acuity, and he was certain Grady was neither naive nor a fool. William smiled to accept the moment. He took up the ruby and placed it in the stainless steel saucer of his electronic scale. The red numerals of the readout said 42.3 carats.

They went on discussing the cut.

Julia remained silent. Her impatience crossed her legs, bobbed her foot, extended her legs, crossed her ankles. If only she were more interested in gems, she thought. Maybe she ought to endeavor to be. When she got back home she could take a course in gemology, not let Grady know, become more and more knowledgeable. She imagined his bewilderment when she dazzled him with a piece of technical information only someone well experienced in the trade would know. How come you know that? he'd ask. She wouldn't tell, or perhaps eventually she would, to take credit for the effort.

She gazed out the glass section of the office partition to the main work area. At the identical blue-shirted cutters, their bent-over backs to her. A mass of pale blue. Her focus fixed upon it, remained fixed and went to blur, surpassed everything within range to be seeing nothing, prolonged that and considered it a blindness of sorts.

She needed only to turn her head to cure it. Brought her consideration back to the office, allowed it to become caught on the framed Japanese print hung on the wall across the way, a nicely done spare shore-scape accompanied by vertical brushstrokes of calligraphy in its upper right corner. The print appeared aged, wasn't tattered but had gone buff. Its colors, subtle to begin with, now nearly indistinguishable. Directly below the print upon the top surface of a cabinet was a roughly fired earthenware bowl of Japanese character with a brown-black gaze. And next to that a female Japanese puppet head, standing upright on its neck, black hair bunned back, little red mouth forever pleasant, a nicked and chipped-off place on its pale, shiny chin. On the near corner of his desk was a folded-up paper fan with a loop and a tassel of red silk. And a shallow, square-shaped lacquer-ware box inlaid with flecks of gold foil. On the far wall, importantly isolated, a framed photo enlargement of a heroic baseball player for the Yomiuri Giants.

There were numerous other things, but Julia for whatever reason had chosen to take notice of only some that were Japanese. Wasn't it a suitable prelude to her more thorough observation of him, this William? Something within her seemed to be chastising her for not having already given him the regard he deserved. And permission was granted her to stare if she needed as she took him in.

His age, she guessed, was somewhere in the late twenties. From those possible numbers twenty-nine came forward in her mind. Not a tall man, five foot ten at most. But his slimness and bearing made him appear taller. A swimmer's physique, that was it. He had the trimly developed shoulders of a devoted swimmer. He wasn't purely Oriental. Japanese and equally something Caucasian. Blessed physically with much of the best of both. The Japanese of him was most evident in his eyes and hair. Straight, strong hair combed straight back, black as could be, and although his eyes weren't lazy lidded, there was certainly a degree of Oriental shape to them, Oriental the way they were set. Their whites were a good healthy white and their irises a surprising deep blue, except for an eighth section of the ring of the right one, which was brown, as though in his being formed that had been a last-minute concession. A pleasing accord of features. Definite cheekbones, a chin neither obstinate nor lost, the center-part nose nearly faultless. Watch him, just watch him. What an appealing manner he has. A sure voice familiar with words, correct with them. Appreciate the hold of his handsome head and his movements, even in his slightest gestures there is masculine grace. Such an advantage to be such a blended man, Julia thought she was thinking.

She broke from her absorption with what she felt was a start but which was actually only a blink. Self-conscious of the side road her mind had just run. It wasn't like her to take such intimate stock of a man, and a stranger at that. She often noticed men, yes, but never, at least not since Jean Luc and certainly not since Grady, had she been so assimilatingly observant, as though something emotional was at stake. What had gotten into her? Could she blame it on her momentary need for distraction? Hardly. The idea that she might be so spontaneously false hearted, that dormant fickleness was coming forth for its turn, made her feel off balance.

"All right," Grady was saying, "which of your cutters would you put on it?"

"My best of course," William replied. "Leave that up to me."

"I assume he won't be one of those who'd need to study the piece for a couple of months before getting to it."

"No."

"I have your word on that?"

"My word."

The last thing Grady wanted was to be back in San Francisco waiting for the ruby to be cut and sent, waiting and phoning and hearing excuses. He doubted that would happen with William, his insight told him it wouldn't, his professional cynicism told him it could. For his immediate peace of mind he went along with his insight.

William quoted his fee.

Grady thought it on the high side but reasonable enough. "Done?"

"Done."

"I gather you're not all that familiar with Bangkok," William said.

"Not really."

"Not *at all* really," Julia put in.

"Do you have plans for this evening?"

"Nothing in particular," Grady replied. "We thought we might wander around, get a taste of the city."

"You might find it too spicy in places," William warned obliquely with a smile.

"I guess we'll just have to take our chances," Grady tossed back in the same manner.

Macho shit, Julia thought.

"Tell you what," William said, "why not be my guests for dinner, then later on you'll have a guide."

"Done!" Julia accepted before Grady had a chance to.

The restaurant William took them to that evening couldn't have been more on the river unless it had been a boat. It occupied a floating platform moored to the bank close by the Phrapinklao Bridge. To get to it one had to contend with a thirty-foot gangway, traditionally in need of repair, an unpredictable side-swiping gangway that presented a formidable feat, especially for ladies wearing high-heeled shoes such as the four inchers Julia had on. The less plucky usually refused, preferring to dine elsewhere, or they unshod themselves and arrived barefoot. Julia, however, hardly hesitated, took it chin up and in stride, not surrendering a degree of temerity to several wobbles and a turn of ankle that was just this side of a sprain.

The owner of the place, an attractive Thai woman whose most recent name was Mahlee Chu, evidently felt the food and ambiance she offered were worth the peril of her gangway. She stood just aboard, maintaining a smile that might have been at least half amusement as she mentally culled the venturesome from the faint of heart and was most annoyed by those women who, taking only shoe-length steps, squealed all the way across, as though their lives rather than their makeup and hairdos were in danger. Whenever there was a plunge into the nighttime, murkier murk of the Chao Phra, it was an event, a cause for immediate, total interruption, a lot of scurry and shriek, drips and razzing. The faller was, when cooperative, brought to the bar, gotten out of his or her wet things to sit in undies and have a double or two of whatever. It happened once, often twice, a month. Three-quarters of the time it happened to someone departing, which spoke well of the pour at Mahlee Chu's.

"When you going to get a new gangway?" was something regular patrons always asked upon arrival, a sort of password.

William was obviously a regular, neither because he asked that, nor because Mahlee replied as always, "Buddha will provide," but because although people were waiting to be seated, the best possible table had been held for him, and Mahlee Chu showed him to it with an arm around. The table was situated in the outermost corner, farthest from the bar, allowed an unimpeded view of the river and all its after-dark aspects.

So, there they were. Grady on Julia's right, William on her left, she facing the river. The preference of a red wine rather than hard drinks was unanimous. William ordered a Bordeaux, an '82 vintage Pauillac, had it served slightly chilled.

They toasted to the only bond they were aware they had, the ruby.

Julia sipped to that but then made Grady and William promise the topic of gems would be avoided from that point on. She had no intention of sitting there ruminating solo while they went on about color, carats and cuts.

"Not even an anecdote or two?" Grady importuned.

Julia yielded to that extent, and now that the terms were set, her mind went searching for subjects more to her interest. Came across plenty but, not to appear presiding, kept them to herself for the time being.

Menus were presented but not looked at. Grady and Julia would leave the choosing of dinner to William, and he would leave it to Mahlee Chu. It was brought in a barrage of courses starting with chicken wrapped in banana leaf and ending with baked moongbean coconut custard and an ample taste of jackfruit seeds. Along the way there were green beef curry, lemon grass prawns, stuffed squid soup and numerous other dishes. Mahlee Chu just kept them coming.

Grady was surprised when Julia asked one of the three waiters who were serving them to identify what was generously submerged in the soup and was told squid and Julia issued an *mmmm* of appreciation and went right at it. As though squid was an old, missed favorite. At another moment during another course Grady noticed Julia had a tiny red pepper clenched between her front teeth. He himself had suffered one of those fiery little devils and his lips felt puffed with blisters, so he thought to caution Julia. However, before he could she bit through the pepper and her tongue emerged and took it all in and he anticipated a gasp from her, but she just chewed and swallowed without even a change of expression.

Some woman, Grady thought observing her, more confounding by the minute. That was by no means a complaint. He wouldn't have her any other way. Her desire for nonexistent natural blue pearls and her immunity to torturous red peppers were incompatibilities he could live with.

Throughout most of the meal the conversation skipped along lightly and neutrally with William in the lead. He dispensing polite charm, as though he had a limitless supply.

One of the topics he hit upon and kept upon for quite a while was the Thai people's extraordinary belief in the supernatural. According to their way of thinking spirits with all sorts of intents were hanging and hovering around all over the place, ready to determine every up and down, path and corner of every life. A winning lottery ticket, an overcooked fish, a head-on collision with a bus: a spirit surely had a part in it. No Thai would think of opening a business, not even a major bank or a high-rise hotel, without first finding out if the spirits were agreeable to doing so on that day. Of course, such unstinting involvement required a multitude of spirits, and there was a multitude, many more spirits than there were humankind. Countless spirits filled the air. There was no getting around them. They might dwell in any object, from a hair curler to a satellite. For some reason they especially liked to reside in clocks and wristwatches, in fact, in any type of timepiece. They'd been known to squabble over better dwellings like Rolex Presidentials and Piagets, frequently stopping those from running until the dispute was settled.

Julia asked William if he had such beliefs.

He laughed self-consciously and told her they were so prevalent that at times it was difficult not to go along with them.

She mentioned having seen the elaborate little spirit house just outside his cutting factory.

He explained it was for the cutters. Without it they'd have only themselves to blame for their mistakes. How did she know it was a spirit house?

Grady too wondered that.

She just knew, Julia said, didn't know how she knew.

William went on about spirits, told how Thai parents normally gave a newborn child an ugly name, a name like *limping toad* or *feeble worm*, hoping to trick the evil spirits into thinking the child was descriptively named, repulsive, not worth the bother.

Julia thought it tragic that anyone should get stuck for life with being known as *limping toad*.

William told her those ugly names were canceled when the child became old enough to fend off bad spirits on his own. From then on he or she would be called by the nice name the parents had in mind all the while. The changing of names was commonplace in Thailand. A person was free to be called what he preferred to be called and without a lot of legal tangle could shed a name and take on a new one whenever he felt inclined.

"Have you ever changed your name?" Julia asked.

The question was so unexpected that William stumbled over his fib. "Uh...no," and then more certain, "no."

"Then you've always been William Shigota?"

William signaled the waitress to bring a fresh pot of tea. The question got lost but Julia had another. "You haven't lived here in Bangkok all your life, have you?"

"Most of it."

"You've family here?"

Another *no* from William.

"So, where's your family? In Japan, I suppose."

"I have an aunt in Tokyo. She owns a shop that sells tennis clothes and, from what I hear, is about to open another. A smart businesswoman, quite successful." Partially true. The aunt in Tokyo was successful at running her placement agency that specialized in bar girls and girls who claimed to be merely bar girls.

"No other family?"

"Some, distant cousins and other relatives. They live in Noto-Hanto prefecture. On an island called Hegurajima. I doubt you've even heard of it."

"You probably go there often to visit."

"Yes." Another fast fib.

"Your mother lives there?"

"My mother is dead," William said levelly, as though merely imparting information. "She died in 1974."

"And it still hurts you to speak of it."

"It doesn't hurt." Another fib. "By now it doesn't."

"What was it she died of?"

William almost said blue pearls. "An accident at sea," he replied. "She was left a considerable amount of money by her father. She bought a boat, a motor sailer, a forty-five footer. We went on a cruise, a long one, she and her sister and I. Down across the East China Sea and the South China Sea, through the Strait of Malacca and up the west coast of Malaysia and Thailand. We'd put in here and there, wherever we liked, no hurry, all nice lazy going, only vaguely sure of where we were, if you know what I mean, not constantly consulting a chart. That's how it was. So the storm, a nasty powerful one, caught us unaware. We saw it coming but by then it was too close and coming so fast it couldn't be avoided. Strange, it was like it was our storm, meant for us, a huge, gray rolling mass of diabolical spirit."

"Really?" Julia inserted to punctuate William's telling. The word was said mainly with interest but colored with a dubious tinge, nearly indiscernible but there if you cared to hear it.

"The boat was swamped. My mother and her sister were drowned. Neither knew how to swim, not a stroke."

An up-the-scale *oh* from Julia.

"I was washed up on an island, a very minor unoccupied island out there somewhere in the Andaman Sea. I could have easily been carried right past it."

"What then?" Julia was hunched forward, forearms on the table, fingers laced. "Evidently you were rescued."

"By a wealthy Burmese man, a merchant of some kind cruising on his pleasure yacht."

"He took you to his home, fed you well, dressed you expensively and provided you with a first-class ticket to Tokyo," Julia imagined.

"He took me to within sight of the mainland, close enough that I could swim to it."

"That was grand of him."

"When I got ashore I found I was in Burma and the nearest place was called Bokpyin. From there I walked and begged my way east over the mountains and into Thailand. Hitched rides north on Route 4 to Bangkok."

"And you've been here ever since."

"I take it you've heard this story before," William grinned wryly.

"Not with the same twists," Julia said, matching his grin.

William gulped some tea, looked to Grady for comment. Grady was content to be a listener and give a good percentage of his attention to the river, the way the reflections of the lights across the way were stretched out upon its disturbed surface in shining yellow pieces. There was also the dark loom and underside of the bridge off to the right.

Julia waited for William to continue, and when after a while he didn't, her interest prompted him. "So, go on. You're how old and in Bangkok on your own?"

"Nine. In most ways a very inexperienced nine. I didn't know how to live the streets like some boys. I did, however, know enough to find my way to benevolence, which happened to be the Wat Po."

"A Buddhist temple."

"The oldest and largest of the many in Bangkok. For the first month I never ventured outside its walls. By day I was just a visitor among the visitors, wandering around the twenty-acre compound with its numerous pavilions and *chedis* and gardens. By night, after the public was gone and the gates closed, I'd rummage the refuse cans for discarded scraps of chicken or pork skin, a few peanuts perhaps, pieces of pickled vegetables and bits of fruit. A quiet little scavenger. Then I'd find some corner in back of a pavilion located in back of everything where I could sleep."

"On the bare ground?" Julia uttered.

William shrugged.

Julia placed her hand upon William's and gave it three sympathetic pats.

Grady noticed, had to tell himself it was only a show of kindness and so what that William was a very good-looking guy.

Julia withdrew her hand.

William told them, "One night I discovered a narrow space between columns that allowed me to get into the Temple of the Reclining Buddha. There it was: a veritable giant fifty feet long, close to twenty feet high, covered completely with gold leaf. No matter that it was a kind old Buddha in repose and hadn't moved an inch in several centuries, through my nine-year-old eyes the way the flames of the many candles around its base flickered reflections on its gold skin it certainly appeared animate enough to sit up and demand to know what I was doing there. Then I noticed at the base of the figure, among the great many candles and lengths of incense and joss sticks and garlands, worshippers had also placed as offerings bits of things to eat. Choice chunks of chicken and beef and pork, all fancily prepared and presented to please Buddha. All sorts of delicacies. Bowls of sweet sticky rice, oranges in syrup, bananas in coconut milk. Needless to say, my appetite overcame my trepidations. I remember gazing up at the plump golden face of the Buddha while my mouth was stuffed, trying to convince myself that he approved and was inviting me to return.

"Which I did, of course. About ten nights in a row. I was caught then by one of the monks. He wanted to toss me out into the Jetapon road, but another monk was against that, took charge of me, had me bathed, had my head shaved, provided me with a white cotton wraparound skirt and a white shirt, showed me how to sit without exposing my feet, and otherwise transformed me into a novice.

"It was, obviously, a major change for me. I got to sleep in the monks' quarters and was provided with a metal alms bowl like all the monks had, so I could go out to the gate each morning and allow people to give me food in exchange for merits toward a better next life. Wat Po was good for me. I did my tasks, was ordained and given saffron-colored robes, was taught among other things how to read, write and speak English. Not just the basics of the language but also its many incredible double meanings. I remained at Wat Po until I was eighteen. The last three years were stressful in one regard." William left that hanging.

Are we supposed to guess what that regard was? Grady thought.

William told them, "A Buddhist monk is forbidden from ever touching a woman or being touched by one. That applies even to his mother. Only an unintentional brush by a woman in a crowd is excusable."

"What a pity!" Julia blurted.

Grady thought, What this William was saying was he got so horny he couldn't hack it. No blame for that. Probably still a horny sort. He hadn't so far made a move on Julia but... "When did you get into cutting?" Grady asked.

"Soon after I left Wat Po," William replied. "I met a man named Carl Kleckner, an older man, a Belgian. He thought I'd make a good cutter, said I had the hands and the preciseness for it. Although I don't see how he could have known that. He was extremely patient with me, showed me how to visualize a gemstone, foresee the geometry that determines a better cut, all the fine points of the trade. Earlier on he'd lost his only son and no doubt I was the surrogate. Ten years ago he sold me half the business for about a quarter of what it was worth and a less than fair percentage and went back to Antwerp. We keep in close touch."

"Was it always the Lady So Remembered Gem-Cutting Factory?" Julia asked.

"No, it used to be just Kleckner's Gem Cutting. I changed it."

"And who may I ask is the Lady So Remembered? An old flame?"

"Definitely."

"Your mother perhaps."

"Perhaps."

Julia was obviously pleased. "You're married, aren't you?"

"No."

"Not at the present time or never have been?"

"Not yet."

"Living with someone?"

"Let's just say I'm looked after."

"By someone special."

"A Thai woman."

"Girl or woman?"

"A woman who looks like a girl. Typical Thai."

"I suppose she's very pretty?"

"Most Thai women are."

"How long have you been with her?"

"Two years."

"You consider that quite a while?"

"No."

"But she does?"

"I believe so. One night I'll come home and she won't be there, but everything will be good right up to then."

"I like her."

"You don't know her."

"Okay, I think I'd like her if I did. Would she come to the hotel one day and have lunch with me?"

"I doubt it. Anyway why would you want that?"

"What does she do with herself while you're at the cutting factory? I mean other than keep house, cook and all that."

"She makes paper umbrellas. Baw Sang, where she was brought up, is well known for the making of hand-painted paper umbrellas. She's particularly good at it."

"Baw Sang, is that what you said?"

"Yes."

"Where is it?"

"Up in Chiang Mai."

"Why would she leave you?"

"Perhaps in order to always be able to know she was true to me."

Julia nodded just perceptibly. "What did you say your mother's name was?"

"I didn't."

"Then, what was it?"

"Emi." He spelled it for her.

"Was she pretty?"

"Beautiful."

"But how was it she couldn't swim?"

"She never learned. Having her head underwater terrified her."

Julia had a sudden impulse to chastise William, to slap him. Her hand seemed compelled, separate from the rest of her. The impulse subsided. "When were you last in Hegurajima?"

"About a year ago. You know, you pronounced that correctly, can you do it again?"

Julia purposely mispronounced it. "You should go there more often," she advised. "It must be a peaceful, quiet place."

"I'm not yet that much in need of peace and quiet."

Grady sighed loudly. Actually it was more of a signal than a sigh. He noticed his napkin had slipped to the floor. Didn't retrieve it. He glanced over the railing to the water. Directly below in the low light was a crude wooden boat with three persons in it, a man, a woman and a sleeping child. The woman in the stern was using a paddle to keep the boat from hitting against the restaurant's floating platform. Grady surmised that if their presence was detected they'd be shooed away. He wished he had some food to give them. There'd been so much, so much left over. But the table had been cleared of everything except the tea, and a bowl of sugar cubes. He reached for the sugar bowl, brought it to himself. Appeared to be merely providing his hands with something to do. Took three cubes from the bowl. As inconspicuously as possible he folded a five hundred baht note (twenty dollars) around each of the cubes. He'd gotten the purple-colored notes at the exchange at the hotel. They were brand-new so they folded crisply, tight. When he had the three cubes done he glanced at Julia and William. They were still going at it, hadn't noticed, wouldn't. Grady planned to toss the money-wrapped sugar cubes to the lesser fortunates in the boat. It was going to make him feel better. He imagined how much it would mean to them, pictured their faces when they realized what he'd tossed.

He looked over the rail.

They weren't there. Nothing but the river and night. They'd given up on him.

A couple of hours later Grady and Julia were in the dark in their suite on the twelfth floor of the Oriental. Taking up only about a third of the king-size bed because Julia was way over on Grady's side, most of her bareness in touch with his.

"What the hell was that all about?" Grady asked.

"Which that?"

"The way you went on and on with him, William."

"I just felt like talking."

"That wasn't talk. It was an interrogation."

"Was I that bad?"

"You don't remember?"

"Of course I do, but was I that bad?"

"I think you were. You really grilled him. I've got to hand it to him though, he held his own."

"He did, didn't he?"

"For a moment there you came close to getting into his sex life. Do you want to get into it?"

"Hell no."

"He's a good-looking guy, isn't he?"

"Very."

"Intelligent too."

"Yeah."

"So why shouldn't you be interested?"

"Stop fishing."

"I'm just asking. You kept hitting him with all those questions, pumping him."

"I don't know what got into me."

A fairly long silence, a hitch in the night talk, setting the background for Grady to ask, "Do you love me?"

"I've begun to."

"When was the beginning?"

"I don't know exactly. Sometime along the line. How about you?"

"Me?"

"You love me?"

Grady put off replying in order to enjoy her question. "I'm afraid so," he said. If it hadn't been for the dark she'd have seen his grin.

She gave him a sharp poke in the ribs. "When did you start being afraid?" she asked.

"As I look back I think it was in Browderbank's office." That first day at his attorney's.

"*Coup de foudre*, huh?"

"Knocked my socks off."

"I suspected as much."

"Don't get smug about it."

"Why not?" She kissed his shoulder, a series of adoring, nibbling kisses. "I was wondering, did you believe everything William revealed about himself?"

"I only half heard about half of what he said. By the way, you were terrific on the gangway."

"Wasn't I though?"

"Besides, why should he lie?" Grady thought aloud.

"You tell me."

CHAPTER THIRTEEN

The following morning while waiting for room service to bring some brioche and over-easies, Grady phoned Doris. Because of the difference in times he reached her at home.

"I tried to get ahold of you this afternoon," she said, "at the hotel in Rangoon. They paged you for a long while and finally decided you were in the swimming pool. Is that where you were?"

"We checked out yesterday."

"So where are you now?"

He told her.

"I assume that means Rangoon was shit city."

"You'll see."

"You scored? What did you get?"

"I said you'll see. How's everything at the office?"

"In capable hands. I took fifty out of petty cash yesterday because there was a shoe sale at Saks."

"You called to tell me that?"

"No. Also, I was in the elevator with Harold day before yesterday. Monday, I think it was. As far as he was concerned I was invisible. The prick. He had Gayle with him. She was sunken eyed. Sniffling and her nostrils looked raw, but I don't think she had a cold, if you know what I mean." Without a pause she asked, "How's the honeymoon going?"

"Swell."

"Like swollen?"

"You've got it."

"Foreign places usually upgrade the libido. Me, I only have to go from one room to another."

"I'm sure you're getting your share."

"I'd prefer a little more quality. Seriously, how's it going?"

"Seriously."

"Need I remind you that you don't do so well with marriage? Anyway, promise me you'll think twice, no, three or four times."

Grady promised.

"The reason I was calling, other than to disturb you, was Phil Prentis was in the building and dropped by. He used to do some now and then business with you when you were at H and H, remember him?"

"Yeah."

"I happened to mention where you were and he said maybe that could be a profitable coincidence for both you and him because he's trying to locate some yellow sapphires. There are plenty here but they're not special enough. He'll pay top price."

Grady clearly recalled Prentis. He always wanted best quality, always paid within thirty days. "What exactly does he want?"

"Forty graduated pieces from twenty carats to four carats, matched canary color, on the light side, but with flash."

"Ovals?"

"Rounds."

Such a suite of ovals might be findable but rounds would be tough. Not out of the question, though. Not here in Bangkok. "I'll see what I can do," Grady told her.

"I'd like to see what you can do."

"You never let up."

"Not until I'm whipped and on certain occasions especially not then. When are you coming back?"

"I had thought of trying for a flight today but now there's the yellow sapphires. Maybe I'll find them today or tomorrow. Soon as I do or feel sure that I won't I'll be out of here."

At the very moment Grady hung up from talking to Doris the breakfast arrived and also at that very same moment Julia came from the bedroom dressed in lightweight white and sandals, looking fresh and ready for the day. Grady thought this was going to be one of those really good days when everything is in sync. Days like that were seldom, but this was starting out to be one. He and Julia had made early morning love, one portion each, and been right together with it at the finish.

The waiter laid out the breakfast and stood by. Julia dismissed him, did the serving. "My eggs are cold and rubbery," she said, more of a description than a complaint. "How are yours?"

"Mine are fine, here, have mine."

"No."

"I'll call down for another order." Grady started to reach for the phone.

"Never mind. I'll just have brioche and marmalade. That's about all I want anyway. The coffee's good," she said after a slurp of it. "Who were you on the phone with?"

Grady told her, also told her about the yellow sapphires he'd be looking for.

"That'll take you most of the day, won't it?"

"Possibly. Why?"

"I don't want to be tagging along."

"What do you want to do?"

"Nothing special, just look around, shop."

There goes the sync, Grady thought. "You have some money?" he asked.

"I've plenty, thank you."

They went down in the elevator. It made three stops to take people on. It was as though speaking were forbidden during the ride. Outside at the hotel's entrance Julia agreed they'd meet at the suite at five or sooner. But no later than five. The doorman beckoned a taxi. Julia would walk. Grady got a possessive peck on the cheek from her before he was taken away.

He didn't find Prentis's suite of yellow sapphires that day, looked at many yellows but most were too chrome, others too pale. He knew precisely the gentle but bright yellow Prentis wanted. For lunch he had a bowl of noodles and some satay chicken at a street stand, got caught in the daily afternoon

downpour, incessantly wondered what Julia might be doing. He
returned to the hotel at five sharp, more than half expecting she
wouldn't be there.

But she was.

On the sofa, reading. Sandals kicked off, legs elevated, skirt
hiked up shamelessly. On the rug within easy reach was a tray
holding a bottle of Evian, glasses, lime quarters, and a bowl of
fruit. Grady caught the hello kiss her lips threw at him. "Find your
sapphires?"

"No."

"Good."

"What?"

"I didn't say anything."

"You said good."

"Did I? I didn't mean to."

Grady helped himself to the Evian. Squeezed in some lime.
"What did you do today?" he asked, sitting on the rug with his
back against the sofa.

"Lots of things."

"Like what?"

"I earned some merits. On the street just a couple of blocks
from here a woman had a stack of little wooden cages with birds
in them and a sign promising merits toward a better next life to
anyone who'd set them free."

"For how much?"

"A hundred bahts each. What's that? Four dollars? I went for six
cages. The birds flew right out, took off like they were a hell of a
lot happier."

"Yeah, and they probably flew right back as soon as you were
gone."

"I doubt that. Anyway, twenty-four dollars was cheap enough
considering what I possibly had to gain. Or perhaps you don't
think so. We've never discussed such things, have we, souls and so
on?"

A shrug from Grady.

"Then, after the bird woman, I had my palms and my feet read."

"Your feet read?"

"Two holy-looking guys in orange robes were doing it from the
tailgate of an old station wagon. One did palms, the other did

feet. The one who read my feet spent a lot of time doing it, said I was an extremely complex person, more complex than I knew. He was particularly fascinated with the crease between the ball and the second toe of my left foot. Took off his dark glasses to get a better look at it. I was artistic, he said, and very angry, which I don't understand at all, but at least he was half right."

"Did you manage to do any shopping?"

"Not much. At a bookstore I found another Alice Bailey and I bought a paper umbrella from a vendor on the street. The man said it was the kind from Baw Sang so possibly it's one that William's live-in did." She reached back around the end of the sofa for the umbrella, opened it and held it above her. It was bright pink, four to five feet in diameter, hand-painted with leaves of green and blossoms of orange with purple centers. The happy colors were infectious. Julia got up and did a haughty walk and some snappy pivots, a fashion model's phlegmatic show-off strut while spinning the umbrella so its ribs and floral pattern blurred and blended. Finally she dropped backward over the fat arm of a chair and deep into its lap, her legs shooting nearly straight up.

Grady applauded with his eyes. "So that was your day, huh?"

"Not all of it. The best came last. I wanted to go to the Wat Po, that temple William spoke of last night. To see where he stole food from the big reclining buddha. I asked a man on the street for directions but he must have misunderstood, or, now that I think of it, perhaps he didn't, because I ended up in an out-of-the-way patch of overgrown plants and trees where there was a stone shrine about the size of a doghouse and what must have been a thousand phalluses."

"You're making this up."

"I am not."

"It sounds invented."

"Maybe that's because the word *phalluses* didn't exactly trip off my tongue." Her grin was a fraction wicked. "I don't believe I've ever before used the word. It's self-conscious and archeological. Would you mind if I synonym it with something more comfortable, like *dick*, for instance?"

"Whatever." Grady was enjoying this just exposed side of her.

"Well, as I said, there was this little untended gardenlike area with a shrine in it, and all around were these dicks. Hundreds and hundreds of idealized hard-ons, much, much, and I mean much larger than life. Picture if you will"—Grady was indeed picturing—"a shiny red lacquered dick about seven feet tall propped against a tree. There were several like that."

"Bet you got out of there in a hurry."

"That was my initial inclination but I brazened it out. The fat, stubbier wooden dicks nearest the shrine had a lot of bamboo joss sticks stuck in them. It looked painful. And I couldn't help but feel sorry for the old wooden ones that had tumbled over and were rotting away."

Grady went into the bathroom and washed up. Inspecting in the mirror he realized that his shave wasn't lasting as long as his shaves usually did. The humidity was to blame, he decided. Also decided against a second shave inasmuch as there'd been morning lovemaking. Thought they might try for an American restaurant that night. Two consecutive nights of authentic Thai would be an overdose. Wondered what William was doing. He'd sort of expected they'd be hearing from William.

"Are you still going out looking for those sapphires tomorrow?" Julia called in to him.

"Yeah, why?"

"Just asking."

The next two days, Friday and Saturday, went about the same.

While Grady sought the yellow sapphires, Julia plied the mystical mélange of Bangkok. She had spiritual readings with three *maw dos* (doctors who see) and came within a fraction of impulse of getting a protective tattoo. When she told Grady about how close she'd come to having a fierce-looking rendition of Mae Khongha, "Mother of Water," inked forever on her right buttock to ward off evil spirits, she expected reproach. However, all she got from him was a rather unimpressed *really?*

Grady figured she was helping herself to such a concentrated dose of spiritual beliefs that she'd soon wear away her enthusiasm. Besides, the phase would dissipate once they were back in San Francisco out of range of so much exposure.

On Sunday they slept late and took an afternoon walk to Lumpini Park, named for Buddha's birthplace, where they watched the flying of intricately constructed kites and looping, diving aerial fights between certain ones designated male and female.

Monday everything happened.

Right off, the first dealer Grady called on had the round-cut yellow sapphires. Not the entire forty-stone suite but about thirty of it with enough matching rough on hand to finish the rest. Though the dealer must have gathered that Grady was eager for these yellows, he didn't take advantage, asked a fair price and was reciprocally answered by Grady paying him half then and there and pledging the balance in cash upon delivery of the goods in San Francisco within the month.

Done?

Done.

Grady, light of heart, hurried back to the Oriental. Catching a flight home foremost in his mind. He'd spend tomorrow night getting over lag in his own bed.

Julia wasn't at the hotel. Grady hoped she wouldn't be out all day. He tried phoning Singapore Airlines for a reservation. Its circuits were busy. Decided he might as well pack, his things, not hers. He wouldn't even attempt to achieve the degree of neatness she'd insist on. He was stuffing worn-once socks and rolls of belts into the toes of shoes when the phone chirped. It would be Julia, he thought, using her good sense, calling in.

But it was William.

As few as possible words were wasted on their opening exchange. William was anxious to tell him: "Your goods are ready."

Unexpected marvelous news. Grady had been under the impression the rubies wouldn't be cut for a month or more. "How do they look?" he asked, toning down his anticipation.

"You need to see."

"Will you bring them or what?"

"Best you come here."

"I'm on my way." And only a few minutes later Grady was outside the hotel, an impatient fourth in the waiting order for a taxi. He'd improved his standing to next when a taxi arrived to deposit Julia. Grady told her where he was off to and why. She reminded him that William had advised taking a water taxi. Grady had forgotten that. The doorman directed them to the hotel's own pier on the river a short walk away.

A dozen or so water taxis were there, awaiting a fare. They were very similar, about twenty feet long with shallow drafts and sharp, extended, upswept prows. Black canopies above their seating areas. Three wide boards situated from side to side served as seats for passengers, six the normal limit, two behind two behind two. The taxis appeared well kept, were painted an olive shade with an aqua and black stripe at the waterline.

The only apparent difference among them was the drivers, particularly the way they were dressed. The orchid-patterned shirt and orange sailor hat one driver had on drew Grady's and Julia's attention to him.

They stepped aboard his taxi, chose the seat nearest the stern. Grady again used William's business card to convey the desired destination. The driver held the card about six inches from his eyes, frowned at it and then all at once transformed his face from frown to smile—an unfortunate smile that activated a lot of chasmic creases and revealed that five of his front teeth, three lowers and two uppers, were no longer with him. He was, Grady now saw, a much older man, dressed a bit too gaily for his years. The turned-down brim of his orange sailor hat nearly concealed his eyes, his lids were a watery pink, the whites gone creamy. Possibly he wasn't as old as he looked, Grady thought, possibly the sun had taken an early extreme toll on him, if not the sun a dissipating life. Didn't matter, Grady told himself, in fact, an older man might be a more experienced driver and would know this river, which appeared wide and something to be reckoned with now that it was slipping directly below just a thin hull away.

The driver nonchalantly started up the engine, gave it more than ample throttle, causing two shotlike pops from the exhaust. The water at the stern riled up, as though angry at having been awakened. For a long moment the driver kept the boat in place.

Grady expected they would gradually pull away from the pier, not get up to any appreciable speed until they were out a ways. And even then it would be slow going.

However, the engine was allowed to have its way all at once. The boat leaped forward, its prow sprang up. A sharp, banking turn was executed and they were under way, headed upriver, skimming along at what Grady guessed had to be a good twenty miles an hour. He glanced back to confirm the driver, who seemed in complete control of both himself and the craft. Grady also took in the engine. It was a small, inline, six-cylinder Chevrolet engine from a midfifties model. A hundred horsepower perhaps, plenty of go. It was mounted on a long drive shaft that extended down into the water. On the business end of the shaft was the propeller. The boat had no rudder. That which propelled it also steered it by being swiveled to the left or right, something the gambrel device allowed. Grady, adequately assured that nothing was amiss, settled down, hugged Julia to him and took in the near shore. Noticed, among numerous other worth-noticing things, a woman washing clothes in the river a short ways from another woman taking a drink from the river not far from still another woman urinating in it.

Just before coming to the Phrapinklao Bridge the driver cut across the river to its west bank for the Klong Bangkok Noi, which was only a third as wide as the river but still a major waterway. After five miles of the Bangkok Noi a change of course to be on the Klong Bang Kruat, and after only three-quarters of a mile came a lesser canal followed by a swift series of lefts and rights within a bewildering network of ways that were hardly wider than water-filled ditches. A final hairpin turn at no letup of speed and there it was again.

The Lady So Remembered Gem-Cutting Factory.

As William had predicted the trip by water taxi had taken only about half the time and had certainly been more comfortable.

Grady told the driver to wait. His intention was to be there with William as briefly as politeness would allow, keep this strictly business, so they could get back to the hotel, make flight reservations, pack and check out. Perhaps there'd be time for a nice dinner before heading for the airport.

William was in his office, practically lying back in his desk chair with his crossed legs up, eyes closed, face up to the ceiling. Grady and Julia were within a few feet of him before he sensed their presence. He stood immediately. He and Grady did a handshake. Julia, as though William was a longtime dear friend, surprised him with cheek kisses. Which Grady thought was odd of her. He got right to the rubies.

They were lying on a white sorting pad on the desk. Four stones with their weights noted.

An oval, two rounds and a cabochon.

The oval at 6.25 carats was largest and, as good fortune would have it, the best of the faceted. But not by much. The two rounds at 3.95 carats each were also beauties. And the fat, smooth hump of the 10.60-carat cabochon was glowing, as though it had its own furnace.

Grady examined the oval with his ten-power loupe. Saw how clean it was, no obvious inclusions, only a grid of silk that ran vertically so it was barely visible, a mere single thread lost in the red brilliance of the stone.

As for the cut, not even Merzbacker could have improved on it. Not a sign of grain on its facets, sharply defined edges and corners, perfectly even girdle all around. The quality of the cut no doubt had much to do with the stone's extraordinary color and brilliance. Grady felt his heart celebrating. "A beautiful make," he remarked. "Whoever cut it sure as hell knew what he was doing."

No comment from William.

"I'd like to meet the guy."

Still nothing from William.

Grady got it. "You did the cut, right?"

William modestly admitted he had.

At once Julia was interested, wanted to have a look with the loupe, was enthusiastic about what she saw. "How beautiful!" she exclaimed. "I can't see a hint of the awful purple you so dreaded, and you know what an eye for color I have. What a red! Simply beautiful!" She took her time, examined all four stones and came within a word of the mistake of complimenting the little pile of overage, chips and such and what waste was left of where the rough had been zoned. "What a marvelous job you did," she told William. "You must have worked day and night."

"I got into it and couldn't stop," William said.

"I thought you looked a little tired," Julia said and turned to Grady to prompt him to join her sympathy. "Poor William," she said.

"Yeah," Grady said while preoccupied with the two rounds, thinking that their match in size and color increased their value considerably.

"When will you be returning to San Francisco?" William asked.

"Sometime tonight," Grady replied.

"Do we have reservations?" Julia asked, concerned.

"I doubt we'll have a problem," Grady told her.

"Satisfied?" William asked Grady, referring to the stones.

"Very," Grady said.

He paid William the amount they'd agreed on, plus an additional 10 percent that he insisted William accept for best effort and all. "You're one hell of a cutter," he said, "we're going to be doing a lot of business."

William wrapped the stones with cotton and placed each in the folds of a separate yellow-lined briefke, the kind normally used to carry rubies, put the four briefkes into a bright red chamois drawstring pouch, wound and tied the drawstring shut. Handed the pouch over to Grady, who put it in his shirt pocket.

William walked them out to the waiting water taxi.

Farewell cheek kisses by Julia.

Thanks and a parting handshake from Grady.

The taxi got under way. When it reached the bend, Julia looked back, saw William was still on the dock watching them go. It caused a catch in her throat.

The first leg of the return trip, that twisting maze of narrow canals, went without incident. Grady couldn't recall ever being so high on life, so receptive to the brighter side of everything offered to his eyes. The ordinary foliage, wide open water lilies at the foot of the banks, the sun striking on half-hidden teak houses, a woman chasing a hen, which would be supper. His, Grady's, was a more prosperous point of view. He could afford to be generous with appreciation now, with those rubies there in his shirt pocket next to his heart.

What a day!

What a splendid world!

His only regret was having ever been skeptical of the piece of ruby rough. He wished, like Julia, he'd believed in it all the way. He'd owed it that. But wasn't it her inexperience with such matters that had allowed her the faith, while his time in the heat of the trade had cooked him to overdone cynicism? Explanation or excuse?

Anyway, glory be, he had in his pocket what he figured was a million profit, give or take a hundred thousand. The cabochon alone was worth at dealer's price as much as he'd paid the rebel woman in Rangoon for the rough. Buddha bless her! Please see that her next ten lives are soft ones.

Grady pinched himself by patting his shirt pocket, proving the red pouch was truly there.

A believer all the way, he thought.

There would have been profit of a different kind in that.

And wasn't that a good-looking bunch of pigs snouting around in the shade of that house? Best of luck, pigs.

By then, the water taxi had reached the Klong Bang Kruat, where the driver took a right instead of the left that would have been the way they'd come. Grady sent him a questioning look and interpreted what he got back in approximate English that the river was a couple of miles ahead and going downstream on it would be faster and easier. Grady surmised from that the reason they hadn't come this way earlier was the river part of the trip would have been much longer and slower, upstream going. He relaxed, returned to his stratospheric mood, taking in the step-up of color and activity there along the *klong*.

It was like a main street of water, about four lanes wide, in some places less than that, depending on how much the structures along it extended out. Every inch of frontage was taken up, crammed by one- and two-story buildings—houses, places of business, combinations of both. There was no unity to the architecture unless it was its dependency on pilings. Pilings of varying heights studded up by the hundreds along both sides. Even the telephone poles were similar uprights standing awry in the water, as though a gigantic someone had just carelessly stuck them there and strung wires from top to top for support. A confusion of wood wherever one looked, turned a prevailing shade of brown from weather and years. Wood asked to fight and outlast its nemesis, water, some of it sorry wood, dead and eaten, needing to be replaced for the sake of its function as a ramp, a dock, a porch, to accommodate the serving of bowls of noodles, the pumping of gasoline, all sorts of everyday neighborhood commerce.

Added to this were the animate, the inhabitants of the *klong*, those who lived by it, spent hours of each day upon it in one kind of craft or another, not many water taxis, small raw wood boats the most common. Powered only by effort and paddle, the latter were constructed with an equally blunt stern and bow so the person aboard needed only to turn in place for a 180-degree change of direction. So many boats! Scurrying back and forth across the *klong*, vending from place to place, loaded to the gunwales with eggplants and moongbeans, durians and starfruit, and all kinds of fish, including pomfret, hard sun-dried prawns and crispy wafers of squid. Other boats clustered here and there for the exchange of gossip.

Evidently, Grady thought, to these people a paddle on the *klong* was equal to a neighborhood stroll. He was expressing that observation to Julia when the speedboat went by. Doing an insolent forty, and, judging from its sleek lines and the vigorous growl of its engine, it could do more. It was the kind of fiberglass, stern-driven speedboat usually used for water-skiing. In fact, when it was by, Grady saw a pair of bright blue water skis sticking up out of the aft cockpit, and he believed that explained its incongruous presence there on the *klong*. The two men in it were headed for the river to water-ski.

That didn't, however, excuse how reckless they were being, Grady thought. No regard for anyone's safety, not even their own at the rate they were going. Make way for us or else was their attitude. Grady disliked them for it, especially when he noticed how much trouble the smaller boats were having as they coped with the speedboat's wake, how they were abruptly bobbed up on the crest of it and had all they could do to keep from overturning. Even the water taxi was sharply pitched by it, causing the driver to mumble a rapid string of words in Thai that Grady was sure weren't blessings.

Grady watched the speedboat cause the same bullyish disruption all the way down the *klong* until it was a small white, diminishing thing that a distant bend eliminated. He wished those two idiots lousy skiing, a lot of high speed, painful smacking falls, and he thought thanks to whatever power was in charge of encounters for making that the last he'd ever see of them.

The water taxi proceeded to the bend, rounded it.

There was the white speedboat. On the opposite side of the *klong*, idling with its bow pointed out, as though waiting, sure of itself and waiting. On the pilings nearby tin advertising signs were nailed up for the everything kind of store located on the dock.

They'd stopped at the store for some reason, was Grady's first thought, most likely beer. They were standing in the forward cockpit. All Grady could see was their heads and a little of their bare shoulders above the windshield. They were young men, Caucasians, similar in appearance, not quite twins but close to it with their darkly tanned skin and variegated blond hair. They even had similar hairstyles, cut close along the sides, long and layered on top, sort of ecclesiastic. Sunlight flared off the mirrored lenses of their identical sunglasses.

Grady half expected they would shout something, probably something obscene, but coming from the speedboat all he heard was the flatulent gurgle of its exhaust along with some heavy metal rock. A cassette in a boom box. The music was suddenly turned up to peak volume, strident, ugly.

Grady gave the two young men the attention they seemed to be clamoring for, glared contemptuously at them across the canal. Because of their sunglasses he couldn't tell whether or not they were looking his way. They seemed to be but perhaps not, perhaps his silent reproach was wasted. Finally they smirked and raised their bottles of beer to him, and Grady realized they'd delayed reaction on purpose, that it was their way of transmitting superior contempt.

Smartass punks, Grady thought, they'd brought him down, spoiled his high with their spoil. They were probably some diplomat's boys, taking advantage of immunity. Shouldn't have let them get to him that much, Grady told himself. Anyway, they were left behind now as the water taxi continued on with not far to go to where this *klong* gave to the river.

Grady tried not to look back. He didn't want to know the speedboat was no longer stopped at that store. Then he heard it, the growl of it under way, and he couldn't resist wanting to see where it was.

Which was about fifty feet behind the water taxi, just tagging along at the same speed. It seemed taunting, intent on intimidating, biding its time with a bit of foreplay until it grew bored with that and became in some way more malicious. Grady was visibly disturbed by it. Julia, realizing that, hooked her arm to his and attempted to distract him by pointing out a young couple making alfresco love on a dock. The man seated with his legs over the edge, the woman astraddle him, kept from falling into the water by his hold around her. They were fully clothed, the man's trousers in place, the woman's skirt naturally gathered up around her by her position. At first glance they appeared to be merely kissing, however the giveway was the cadent up and down cantering motion on the part of the woman, punctuated by a series of rotations and the way when she broke from the kiss she let her head fall back as though she lacked the strength at that moment to sustain it.

"Don't you wish you could be that oblivious?" Julia said.

"I could be," Grady contended. "Given the right circumstances."

"Conditions, conditions," Julia needled.

The speedboat came on.

Came up even with the water taxi and ran alongside less than ten feet away.

Grady got a better look at the two young men and they got a better look at him. It seemed they were checking him out, verifying him. Maybe, Grady thought, he was wrong about that; there was no reason for it. The one at the helm was good with the boat, sure of it, Grady noticed. He also noticed the other one had a thin gold chain around his waist, swagged there, kept from slipping off by the studs of his hip bones.

The speedboat dropped back but only to get a running start so with a lot of throttle it could swoosh by the water taxi, causing it to have to contend with a wake so severe it came within a few inches of taking on water.

The taxi driver was incensed. So was Grady, who called them *young shits* while the driver called them worse in his language. Futile cursing because they were well out of hearing range and, anyway, its engine would have drowned it out.

The speedboat was down the *klong*. It turned around, came back and hounded the water taxi again, came alongside again, matched speed and maintained it about twelve feet away. The young man wearing the waist chain had moved to the aft cockpit, was standing there facing in the direction of the water taxi.

Grady sensed a change in the young man's attitude. It was as though he'd shed his layer of spiteful amusement and was down to a serious self. No mere hell raising in his eyes now, and there was a grimness to the set of his mouth.

The water taxi driver was livid. He stood, shook his fist at the young men. Let go again with his string of invectives, spitting them out so rapidly and with such rage that particles of saliva sprayed out along with the words and caught the sun in the air around his face.

Grady didn't see the gun, not at first. For one thing it was entirely unexpected. It was just something black on the end of the right arm of the young man in the stern of the speedboat before it became a gun, before it was raised up to hip level and pointed.

A nine-millimeter machine pistol was what it was. With a silencer attached so that when the trigger was pressured what was heard was merely a spewing of seven or eight *thumps*.

At least four of the shots struck home. An up-to-down pattern. From the water taxi driver's throat down to his crotch. The impact reeled him, drove him against the hot bare engine and crumpled him into a contorted heap in the limited space back there.

Grady couldn't believe it. A situation of mere harassment and peeve had suddenly turned deadly. Next he and Julia would be raked with bullets. However, the young man didn't shift his aim, actually relaxed the pistol, hesitating as though to appraise and appreciate what he'd done to the driver.

Grady and Julia dropped to the latticed deck of the water taxi. There was no way to hide, really. The upper part of the hull, the free board, barely kept them out of sight. The speedboat needed only to come a half dozen or so feet closer to have them visible, and the young man would shoot them point-blank.

The only possibility, Grady thought, would be to wait until the speedboat was coming alongside. There'd be an instant, perhaps, when it wouldn't be quite close enough to suit the young man but close enough for Grady to loom up suddenly and leap from boat to boat, leap right at the young man and get to him before he had a chance to fire. Could he risk a peek over the gunwale to see if the speedboat was within leaping range? Sure, and get the top of his head blown off. He'd just have to guess it, time it just right. Maybe there'd be a sound that would help him decide when. At best it was going to be the most desperate kind of move. How different it would be if he had a gun, he thought. If the situation wasn't so one-sided. If he had a gun and let these men know it, just fired it in the air to let them know it, they'd probably run. No fucking gun.

Julia was faced away. She turned her head to be eyes-to-eyes with him. Hers were showing more of their whites than usual, and she was breathing through her mouth, like she was a bit winded. For Grady there was a sadness to her fright, the idea that Julia was about to be deprived of the rest of her time, the currency of her existence to be squandered, infuriated him and, in turn, his fury made him feel even more helpless.

He waited, listened, would attempt the leap.

The young man fired off two volleys. One group of bullets struck around the waterline of the taxi. The others went much higher, tore through the canopy several feet above Grady and Julia.

Intentionally wasted shots, Grady believed. To keep him and Julia as they were, cowered down. But why? Why wasn't the speedboat being brought alongside? They'd witnessed the killing, could identify the young men. Maybe those two didn't care, were privileged enough not to care, Grady hoped they were, hoped they were through and by now headed away.

Something flew through the air.

Thrown from the speedboat.

Landed within inches of Julia's head, scraped across the plain surface of one of the plank seats and found nothing to grab onto. It was a five-pronged grappling hook, a ten pounder attached to half-inch nylon line. Like some awkward, galvanized crustacean it proceeded to the interior of the hull, tried to get the gunwale, groped along it and finally got a hold on one of the upright steel pipes that supported the canopy.

At once the nylon line was made taut and Grady heard the speedboat's engine answer the demand for more power. Felt a sudden surge. Took a cautious look at the situation.

The young man who'd had the machine pistol now had an automatic rifle. At the ready. He was standing in the rear of the speedboat, alertly facing back to the water taxi, which was now being towed down the *klong* in the direction of the river. Going at a fast clip. About twenty feet of line connected the two vessels. Because the grappling hook had the water taxi caught back a ways from its bow, the water taxi was being dragged along at an angle and the resistance of its hull to the water was causing shudder.

Grady considered going overboard, making a swim for it. He

asked Julia what she thought of that. She was all for it. He gave it
a second and third thought: maybe when they rose up and dove
in, no matter how swiftly, the young man would get off a spurt of
shots and not miss. And, even if he did miss, before they could
swim to the bank the speedboat would turn around, come back,
and have no trouble killing them in the water. Alone, he would
have risked it. But he didn't want to risk her. Besides, he had no
idea how good or bad a swimmer she was. For all he knew she
was a dog paddler.

A short distance farther on they reached where the *klong* joined
the Chao Phray River and the idea of swimming to safety was no
longer a reasonable option. No matter how well they swam, with
the wicked currents of the Chao Phray it was doubtful they'd
make it to shore.

Why, Grady wondered, had they resorted to towing, and where
to? Going like hell downriver. It wasn't far to the sea. Maybe they
had extemporized their maliciousness, had been inspired by it to
take him and Julia water-skiing, mix fun and fatalness. That would
be their style. Whatever, considering the way the driver had been
so deliberately killed...

Grady glanced at the dead driver, whose lavender shirt was ugly
brown where the blood had seeped and was already coagulating.
What, considering the circumstances, would the driver do if he
were still alive? Grady asked himself. Speak to me, driver, he
thought. You know the fucking river; you know this fucking water
taxi. You're an old bag of tricks. Yeah, you're an old *dead* bag of
tricks, gone to the place where they dole out next lives. You're no
help at all.

But wasn't it possibly some aspect of the driver, some ability
that he'd acquired since death, that spoke into Grady's head, gave
him instructions in the form of an idea?

Grady slithered over the rear passenger seat to the driver's spot,
shoved the lifeless old man out of the way. Kept low while he
studied the engine, its controls and the steering system. It could
hardly have been simpler. A switch for on or off, another for
forward or reverse. A horizontal steering arm with a throttle on
the end of it—a rotating section such as commonly found on
motorcycles.

Grady peeked around the side of the engine over the stern.

There was the twelve-foot-long shaft that reached back and down diagonally to the water. With the propeller on the end of it. He tried the steering arm, moved it laterally to the left. The engine, shaft and all, moved with it, swiveled so the propeller was off to the right. He moved the steering arm laterally to the right to have the propeller off to the left. Nothing complicated about the steering.

It occurred to Grady then that the engine should be on. They'd been under way when the driver was killed, so it should still be on. Had the driver hit the on/off switch when he'd been slammed back against the engine, or perhaps when he so suddenly released his grip from the throttle had the engine stalled? Anything was possible, including a malfunction.

Grady glanced at Julia.

She drew a question mark in the air.

Grady shrugged. Which was true. He wasn't sure. It seemed as though he was making this up as he went along, and yet, it equally seemed as though he was obeying instructions a step at a time.

Such as now. He was to switch on the engine.

It started right up.

He gave it just enough throttle to keep it idling. Craned up for a peek at the young man in the stern of the speedboat, who apparently was none the wiser and wouldn't be able to hear over the roar of the engine beneath him.

They were surely on the river now, going down it, somewhat favoring the left half. There was considerable traffic. Four boats, extremely narrow for their length, the makeshift fat-beamed boats of families that lived on the river, water taxis buzzing about, of course, and many barges, tugs laboriously pulling strings of four to eight of those. Most prominent were the huge rice barges, semicylindrical shaped with corrugated tin roofs. Given wide berth by all the other vessels. In fact, every floating thing kept a generous distance from every other floating thing.

It was that afternoon time when the accumulated heat was about as high and thick as it would go. The sky was ambivalent, had blue patches, but directly overhead leaden clouds had amalgamated and were swiftly gaining weight for the daily downpour.

Well, do or die, Grady thought. He twisted the throttle up full and shoved the steering bar as far to the left as it would go.

The stern of the water taxi swung left, making an advantage of the angled way it was being towed, increasing the angle so the bow caught more water and was forced even farther right.

Which, in turn, brought the stern around sharply. And now the water taxi was perpendicular to the speedboat, being dragged along sideways by it like some unwilling charge.

The nylon towline was quivering with tension. It wouldn't break, could take at least ten times the strain now being put on it.

Grady in the driver's place was exposed now, not entirely, but enough so the young man brought the rifle up to aim position and pulled off several short bursts.

Bullets cut the air close around Grady. Others ricocheted off the head and block of the engine. Grady expected any moment to experience what it was like to have a bullet smash into him, most likely into his skull, the most evident target.

He flipped the switch.

From forward to reverse, from full speed ahead to full power back.

Causing a sudden additional surge of resistance.

The grappling hook kept its hold on the upright support of the canopy. However, the support couldn't take the pull. It gave way, as Grady had hoped. The four long screws in the flange where the upright was attached to the flat upper edge of the hull ripped out, and that section of the canopy collapsed. As though settling for any sort of grasp, the grappling hook got into a tangle with the canopy and its steel frame, and, next thing, the entire canopy and frame were torn away and that was all the speedboat was dragging downriver.

Grady had only an instant to appreciate that. Because with the abrupt release at full throttle in reverse the water taxi was out of control. Headed for collision with a forty-passenger tour boat.

Grady had to switch to forward and swerve the taxi sharply.

Too sharply.

The bow of the taxi reared up, high up. For an instant only its stern was in the water. It did a partial, off-balance pirouette and came down more overturned than not.

Everything loose in the taxi was all at once in the water, including the body of the driver. Grady and Julia were plunged in and under so awkwardly that for a while they were disoriented, didn't know which was the way to the surface.

Julia wasn't panicked. Ordinarily, being underwater was not something she found pleasant, or safe, even when she was in a nice, clear swimming pool. However, now she felt unexpectedly capable of coping with the situation. Actually, she was more concerned with Grady's safety. Where was he?

The river water was murky and there was no sunlight to help visibility. Julia could barely make out the body of the driver, his lavender shirt, as it sunk off a ways to her right. Then, also in that direction, she spotted something else.

Bright red. The drawstring pouch containing the rubies. It must have come out of Grady's shirt pocket.

Julia's immediate reaction was to swim to it, to retrieve it, and, after only a couple of strokes, there it was within easy reach, sinking slowly because it was lightweight and not yet saturated.

She didn't grab it. She watched it, as though fascinated with its descent. Her thought was she could have it in her grasp whenever she chose. Treading water, she kept her gaze on the red pouch, picturing the rubies she knew it contained, how important they were to Grady.

She reached for the pouch.

But only mentally.

It was as though her arms were paralyzed. She couldn't work her arms. They wouldn't move. Why, for God's sake, why?

The pouch was soaked now, sinking more rapidly.

Julia commanded her arms to allow her hands to seize it.

They disobeyed.

CHAPTER FOURTEEN

Y ou moping?"

"Just thinking."

"You've never struck me as the sort who'd mope. Even if it was over a loss of a million or two."

"You called the airline?"

"All of them. Want some bread and wine?"

"No."

"Anything I can do for you?"

"Get us a flight home."

"There's no available space, except as far as Hong Kong. We'd have to lay over there until tomorrow night, maybe even until the next day, nothing could be promised."

"Fuck Hong Kong."

"My sentiments exactly. One airline, I believe it was Singapore, said it would put us on standby. But do you want to do that, hang around the airport praying for no-shows?"

A negative grunt from Grady. The last thing he wanted to do now was subject himself to airport hours. That, he thought, would likely cause him to go mad.

They were in the bedroom of their suite at the Oriental. On the
floor in a pile of pillows with neither clothes nor lights on. That
afternoon when the river police pulled them out of the Chao
Phraya, Grady had decided the episode with the young men in the
speedboat was too complicated and implausible to explain. He'd
let the police assume what it appeared to be: merely another case
of near drowning. Besides, he'd discovered right off that he'd lost
the rubies and was in no mood for words.

So back to the hotel they'd come, sopped to the skin, catching
every eye as they squished and dripped across the busy lobby and
up. They got out of their wet things and took a shower, which
improved their comfort but not Grady's disposition. Julia sensed
he needed or, anyway, wanted quiet, didn't press for conversation.
He hardly said anything, nothing consequential and that was how
it went throughout the early dinner that he left her to order up.
He ordered the wine. For some reason, without giving the wine
list more than a glance he chose the most expensive red on it. An
'82 Cabernet Sauvignon Grand Cru. Then he sipped down only a
half goblet of it. Had he asked her preference she'd have told him
her state of mind called for a crisp, delicate white, a Riesling or
Gewürztraminer perhaps, something more reasonably priced.

The high point of the evening thus far had been when the valet
came to return the clothes they'd worn that day. Clean and hand
pressed and none the worse for the river dunking. He must have
known from the silt caught in the pockets and seams what had
happened, however he remarked that he was kept particularly busy
during that time of year because guests were constantly being
drenched by the rains.

Grady appreciated the valet's tact. For a moment.

And now, here it was, close to ten o'clock and he was all
pillowed up with extras supplied by the housekeeper. Within
touch of Julia yet not touching her, resisting that rather sacrificially,
and she was again asking was there anything she could do for him.
"A foot massage or something?"

"No."

"I could turn on a light and read you a page or two of Alice A.
Bailey, what she had to say about ambivalent souls. I think you'd
find it interesting."

"No."

"You're nothing but a bunch of nos," she said with an air of subtle reproach followed by a stab at assuming control. "I'm going to call down and have someone up to give you a real professional foot massage. I understand they spend as much as an hour on each foot."

"Ever had it done?"

"Never to that extent."

"And never professionally."

"You know the best would be to get back on normal track again right away. Brooding is like quicksand."

"I'm not brooding."

"You're doing something."

"Thinking, I told you."

"Meditating?"

"Whatever."

"Well, if it's just thinking, how about letting me in on it?"

"Okay, you're in on it."

"I feel as though I'm out."

"Believe me, you're in. Give the airlines another call."

Julia refused by not moving or saying anything. After a while she said, "I'm beginning to become an avid believer that everything, good, bad or neutral, happens for a reason."

An indulgent sigh from Grady.

Julia disliked that sigh more than anything about him she'd ever disliked. She got up quickly and went into the sitting room to the table that had the remains of dinner on it. Poured herself a goblet of the wine, took it and the basket of dinner rolls back into the bedroom. Resumed her place on the floor among the pillows. Broke off a hunk of a roll, dunked it into the wine and ate it. It was something she'd been doing with wine and bread ever since her long-ago days with Jean Luc. In fact, Jean Luc introduced her to it. At the Café Flores. Their own special communion Jean Luc had called it as he dipped and extended to her. High priest Jean Luc, determiner of heretics. Fuck those memories. She was creating new, choicer ones.

Although not at the moment.

She thought about offering Grady a dunked bite. Maybe he'd get the communion inference and come out of his cave, come out into the sunshine of them. She'd love it if right then he'd come out of it, grab her and giggle her and roll her around the floor. Would that she could will it, perform such emotional telekinesis, move him in an instant to realize he wasn't so awfully alone.

Get me, she thought, me, the convert-suicide trying to do the impossible, dispel someone's insularity. She was certain that was the bout he was fighting. The loss of the rubies had triggered it off and, of course, being shot at. She studied him withdrawn. He looked eerie in the neonized Bangkok atmosphere being reflected into the room. Even temporary hermitism can change the hell out of a person, she concluded and placed the wineglass aside while she plumped her pillows, rearranged them and then herself.

To do some thinking of her very own:

That incident in the river, when, at the crucial moment, she'd temporarily lost the use of her arms. It was weird, the weirdest thing that had ever happened to her. She hadn't mentioned it to Grady, might never. How could she ask him to understand when she herself didn't? She wasn't altogether sure it hadn't been purely physical, a lapse, for instance, in that part of her brain having to do with motor control of her arms. A thirty-second stroke? If not that, what? Could it have been that she'd wanted Grady to be less eager about running home right away to San Francisco with those rubies? Which was what he'd told her he intended to do. That would mean she'd let the rubies be lost just so she could have her way. Did she have such connivance lurking in her cerebral mechanism? Ridiculous. That just wasn't her. But, she had to admit, it would fit her wanting to stay on here in Thailand awhile. She was well aware of that desire and also aware that seeing more of William was a part of it. How strangely he affected her. She'd done some libido searching and found her attraction to him was not sexual, not in the ordinary sense. She'd wanted to kiss him, yes, embrace him, yes, and there'd been nothing erotic in those urges. Anyway, the certain thing amidst all this muddle was her love for Grady. As equivocal as it might seem, that was flourishing in her, had already grown beyond the boundaries she'd predicted. How long, she wondered, would he remain in this miserable mental state? Communication was called for, but she knew from experience that it seldom eased real woes. And wouldn't it be hypocritical of her to commiserate when she'd contributed so substantially to the need for it?

What the hell, it was worth a try. "One way of looking at it," she said, "is you're out the fifty thousand you paid for the rough. That and a few new dreams. With a little hustle and hope you'll make both up in no time."

"Sure," Grady said, because it was easier to agree.

The thinking he was doing was the sort a guy normally would do seated alone at a bar on a rainy Tuesday night or during a long, late-night-anywhere walk or while mowing a lot of lawn.

Taking interior inventory.

And considering rearrangement.

It might have appeared that he was sulking, moping or whatever, and, sure, he felt bad about losing those rubies, but that incident alone wasn't what was getting to him. Rather it was that incident plus the aggregate of all such blighted hopes over his gem dealer days, and he just couldn't be in the lighter-hearted here and now with Julia and cope with all those replays.

His Larkin years for one.

Even then, during his pleasant, clean-slated start with Larkin, there'd been instances that had caused some of his faith in fairness to leak out of him. Early on it had been easy for him to apply a patch. There wasn't all that much deliberate deceit in the gem business, he'd told himself. Dealers were being honest when they bragged about their tradition of honesty. The sleight-of-deal tricks they pulled, as premeditated and perverse as they might be, were for professional amusement as much as profit. Sleight-of-deal was a given, the soul of competitiveness. Just expect it. It was gamelike. One had to know how to dupe in order to avoid dupery. Bluff to keep from being bluffed. Know the old and new ways to fuck over to not get fucked over.

Don't learn the hard way that emeralds were frequently impregnated with oil to obscure their inclusions and give them a livelier green; that among a lot of rubies there might well be a few carats of synthetics mixed in (pure profit); that sapphires were, more probably than not, cooked, heat treated in extreme high-temperature laboratory-type ovens to improve their blue; that GIA (Gemological Institute of America) certificates, as authentic as they appeared, might be forged; that not every fine white diamond claimed to be of Russian origin (and therefore more expensive) had really come from the tundra.

Such misrepresentations went on and on and were attempted even when the chance of their being believed was slim. The smart kept on trying to outsmart the equally smart. The not so smart sooner or later got victimized, ridiculed, and sometimes seriously hurt.

It hadn't taken long for Grady to become habitually wary, for distrust to become his marrow. Larger patches were required, and often they wouldn't stick.

That was especially true when he became associated with Harold Havermeyer. Harold personified the respected gem dealer. He was by far the most insidious and slighting dealer Grady had ever encountered. Harold's reputation in the trade included those qualities, and they seemed mainly to be what had brought him the respect. Now that Grady had put some space between himself and Harold he thought it likely that the reason Harold had given up on him was Harold had detected a reservoir of fairness left in him. Perhaps Harold had watched and waited for it to dry up, and when it didn't he just couldn't have it around. The last thing a dealer such as Harold would trust was fairness.

Another, more recent, of the replays was the Rangoon Emporium. Grady doubted that he'd ever been made to feel so ineffectual. Out of place and small time, bullied by the more established dealers and their deep pockets. He was sorry that he'd attended the Emporium, but, on the other hand, perhaps it was a lesson learned and for the best that he accept his true size.

As for the clash that afternoon on the river, he'd by now had a chance to review it and was close to believing it hadn't been merely an episode of random terrorism by a couple of privileged cretins. There were too many inconsistencies for that explanation.

Why, for instance, if those two had been out for thrill kills, hadn't they kept on right after they'd done in the driver? That hesitation by the shooter, which allowed Grady and Julia to drop down out of sight, could have been intentional.

And then, why hadn't the speedboat been brought close alongside to accommodate a point-blank finish?

And then, why had the shooter, who'd been such a sure shot when he dispatched the driver, not been able after that to hit anything but air and water? Even when Grady was tending to the engine and steering and such an easy target? Misses on purpose?

Seemed so. And, if so, where was the water taxi being towed to? And the larger question, why?

They were after the rubies, Grady thought. Had to be. Possibly those two had a regular thing going, waylaying precious stones after they'd been cut way out there at the Lady So Remembered Gem-Cutting Factory. That, of course, would require someone at the factory to let them know who and when.

One of William's cutters?

William himself?

It was William who'd suggested, practically insisted, they take a water taxi. The only other person who'd known of the rubies was Reese, the dealer who'd recommended William. Of the two, the shadow more likely fell on William.

William and his winning ways, all charm and candor and eager cooperation. Shouldn't have trusted him, Grady thought. Should have seen the setup coming. It was obvious now why William had taken the cutting and faceting of the rubies on himself. The reason he'd done the stones so swiftly and well had been self-serving. He needed to have them done before Grady departed for San Francisco, or else he'd have had to ship them by air insured, not giving his boys a chance to steal them.

As neat and tight a fit as that scenario seemed to be, Grady didn't want to believe it. Because, he realized now, he'd been on the way to liking William, and, also, because he felt as though he was fresh out of patches.

No more patches.

But no paucity of options.

What if, he thought (and it was by no means a new thought), he were to get out of the gem business? Not sometime soon or later on but tonight, in fact at that very moment. Chalk up the years he'd spent in it as a long-term misdirection. He couldn't recover the years, of course, but it was in his power to return to the moment when he'd been captivated by gems and instead, this time, be merely appreciative of them and get on with his first chosen profession.

He would buy a sound Federal-style house somewhere close to Litchfield, close to home. Give it a fresh coat of white and all the new black shutters it needed. A brick walk in a herringbone pattern to its front door, twelve-over-twelve windows, screened-in side porches. Barns too, it would have to have typical fat, red barns. And huge maples, grateful for the nourishment he gave them and that he knew how to install steel rods to help support their one-hundred-and-fifty-year-old main leaders. He would plant ten thousand jonquil bulbs in the lawn and carry on a territorial war with moles and mice and the place would be admired, especially each April, pointed out as where Grady Bowman, the landscape architect, lived.

With his wife, the artist.

Or where Julia Bowman, the artist, lived with her husband, the landscape architect.

Either way would be fine.

He would establish himself by casting some bread upon the water, charge no fee for planning and doing the grounds of some new important estate down in Greenwich or someplace in northern Westchester County. Put his heart and future into it. No matter that it took six months or even longer, do it right, have it admired. No topiary. He'd still live up to the aesthetic pledge he'd made when he was twenty to never shape a swan out of a boxwood or a mushroom out of a yew. He'd have every plant, tree, shrub appear as though it was having its own wild way and altogether create the illusion of nature on the verge of chaos. That sort of symmetry was acknowledged as the most difficult to achieve, but he'd do it, be happy doing it.

He would, he thought, begin really thriving again the moment he again stomped the blade of a shovel into a bed of loam, as soon as he felt acorns underfoot while walking a Connecticut woods, as soon as he was at a drafting board determining the locations of terraces, paths and walks.

He would do his landscapes and Julia would do hers.

He would get on the phone and place a call to his family. He would bounce his voice off a satellite and into their ears and hearts. Let them know what he'd decided and to expect him and Julia soon.

He stretched to reach for the phone on the nightstand. Julia was in the way and his hand got sidetracked by the back of her neck, that place so susceptible to attention. His touch immediately moved her to him. Her foot overturned her wine goblet and at precisely the same moment there were two raps on the door.

Room service come for the dinner cart, Julia thought, inclined to ignore it and anything else now that Grady had broken his ice jam.

On the condition that this would be the last such disturbance of the night, she got up, slipped on a robe and went to the door. Was about to open it when an envelope fell from the message slot onto her bare toes. She picked it up. Switched on the sitting room lamps. Saw Grady's name, just his name, on the face of the envelope written in black with a wide-nibbed pen by a bold hand. Expensive stationery, she knew from the substantial feel of it, the envelope unmistakably lined.

She took it to the bedroom to Grady, who was now slouched and sunk down reconditely among the heap of pillows. It appeared she'd lost him again and thought she had the damn interruption to blame for that. She dropped the envelope onto one of his few exposed areas and switched on the near lamp.

Grady squinted at his name as though it were entirely unfamiliar. The envelope was politely sealed at only the point of its flap. The note within read:

Dear Mr. Bowman:

I have only just this moment learned that you were here in my part of the world. We have never met, however, I would like to remedy that by inviting you to be my guest for a stay at my home in Bang Wan. Your schedule permitting, of course.

No need to reply. My driver will fetch you tomorrow morning at nine.

Respectfully,
Hattori Kumura

Grady read it twice to himself and a third time aloud. A chance to meet Kumura, he thought. He'd probably never get another. Hell, Connecticut could wait! "Want to go?" he asked Julia.

"I thought you were itching to get back to San Francisco."

"Do you know who Hattori Kumura is?"

"No, but I gather from the tone of this note he wants some-thing. Is he wealthy?"

"I guess."

"Wealthy people seldom if ever write fan letters."

"That what you think this is?"

"Sure. This Kumura guy doesn't know you but infers that he knows of you and that he likes what he knows. Oblique flattery is often more compelling than the frontal kind."

"What makes you so good at reading between the lines?"

"Well," Julia arched, "I do have talents other than those I use to gratify you."

"But I'd settle for the latter," Grady grinned.

"So, who's this Kumura?"

"Kumura pearls."

"Is that good?"

"In my estimation, but not only mine, Kumura pearls are unexcelled."

"You sound like a testimonial advertisement in *Town and Country*."

He tried to fix her with a look of reproach. "I'm putting up with you right now. Do you realize that?"

She smiled. "Tell me about Kumura pearls."

He did. She listened.

Then she read Kumura's note again, noticing his use of the word *fetch* and thinking that odd. She got the hotel's complimen-tary map of Thailand from the desk drawer. Shared it with Grady. The map didn't have an index, so there was no easy telling where the place mentioned in Kumura's note was located. Finding it became an undeclared competition. Grady thought logically it would be somewhere in the environs of Bangkok. Julia, mean-while, searched all over the map. "Thailand's got a lot of Bangs," she remarked as she saw village after village with that first name.

Then she found it, kept the tip of her fingernail on the tiny lettering that designated Bang Wan. It was situated on the west coast where Thailand narrowed, about two hundred and fifty miles to the south. "Shit," Julia said sobering. "That's by no means a short drive." She traced the ocher-colored highway that the map indicated was the only way to reach Bang Wan. "And the road's no interstate, either," she added.

Grady merely glanced at where Bang Wan was, and he only

half-heard Julia. He was distracted by the name of a village he'd
come across on Thailand's east coast. An out-of-the-way settlement, nothing important or large close to it. "Here's that place
you mentioned," he said.

"What place? When?"

"When we were in Rangoon checking in. You said you'd stayed
in a better room in Lam Pam, remember?"

"Nothing of the sort. You've insisted on this before, but believe
me those sounds have never come out of my mouth."

Grady looked her straight in the eyes.

Her eyes defied him to see Lam Pam in them.

Grady had the feeling that he did.

CHAPTER FIFTEEN

At nine the following morning when Grady and Julia went down with their luggage Kumura's car was waiting in front. A white Bentley Turbo R, stretched to order and otherwise customized. The driver was standing his best attentive stance at the open rear door, had a hold on its handle ready to perform the duty of enclosing. He was tastefully liveried in a perfect fit of dove gray gabardine with black accessories, kid gloves and all. He was a Korean, typically chunky, his broad nose and chin emphasized by the shiny black overhang of the beak of his cap.

As soon as Julia stepped into the roomy plush of the Bentley, her concern over having to endure a daylong drive to Bang Wan was considerably lessened. She took a whiff of the sprig of jasmine that was in a tiny crystal vase permanently attached near the window on her right. She thought there'd surely be a thoughtfully packed lunch in the burled chestnut cabinet. She felt the smooth regardful surge of the Bentley as it got under way. She decided it wasn't too soon to remove her shoes.

However, twenty minutes later she was slipping her feet back

into them as the Bentley arrived at a private area of Don Muang
Airport where a Falcon 50 jet was all checked out, warmed up and
idling sibilantly.

From an impeccable takeoff to an impeccable touchdown at the
airport at Muang Mai took only a half hour. There, a similar
driver and another white Bentley awaited to transport Grady
and Julia, as though they were precious, fragile cargo, up
Thailand Route 4 and across the Sarasin Bridge and onward
north. Over a paved swath through verdant countryside and
every so often a village (Klok Kloi, Wang Thang, Lam Pi and
Phan Yai) that speed both brought into view and within seconds stole away.

Forty minutes of that.

Then the Bentley turned off Route 4 to be on a freshly paved
private road, which after a short ways presented what had to be
the start of a developed property—a woven steel fence not quite
concealed here and there by a crowded growth of oleanders.
Twenty-foot-tall oleanders fronting a twelve-foot-high fence.
The sort of perimeter a discrete institution would have, Grady
thought, to prevent some from getting out, others from getting
in.

He assumed this was Kumura's place, didn't care for the feel of
it. He acutely wished he hadn't been persuaded by his curiosity
and Julia to make the trip. All the way he'd been on the verge of
that feeling but this was as close as he'd come to retreat. *Stop!* his
imagination ordered the driver, *turn around and take us just as
nicely back to Bangkok so we can get on with our better life*. But to
turn back now that they were within a throw of their destination
would require a spectacular excuse, he thought. Even if he convincingly feigned something like a slipped disc he'd surely be taken on
to Kumura's.

He gazed at the monotony of oleander and fence and, finally,
those were interrupted for a gate, a heavy high gate with imposing
piers. The Bentley didn't slow for it, proceeded on for at least
another mile of oleander and fence before coming to another gate,
this one as impressive as the first but for some reason not with the
same forbiddance. Perhaps the reason was the pink jasmine that
was climbing frivolously up its piers or the more delicate design of
its lighter-gauge grillwork, or perhaps it was the way it parted and

swung open voluntarily with what seemed to be more hospitality than ritual. Next came the crunching of the pebbled drive beneath the wheels and two gentle bends. The second brought the house into view. It was miniaturized by distance, situated beyond twenty tended acres mainly made up of lawn. The sort of estate-size house one would expect to find in Palm Beach or Santa Barbara and even in those places in an age past. No less than thirty rooms distributed over various levels, winged out and, in the main section, two storied. White stuccoed exterior, red tile roof, arched double windows. Though hemispherically out of place it appeared comfortable here, congruously settled.

The drive carried into an ample stone-paved courtyard. The Bentley stopped precisely at the main entrance, which had four wide, deep steps up to a landing.

There was Kumura.

As the Bentley's rear door was opened Kumura came with a smile down three of the steps, meeting Grady and Julia more than halfway. "How delightful that you could come," he said with moderate enthusiasm, as though their arrival hadn't been a certainty.

Grady was sure Kumura had been assured of their coming every phase of the way.

"And on such short notice," Kumura added a bit apologetically.

He and Grady shook hands. Grady introduced Julia. Julia extended her hand for an equal shake. Kumura pumped. "I trust it wasn't a trying trip," he said.

"Quite the contrary," Julia tossed brightly, "we never had to lay a hand on our luggage." It was evident to her now why Kumura had used the word *fetch* in his note. He spoke with an educated British accent.

In appearance, however, he was unmistakably Japanese. Somewhat taller than average but typically slight. His hair was white, not variegated or here and there, but every strand white. Fine hair, a bit receded and sparse. He wore it middle parted. White as it was it helped his impression of immaculateness, possibly even purity. As did his complexion, so scrubbed and healthily pampered it seemed nearly to have a translucency. When he'd greeted Grady and Julia he'd removed his gold wire-framed sunglasses so the warmth of his reception would also be discernable in his eyes. He hadn't especially dressed for their coming, was wearing white slip-on sneakers, a pale pink short-sleeved linen shirt and tan shorts held by a web belt of a cerise shade.

Grady put Kumura's age somewhere on the other side of sixty but not beyond sixty-five.

"I've been looking forward to your visit," Kumura said as he led the way into the house. "There are so few people I'm able to exchange interesting discourse with these days, particularly in these parts." He hesitated for a second thought. "But I suppose that's equally true wherever I might be. Except London, of course, and on rare occasions New York. I invariably get my fill in London."

The man seemed to have the world, if only his own, by a string, Grady thought. He'd had no preconception of Kumura, hadn't, in fact, pictured a Kumura person. It had always only been the pearls, with whoever was behind them anonymous and unapproachable. If he had visualized someone it certainly wouldn't have been this man who was, now that Grady considered it, too much on the money, analogously pearllike with his pure white hair and rather translucent complexion.

They were now inside the house, pausing in the spacious reception hall to get used to the sudden gentler half light. The dark patina of polished terra-cotta tile floors and walls of plain white assisted in sustaining the airy coolness of the atmosphere, and like all houses, even those of grand size, this one had its distinctive fragrance.

Julia inhaled deeply to enjoy the arrangements of cut flowers that occupied the matched pair of gilt consoles off to each side. Grady glanced up at the crystal chandelier, so huge it made him uneasy to be directly beneath it. Ahead were left and right staircases that curved up to a second-floor landing.

"Take whatever time you need to get settled in," Kumura said, "then come down and find me on the main terrace."

Two servants saw to the luggage and showed Grady and Julia the way. Up to the second-floor landing and a wide hallway, past what must have been a dozen closed doors to a large room that was considerately remote. All its windows and doors were as open as possible, and the playful breeze that was entering had the sheer white panels billowed and the mosquito netting around the bed waving at itself.

Grady looked out the window to get his bearings. Down an easy slope about two hundred yards from the house was a beach, marked by several sizeable cabanas, the portable European type, bleached muslin fitted over a metal frame. The long blue and green split pennants that streamed from the peaks of the cabanas provided a festive touch. The beach wasn't right on the ocean, but rather on a bay of it. Two miles across the way was what made it a bay, a barrier strip of land, only visible now through the haze because of its darker color. Beyond that, Grady decided, would be the open sea. A nice layout, he thought.

"Well, shall I unpack or what?" Julia was saying. She had the luggage zipped open.

"Huh?"

"Are we going to stay or just stay overnight?"

"I don't know."

"If it's going to be only overnight we could rough it, don't you think, live out of our suitcases? At least I know I could." She toed off her shoes again. "You, though, I don't know how you'd be able to find what you need in this mess." She plucked a soiled sock from his crushed and disordered things. "Are you all out of clean undies too?"

"Yeah. I'm wearing the not too awfully dirties."

"Can't have that."

"I figure as long as I keep my person clean I'll last until home."

His person, she thought. Her person, she thought. An old heavy thought. She dropped it. "So are we or aren't we?" she asked. "Do I or don't I?"

"You call it."

No indecision. She went right at it, transferring things neatly to the drawers of the commode and hanging whatever required hanging in the closet. She was sure his suits, especially his linen jackets, were wrinkled beyond recovery.

Grady, meanwhile, had flopped deadweight faceup on the bed. "I could do with a nap," he said.

"You slept well last night."

"How do you know? You were sleeping." He did a major sigh. "I feel wasted, really."

"Low blood sugar," said Julia, giving her diagnosis.

"Low, that's for sure," he mumbled.

"How's the bed?" she asked.

"Better than Burma but the mattress is too soft."

"Want me to ask for some boards?" she said with a tinge of strained tolerance.

"To put under it you mean?"

"Yeah." She was unpacking nonstop. "Is it the kind of mattress that we'll both end up sunk in the middle of?"

"Won't we anyway?"

"Not if you're wasted."

"I'll revive. You're probably right, low blood sugar."

"Doesn't matter, not as far as I'm concerned. I'm for a fortnight of celibacy."

He waited a long beat before saying "Me too," drawing the words out as though at last he was reprieved. He got up and hugged her from behind. She used total impassivity to get free. He did a nonchalant shrug and decided to help by taking their toiletries and other such needs into the huge marble bathroom. "What do you want, the left or the right sink?" he asked out to her.

"The right," she said, definitely, as though it mattered.

Ten minutes later, after freshening and changing into shorts, they went down and found their way to the main terrace. It was hardly missable, as the better part of the rear of the house opened onto it. A linear terrace thirty feet deep, two hundred long, the roof of it supported by a series of graceful arches. From anyplace along it the rear grounds, lawn, planted beds, cascades and all, were accessible by way of eight shallow steps. Blue wisteria and pink bougainvillea had captured the columns that formed the arches, and huge to incidental stone planters were grouped around to have mock orange, camellias and hibiscus close by.

Kumura was at the far end of the terrace seated at a large round table covered by pale blue linen. He noticed Grady and Julia immediately and beckoned them to him, as though anxious to have them near. He dabbed at his mouth with a napkin as he stood for Julia and acknowledged Grady. Thus far, none of his mannerisms or gestures had been Oriental. He offered them chairs with a sweep of his arm. "Normally," he said, "I breakfast late or lunch early, whichever suits the whim of my appetite. You'll have to tolerate me."

It occurred to Grady that if he had Kumura's means he'd sure as hell set his own hours. He noticed an edition of the *Manchester Guardian* lying on the table and folded just so; propped up in a silver holder to permit reading it hands-free was a *London Times*.

"I do hope you're hungry," Kumura said pleasantly. "I certainly am. Mind if I continue?"

"No, please do," Julia told him. "I'm famished and Grady has terribly low blood sugar."

No sooner said than the servant standing by at a side table prepared two plates with portions from several covered sterling silver dishes. Shirred eggs, Irish bacon, Scotch sausage links and scones. The scones were nearly split through. Grady watched Kumura load one with strawberry jam and dollops of cream. Grady followed suit.

"My favorite, Devonshire splits," Kumura said.

"Mine too," Grady fibbed.

They toasted with their scones before taking bites. Grady found it impossible to not be sloppy, got jam and cream down his fingers all the way to his palms. Kumura was practiced, didn't nibble but his bites were gentler.

"Fortnum and Mason sends me things each week," Kumura said, "delicacies and what I consider staples, certain spreads and tins of stuff. It knows my tastes by now. I bloody well panic when at least one cupboard isn't full."

A concurring *mmmm* from Julia, as though that had also been her experience. Now, having heard Kumura more she was even more off balanced by his long *a*'s and *o*'s and short *i*'s. No doubt, she thought, he'd been educated in Britain, probably sent there by his family, however that wouldn't have entirely swept the Japanese from the corners of his vocabulary. He must have gone on practicing and perfecting and erasing accent long after his school and university years.

Kumura paused from eating, looked Grady's way, anticipating what would be next because it was time for it. The question.

"How did you know I was in Bangkok?" Grady asked.

"An acquaintance, well, actually I should say a connection at the

Oriental informed me. When anyone of interest or importance stops over there I'm apprised of the fact."

"Why?"

"In case I might consider it useful."

"Useful?"

"Being in this off-track part of the world for any length of time has its pleasures and advantages, however it can get to be a sort of creeping mildew if you allow it. Thus, one must reach out for diversion, make the most of what comes."

That seemed reasonable to Grady. Interest or importance Kumura had said. Grady doubted he qualified for either, considering Kumura's league. "What do you know about me?" he asked straight across, expecting Kumura either to admit he knew nothing or, more kindly, claim having heard good things generally from various people and hope Grady would let it go at that.

Instead, Kumura recited, without commentary, Grady's past fifteen years in one unpunctuated sentence, from when Grady chose Larkin and gems over landscaping to his severance from Havermeyer and Gayle and even on to Grady's efforts to establish his own business in the Phelan Building. Kumura ended it with a signal to the servant for more coffee.

Grady was overwhelmed and perplexed and flattered that so much of him had been in Kumura's head. He decided to heed his dealer's side and not ask Kumura to take him further down this road. There was a lot more to it, had to be, but it would come out.

"Now me," Julia challenged. "You know absolutely nothing about me."

"Ahhh, you," Kumura charmed, "you're like a Foujita sketch in invisible ink."

Julia enjoyed that.

Grady was feeling much better now that he'd eaten. Perhaps low blood sugar really had been his problem. More likely the restorative had been Kumura's words. Whichever, he was thoroughly relaxed and it had been a good five minutes since he'd given a thought to either the lost rubies or San Francisco.

Julia and Kumura were now discussing the merits of Tsuguharu Foujita, who'd lived and painted in Paris in the early years of this century. That was out of Grady's conversational repertoire, so he just let them go at it. He looked down to the bay. The sun was striking it differently now, and he could see several small motorized boats on it, some stopped, others buzzing around. Also, the surface of the water, the uniform texture of it, was interrupted in some places by rectangular sections of some sort of floating material. The distance prevented Grady from deciding those were bamboo rafts, until Kumura told him. "This afternoon I'd like to show you around our operation."

"You're pearl farming here?"

"Yes, of course."

"Is that well known?"

"It's far from a secret, but we do keep a low profile."

"Looks to me like a great location for it," Grady said to help the impression that he wasn't totally unknowledgeable. What he knew about pearl farming was what he'd read, which was considerable, but here with Kumura he was on actual unfamiliar ground.

"I have a hundred-year lease on the water and I've owned outright the land all around since 1970," Kumura said. "The instant I set eyes on this bay I realized how ideal it would be for the growing of pearls." It was one of Kumura's business victories, and he liked talking about it, went on to describe the special characteristics of the bay, how it was protected from the temperament of the sea and the fury of storms. "We had damage from a particularly vicious typhoon several years back but that's been it. More than I can say for the original Kumura installation at Ago Bay."

The pearl farming in Ago Bay on the southern coast of central Japan was what Grady had read and knew most about. It was there that the Mikimoto firm and numerous prominent others were located. Grady understood that the water of Ago was becoming polluted and, as a result, first-quality pearls were becoming scarcer. Prices were up.

"If there's a better location than this for growing pearls I've not seen it," Kumura said. "The tides are never a problem. The water is gently circulated by way of an inlet to the north and an outlet on the south. The bottom is clean and sandy, swept by the currents. Ago Bay, as you may know, has a problem with silt. When stirred up by a storm, silt can be a major problem. Pearl oysters are temperamental as hell, they seem to sulk and refuse to produce unless conditions are just so."

Grady pictured the bottom of this ideal bay. Inhabited by contented, pearl-laden oysters. He also thought about the favoritism of fate. Here was Kumura, a man in the line of a family that had year after year for nearly a century made a fortune in pearls. Hundreds of millions. If he never grew another pearl it wouldn't matter. But it's he, rather than someone needful, who happens upon this bay. And, of course, he had the wherewithal, the clout and finances, to make the most of it. What if instead of Kumura, he, Grady, had been the first pearl-appreciating person here? He could see himself scuba-diving the bay, skimming along the dappled bottom, delighted as, for his benefit, oyster after oyster opened to show its perfect treasure.

"Oddly enough," Kumura said, "there weren't any oysters here to start with. Except for a few strays. We had to bring some in, plant them, so to speak, allow them to proliferate on their own."

"You brought them from Ago Bay?"

"Heavens no. Ago Bay oysters are the species *Pinctada martensii*, what we call Agoyas. They'd be extremely unhappy in this warmer water. Besides Agoyas rarely produce pearls larger than nine millimeters and they run yellowish, must be bleached. We wanted to try for double that size and white on their own."

"So, what did you bring in?"

"*Pinctada maximas*, silver lips."

"From where?"

"That, my boy, is another story," Kumura said, not evading, just arbitrarily concluding this installment.

Two explosive pops.

From somewhere down on the beach.

Sounded like gunshots to Grady. He looked to Kumura, who wasn't the least distracted from slathering jam and cream on another scone.

When after a while Grady again looked in the direction of the beach he saw a man and a woman headed up the slope. The man carrying a shotgun. Cradled across his chest in the manner of a serious hunter. The woman had on a floppy-brimmed straw hat. They came all the way up and onto the terrace.

Grady presumed Kumura must have been expecting them, as he

was neither surprised nor elated, merely accepted their arrival. He did the introductions matter-of-factly.

The woman was the Marquise Paulette de Sablier, the man, Daniel Lesage. Both were French.

Paulette delivered ritualistic cheek kisses to Kumura, an extra for good measure. She sat and removed her hat condemningly, like it hadn't served her well enough. She requested in a demanding tone a goblet of Evian *sans glace*, then changed that to a *citron pressé*.

Lesage propped his shotgun against the nearest column and, without being offered and ignoring the servant, helped himself to sausage and eggs from the side table.

Paulette complained about the heat with typical French umbrage. Blew out a breath that, Grady thought, in keeping with her complaint should have come out as steam. "I'm moist all over," she frowned. "I really didn't want to go shooting today, would much rather have splashed around in the pool, but Daniel insisted."

Grady glanced at Lesage's shotgun. It was a Holland and Holland twelve-gauge over and under, elaborately engraved. At least a ten-thousand-dollar gun. "You were shooting traps?"

"No, no, no," Paulette replied, "but it is very much like trap shooting. I scale slices of bread into the air as high as I can. The gulls catch the bread. At that perfect moment Daniel shoots the gulls. Twice today he got four gulls with one shot. I like him to shoot. It improves his disposition."

"Monsieur Lesage is my partner," Kumura explained.

"Limited partner," Lesage corrected dourly.

"Limited," Kumura confirmed to all but aimed the word at Lesage, who begrudged with a toss of his head and a grumble around a chew of sausage.

Lesage was a good-looking, tall man in his early fifties. Despite his large-boned physique he had a well-bred sort of face. His nose was narrow, pleasingly shaped but not totally lacking in interest; his brow ridges were just prominent enough and his cheekbones and chin were definite. Light brown hair, plenty of it. It had gone gray at the temples, distinguishing him, and for some reason at the moment he had a three-week beard, which was entirely gray.

A kind description of Lesage's bearing would have been confident or very self-assured, and, at times, when he made an effort, that was the extent of his uppishness. However, the attitude that those around him saw regularly was one of careless presumption. A life of privilege was to blame, it seemed, for having developed in him an outlook that could not be expressed without a degree of disdain. He was seldom pleased enough to admit he was pleased and when he couldn't avoid such an admission he was embarrassed. Sentiment was a stranger to him. He refused to recognize it in others. Guile, however, was an old, usable secret friend.

After the first few minutes of exposure (actually from the point when he'd heard about the gull hunting) Grady didn't like the Frenchman and was grateful that he'd never have to. The way Grady looked at it, Lesage was a temporary, the most transient kind, would be forever gone from his life in not too many breaths. He watched Lesage use the nail of a little finger to extricate a grain of fresh ground pepper from between two of his too perfect, unbelievably white, front teeth. Noticed how Lesage's hands contradicted, were not just huge, but coarse knuckled, ugly peasant hands.

As for Paulette, anyone in her presence, man or woman, would have found it impossible to disregard her. She was that physically beautiful. Paulette had a remarkable effect on a beholder. The mere sight of her, particularly when she was at her best, would dilate the pupils and send such strong impulses along the optic nerve to the occipital lobe of the cortex that the image of her wasn't just immediately clipped and filed away in one of memory's cells. Rather, an afterimage remained, as though the receptors did not want to proceed to what was next being looked at.

That happened when Grady assessed her. Not to be caught staring he nonchalantly looked away, looked at Julia. The afterimage of Paulette persisted and for a long moment what it seemed he experienced was a double exposure, Paulette and Julia.

Paulette's was a fierce beauty. Without moving a lash or pupil or lip, capable of siege or incursion. Her eyes were a good part of her influence. Brown eyes, not exceptionally large but eloquent, so deep a brown in many lights they appeared black. She made the most of them, of course (knew her weapons), deepened the set of them with perfect dark smudges below and above her lids (no hard lines), plucked her brows and otherwise helped them into the shape of astonishment, skepticism, hauteur, any number of statements, depending on how they were read and who was reading. On her noble, her marchioness's head, was hair the color of wet coal, disheveled just so to suggest she'd come (not taken time to repair) from a vigorous entanglement.

Grady searched for the error of Paulette. If anything, he decided, it was her ears. They were proportionally correct but a bit too intricate, more convoluted than ears usually were. Still, they weren't unattractive, and he was made to think of them as maelstroms in which perhaps a million compliments had drowned.

He also couldn't help but speculate on how much passion she'd caused and received. The quality of it. A midthirty-year-old prime-time woman with such resources. How aggressive could she be? What would cause turnabout, set her off? Was there one ever so slight but extraordinary thing that could touch off her current? Her secret switch, so to speak, or perhaps not so secret, perhaps if one were able to remain objective enough while with her the requirements could be detected. Who knew? This Frenchman Lesage? Grady preferred to doubt that.

Lesage brought out a pack of Gauloises, took one from the pack with his lips and used a gold Dupont to light it. "Do you mind if I smoke?" he asked Julia within the exhale of his first puff.

"It's your funeral," Julia smiled, as if she'd enjoy hurrying that eventuality.

Lesage took it as a jest.

More coffee was poured. It was regular brewed coffee. Paulette requested espresso and it was hurriedly prepared, served in a Limoges demitasse with a sliver of lemon peel. She spooned in five heaps of sugar, counted them aloud in whispers, which was her habit or superstition. She stirred and stirred, the spoon caused scrape and ring on the fine china.

The conversation had gotten to this house of Kumura's, how exceptional it was and so compatibly contrary in this setting.

"I have the same sort of mansion down the way," Lesage said.

That explained that first gate on the road, Grady thought. He wondered why Lesage had chosen to refer to his house as a mansion, even if that's what it was.

"Both this place and mine are by Addison Mizner," Lesage said. "You know, Mizner, the architect who was so much in favor with the American wealthy back in the twenties."

Julia gave that information the slightest possible nod.

Grady gave it a glance up to the terrace's colorfully tiled ceiling. He spotted two places where tiles were missing.

Lesage was pleased to relate that the original houses had been built by Mizner in Palm Beach and had since been demolished. The architectural plans had survived, however, and he'd managed to obtain them for five thousand a set from a financially forsaken descendant of the original owners. "I'm superb at coming up with such valuable things," he said, and when neither Grady nor Julia were impressed enough to suit him, he was prompted to tell them, "in fact, if it hadn't been for my resourcefulness there probably wouldn't be more than a dozen pearl oysters in this whole fucking bay."

Kumura looked away intolerantly.

Paulette's sigh said this was an over-heard story.

Lesage was too primed to stop. He related how back in 1975 when Kumura needed oysters for the bay he, Lesage, had assembled a task force of six deep-sea fishing boats, specially equipped them with holding tanks, hired tough crews and the best divers and made out down through the Strait of Malacca and across the Java Sea and the Indian Ocean (some sailor!) to the northwest shoulder of Australia, a stretch of coast called Eighty Mile Beach. Reconnoitered the pearl farms along there while staying well clear of them and pretending to fish. Nothing was left to chance. He and a few of the crew went ashore for what appeared to be a night of carousing in the town of Broome, and again another night in La Grange. Learned from loudmouths and braggers which pearl farms were getting the better yields. The very next night they made their move. Several divers were sent in ahead with knives to take out the watchmen posted on the rafts. Then the rest of the divers went to work using directional underwater lamps attached to their foreheads. The oysters were suspended under water in rectangular wire cages, on the average twelve to a cage. Silver lips, about the size of a dinner plate, the kind capable of producing South Sea pearls ranging in size from ten to twenty millimeters. At first the divers cut into the cages and removed the oysters, but that went too slow, so they began cutting the suspension lines and sending the cages up loaded. In six hours they just about cleaned out the best of the two best farms and before dawn, before anyone was the wiser, all boats were headed full speed back to Thailand. With fifty thousand Maxis in the holding tanks. The Aussie pearl farmers complained to their government, which complained to the proper Thai officials, who expressed regrets and counted their end.

"As you may know," Lesage said, "oysters normally don't like being disturbed, but these took the trip as if it was a pleasure cruise. We didn't lose more than a couple hundred. The others got strewn into this bay and have been showing their appreciation ever since. More coffee!" Lesage snapped at the servant and lighted another Gauloise as though it was a reward he deserved.

Stolen pearl oysters, a few killings, a bit of corruption, Grady considered. Who would have thought it? Certainly not some decorous woman deciding her will, unable to make up her mind about which daughter deserved which strand.

Paulette changed the subject radically, asked Julia, "Have you spent much time in France?"

"Not lately."

"Perhaps you've been to Saverne."

"I don't recall ever—"

"It's a short distance from Strasbourg partway to Nancy. I'm from.there, Saverne."

"I spent a few days in Nancy years ago."

"So, chances are we came within seventy-five kilometers of an encounter."

"Possibly."

Paulette slashed Grady with a glance before aiming exclusively at Julia with: "Have you ever given thought to the spaces you've created throughout your life, how you've disturbed the air? For instance, now, there you sit, the air pressuring around you, the shape of you. Let us say you vacate that space, move to another chair or whatever. The instant you move the air rushes in to fill the space you've left, the air collides and causes reverberations that never cease. No matter how unmeasurable they might be or how more unmeasurable they might become, those vibrations, so to speak, continue eternally. It is interesting, *n'est-ce pas?*"

Julia thought this was something Paulette had said numerous times before, a seemingly offhand demonstration of a philosophical side to prove there was more than physical reason to desire her.

The validity of the premise wasn't as important as whether or not Paulette had thought it herself. Had she merely read it and remembered it for future use? Julia gave her the benefit of the doubt, although she'd known women (and men, too) who gathered up and carried along with them a supply of such cerebral displays. Didn't she herself have a reliable few?

"Being from Saverne makes me Alsatian," Paulette said. "The usual comment is I don't look Alsatian and I happen to agree, considering my coloring as well as my moral temperament. I believe I must be a throwback from the Dark Ages or some such time, from an Italian rapine perhaps. Or"—she laughed—"from nothing quite so spectacular, a trip my sexually suppressed mother made alone to Milan might be all there is to it. Don't you adore lurid possibilities?"

"Possibly," Julia arched.

"Daniel and I didn't meet in Saverne," Paulette volunteered. "We met on the Paris to Lyon run of the TGV going one hundred and sixty miles an hour."

"TGV?"

"*Train à grande vitesse*. In first class, of course. I had noticed him, or rather we had noticed each other earlier in the restaurant of the *gare*. Just a catch of the eyes but it was enough so that when we encountered on the train we felt acquainted. We had splits of champagne, two each. He had on a smartly tailored gray suit and an eccentric necktie. I adore the TGV. It resembles a striped orange, gray and white snake, *très chic*."

As Paulette related this the volume of her voice diminished decibel by decibel, so gradually that Julia didn't realize she was leaning closer and closer in order to hear. By the time the words *très chic* came from Paulette's exquisite lips, her and Julia's faces were only inches apart.

Julia wasn't daunted, didn't draw back. "Why this?" she asked privately.

"So I may smell you," Paulette whispered. "You have a personal scent *provocant*."

Lesage was talking dinner. "There'll be five of us."

"Six," Kumura corrected. "That is, if you don't mind. A dealer from Bangkok is having someone bring me a little something and I've promised to put the fellow up for the night."

"Six, then. And instead of *don't be late* you can be as late as you wish. I prefer dining late."

"This afternoon I'm showing Grady around the facility," Kumura said. "Julia, you're more than welcome to come along."

There was nothing Julia wanted less. "What are my other options?" she asked.

Paulette rescued with, "Our place for a swim."

"Yes," Lesage hissed.

CHAPTER SIXTEEN

G rady and Kumura walked along the edge of the bay with sneakers tied together by the laces and slung over their shoulders. The tide was ebbing and the sand was fringed wet and packed, punctuated with fragments of scallops and cowries, and mites and parts of crab shells that had been pecked clean. Kumura had loaned Grady a top-open cap with a magenta-colored clear plastic visor, so whatever Grady saw was affected by that softening, pleasant shade.

Their pace was slow, an observing pace. No need to hurry; they had all of the afternoon. For the first five or so minutes they remained silent, and it was during then that Grady had gotten to thinking about where he was geographically: there on the beach of this pearl-oyster-laden bay in Bang Wan, a village he'd never heard of in southern Thailand not far from either the border of Burma or that of Malaysia. He tried to visualize the immediate area, the houses, bay and all, as it would appear from above, from, say, a couple of thousand feet. Then what he got was a mental map of Thailand, which more or less expanded on its own to include all Southeast Asia and next, like a demonstration of the powers of distancing perspective, that flat map changed into the ball that was the entire world, the blue and white, clean-looking and flourishing-looking world as seen from the moon. God, wasn't he ever infinitesimal and inconsequential!

The fragment of a sharp shell he stepped on snapped him back to proper relativity and he said *Grady Bowman* to himself four times, like it was the prominent chord in a vast orchestration. The breeze was for him, the sun was for him, the hoochie-koochie of the air above the baking beach ahead was for him. As also were Kumura's words at that moment. "How much do you actually know about pearls, Grady?"

"Not all that much," Grady believed he was tactically right in admitting. "Anyway, not as much as I pretend."

"How about the market?"

"I keep up."

"I'm sure you do," Kumura said, inferring that was another facet of Grady he knew about, his ability to overview.

"Strong market right now," Grady said.

"Yes, the demand for pearls has never been so great, however . . . the situation for pearls has never been worse. Quite a paradox."

"Because of pollution?"

"That, but not only that. Sure, industrial waste, chemical fertilizers and so on are spoiling the pearl-growing waters, but the pearl farmers themselves are also to blame."

"How's that?"

"Ever heard of the Japan Pearl Exporters Association?"

Grady had but he sensed it best that he ought to just let Kumura go on.

"It's a government agency established in the early sixties," Kumura said, "to oversee the pearl industry. I happened to be among those who pushed to form it. Its purpose was to set standards of quality and make sure they were lived up to by the pearl farmers. All pearls intended for export had to be inspected and approved. If a batch wasn't good enough in one way or another, it wasn't allowed to be shipped. Instead it was confiscated and destroyed. You thirsty?"

"Yeah."

"So am I. We should have brought along a thermos of orange squash or something. Thoughtless of me."

Kumura went to the water and cupped a double handful. Didn't drink it, just took some into his mouth, swished it around and spat it out. He continued walking and talking. "Although the standards were high and rigidly enforced the pearl farmers for the most part realized it was for their own good and went along with it. Sure, there was some grumbling and disputes and incidents involving corruption, but the export inspections prevailed. For about ten years. That is, until pearls became such a staple of fashion and the demand heated up."

Kumura stopped again, this time to hitch up his shorts. He took a couple of Callard and Bowser licorice toffees from his pocket. "Forgot I had these," he said. Didn't ask if Grady wanted one, just assumed and tossed it. They remained stopped while they unwrapped and put the toffees in their mouths. Grady watched Kumura take the time to fold the silver and black foil wrapper into a tiny triangle, sort of origamilike. He put it to pocket for discard elsewhere. Grady crushed his, rolled it into a ball and had it for his fingers to play with as they went on down the beach.

"Last year, how many pearls do you think were exported to the United States from Japan?" Kumura asked.

Grady knew roughly how many but said he wouldn't even venture a guess.

"Thirty million mommes were officially shipped. Two hundred and fifty thousand pounds."

"A lot of pearls," Grady commented, trying to visualize such a heap.

"Worth a lot of money," Kumura echoed. "Close to a billion dollars."

Another unimaginable heap for Grady.

"The demand is actually too strong," Kumura said. "In order to meet it, or, I should say, take advantage of it, the majority of pearl farmers have said to hell with standards. They've overcrowded the waters of their farms, drastically shortened the culturing periods. At the same time the pearl export inspection agency has become accommodatingly myopic. Batches of pearls that would never have passed inspection before are now getting a mere glance and an approving wink. Even trash pearls, the most inferior quality, have a market. Instead of being destroyed as regulations stipulate, they're being shipped to Hong Kong and sold on from there. It pains me to think of it."

"But prices are up," Grady reasoned.

"Not across the board, only the prices of better goods, and that's because better goods are scarce, and getting scarcer. When I was last in New York I dropped in at a retail store on Madison Avenue. Didn't introduce myself. Asked to see pearls and was shown some medium-grade strands. When I seemed reluctant the saleperson took that to mean my concern was the price and proceeded to show me some that were less expensive. I examined those closely. They were not only blemished in various ways, they had such little nacre I could, with my bare eyes, make out the beads implanted in them. It infuriated me."

Grady understood. He also hated seeing such bad goods.

"How long do you think farmers used to allow their oysters to grow pearls?" Kumura asked.

Grady figured it was about time he admitted to knowing something like that. "Three years."

"Yes, but nowadays many are putting a crop into the water in June and harvesting it in December. The pearls they're getting have only about two-tenths of a millimeter of nacre. Compared to the full millimeter a term of three years would bring. As you no doubt know, the more layers of nacre the greater the luster."

"Yeah."

"Pity the poor lady who buys for herself or receives as a gift such inferior thin-skinned pearls. At first they appear all right to her, lustrous and gleaming, but within a year or less they start to die. They go dull, and, when she wonders why, she's told the cause is her perspiration and the perfume she's been spritzing."

"Pity," Grady agreed, meaning it.

"Pearls for the masses," Kumura verbally shrugged.

By then they were a mile up the beach and the Kumura facility was in view. It consisted of two similar structures of black steel and reflecting glass. There was nothing architecturally attractive or unusual about them, and Grady's initial reaction was they didn't belong here, Silicon Valley maybe, but here they were spoilers. Not until he got closer did he realize how gigantic one of the buildings was. Not tall, four stories at most, but plenty long and wide. It extended from the shoulder of the beach out into the bay, sort of like a contemporary office building that had toppled over and landed in the water just right. The second, smaller building was oppositely situated. It ran inland from the shoulder of the beach. It wasn't landscaped, and tropical growth, banana trees and such, concealed much of it.

Grady and Kumura put on their sneakers and entered the inland building. At once they were in a spacious area bathed in softened sunlight. The roof was made up of diffusing glass panels. Also overhead was an irregular lattice, a confusion really, of white PVC pipes. They ran in every direction, were numerously elbowed and, as well, accented with red valves and green levers.

Vertical pipes, connected to certain of the horizontal ones above, extended down to vats. Heavy-gauge, extruded plastic vats, about six feet square, four feet deep. The floor was smooth concrete inset with steel grate drains. Although the place was very clean it smelled strongly of the sea and sea creatures. There were twenty or so workers about. Kumura acknowledged them with what could pass as a bow or merely a deep nod.

He explained to Grady that half the vats here were for holding mature oysters ready to be nucleated. The other half for holding spat, newborn oysters, that needed looking after for a couple of months before being placed in the bay, where, he hoped, they too would mature in two or three years. "By the way," Kumura said, "as you probably know oysters are hermaphroditic."

Another bit of information Grady knew but let Kumura have the enjoyment of imparting.

"Oysters have both male and female sexual organs. They go through phases during which they apparently prefer one over the other. Marine biologists have all sorts of theories about why they switch as they do. I like to believe it's a matter of whim. Anyway, the oyster that was a mother last month may be around spreading sperm this month," Kumura grinned. "Quite a fucking arrangement."

"Yeah."

"Can't help but envy it, considering our human plight. I mean the difference between the genders when it comes to the allocation of potential passion."

It was a lighthearted gripe, but Grady didn't miss its acrid under-edge.

They proceeded to an adjacent area, where, Kumura said, the

implanting was performed. The concrete floor there was enameled a stark white, helping the impression that it was cleaner, even sanitary. Twenty workbenches were precisely lined up in rows of five. Their top surfaces were stainless steel and they were rib cage height to make it easier for the workers, so they wouldn't have to stoop.

The workers, one to each bench, were wearing green medical-type smocks and had their hair contained in the sort of unflattering caps used in hospital operating rooms. Nearly all the workers were women, Thais and Malays and Japanese.

Kumura stopped at the workbench of a Japanese woman he introduced simply as Naomi and in the same breath said she was one of the best at implantation. Naomi didn't have much of a nose and a crowd of unfortunate, tea-stained teeth. She smiled unselfconsciously and waited for Kumura to gesture that she should continue her work.

In the tray on her left were several oysters, South Sea silver lips, each about twelve inches in diameter and four inches where they were thickest. Their gray to black and dun to brown exteriors were concentrically but roughly ridged, not in any way attractive.

Naomi randomly chose one of the oysters. She placed it before her on an especially constructed metal stand so it was braced and positioned in such a way that its valves, that is, its upper and lower shells, were diagonally in line with her eyes.

It first appeared to Grady that the oyster was firmly closed and that it would probably take some hurt and damage to get it open. However, now he realized a slight slit.

"Oysters are gregarious creatures," Kumura said. "When not in a gang and, as well, a bit hungry like this one, it expresses its discontent by opening up to the world."

Naomi took advantage of the oyster's sparse opening, inserted a little hardwood wedge. The oyster responded by opening a degree wider. Naomi inserted another, thicker wedge and removed the first. When the oyster opened still wider, in place of the wedge, she inserted a stainless steel protractor. She squeezed the protractor firmly, very gradually increasing pressure.

"The trick," Kumura explained, "is not to put too sudden or too great a strain on the adductor muscle." He indicated where the shells were hinged. "That's just about the worst trauma one can inflict on an oyster. It's like breaking its spine. When that happens it gives up completely."

The oyster was now open enough for Grady to see its black, brown and pumpkin-hued mantle, the flimsier somewhat gathered edging of flesh nearest the lip of the shell. Farther in were its other glistening components, stomach and feet and all, slickly and comfortably arranged on the iridescent inner surface of the shell.

Naomi worked swiftly, not wasting a motion. The procedure was obviously one she'd performed countless times.

She took up a scalpel from her instrument stand. Made a three-quarter-inch-deep, three-quarter-inch-long incision in the oyster's mantle, precisely where its ambivalent gonads were located.

"Care must be taken not to make the incision too close to the lip," Kumura commented, "or else the pearl we get will be misshapen."

Next, using a special thin instrument with a cup on its end, Naomi reached into a little bin labeled *14mm*. Chose one white head from the identical many that were in the bin.

"Those are from the Mississippi River, right?" Grady said.

"Yes," Kumura replied, having just had words taken out of his mouth.

"Shaped from the shell of the washboard mussel," Grady added before reminding himself not to be a know-it-all, in fact, to remain a catcher not a pitcher.

With a steady hand, Naomi extended the instrument cupping the bead into the oyster, inverted it and dropped the bead precisely where she wanted. Pressed the bead gently into the incision she'd made, making sure it was well in and snug.

She turned her attention to an oyster in a shallow tray to her right. Its upper shell had been intentionally broken away, so it lay there entirely exposed, still alive but about to be sacrificed. Using the scalpel and a pair of surgical scissors, Naomi amputated a portion of its mantle, a cube-shaped piece that she trimmed to correct size before transporting it with tweezers to the incision of the first, more fortunate oyster. She tucked that snip of flesh into the incision, adjusted it neatly around the bead.

Removed the protractor.

The oyster closed immediately, as though irritated at having been put through such torment. Naomi dropped it into the oxygenated and salinated water of a nearby tank to recuperate along with the other oysters she'd implanted that afternoon.

Grady had never expected to witness an implantation. He'd been fascinated.

Kumura thanked Naomi. "Three years from now," he said, "God, Allah, Buddha and everyone else willing, we may be blessed with another sixteen-millimeter beauty."

The tour continued.

They left that part of the facility for the other building, the larger one on the bay. Grady at once saw the reason for its dimensions. It included a pair of slips, each plenty wide enough for two good-size vessels to pass or lay side by side. For most intents and purposes the structure served as a huge docking shed. It was where the various sorts of boats needed by the pearl farm were serviced and maintained. It was where the rafts were constructed. It was where the boat crews and other workers were quartered. Four stories up along each side were steel grate ramps that gave access to the rooms in which they lived.

It was also where Kumura and Lesage kept their personal vessels. Such as Kumura's 130-foot power yacht. There it was, with the name *Zephyr* in gold and black lettering on its stern along with its port of registry, Singapore. So white, impeccable and polished it appeared brand-new.

Grady asked if it was.

Kumura told him it wasn't. He'd had it designed in England and built in Rotterdam ten years ago. "But that ketch there is a Hinckley that was delivered just last month," he said, calling Grady's attention to a fifty-foot motor sailor named *Sea Cloud* that was tied up a short ways farther on. "It has everything." They paused to look it over. "Personally, I think I'm going to prefer it over *Zephyr*. When out on the water I enjoy not striving for total comfort."

Grady appreciated the ketch. And coveted it. Like most guys he carried the someday desire to own such a boat, and also like most, that space in him was shared by the squelching realization that chances were he never would. Cost as much as a house, such a boat, and on top of that would be the bruising expense of upkeep. Substantial, wanted things were like that, turned on you with encumbrances before you even owned them, Grady thought.

He gazed across the shed to the other slip, where there was another power yacht. This one larger and newer and with sleeker lines. Italian design, Grady guessed and then guessed aloud it belonged to Lesage.

Kumura told him it did.

"What about that sloop over there?" A really handsome motor sailer with a blue hull.

"Also Lesage's."

Grady thought, a bit jaundiced, that the limited partner did all right for himself.

They went on along the slip, past where a crane had a motorboat lifted and was placing it upon a scaffold so its hull could be worked on, past where there was the clanging staccato of metal being hammered and the shouting of various languages, past where the acetylene blue sparks were popping about and the air smelled of hot metal and Thai cooking.

Grady, taking it all in, noticed three young men leaning upon the rail of the steel grate ramp forty feet above. They were observing him and Kumura, but especially him. The three were bare to the waist, deeply tanned. Their blond hair was nearly shaved on the sides and in back but long on top. Acorn shaped. They were staring down. Grady stared right back up at them and thought how much they resembled the young thieves who'd given him a hard time on the river. They might very well be, except it didn't make sense. That had been in the combat zone of Bangkok, this was Bang Wan, peaceful place of pearls. Because of the angle and distance Grady couldn't see their faces distinctly enough, tried for a long moment more before deciding to chalk up the resemblance to coincidence. No, style, that's all there was to it, a matter of style. Guys that age were always into a trend.

At the far end of the shed the two slips gave to the open water of the bay. Several speedboats and some wide-beamed, clumsy-looking vessels were tied up there. Maintenance boats.

"We'll take one of these tenders," Kumura said and stepped aboard. Grady followed and, in moments, with a dark-skinned Thai at the helm, the tender chugged from the shed, headed out into the bay.

The channel, Grady saw, was well marked by green-striped and red-striped buoys. The buoys had strobe lights on them for negotiating the channel at night. It wasn't a straight channel but ran through a maze of bamboo rafts all the way across the bay.

There were many more rafts than Grady had thought when he'd noticed them from the terrace. A hundred was now his estimate. Each raft was twenty feet by twenty feet, and, joined as many were, they formed long, rectangular sections.

Kumura had the Thai stop the tender at one such section where work was in progress. That allowed Grady to see that the rafts were constructed of twenty-foot lengths of bamboo six to eight inches in diameter. Two layers of these runners, the top layer at a right angle to the bottom, latticelike. Spaced four feet apart, they formed individual openings. Wire mesh cages of dimensions that allowed clearance were suspended from the openings to below the surface of the water.

At that moment a cage was being manually hoisted up through one of the spaces. The cage had no top, was really more like a square, sharp-cornered basket.

Grady counted the eight oysters it contained. A worker removed one, handled it as though it had no more prospect than a common hunk of rock. He propped it up on the edge and chopped at it with a cleaver, hacking away the crusty material that had attached to the shell. Another worker used a hose to wash off algae.

"Once a month every oyster gets a beauty treatment," Kumura said. "Keeps them healthy."

"And happy," Grady added.

"And happy," Kumura concurred.

As the men continued cleaning and washing down the oysters they came to one that had a small starfish clinging to it. "Starfish adore oysters," Kumura said, "that is, they adore sucking the life out of them. An octopus will do the same. We're constantly having to battle those two."

The worker cleavered the starfish.

The tender got under way again along the channel. After going a short distance it turned in between two sections of rafts that were being worked on. Stopped close alongside the one to starboard. Kumura stepped over the gunwale of the tender to be upon a raft. "What we have here are some of our three-year-olds," he said, turned and stepped confidently along a length of bamboo, making it look easy.

Grady didn't try to keep up. Not only was the bamboo round, thus offering a meager surface, but also slippery wet. Rather than risk falling in among the oysters he limited his going to heel-to-toe lengths. Told himself that neither Kumura nor the workers were amused by his inching along. Shit, he'd never walked a wet bamboo pole.

By the time he got to them they had a cage up and out. Kumura told Grady to choose one of the oysters the cage contained. They were as identical as silver lips could be, equally big, equally ugly. Grady heeded whatever it was in him that told him to pick the third from the right.

One of the workers used the blade of a primitive hatchet to force that oyster partially open. He held the oyster up with the flat of both hands. Kumura peered into it. Then reached into it.

It was, for Grady, like sleight of hand when he saw Kumura's fingers emerge with a pearl. White as could be pearl, translucent and lustrous as could be pearl, an approximately sixteen-millimeter South Sea pearl, and round enough if not perfectly round.

Kumura examined it, rolled it between thumb and second finger for an all-around look. Was apparently satisfied. He handed the pearl to Grady, who examined it thoroughly before extending it to Kumura.

Kumura refused to take it back. "It's yours," he told Grady casually.

"You're kidding."

"No, I want you to have it. In fact, I insist. A memento of your being here."

Grady couldn't refuse, didn't want to. He'd begun to like Kumura and now he liked him one sixteen-millimeter, top-grade Kumura pearl more. Maybe, he thought somewhat like a vow, he'd keep it forever.

They went back aboard the tender and proceeded along the twisting channel. For whatever reason, his increased familiarity with the place, Kumura's camaraderie and generosity or what, Grady was beginning to feel personally connected to this pearl farm. It was a feeling that bordered on proprietary. Grady knew how unreasonable that was.

When they reached where the channel and the sea took and gave they headed back to the docking shed. It was then that Kumura found another couple of toffees and said, "Grady, I hadn't intended to get to business for at least two or three days, but sometimes when people such as we get together and get along things accelerate. Haven't you found that to be the case?"

Kumura kept looking straight ahead as he said this, Grady noticed. As if he were talking to the wind. There was a space for Grady to put in a *yeah*, so he did.

"Frankly," Kumura said, "I had more than your company in mind when I asked you down here."

Here it comes, Grady thought.

"I'm of a mind to want you to hook up with Kumura. You can gather from that I'm not a hundred percent sure it's a right move but I'd say I'm in the high nineties."

"What do you mean by hook up?"

"Kumura is in need of fresh representation in the United States market. Not a dire need but nonetheless a need. Our problem is we're not first in the minds of the dealers as we should be. Anyway, that's my opinion. The same applies, I think, to a great many of the retail outlets that handle our goods. They're not all Neiman Marcus. Too often what they do is take a piece or two of ours to use as upscale leaders. Show them with the intention of shaking a customer down to something they say looks almost as good and is much less pricey. Have you known of that happening?"

A nod from Grady.

"We need to find a way to inspire the market, convince it that selling quality will benefit everyone."

That was one of the oldest sorts of wishful thinking, Grady thought, recalling some of the powerful, slick, hardass dealers he'd known, some of those whom he mentally called his groaning moaners. Still, Kumura was on the brink of a proposal, and what gain in crapping on it? "The dealers would be the key," he told Kumura. "They hate knowing or having it known that they're being used, even if it's for their own benefit. But they love being catered to, even when they know there's an ulterior motive. It's amazing how large their appetites are when it comes to eating up a guy's time."

A pleased smile from Kumura. He believed Grady's wheels were already spinning. "You'd be in charge of the entire U.S. market for Kumura."

"Who'd I be answering to?"

"Only myself."

"Not Lesage?"

"No."

"I doubt I could get along with Lesage. He may be as resourceful as he claims but for me the chemistry's all wrong. Sure you won't spring him on me after the fact?"

"I promise I won't. Furthermore, I'd see that you were smartly installed in San Francisco, which is where I assume you'd prefer to be located. First-rate offices, showroom, staff and all."

"Why me?"

"Why not you?"

Good question. Grady imagined the offices. He imagined Doris. He imagined Harold.

"You haven't asked about your compensation. On purpose? Even so, it's impressive, I must say."

"All right, tell me."

"Tempt you? That what you said?"

"No, tell me."

Kumura pulled a figure out of the air, but it sounded as though it was an amount he'd given serious consideration. "Six hundred thousand a year with increases negotiable yearly. An expense account that will allow you to live extremely well. A company car, a Bentley, and driven if you like, and an apartment in keeping with the Kumura image."

Better than having to hustle and hondle around for goods that he might be able to margin, Grady told himself. Better than crying over spilt rubies. "When do you have to have my answer?" he asked.

"No hurry. As I told you, I haven't quite made up my mind about you yet."

CHAPTER SEVENTEEN

Julia was out of the shower and towel drying her hair. Humming a bright, every song. She still had her makeup to do, and Grady figured she was at minimum a half hour from being ready, maybe an hour if she got undecided about what to wear.

She'd just returned from her swim with Paulette, brought back by Paulette in that year's Rolls Corniche, top down. Grady had gotten back much earlier with the almost job offer by Kumura centrifuging in his head, anxious to tell Julia about it. When she wasn't there and didn't show up for a couple of hours it got anticlimactic, had lost so much edge that in telling he was offhand, and when she reacted enthusiastically and said she and her intuition, or whatever it was, were certain Kumura would be 100 percent sold on Grady before the night was over or within another couple of days, it didn't have the positive effect on him it should have.

"How was Lesage's mansion?" Grady asked.

"Not special," she replied.

"Did you swim?"

"Yeah, and I got a little too much sun."

Her skin looked hot, tanned but pinkish. Grady noticed there weren't any demarcating paler areas that her bathing suit should have covered. He decided not to mention it. Instead, he casually asked, "Was Lesage around?"

"Off and on. Had his nose in a *Wall Street Journal* most of the while."

Checking out the figures, Grady thought and nearly said. "What about the marquise?"

"She's rather nice. In short doses. As a have-around friend I imagine she'd be a bitch. She is a stunner though, isn't she?"

"Yeah."

"How dreadful to be so handicapped."

Grady stifled a scoff.

"I mean most people must be so zapped by her looks that they assume she's shallow. Actually, given the chance, she has a share of depth. She's no Simone de Beauvoir by any stretch but, still, a few fathoms."

"How great is her body?" Grady was trolling for a rise of jealousy.

"From that I take it you've already found it great and just want to know the degree."

"Whatever."

"Anyway, you saw."

"Not as well as you.'"

"Want a mole by mole report?"

"If that's what it rates."

"Let me just say the body goes well with the face."

"I imagined as much."

Julia pretended exasperation, tightened her lips and vigorously transformed her damp hair into wild blond tendrils. "At times I don't know how to take you," she said.

Grady disagreed lovingly. "You always know."

"Damn it!" Julia exclaimed, feeling the temperature of her shoulders and then presenting her face to Grady. "Is my nose terribly red? It is, isn't it?" She scrunched it up. "I'll bet anything it peels. Nothing less attractive than a peeling nose, and what a time to have one."

A flare-up of vanity provoked by the proximity of Paulette, Grady surmised.

"I wish I'd thought to bring along some aloe vera lotion," Julia said. "Might Kumura have an aloe vera around?"

Grady recalled vaguely having seen some aloe vera plants along the drive.

"Go out and look, would you?"

It occurred to him that he'd need a knife to cut the aloe vera. It was meaningful, he thought, that he didn't carry a pocketknife these days, indicated a change of heart, perhaps a hardening. Throughout most of his young life he'd possessed such convenient little knives. One of sterling silver from Tiffany that had been a gift from himself stood out in his memory. He'd lost it just as he'd lost all the others. Even when he took special care not to lose them they slipped from his trouser pockets to hide in the crease of the rear seats of taxis as if they couldn't wait to escape him.

He got a nail file from her toiletry case and went out. He was already dressed and everything for the evening, had on a cream-colored linen suit, nearly matching voile shirt, no tie and a pair of woven, white leather loafers. Some of the wrinkles had hung out of the suit. Maybe it didn't still look as though it had been slept in, only as though it hadn't been taken off for a nap.

He was feeling too white and creamy to go mucking around the grounds. Some of the sprinkler system was on, he noticed. Still, this was a mercy mission for his lady and perhaps his motive was more macho than chivalrous, but either way or both he wasn't going to just stand out there a long enough while and then go back up and tell her no aloe vera. Besides, how would he explain if later on she spotted one of those fat-speared plants, he being a landscape expert and all that.

He walked down the pebbled drive quite a ways. Saw a red car coming in. As it drew nearer the car became a Porsche convertible, and then when nearer still the driver became William.

William stopped the car and was quickly out of it. Bringing a genuine smile, offering his right hand, glad to see Grady.

Grady kept his right hand to himself.

William's smile vanished. "What's wrong?"

"You fuck!"

"What's the matter with you? What the hell are you doing here? I didn't expect—"

Grady clutched William's shirt front with both hands, drove

him against the trunk of a nearby tree, hard. "You set me up, you
son of a bitch."

William allowed the manhandling. "What are you talking about?"

Grady jerked William away from the tree trunk so that he could
again slam him against it.

That really hurt. William had had enough. He brought his
hands up through Grady's hold, breaking it. Within the same
motion he got Grady by the arm, twisted it in such a way that the
rest of Grady had to go with the twist.

Grady was surprised to be in the air, surprised when he landed
in a front-down sprawl on the damp grass. Dazed by the impact,
he managed to get up on all fours. With an efficient side kick,
William swept away the support of Grady's arms, dropped Grady
and rolled him over. Next thing Grady knew William was above
him, had his right arm straight up and rigidly locked, just short of
causing severe pain and damage. Also, William had a knee pressed
into Grady's neck with some weight and threatening more. Grady
thought of trying to break the hold, but his immediate second
thought was he'd be better off just lying there.

"Now," William said, "what's your problem?"

Grady related, with as little breath as he was being allowed, the
run-in he'd had on the river, how it had caused him to lose the
rubies. He didn't repeat the accusation that William had been
behind it because, now, as the account of it came out, that
reasoning deserted him. He tried to convey that with his eyes, and
when, after a deciding moment, William smiled a little, Grady
knew he was going to be let off without having to apologize
outright. William released him and he got up. They walked over
to the Porsche and leaned against the driver's side.

"What made you think I had something to do with it?" William
asked.

"I ran down the possibilities and you came to the top."

"That's insulting. I should have broken your arm."

"Someone set me up, someone at your factory maybe, one of
your cutters."

William doubted that. "Finished goods leave my place practically every day, so why hasn't it happened before?"

Grady thought it probably had, said so.

"It would have gotten back to me," William contended. "Sure, people sometimes get harrassed on the river, but not hijacked. In my opinion what you were up against was a couple of free-lance bullies, *farang* assholes out for the pleasure of scaring."

"Scaring shit, they killed the water taxi guy, point-blank killed him. And they took at least fifty shots at Julia and me."

"They might have been on drugs."

"The universal excuse."

"What makes you so sure those guys even knew you had the rubies? Did they say or do anything to indicate that?"

"Not really."

"The fact is they didn't jump aboard the taxi or even try."

"No."

"And, bottom line, they didn't steal the stones, *you* lost them."

That was true, that bottom line, Grady admitted to himself. He'd been in need of someone to blame other than himself. His inward-aimed anger had turned and burst out and in its place now was regret and embarrassment. "Christ, you threw me ten feet like I was a featherweight. I should know better than to mess with a puny Oriental."

"Half Oriental, or I could have thrown you twenty. I'm sorry about your suit."

Grady took stock of it. The cream linen was badly grass stained at the knees and elbows. "How'll I explain? Think they'll believe I tripped over a sprinkler?"

"Looks more like you've tripped between some hot Thai girl's legs."

"Does, doesn't it?" Grady smirked.

"I phoned your hotel and was told you'd checked out. I thought you'd left for San Francisco. Is Julia here with you?"

"We're houseguests. Do you know Kumura?"

"By reputation, of course. What business he and I have done in the past has been through one of his middlemen. This time he was in too much of a rush to be bothered with that sort of arrangement, so I volunteered personally to make delivery. In return he insisted I stay over, at the very least for dinner."

"Oh, so you're the sixth I've been wondering about. Great! C'mon, help me find an aloe vera."

CHAPTER EIGHTEEN

The table was brought out and placed in the inner courtyard, and because of the antique pavers there, the unevenness of them, the servants had to place wedges beneath the legs to make it steady.

That was always a problem when Lesage decided the inner courtyard was where he wanted dinner served. It took two servants over an hour to get the table so it didn't wobble, and while they were at it they risked mumbling how unreasonable it was that Lesage hadn't chosen elsewhere for dinner, such as the smooth-surfaced loggia or the balcony outside his second-floor study, two places he more occasionally favored.

It wasn't that Lesage didn't have a proper dining room and a fine mahogany table that could seat fourteen roomily and eighteen with only cozy squeezing. In fact, the dining room was where he'd usually eaten with or without guests—before Paulette came upon his scene to suggest he be not so conforming in that regard and, as well, in numerous other ways. "Give in to whim," Paulette advised, "you'll be surprised what you can get away with and the *puissance* you'll feel."

This night was a good example of how much to heart Lesage had taken Paulette's advice. He couldn't have been more vague about what time dinner would be, simply because he wasn't of a mind to be precise. "Possibly around nine or perhaps later" was what he'd told his majordomo. He'd also expressed his preference of which silver service he wanted used, then changed his mind from the Christofle to the Puiforcat to the Buccellati, and the crystal from the Baccarat *Harcourt* to the Saint Louis to the Waterford, merely to give his prerogative a little exercise.

Now it was ten-thirty. The table was set and the three Thai servants who would do the immediate attending had been standing by, practically stock still, since eight. Their lower legs were burning and they were close to giving in to a relieving few minutes of sitting on the edge of the courtyard fountain. They'd tried chants and meditations and appeals to various good-natured spirits. They'd even tried willing desensitization of their bodies from the hips down by disregarding all else but the music that was emanating from the house—alternate five-minute, transition-free segments of Debussy and Reba McEntire.

One reason for the late dinner was that Lesage had had a substantial cheese and charcuterie snack around six o'clock, and his appetite was only now approaching the outskirts of hunger. Also, he was getting more enjoyment than usual out of showing what he owned.

The evening had started at nine in the salon with a decreed choice of cocktails. Scotches and sodas and vodkas on the rocks and such were disallowed. More *divertissant* to begin with sidecars, daiquiris, Lesage said, and recommended the martinis, which he personally concocted, calling attention to the dribble of cognac that went first into the glass and was swirled therein vigorously so it coated the inside before the pouring. He insisted Grady and Julia sip a taste, awaited their approval. Grady, out of spite, nearly scrunched his face and declared it tasted god-awful. But it didn't and he didn't and Lesage martinis (as Lesage called them) were what he and Julia chose to have.

As for Lesage's house, Julia's blasé response earlier on when Grady had asked about it had been way off. The house was every square foot prime Mizner, exquisitely detailed with difficult graceful arches, groin-vaulted ceilings and other features. It was a good

third again the size of Kumura's house and more intensely decorated. Not with a mere introduction of elegance here and there,
rather a crowding of it throughout, many things competing for
admiration. Who, for instance, could decide that Regency console
over there was less deserving than the pair of Meissen yellowground
chinoiserie vases placed on its *brèche d'alep* marble top, or more to
be appreciated than the Louis Quinze ormolu two-light *bras de
lumière* that were flanking a George II giltwood mirror? Were not
that pair of Gaillard tabourets worthy of four hundred dollar a
yard silk? And in the same seating area, the two matching *fauteuils
à la reine* miraculously rescued with petit point upholstery intact
from the ravages of the revolution.

"Those *fauteuils* are signed Jean Avisse, 1745," Lesage mentioned,
just mentioned as though it might, just might be of some interest.
Years ago, before Paulette, he'd crowed those same words.

Kumura lingered in the salon while Lesage nonchalantly guided
Grady, Julia and William through the ground floor areas. Lesage
was particularly *dégagé* when they were in the gallery. With the
merest lift of his well-bred chin or with a single slight flourish of
his peasantlike hands he presented the paintings he was most
proud of, making remarks he'd practiced and had down pat by
now. "That's a fair enough Degas" and "Tissot always painted
women seated, didn't he?" and "I'm a bit taken by Boldini, as you
can gather" and then a contemplative gaze at a Fantin-Latour still
life of nasturtiums before remarking as though alone, "I'm not
altogether sure of this one now that I've had it hanging for three
months. I might replace it with a fine Bouguereau or a Draper.
I'm becoming partial to fin de siècle. Are you familiar with
Herbert Draper?"

Grady deferred to Julia who deferred to William so no one
replied. What shit, Grady thought and believed Julia was probably
reading his mind and agreeing from the way she sneaked him a
wink.

Lesage proceeded down the long gallery, passing a couple of
lovely Boldinis and a Matisse without so much as a glance. He
didn't pause or suggest that everyone go out and be seated at the
dinner table, just continued at his meandering pace out the french
doors that gave to the courtyard, assuming they'd all follow.

Which they did and were made to stand around a long moment

while Lesage decided on the seating arrangement. He chose to have Julia on his right next to William next to Kumura next to Paulette next to Grady, thus putting the latter on his left. As they were about to be seated Paulette asked William if he'd mind exchanging places with her. William did mind, preferred being next to Julia but he could hardly refuse. Paulette offered no reason for wanting the exchange and Lesage suddenly let it be known he couldn't care less where anyone sat. *"Commencez!"* he impatiently ordered the overseeing majordomo.

The table was round so it had no head, but there was no doubt, however, who was presiding. Throughout the hors d'oeuvre (a *fois gras en terrine*) it was Lesage who began and terminated the topics of conversation.

At one point a contribution by Julia happened to contain the word *cathedral*.

Paulette jumped right on that, submitted that she and Lesage had first met at a cathedral in Senlis. Everyone, of course, was familiar with the town of Senlis, in Oise, thirty miles north of Paris.

"Oh, that Senlis," Grady remarked wryly.

Paulette went right on like a *Guide Michelin* informing that at one time besides the cathedral there were three other churches in Senlis, so many because of the abundance of good hard stone available nearby. But now the three other churches, despite their religious structure, were a market, a cinema and a garage. Their crypts had become furniture shops. Come to think of it, Paulette said, it hadn't been in the cathedral that she'd first met Daniel, rather in the church now a market. He, so outstanding, too distinguished-looking for the place, buying four bunches of white breakfast radishes because, as he told her later when they were seated in his Rolls chomping and chatting, he'd suddenly had a craving for fresh radishes on his drive back to Paris from Deauville. She'd suggested then that the craving had been divinely instigated. She still thought so, she said.

Where, Julia thought, would be the next place they supposedly met? This Senlis version was the fourth she'd heard from Paulette. Initially there'd been the one at 165 miles per hour. Then, divulged in spectacular detail, it had been in the warm conducive mud of Montecatini. Followed by the hot, chance encounter during the Royal Club Gold Tournament at Evian-les-Bains. And now radishes. Was the marquise a diagnosable dingbat? Julia wondered. Or was it only that she found it amusing to create contradictions and quandary? Considering it through the lace of three martinis on an empty stomach, Julia gave Paulette the benefit of the doubt, decided the obvious fibs were intentionally obvious, indicative of Paulette's vagarious spirit, one of her ways of combating ennui. Choose what you prefer to believe, not everything I tell you, was Paulette's caution. Not bad.

Julia stole a glance at her. Got caught, but exonerated herself with a neutral smile. Paulette retaliated with a conspiratorial one. Julia took notice again of Paulette's left hand. A ring on each finger and, as well, the thumb. "Poor is not being able to afford an affectation," Paulette had said that afternoon. The stones of the rings were all precious and large. Adjuncts to the claws, Julia thought, like the spurs of a rooster.

Throughout the first course (a cold, creamy potage crécy stylishly served to each place in an individual Limoges tureen) the conversation lagged and raced, hopped and limped along. The factions had no mutual acquaintances to discuss, so for ammunition they resorted to famous persons, motion picture stars, politicians and the like. Those were good for a quarter hour. Then it was on with a stumble to the greenhouse effect, life on other planets, the population explosion, fur coats versus live animals, Lesage's account of a perilous Viet Nam war experience (embellished greatly since it was first told, and by now, for Paulette and more so for Kumura, a stale story they both tried to interrupt and sidetrack).

William's participation in the table talk was sparse. He didn't initiate any subject, limited himself to concurring phrases.

Kumura provided fuel every so often but didn't pour it on.

Grady, who'd also had three martinis and was two goblets into the wine, thought of a lot of comments he wanted to slip in, but kept most of them, especially those that were too sharp or acidic, to himself. He couldn't hold back, however, when Lesage boasted how one of his gardeners had clipped a yew into the likeness of a dog.

"What kind of dog?" Grady asked.

"Just a dog."

"A regular dog is easy. Have him do a breed."

"Yeah, a Shar Pei," Julia put in.

Lesage thought he should laugh, so he did. He cut the laugh abruptly, as though a portcullis in his throat had just dropped, and went back to sliding small bits of his portion of the *gigot farci*. He ate overproperly, held his knife as if it were a delicate tool, cut with just the tip of it and never stabbed with his fork, used the back of its tines for transport.

"I understand you're an artist," he said to Julia, not bringing his eyes to her until the statement was out.

"I paint," she said plainly.

"Like whom do you paint?" Lesage asked, and inasmuch as he'd planned the point didn't wait for her reply. "American painters are blatant derivers, not an original brushstroke ever. Except, of course there's Andrew Warhol and his piss paintings."

Lesage allowed the invisible question mark to form.

"For those of you who aren't familiar with the achievement, what Warhol did was coat canvases with metallic copper paint and have just about anyone who happened into his studio relieve her or his bladder on them. The copper oxidized where it was splattered, creating a green, black and orange pattern. Quite a few American critics, including some quite notable, had praise for these canvases, said they had significant meaning and merit. Others went so far as to propose they expressed an affinity to the staking out of territory by animals."

"In my opinion they were remarkably alchemical," Julia said for spite.

Grady read her eyes and thought Lesage should fear for his life.

The conversation again sputtered.

Which gave Lesage the opening to soliloquize on his knowledge of oysters. Not the pearl-producing kind (species ostreidae) but those for eating (aviculidae). He expounded on the Belons and the Portuguese varieties, the young *claires* compared to the *fines de claires* compared to the plumper, more preferred older *spéciales*. He explained, as though he were tutoring, how the French dealers classified from triple zeros and double zeros (rarest and best) to the less desirable single zeros and ones and twos and finally the small, cheapest threes. Lesage claimed a three had never passed his lips, never would.

From oysters the topic had only to shift slightly to be pearls and all at once a rich, conversational vein had been tapped with everyone taking a share.

"Cultured pearls weren't allowed to be sold as pearls."

"They had to be called beads, didn't they?"

"According to international law."

"Until the crash in 1930."

"Before then the only pearls considered to be pearls were naturals."

"Think of all the naturals there were back in those days."

"Tons."

"And now it's said there might not be more than four or five truly gem-quality natural pearl necklaces in existence."

"That's hard to believe."

"Doesn't seem possible."

"What about all those long strands of pearls women wore in the twenties? I believe Chanel made them fashionable. Women used to twirl them and tie them different ways."

"They weren't naturals."

"So officially they weren't pearls, is that it?"

"Fuck the distinction." From Lesage.

"Dear, the distinction has been fucked." From Paulette.

"Fortunately." From Kumura.

"What happened to all the naturals, I wonder? The regular rich and the royal rich had so many."

"They got stashed away."

"Or mistreated."

"Both. Reminds me of something that's said to have happened in the seventeen hundreds. A maharaja of somewhere, his name escapes me at the moment, possessed a huge fortune in pearls, kept them hidden away in a large cask. When he died his son claimed the hoard, opened the cask and found only peels of nacre and pearl dust."

"The pearls had also died."

"They do, you know, dry up and die unless they get attention."

"Pearls and people." From Paulette.

Grady was now in a more comfortable element, sure that he could hold his own when it came to pearl trivia. For him the evening had now turned enjoyable. "Roman women wore pearls to bed to sweeten their dreams," he said.

"Caligula had his boots encrusted with them."

"And the trappings of his horse, as well."

"Mary, Queen of Scots, owned a great many remarkable pearls, loose and in strands."

"They went when her head did, I suppose."

"Queen Elizabeth got the most and best of them. According to Walpole, Elizabeth wore a mass of pearls in her hair, on her ruff and on a huge fardingale."

"What the hell's a ruff?"

"I know what it sounds like it might be." From Paulette with a wicked smirk.

"A huge fardingale, you say?"

Laughs, a league of laughs.

"In ancient times..."

"How ancient?"

"Ancient ancient. It was believed that pearls grew in the brains of dragons."

"The Japanese tell of a pearl with so much luster that its glow was visible three miles away." That from Julia.

Grady assumed that tidbit was something she'd read and just now was prompted to recall. Or else she'd made it up. What amused him was the wide-eyed, serious-faced way she'd said it.

"I've seen some remarkable pearls in my day." That from William. No one asked him to elaborate and his statement was lost as the verbal sallying continued.

"Cleopatra..." Lesage began.

"Oh Christ, don't pull out that old stale story. Everyone's heard it."

"I haven't," Julia said.

"I'll make it short," Lesage promised and began. "Cleopatra, during the height of her passionate days with Mark Anthony, wagered with him that she could serve him a dinner so expensive it would never be equaled. Indeed, the meal she served was sumptuous, however Mark Anthony found nothing so expensive about it. He thought he'd won the wager, until Cleopatra removed one of her pearl earrings and dropped it into her goblet of wine, where it quickly dissolved, and she had Mark Anthony drink it down. That pearl—"

"Was worth a lot of drachmas."

"Ten millions dollars today." From William.

"You fucked me out of the punch line!" Lesage complained loudly. He was really irked at William, looked at Julia, his lone audience, for support.

She wasn't about to be that generous.

"That never happened, that Cleopatra pearl-in-the-wine business," Grady contended. "It's just a romantic myth."

"What makes you say that?"

"Because pearls don't dissolve in wine," Grady replied. "Except in the movies. In the movies they drop a pearl into the wine and right away the wine starts bubbling to dramatize that the pearl's dissolving."

Kumura agreed.

Lesage challenged. He resented having his story debunked.

"I'll prove it," Grady said. He brought out the sixteen-millimeter pearl Kumura had given him that afternoon. With a little showmanship he dropped the pearl into his goblet of wine, and waited. "See, no bubbles," he said. He brought the goblet to his lips and drained it, peered into the goblet and did a perplexed take. "No pearl!" he exclaimed convincingly, and when Julia laughed rather unsurely he pursed his lips and allowed the pearl to appear.

"Such talent," Paulette remarked cynically.

"However," Grady admitted, "I do believe the old, true accounts are best. The shark charmers, for instance."

"Shark charmers?"

Kumura knew of the shark charmers, but didn't let on, allowed Grady a total audience.

"The pearl divers who took part in the great pearl fishing seasons in the Gulf of Manaar in 1905 and 1906 were—"

"When did you say?" From Julia with keen interest.

Grady repeated the years and went on. "The divers were a superstitious bunch. Easy pickings for certain individuals who exaggerated a mystical demeanor and claimed to be able to provide protection against attacks by sharks. Naturally, some ritual was involved. The so-called shark charmer was locked in a windowless room and would remain there throughout the day while the divers were out in the gulf working the bottom. The only things in the room with the shark charmer were a brass basin of sea water in which there were two miniature replicas of fish made of silver, supposedly a male and a female. The charmer's job was to prevent the silver fish from attacking each other. If during the day none of the divers suffered a shark bite the mystical power of the charmer was the reason. If, on the other hand, a shark bite had occurred, the charmer had any number of excuses to fall back on, that someone had doubted his power, for example, or he was dissatisfied with the pearls with which he was being compensated. For his services the charmer received a twentieth of each day's catch."

"Interesting if true," Lesage commented.

"It's true," Julia asserted firmly.

"*Oui*," Paulette put in, "I've known quite a few such charmers."

Lesage took silent exception to her remark.

Kumura was about to contribute the old belief that pearls represented the tears of unhappiness that would be shed in married life—when Julia beat him to it. "I'll tell one," Julia said and went right on to relate how at one time in Borneo it was believed by the pearl divers that if every ninth pearl found was placed in a bottle along with an equal number of grains of rice the pearls would breed, multiply. The bottle had to be corked with the finger of a dead person. "Practically every house had such a bottle," Julia said.

"How macabre," Paulette thought aloud.

What was it with Julia? Grady wondered. Was she making things up for the hell of it? He'd heard various Borneo anecdotes but never that finger stopper one. It was farfetched. The thing of it was how earnestly Julia had put it across, as though she knew of it firsthand.

"Pearl divers are ignorant, always have been. Otherwise they wouldn't do what they do." That from Lesage.

Julia glowered at him.

"Their exploits have been greatly exaggerated," Kumura said. "For example, I've read sworn, recorded accounts of divers in the Society Islands who've gone down thirty fathoms and stayed under—ten minutes."

"When was that?"

"A hundred years ago."

"Anyone could go down thirty fathoms and stay under...forever," Grady quipped.

"How deep is thirty fathoms?" Paulette asked.

"About a hundred and eighty feet."

"Without diving gear?"

"Just a mask."

"Impossible."

"The best divers are the Japanese amas."

"Think so?" Julia challenged.

"I know so," Lesage told her.

"Then it's true." Julia did a sweet smile. "In fact everything you say is true."

At that moment beneath the table Paulette's hand reached and found Julia's hand. Enclosed upon it and held it captured for a while and then, as though it were an object without a will, brought it to herself and placed it just so, palm down on the bare skin of her inner thigh.

Julia's immediate reaction, even to just the hand holding, was to jerk her hand away, and she would have, however she was undergoing the same loss of control she'd experienced in the river when it had been impossible for her to reach out for the pouch containing the rubies. Again her arm and her hand wouldn't mind her.

She didn't panic. Mainly because this paralytic sensation had occurred before and she wanted to understand it. It seemed her hand and arm were separate from the rest of her. As though they were being persuaded to misbehave, not heed. The persuasion spread to her shoulder and neck and within her head, and she no longer considered that her hand and its fingers, kneading gently as they were, stroking and skimming, upward and downward lightly, were performing against her will. Rather, something told her what they were doing would be beneficial.

Lesage stood suddenly, causing the legs of the table to slip from the wedges and wobble drastically. "We'll have coffee and whatever else you might want up in my study," he said, turned and walked into the house before the others had a chance to rise.

CHAPTER NINETEEN

Lesage's second-floor study was a huge high-ceilinged room with a series of tall french doors leading out to a balcony. It was paneled in antique walnut boiserie. One entire wall was inset with bookcases that held so many leather-bound volumes they looked painfully squeezed. On the surface of the lower shelves was an array of precious little *objets*: lots of shagreen-covered things, boxes, clocks and such, a collection of gold and jewel-embellished ladies' compacts, a premeditated scatter of ancient Greek coins, a few of a hundred litrae showing Herakles slaying a Numean lion.

The *bureau plat* that Lesage now called his desk had originally belonged to someone within personal range of Louis Quinze. Among the things on it was a Sèvres spyglass provenanced to Madame de Pompadour and a silver-framed enlarged snapshot of Lesage and Paulette. Paulette immediately drew attention to it, as though she'd not seen it prior to now.

"That was taken the afternoon Daniel and I met at Lake Como. We were both staying at the Villa d'Este. The Count and Countess Del Vecchio and I needed a fourth for bridge and Daniel obliged."

Julia shrugged and plopped down into one of the plump cushioned sofas. There were three such sofas. Grady sank in next to her.

Coffee was served from a silver pot created by Paul de Lamerie. Cigars were offered from a Buccellati humidor. The cigars were Flor de F. Farach Extras, true Havanas. Grady and William declined the smokes. Paulette took one from the humidor, held it beneath her nose, whiffed it and replaced it. "I prefer them unlit," she said. Lesage bit the puffing tip off one and lighted up. He motioned Kumura to sit behind the desk, and Kumura settled in the antelope skin-covered *bergère* that Lesage's rump had broken in.

Grady gulped the coffee. It was French brewed, extremely strong and nearly viscous. Made the hairs on the back of his neck bristle. He'd have a problem sitting still if he drank more, maybe even get to grinding his teeth. What the hell . . . he held his cup up for a refill.

"Grady," Kumura said loud enough to get everyone's attention. "From what I understand you have a unique ability."

"Such as?"

"I'm told you're one of the few people able to distinguish a natural pearl from a cultured one without technical means."

Grady had reached the assumption the job offer was the reason Kumura had gone to the trouble of looking into him, his background. But it seemed unreasonable that Kumura had dug this deep. He told Kumura, "At times I can tell the difference."

"Anyone could half the time," Lesage contended. "That's just in keeping with the laws of chance."

"I usually do better than that," Grady said. "How about most of the time?"

A dubious scoff from Lesage. "What's most of the time, eighty, ninety percent, what?'

Grady felt like whacking him one. One shot in the gut, a hard right. He did pop him, with his eyes.

Kumura brought out a pearl from his right jacket pocket. Another from his left. He placed them well apart on the surface of the desk.

The pearls were blue. Didn't have merely a bluish cast, they were a vivid blue. Like blue sapphires but with pearl qualities, luster and iridescence. They appeared to be perfectly round, identical in that respect, and of equal size, slightly larger than a child's play marble, about three-quarters of an inch in diameter.

William sat forward to take them in. His eyes stayed fixed on them. No telling what his thoughts were.

Grady felt Julia stiffen and heard her breath catch. She laced her fingers and confined her hands between her knees.

Lesage was indifferent, Paulette just as much so. She was pouring herself a cognac.

"One of these pearls is a natural," Kumura explained to Grady. "The other is a cultured pearl that's been dyed. Can you tell me which is which?"

Grady got up and went to the desk. An afterdinner game, he thought. Kumura was trying to trick him. Both the pearls had to be dyed. There'd never been a natural pearl that size, about eighteen millimeters, Grady estimated, and that blue. If so, it would be worth a fortune. Several million, at least, more probably, depending upon what someone would pay for it. Should he purposely allow himself to be tricked, or show how smart he was? He recalled having told Julia just last week at Reese's when she'd asked for real blue pearls that there was no such thing. "Am I allowed to handle them?" he asked Kumura.

"Of course, but please don't get them mixed up,'" Kumura replied. "I don't happen to have your gift."

Grady took up one of the pearls, enclosed it in his fist. Then the other in his other fist. He didn't close his eyes or roll them back and do anything that might be taken as a trance. Merely concentrated on the spheres in his hands, first one, then the other, and then both simultaneously. Focusing on both at the same time was difficult. His concentration kept veering left or right. The pearl in his right seemed to be talking to him more, claiming it was the natural. It was his imagination probably, but didn't it seem to be throbbing, insistently trying to convince him. It was in on Kumura's trick, of course, Grady thought. He was sure neither pearl was a natural, but if they hadn't been so large and especially so intensely blue, he would have chosen the one in his left because it felt so placid and pure. "Is it all right if I loupe them?" he asked.

"By all means do," Kumura replied and provided a loupe from out of Lesage's desk drawer.

Grady first examined the blue pearl from his left hand. Held it up and saw with ten-power magnification how flawless was its complexion. Its luster was deepened by its body color. He rolled it slowly between his thumb and second finger, examined it all around. It was consistently fine. He did the same with the other blue pearl, the one he'd had in his right hand, the noisy one, as he thought of it. It appeared equally lustrous and symmetrical and free of any sort of blemish. Only one thing about it that caught Grady's eye. One tiny thing. A minuscule speck on its surface that differed ever so subtly from its overall color, just a little darker.

Grady let his imagination run free with that speck. It was where the pearl had been drilled, he thought, with an extremely fine-gauge drill, like a needle. So that it could be dyed. So the dye could get to and permeate all the layers of nacre outside and in. The pearl had been soaked in a beaker containing a blue medicinal dye for as long as it took to attain this color. Then the drill hole was filled in with a compound of pearl dust and cement, then polished. It was a careful, neat job, intended to deceive. Grady had his exceptional gem dealer's eyes to thank for discerning it and providing him with an opinion. Or was it an opinion as much as it was a hunch? He still leaned toward the more likely possibility that both pearls were cultured and dyed. He should say that to Kumura, let Kumura know how sharp he was.

Instead, he placed the pearl he'd had in his left hand on the desk in front of Kumura and told him, "That's the natural."

Kumura waited a long beat before calmly saying, "Right you are. Amazing."

Julia beamed proudly and mentally applauded Grady's rather mystical demonstration. Unnoticed was the flare of malevolence in her eyes as her gaze fixed upon the natural blue pearl.

William, meanwhile, managed a slight smile, contrary to the serious set of his expression and the solemn sorting of possibilities that the verified natural blue had suddenly brought about in him.

"Bravo!" was Paulette's momentarily amused reaction.

No comment from Lesage. Having been relegated to the perimeter of attention, he tried to regain the center by attempting to peel an orange in one continuous coil. It was a performance he'd practiced much and normally succeeded at. However, this time distraction caused him to pare too thin, the peel was severed and the blade of his penknife sliced his thumb nearly deep enough to show blood.

Grady nonchalanted, gave little to his ability to discern natural from cultured. In this instance he believed he'd been clever and lucky more than anything.

A pot of fresh coffee arrived and a dish of chocolate truffles. Also some curly cookies that Lesage enjoyed telling everyone were called *langues des chats*, cats' tongues.

Kumura came over and sat on the sofa next to Grady and Julia. Julia flirted with him a little, fed him nibbles of her cookie. Grady told him, "I was meaning to ask, before, when we were talking about pearl divers, have you ever personally met an ama?"

Kumura said he had, many. "They're not as plentiful, though, as they once were," he said. "Last number I seem to recall there were seven thousand still active. They gather each year at the shrine on Ise Peninsula. It's quite a sight to see them diving all at once, all those heads bobbing in the swells."

"I've read a lot about them," Grady said, "the way they dive and all. I find it fascinating."

"Have you ever been to Hegurajima?"

"That's where William is from," Julia informed. "He has family there."

"Really?"

"Really," William confirmed. All eyes were on him.

"Ama tradition is still very much alive up there, isn't it, William?" Kumura said. "Most of today's amas have resorted to wearing modern equipment, scuba gear and all that, but there are those who refuse to give in to it and dive the old way. That's especially so of the amas on Hegurajima. It's a remote place, one of the lesser spoiled. Worth a visit."

That pleased Julia for some reason. She rewarded Kumura with a truffle, had him open his mouth wide for her to pop it in.

"I enjoy diving," Grady remarked.

"Are you experienced?" Kumura asked.

"It's not something I do every week. In fact, it's been too long since I last dove. I spent a whole month once exploring the reefs off the Dominican Republic. Came across signs of an old wreck and caught the treasure bug. I'm sure that wreck had been worked over before, plenty. All I found was a pair of leg irons, you know, shackles. No matter, it was one of the best months of my life."

"Rather than swim around some old sunken ship that's been gleaned by every other diver in the world, I think it would be much more rewarding to go for pearls," Julia said ingenuously.

"Fat chance," Grady told her. "Finding a pearl oyster on its own would be a long, long shot, much less one containing a pearl."

"You've looked I suppose," Julia defied.

Kumura interceded. "He's right, to a point. The waters near here were pearled out years ago. That's not to say you wouldn't find a few strays here and there but the prospect of a crowded bed is highly unlikely. The same might be said of the area north of here. But in Burma waters I believe one would have better luck."

"Why?"

"Only because Burma's been so self-isolated and the government hostile. Burma may not make the most of its riches but it surely doesn't want any outsider taking advantage."

Grady imagined what it would be like, diving for pearls, finding one, even just one. It was an old dream he'd given up on. "What a kick it would be," he thought aloud.

"Yeah." Julia fueled his notion.

"Even if for no other reason than to be able honestly to say you'd done it," Grady said.

"That's the right attitude."

"It is, isn't it?"

"You feel that strongly about it you ought to do it."

Grady shook it off. "It'll never happen."

"It could if you wanted it to," Kumura said. "The Andaman Sea is right out there. My new ketch could use a shakedown. How good a sailor are you?"

"Fair enough."

"That Hinckley practically sails itself."

Grady turned it over in his mind, told Kumura, "Thanks, anyway."

"Some guys only talk adventure," Lesage remarked.

Grady ignored that. Christ, he thought, this is getting to be a thing actually to do. Now did he really want to?

A nudge from Kumura. "What have you got to lose?"

"The better question is what's there to find," Julia said optimistically. "Me, I'm all for going."

Grady looked to William, who was seated on the sofa opposite. "Not me," William said. "I'm not much of a swimmer."

"Thought you said you were," Julia said with a sly admonitory tone. "From what I understood it was your mother who wasn't the swimmer."

"Anyway," Grady said, "we don't have any scuba gear."

"Lame excuse," Lesage goaded.

Fuck you, Grady thought. His more lenient self told him some underwater peace would do him a world of good. Hadn't he been longing for it? He'd consider it a holiday, time off, time out. It wouldn't matter whether or not he even saw an oyster. Besides, why should he deny Kumura the pleasure of being generous? His future boss, maybe.

He looked to Julia. They'd make love on deck at night. They wouldn't necessarily limit it to night. He could practically taste the salt on her skin.

Julia seemed to know his thoughts, there was wickedness in her eyes. "Let's," she whispered.

That settled that.

Kumura was pleased.

For some reason so was Lesage.

Paulette and Julia left the study, ostensibly to make feminine repairs.

William was up and pretending his attention was on the contents of the bookcase, removing volumes at random, opening them to any page, not actually scanning the printed words. He was agitated, feeling the need to be apart from the others in order to put his mind straight.

The sight of those blue pearls had set him off. Like a switch in his head had been thrown, causing an arc of a long-contained current. Now he was charged with it, his eyes possibly sending out electrical sparks, bolts coming from his fingertips as he snapped shut Proust's *Remembrance of Things Past* and replaced it in the vacancy he'd caused. He closed his eyes, shoved his hands in his trouser pockets and shifted his weight so it was the responsibility of both his legs.

He left the books, moved on to the adjacent wall where a portrait of an eighteenth-century gentleman was hung. Lesage had claimed the man was a forebear on his mother's side. Well-done portrait, well-off gentleman, vague resemblance to Lesage. It struck William that the location of the portrait was strategic, acting as visual prologue to the good-size niche that was next, an architectural intention, not an afterthought, meant for no other reason than to contain Lesage's most personal and defining keepsakes. Shrinelike.

Hung on the walls of the niche were numerous well-framed and neatly matted watercolor sketches by Alexander Sauerweid. Of Napoleonic soldiers slain and alive with sabers, carbines, horses. They set the military ambiance for the photographs situated among them, snapshots turned sepia, others a better quality, professionally taken, all captioned in typeset.

Of young Lesage as a cadet at Saint Cyr in full dress, plumed casoard and all.

Of young Lesage and several fellow cadets out on a good time.

Of young Lesage in his Saint Cyr days behind a machine gun during field maneuvers at Coetquidau.

Of Lesage as a *sous lieutenant* wearing the *képi blanc* of the Foreign Legion.

Of an older Lesage as a *subalterne*, a *capitaine* standing with his company.

Another of those in paratroop gear.

A rack of happy-hued medals encased in a glass frame, including the Légion d'Honneur.

The framed colors of the Thirteenth DBLE (*Demi-Brigade de la Légion Étrangère*), a cap badge of the same.

An elaborate saber.

Numerous letters of commendation, citations.

Lesage's honorable discharge from the Legion.

There were many more, but it was at that point William came across the knife.

Knife like no other.

Kept under glass in a boxlike frame.

Knife with a curved blade, striations visible along its cutting edge from having so many times been honed.

Burmese knife with a carved whalebone handle...

...bearing the inscription *Buddha is generous*.

CHAPTER TWENTY

The man now known and credibly documented as Daniel Lesage was born at the Château de Montal near the village of La Chaise-Dieux in the Haute Loire. Not within the château itself; that would never have been permitted. Even had his mother, Claire, become overcome with labor pains during her duties and unable to move on her own from the laundry room, she still would have been carried out to her room at the rear of the barn.

The man now known as Lesage had been an unintended child, and later on in his life he'd not be able to recall a moment when he wasn't aware of being unwanted. A mere week after his birth, although Claire hadn't healed enough nor regained all her strength, she made off with a local vineyard worker who'd been waiting four months for her to become unburdened. Her departure wasn't unexpected by Gilbert, the father, inasmuch as Claire had always had an exaggerated opinion of herself, her looks, and had never believed mirrors. She'd loathed being a laundress and said that her hands were red and sore in protest of the low tasks demanded of them, the scrubbing and bleaching of bed linens to remove the stains of monthly blood and nightly coitus.

So, she was that soon gone, leaving the father with the responsibilities, including the naming of the child. He settled on Leon-Charles and saw that it was legally recorded on a certificate of birth.

Leon-Charles Bertin.

Gilbert Bertin, the father, had been employed at the château for ten years and hoped to continue on. He had no specific duties, was expected to do whatever might be necessary around the place, from light work such as unstopping a toilet to such heavy work as extracting a tree trunk. For impression the owners of the château, Monsieur and Madame Rocard, sometimes referred to Gilbert Bertin as their caretaker. Ordinarily he was only the oafish hulk of a man who was convenient to have around. His most appreciated virtues were he kept to himself, said little and was satisfied with a wage less than would need to be paid to someone else.

Thus, the boy Bertin grew up in the shadow of the thirty-room eighteenth-century château. He wasn't permitted inside and there were strict limitations on where he could set foot on the grounds. The gardens were especially off limits to him and so were the orchards and arbors. The barnyard, the animal pens and the thickly wooded acreage beyond the barns were his domain.

As a small boy he accepted these territorial decrees, abided by them. It wasn't until he'd added years and growth that he began stealing peeks through the ground floor windows of the château, ducking down in the shrubbery and cautiously popping up to have a look in. The comforts and luxuries he saw inside made him question why he should be grateful and resigned to his meager lot, excluded.

Being on the outside looking in became more and more unbearable for Leon-Charles. As he grew, so did his rancor. It got so he could think of little else other than his getting back at these dictatorial people and the imposed confines of this place. He'd certainly have his way and leave when the time and circumstances were right.

As it so happened they were on that Saturday during the same month as his fifteenth birthday. Monsieur and Madame Rocard were away on an extended holiday in Antibes; the servants had been given time off. Leon-Charles broke into the house, helped himself to it. In the pantry he took a bite straight from an intact wedge of Cantal. In the library he swigged very very superior cognac straight from a decanter.

Upstairs in the main bedroom he took off his shirt and trousers and flopped down on the Madame's *chaise de la reine*. Plump of cushions, slick of silk.

He lay there in the late afternoon light mimicking arrogance and languor. At dusk a strip of light across the Savonerie carpet caused him to realize that the Madame's dressing room door was ajar. He got up and went in. Obviously the Madame had dressed and departed in a rush. Not only had she left the light on, but also her silk nightgown and robe and high-heeled slippers were strewn about, her makeup and various little brushes were scattered on the surface of her vanity. A tissue she'd used to blot her lips had missed her wastebasket. The door to one of her closets had been left open, the closet where she kept her shoes and handbags, where she kept her Boule-worked jewelry case.

The case contained what the Madame called her better everyday jewelry. To Leon-Charles it was a treasure. His fingers got right into it: a straight-line emerald bracelet, a pink topaz and diamond crucifix, a Cartier tortue watch, a pendeloque aquamarine pendant, black opal ring, diamond double-clip brooch, diamond tremblant, gold bangles, various other rings. And more.

Leon-Charles grabbed out the valuables and placed them in the center of the Hermès scarf he'd spread on the floor. He was kneeling, gathering and knotting together the corners of the scarf, when Monsieur Rocard appeared in the dressing room doorway.

Caught! Stealing and naked.

Leon-Charles tried to charge past the Monsieur, however the Monsieur got ahold of his arm and flung him, sent him reeling over the chaise and down hard in a sprawl on the hearth of the marble fireplace.

The Monsieur was furious, rushed to press his advantage. He would have stopped in time and out of range if he could have, but his momentum carried him into the arc of the swing of the heavy metal fireplace poker on the end of Leon-Charles's arm. The poker caught the Monsieur on the side of the neck below his left ear. The impact took the Monsieur's legs out from under him, and he was on the way down, already unconscious when a second blow in nearly the same place killed him.

Only then did Leon-Charles realize the Madame was there in the room. She rushed for the door to get out. Leon-Charles got to it first.

There were no reasoning nor pleas from the Madame. She glared ascendantly at him, straight into his eyes, down at his nakedness.

He swung the poker.

The arm she put out to fend it off was fractured at the wrist. The blow was barely impeded. The force of it continued on, crushed her right hip.

The Madame went lopsided, was turned sideways, her head snapped back from the pain. To Leon-Charles it seemed from her position that her head was being offered. He brought the poker down full force upon her profile, across the bridge of her nose. Smashed her nasal spine and drove the nasal process and other encasing bone back into her brain.

She lay dead on the carpet. In a contorted position, legs apart, crotch exposed, white underpants visible.

Leon-Charles bolted the door. He arranged the Madame's legs so he could pull off her underwear. Saw that she was menstruating. Spread her legs enough, stroked himself to hardness and got between. He didn't try to pretend she wasn't dead. Even if she had been alive only his own sensations would have mattered.

He came almost at once. Used her dress to wipe her blood from his penis and testicles. Got dressed, gathered up the jewelry-laden scarf and went out. Took one of the cars from the garage, the blue Mercedes sedan. He'd driven it a few times up and down the private roads of the château, teaching himself. It had an automatic shift, was easy.

When he was past the point where the château's drive gave to the public road he felt he'd gotten away. He didn't look back, not even mentally. He followed the road signs to Le Puy and from Le Puy to Valence and then on down alongside the Rhone to where the car ran out of gas twenty miles from Marseilles.

He slept in the car, slept well, and early the next morning hitched a ride into the city. Found a likely looking jewelry shop on a side street off the Boulevard de Briancon and believed the fifteen hundred francs (three hundred dollars) the sober-faced lady there paid him for Madame Rocard's jewels was a fair price. After all, he'd never had more than ten francs in his pocket at any one time.

He bought a pair of better shoes, a football jersey. Hung around the streets, especially the Quai du Lazaret and the streets of the Port Moderne. Fascinated by the large ships, he tried to sign on one as a deckhand for a trip to anywhere. He was tall and hefty enough for his lie about his age to be believed. The reason he was turned down was he didn't have any papers, either personal or union, and no passport.

His money was soon down to thirty francs. He needed papers. Where could he go without papers?

A barman told him.

Leon-Charles went that same day to the recruiting office located at the Bas-Fort Saint Nicolas. The recruiting corporal didn't ask for any papers, just asked a lot of personal questions. Leon-Charles replied to all but a few with lies. His name, he said, was Raymond Sorel. He was eighteen. The corporal wasn't there to disbelieve. He issued Raymond Sorel a black two-piece track suit and had him sign a five-year contract. Raymond was taken by truck to Aubagne, the holding station, as a potential for the Légion Étrangère (Foreign Legion).

He was big enough, strong enough, mean enough. Week by week, the grading band on his arm went from yellow to green and, finally, to red. He was in. His *le paquetage* (uniforms and equipment) was issued. He was sent for training at Castelnaudary, located between Carcassone and Toulouse.

As an *engagé volontaire*, as the Legion calls them, he ordinarily would have undergone four months of training. However, due to the dire situation in Indochina, training was accelerated, cut to two months.

Raymond hated the service from the moment of his first salute. He kept that and all his complaints to himself, however, maintained the image that he had the makings of a good Legionnaire. Why the fuck should he care about tradition and the other shit they tried to stuff into his head?

In February 1954, on the Wednesday prior to the weekend that Raymond planned to desert, he was shipped out. One of the reinforcements for the Thirteenth DBLE (*Demi-Brigade de la Légion Étrangère*) in Dien Bien Phu.

War? He wanted no part of it. Fellow Legionnaires talked about the glory of dying and how outnumbered they were. Casualty figures were quoted as though they were something to boast about. Raymond felt neither his life nor his death was his own, blamed lousy circumstances for suckering him into this situation. He was assigned to a 120 millimeter mortar crew dug in on a strong point named "Beatrice."

The French garrison consisted of 11,000 men.

The Vietnamese under General Giap had three divisions of infantry and one artillery division, altogether about 50,000 men, and were supplied by 100,000 coolies.

It seemed to Raymond, when the attack began at five in the afternoon of March thirteenth, that all 50,000 enemy were coming at him. He wasn't hit, not a scratch. He pulled the twitching bodies of dead Legionnaires over him like a blanket. Their final defecations were suffocating, their blood soaked him. He didn't move, barely breathed. At nightfall the battle was still raging, but his position had been overrun. For the moment, at least, and merely by a fluke he'd been spared.

He crawled out from under, ripped off all his insignias, threw away his helmet. Thought how fortunate it was that he hadn't gotten tattooed with a regiment designation as so many of the other new guys had during the last leave. There was nothing on him to identify him as an enemy. Except, of course, his battle fatigues. He kept down, moved in a crouch, crawled, and finally reached the cover of some undergrowth. Came across a dead coolie, whose plain shirt and trousers were too small for him but were safer than his own battle fatigues. He was reluctant to give up his combat boots but knew they'd be a sure giveaway.

The impression he hoped for was that of just another French civilian with Vietnamese sympathies. Caught up in the war. He invented the details to substantiate that, new name and all, and made his way south, kept to the narrow, circuitous paths until he was far enough from the action to risk the roads, went begging and taking from village to village.

When the French forces pulled out in defeat in May, Leon-Charles Bertin who'd become Raymond Sorel (missing in action) was one George Gaucher with stolen, incomplete but adequate papers to prove it. He got hired aboard a shorthanded freighter out of Kampot, Cambodia, bound for Java.

Over the years Bertin learned Asia, sometimes the hard way, at other times the soft. He became increasingly chameleonlike, able to blend against nefarious backgrounds and circumstances, altogether a tough Asia hand. Quite a few times he came within a little more nerve or luck of making what he thought of as his big score. The problem was he never recognized these situations as big scores until they were past him. Usually he ended up having to fall back on some menial job, such as sacking oyster shells in Tuamoto.

Then, in 1974, Bertin won half of the boat in the poker game in Bangkok and killed for the other half and went on the pearling expedition with the two amas and the boy in the Andaman Sea. The natural blue pearls he came back alone with transformed his life.

He sold one of the smaller blue pearls, a nine millimeter, to a Bangkok dealer for ten thousand dollars. That staked him to a better presentation of himself and got him up the line to Kumura. He knew with Kumura he was in the presence of top dollar. He placed all the larger blue pearls before Kumura. They measured on the average about eighteen millimeters. Kumura examined each pearl thoroughly and asked if there were more. Bertin had planned on keeping the others, the smaller and malshaped, to sell to someone else, however, under the pressure of the moment he brought them out and showed them.

Kumura offered fifty million dollars for the lot.

Bertin was stunned. A spurt of adrenaline made his throat go dry. All he could manage to say was: *"D'accord."*

He wouldn't divulge to Kumura where the natural blues had been found. Kumura tried various ways to get it out of him, but all Bertin would reveal was they'd come from an island in the Andaman. It wasn't difficult for Bertin to stick to that because that was all he knew. He had only a vague idea where the island was located. Every so often he'd get to thinking about it, the wealth that was still there, and his determination to find it would get worked up. He'd sail off and find other similar islands but not the one.

Each time Bertin left on one of those sails, Kumura anticipated that he'd be bringing back another batch of blues. That prospect, not the appropriating of the Australian silver lip oysters, was the main reason Kumura cut Bertin in on the Bang Wan Bay farm. The limited partnership kept Bertin around and kept hope in Kumura's outlook.

With the fifty million paid by Kumura and sizeable profits from the cultured pearls from the farm, Bertin could afford anything he might want or want to become. While his Mizner house was being built he went to Geneva and underwent a series of cosmetic surgeries. Didn't just have his nose idealized and the dissipation removed from around his eyes, but got himself an entirely different, more attractive face. Chin, cheekbones, brow ridges, ears and all. For a coinciding smile he had his crooked teeth extracted and replaced with believable implants. He'd explicitly told the surgeons the well-bred look he wanted and that was what they gave him.

Bertin's manners and personal style were bought. And Paulette helped finish him.

And now there he was in his second-floor study of his large, luxuriously appointed house with a true, twenty-five-dollar Havana being brought to the slicked hole formed by his lips so he could enjoy causing a plosive sound and a miniature thunderhead around him. "I believe," he was saying, "our sense of self is influenced most by those things we possess. One must own to be one's own."

William, from across the room, just outside the niche containing Daniel Lesage's various verifications, fixed on the man. He mentally reconstructed the face, added brow, added chin, coarsened the nose and reshaped the cheeks. William's memory confirmed the voice and the mannerisms and he was nearly certain who Lesage truly was.

Lesage must have sensed William's stare. He brought his eyes around to William's and they were opposed, eyes-to-eyes, for a long moment. William shifted his attention to the photographs of Lesage in the Légion Étrangère. With the keen, analytical vision of a gem cutter used to determining flaws, he studied the photographs closely and noticed how often the Lesage faces were identical in perspective, expression. Someone had done an excellent job, spliced the negatives, printed the photographs, retouched them, copied them and printed them again, so Lesage could confidently display them here. Captain Lesage, hero Lesage, fucking Bertin, William thought.

He again looked across the room at Lesage.

Lesage's eyes were still on him.

Had Lesage recognized him? Unlikely, William thought. He'd been only eight. Now at nearly thirty he was considerably changed. As a test William smiled amiably and nodded. Perhaps Lesage believed William was commending him for what was displayed in the niche. He returned the smile and nod.

What should he do? William thought. Expose Lesage then and there? (Who would believe or care?) Confront him one on one? (Such privacy would be too lenient.) Kill him? (What else?) With a gun? (He deserved a knife.) There were so many voices in William. Which should he heed? Whatever he decided on, he told himself, he shouldn't decide now.

He went out onto the balcony.

Grady was there out of range of the cigar smoke. Leaning on the railing of the balustrade, observing Julia and Paulette. They were directly below on the smooth decking of the swimming pool. The piece of music that was playing and had been playing over and over, as though it were a part of a conditioning process, was Diane Schurr's rendition of "Nobody Does Me Like You Do." Julia and Paulette were slow dancing to it, pressed and barely moving their feet. Neither was leading. Their arms were around.

Julia seemed oblivious to anyone watching. Paulette, however, was well aware that Grady was up there. Three times she'd glanced up at him, not to convey he was being romantically eclipsed, just to ascertain that he was still there. It seemed his presence was essential and, in that respect, he wasn't excluded.

Not to worry, Grady told his possessiveness, he knew his Julia.

"Are you serious about going pearling?" William asked.

"Yeah."

"When?"

"If possible tomorrow sometime. Soon as Kumura or someone checks me out on that ketch. Why?"

"My mind got changed," William told him. "I better go with you."

CHAPTER
TWENTY-ONE

In the three o'clock dark of the next morning, one of Kumura's white Bentleys arrived at his big house in Bang Wan. Bringing a female visitor.

Arrangements had been made for this visit a month ago. Through the intermediary in London who usually saw to such affairs on Kumura's behalf. As always before there'd been the telephone conversations between Kumura and the female, the purpose being to confirm in his mind that she was neither stupid nor pretentious, qualities that even in the long-gone best of times had dampened Kumura's erotic spirit.

Kumura had rated her fascinating, which, according to his scale, was on the higher side. For instance, when he'd asked her name she'd been quick with the suggestion that he give her one. When he'd asked her age, just as quickly she'd thanked him for the opportunity to fib, said she loved to lie as much as she lied to love, was good at it because she had an excellent memory. Was he such a masochist that he insisted on the truth?

Kumura was amused. He decided to call her Celia, an Anglo

name that had always appealed to him, and, according to the photographs of her he'd been sent, he believed it suited.

Now this stranger he'd christened Celia was in the house and up the stairs and on her way down the long hall to Kumura's bedroom suite in the south wing. Kumura heard the clips of her high heels on the adobe tiles, drawing closer.

He'd been informed of the progress of her journey from when she'd been picked up at her Belgravia flat and driven to Heathrow to a short while ago when his Falcon 50 had landed her at Muang Mai. In the interim she'd been allowed a two-day stopover in a suite at the Peninsula in Hong Kong. To recover from the long air trip. From one point of view that was thoughtful of Kumura, from another, to his benefit: she wouldn't be tired and lagged. Experience had taught him that bought, temporary women, no matter how promising their dispositions at the outset, could turn and make matters ugly when not feeling up to par and their margin of tolerance was thin.

The cadent clip of her heels was louder, more definite now, bringing her to him. His anticipation was peaking. He'd come to believe in the importance of anticipation in these sexual dramas. The eventual encounter and even the culmination ofttimes hadn't been as enjoyable for him as his anticipation. That was why he'd insisted on reports of her on the way. To anticipate her, to accumulate in his mind impressions of the effort she was expending to get to him.

She, this Celia, was at the door now. Kumura thought the thought that usually occurred to him at this juncture: that he should have bolted the door, allowed her rap on it to become a pounding, her insistence to increase to such an extent she became desperate and began sobbing.

Her rap was a polite one.

He didn't go to the door, remained across the room from it so his first sight of her would be a full-length view. Told her to enter.

She was in white, fashionably dressed, had on a short skirt that underslung her buttocks and conveyed that she knew how good her legs were. A tall blond with the sort of tight, conscientiously maintained body needed for success by women whose callings required exposure: showgirls, strippers and such.

She was more attractive than her photographs had shown. And

she moved well, Kumura saw, as she came to him with her hand extended and introduced herself as Celia. Her hand was moist, which gave away she was nervous, but there was no other indication of that, and if she was under the influence of a drug it wasn't apparent.

They sat across from each other. She asked permission to smoke, lighted a Dunhill with a cheap, throwaway lighter. Exhaled so vigorously her mouth was momentarily ugly. That was her first and, Kumura hoped, her last self-betrayal.

The beginning was eased by discussion of her trip and London. Kumura inquired about where in England she'd been brought up and about her family, but he didn't expect truthful replies. It struck him how spurious this entire encounter was. He fought off the thought by contending to himself that he'd be able to cause her pleasure.

"How long will you want me here?" Celia asked.

"I don't yet know."

"It doesn't matter."

"Why did you ask?"

"Merely to get things arranged in my mind. I'm not in a hurry, it's not that."

Now, Kumura noticed, she had less composure than she'd had initially. Perhaps because of his Orientalness and the possibility of bizarre requirements. It made him wonder what she expected he'd want done and, on the other hand, what genuinely to arouse and please he could do to her. This was the guessing game with rules assumed: to inquire or divulge outright would spoil. Best to discern and tacitly disclose, send subtle signals.

"Would you care for something to drink, some wine perhaps?"

"Not yet," she said.

"You'd like to freshen up?"

"Yes."

Kumura rang for a servant.

"Will we ... will I be coming back here?" she asked.

He told her she would. The servant showed her out.

At once Kumura gave his attention to the blue pearl. He'd wanted some prelusive time with this Celia, to ascertain that she was appealing enough before preparing it. If she hadn't been, if she'd been crass or brittle or dowdy he'd have sent her away and left the pearl intact.

There it was, on the surface of his desk, the last of all that many he'd bought from Bertin. Initially, when he'd believed Bertin could supply him with more, he'd used them with a frequency close to wasteful. Then, when he realized no more were forthcoming, he'd rationed them to himself, and now, it had come down to this last one, his last eighteen-millimeter blue.

Kumura cringed when he considered what lay beyond it, the inability without recourse. He remembered all too well what that had been like for him. In fact, he was able clearly to recall the first time impotency had chosen him: in the bed of a suite at the Carleton in Cannes with an Italian woman whose pleasure would have been his achievement. He'd been embarrassed rather than alarmed because it had never occurred to him before and, he thought, it wouldn't again.

But it did. It happened frequently. Then it happened more often than not. His penis became undependable, and because it couldn't be depended upon it became predictably undependable.

He consulted some of the most prominent London doctors, went from one to another along Harley Street. They expressed various theories regarding his condition but avoided offering diagnosis. How many medical hands clothed in powdered rubber gloves fingered at his flacid member and thought *there but for the grace of something or other go I*.

Urologists asked: did he have an erection upon awakening in the morning? Some mornings? Did he have nocturnal emissions? Was he able to masturbate? Would he consider a penile prosthesis, a sort of splint to aid insertion?

No, no, no, no, definitely not, were Kumura's replies.

Psychiatrists poked around among his childhood experiences and impressions. There was likely something causal there but they didn't find it. One psychiatrist, a Swiss with Luther in his gray matter, had to bite his tongue to keep from commenting that Kumura was a womanizer and by being made impotent he'd gotten what he deserved.

In many cultures, especially in the innately ashamed West, Kumura might well have been branded a womanizer. In Japan, however, his vigorous libido was a distinction. He was a swordsman to be reckoned with, a carnal samurai. He'd adored women all his life, it seemed, had been erotically aroused by them since infancy when his mother had shown off his penis to her female friends and allowed them to pinch it, boasted about his *ochinchin*, honorable tinkle-tinkle.

He'd been sexually precocious, actively so, knew how to satisfy and did before he himself was able to orgasm. When that capability was his and for years after he thought of it as a physical fortune that never depleted, that only required an interval, often hardly more than a pause, to replenish.

There were numerous *pichi-pichi-gyaru* (lively girls) in his young life. He preferred a *pikaichi* (dazzler) over one that was *kawaii* (cute) and he was wise to their guile, wanted to believe but seldom did when they asked him demurely to be *yasashi* (gentle) because their *kuri-chan* (little clit) was so sensitive.

School in England was supposed to temper him but, of course, it didn't. His parents believed the apparent propriety of the British would rub off on him. He, however, soon enough saw right through the British, disregarded their airs and got to their lust.

The women he encountered in England appealed to him far more than the women he'd been with in Japan. Those perennial Japanese schoolgirl pretenders with their wistful confusion and reliance on demureness couldn't hold a candle to the lithe and elegant English beauties who transformed so extremely in the little time it took to go from the drawing room to the bed.

English women. He loved their polarity. He would lie in the perfectly contrived light of some luxurious West End female lair and, while making the most of another afterfloat, feel sympathy for his former comrades half a world away; who, no doubt, were still enduring brothel and bar, hanging around the Mikado hoping for a night, or even an hour of sensual largess from one of the rare hostesses considered beautiful. Oh, the energy expended in search of a smile genuinely naughty, an assertion that couldn't be denied, a moan, shriek or wiggle truly induced. Unfortunate fellows, Kumura would think, as, beneath the sheet, long tapered female fingers found him and kept hold to enjoy even the first stirrings of another erection.

This being Kumura's nature one can well imagine the impact early impotency had on him. He was bereft, uninspired by everything, a huge portion of his existence, the most gratifying, fervent portion, had been obliterated. He stood naked before mirrors and gazed at his disinclined member. How much it had been loved, tactilely worshipped, how swift it had been to reply whenever called upon. And now...

What was he to do inasmuch as medicine and psychiatry hadn't supplied an answer? Was he to spend the rest of his life feeling the fraud, avoiding heated demands, scheming to dodge them?

There had to be an answer. Perhaps he could find it. Might it be in a certain type of woman, in some particular aspect of a certain type. A quality of her voice, a shade of her eye, an ever so slight, subtle thing as her graceful or possibly ungraceful way of sitting? No use putting his hope there, he decided. He'd previously culled his preferences.

Then aphrodisiacs.

He thought he'd try anything, however his logic prevailed when presented with such purported panaceas as: male beaver fat, the ashes of frogs' legs, mandrake root, alectoria stones and swallows' wombs. A so-called sexpharmacist in Tokyo guaranteed results from both rhino horn and monkey testicles. Costly stuff. When neither had the slightest effect he was amused at himself for having tried them, reasoned that he hadn't been ignorant enough for them. He heard tell of a substance newly developed in a research laboratory in France as an anesthesia, which in small doses affected the part of the primitive human brain where sexual impulses are based. He followed down the lead and found it was not newly developed, rather *nearly* developed, which meant that one of the ingredients of the substance was hope. The next time he inquired he was told the laboratory was no longer pursuing that project.

It was by coincidence that blue pearl became a consideration. Kumura happened to be visiting his widowed mother in Hagoya for a few days. Late one night he was in his father's library, which contained a collection of very old to most recent books on pearls and pearling. He happened to slide out a volume entitled *Pearls as Remedies*. He broke the book open to any page, which turned out to be the third page of six pages devoted to excerpts from Robert Lovell's tome entitled *Panmineralogicon*, published in Oxford in 1661. The paragraph his eyes chose to fix on dealt specifically with the efficacy of blue pearl in the treatment of various ailments such as those involving the heart, eyes, nerves, and blood. It was, according to Lovell, exceptionally effective in reversing sexual dysfunctions.

Kumura was mildly curious, mainly amused. It smacked of dried monkey gonads, he thought, otherwise wouldn't Lovell have been more specific?

A footnote referred him to another page farther on citing the Pharmacopeia of India, which stated that beyond doubt blue pearl was a sexual stimulant and a panacea for impotence. The recommended dosage was one-quarter to one-half grain, powdered.

Blue pearl was also prescribed for impotence by Marabari, a noted thirteenth-century physician of Kashmir. By Li-Shu-Chin, the sixteenth-century naturalist. By the 1877 catalogue of the Nate Exhibition in Yedo, and as well by the nineteenth-century physician to the Maharaja of Tagore, one Sowindro Mohun, who claimed for blue pearl the curing of various disorders, including, most emphatically, sexual weakness. There were three entire pages relating case histories in which blue pearl had done the trick.

Who would have thought it?

And who was thinking it now?

Not he, his well-educated sensible mind scoffed. The desperate ego-tattered side of him was only slightly less pragmatic.

He read on and fell asleep there in the library with the volume *Pearls as Remedies* across his chest. But he didn't sleep well. Imagination invaded his unconsciousness with blue pearls, had them ricocheting around in the container that was his head, being spat at him with machine gun rapidity by hostile oysters.

Bright blue pearls.

He'd never seen one. Though pearls had been the family business since 1874 and made the family fortune, he'd never heard mention of one by either grandfather or father. He asked his mother if to her knowledge there'd been any blue pearls. She started at the question, studied him for a long moment and pulled up the corners of her mouth into what could be taken as either a knowing grin or a commiserative smile.

That reaction by his mother motivated him to put word out to the trade that he'd pay well for any natural pearls of blue. In response he was presented with quite a number of pearls that

appeared a bit blue, had a hint or cast of blue as opposed to the
usual white, pink or cream. None, however, were the deep, lively
blue specified in the remedy book.

Months went by.

Blue pearls forfeited their place in the front of Kumura's mind.

A Burmese dealer showed up with two he'd obtained from an
alcoholic beach person who'd found them among other tidal
leavings in Mergni. They were only about the size of baby garden
peas, were lumpy and ulcerated, so malformed they looked like
some melted man-made substance. Nevertheless they were pearls
and bright blue and that was what mattered.

Kumura paid five hundred for them.

The Burmese dealer thought perhaps Kumura had lost his mind
and, just in case, demanded cash.

Kumura put off trying the blue pearl remedy. He believed it
would turn out to be merely another grasping measure and that
the most he'd get out of it was temporary hope. No more than a
speck of hope but better than none, so might as well prolong it a
couple of weeks.

The time came. Kumura didn't make an important production
of it. Alone, in the gloaming of a Saturday evening, he put on a
silk robe and sat in a chaise on his terrace overlooking the sea.
Sipping a brandy and soda laced with blue pearl while his hearing
divided its attention between Mendelssohn's Concerto in E Minor,
Opus 64 and the birds chirping at the evening light.

He drained his glass, closed his eyes.

His thoughts wandered and decided on a road that returned
him to an experience he'd had back in his virile days. January in
Paris. At the Crillon with an American fashion model he'd met
earlier at the Ritz bar. She was there in Paris to work in the Spring
Collections. He was there on the excuse of business but really on
the chance of the likes of her. She was a good half head taller than
he in her stocking feet. Perfectly thin for the sake of clothes, with
the small breasts that were mandatory then. How craving her
breasts were, as though they'd been neglected. He loved them,
gave them their due. The entire length of her body was greedy for
sensation, the backs of her knees, her wrists and other pulse
points, the pits of her arms. She was too proud to be ashamed, a
private exhibitionist. She lay back gracefully, as though his eyes

were cameras. Her well-tended fingers unfolded her vagina for
him and he saw a reason other than passion for her immodesty.
She was lovely down there, dainty and lovely, a delicate fleshy
orchid, with her clitoris come out. Was she aware of how lovely
she was down there? Aware by sense or comparison? he'd wondered.
Though worthy of the tenderest homage, she was one of those
who preferred less of tender, let him know in candid terms what
she preferred, a trace of command in her tone but her voice never
raised above a whisper. Let him know what she was feeling as he
did those preferred things to her, whispered her descriptions in a
surprisingly pleasant medley of sweet talk and obscenities.

At the time he'd suspected she'd be one he'd not forget, so he'd
made the most of her.

He returned to himself on the chaise, opened his eyes. Didn't
trust the feeling, thought it might be imaginary, a phantom
sensation, like people have who've lost a limb and feel as though
it's still there.

But it *was* there, had gorged and distended and forced itself up
and out through the overlap of his robe below where the robe was
sashed. It was hard and usable and had transformed to that
condition by his merely mentally meandering to a memory. That
memory had come forward for its portion of reliving numerous
times previously and all it had ever done was exemplify for his
regret what used to be.

Neither had the miraculous occurred. It was incredible but not
miraculous, had a rational explanation. He'd just happened upon
a remedy, that was all there was to it: an ancient passed-over
remedy too esoteric for contemporary consideration, he thought,
accepted, concluded, end of doubt.

Blue pearl.

A month later, fate had proved how timely and provending it
could be when Bertin/Lesage had sought out Kumura with a
bagful. How little Bertin understood their true value. And now,
so many years later here was Kumura in the bedroom of his
Mizner house in Bang Wan contemplating the last of those blues.
No outlook for another supply. After this time, after this Celia,
at 14.8 grains per dose (the Pharmacopeia of India had been way
off on that point), there'd only be enough for nine more instances.

He tried not to think of that, to focus his mind on the pleasure at hand. He unfolded the briefke that William had delivered, examined the pink sapphire it contained. A cushion-cut pink Ceylon of ten carats, a nice one. It was intended for Celia. The arrangement was *service-compris* but it had become his custom to throw in a little extra when deserved.

He put the sapphire back into hiding and took up the eighteen-millimeter blue. With extreme care, but no concern for its value or beauty, he fractured it with the jaws of a nickel-plated monkey wrench, making sure the larger pieces and fragments of it fell into a smooth marble mortar. Using a pestle, he crushed the pearl into a powder, then transferred some of the powder to the plate of a small electronic scale, adding a bit more at a time until the readout told him 3.7 carats precisely (four grains equal one carat).

While he was at it he measured out nine more such portions and enclosed those in briefkes, placed the briefkes (his immediate potent future) in his wall safe among other precious things.

He poured a goblet of claret, a 1969 Haut-Brion Graves, and dropped in the remaining portion of powdered blue pearl. Stirred the concoction well with a forefinger and gulped it down, feeling the grit of the fine powder on the membranes of his throat. There was, he saw, still a slight powdery residue in the goblet. He splashed in more wine, swirled the goblet vigorously and drank before there could be any settling. Examined the goblet to make sure he'd gotten every particle.

Enjoyed an additional twenty minutes of anticipation before ringing for this Celia.

CHAPTER
TWENTY-TWO

The Andaman Sea was having one of its kindlier days. Its regular conspirator, the wind, was being lazy. Gusts, offsprings of the wind, were playing on the sea's surface, swirling and skipping about. Only a wave here and there was high enough to have a crest. Flying fish used those for lift and momentum, to get their winglike fins spinning. They were accustomed to more launch in the Andaman. The sky was also at its best. So whole and indefectable it might have been overall a piece of fine cloth, or the encompassing membrane of an enormous pure soul.

With a prevailing wind of less than four knots Grady had set only the ketch's mainsail, and that only for stability. The mainsail, deprived of bellow and not even catching enough wind to crowd out its slack, didn't look as though it was enjoying itself. The *Sea Cloud*'s eighty-horsepower diesel engine was doing its thing. Eight knots steady.

Grady was at the helm. Julia and William were close at hand in the padded cockpit. There wasn't anything to do but keep on course. How right Kumura had been when he'd said this new Hinckley fifty-footer would practically sail itself. It was equipped

with the most recent sailing and navigating devices, such as a
furling system to unwrap and wrap the headsail, and a Magellan
GPS (global positioning satellite) NAV5200 receiver to reckon in
degrees and minutes precisely where the boat was at any instant.

That morning the skipper of Kumura's motor yacht had met
Grady in the docking shed and thoroughly checked him out on
the *Sea Cloud*. Explained all the electronic devices and shown him
where everything was stowed. The boat's interior was extremely
well designed, not an inch of wasted space and yet it didn't seem
cramped. Lockers, bins, shelves, drawers. Life preservers were in
here, spare sails in there, extra anchor here, flares there, firearms
here. The latter consisted of an automatic rifle, machine pistols
and a pair of Glock .40 caliber semiautomatics. Several loaded
magazines and clips and boxes of rounds. Grady wondered why
such an arsenal but didn't ask, figured it was Kumura's boat and
Kumura knew what comforts he might need.

Kumura was also concerned with Grady's needs. While Grady
was getting checked out on the *Sea Cloud*, diving gear, wet suits,
backpacks, fins, regulators and everything else needed were brought
aboard and stowed. Grady had planned on him and Julia and
William driving to Phuket that afternoon to buy the equipment
and supplies they'd need, however Kumura had seen to it. At least
he'd seen to having someone see to it. A dozen air tanks were
lugged aboard and strapped securely in place. After the tanks came
the galley supplies, staples and delicacies. And a supply of liquor
and soft drinks, cases of Evian. Servants were still bringing aboard
and making everything right when Grady returned to Kumura's
house to fetch Julia and William.

So, they'd been able to get under way at noon that day rather
than tomorrow. They were now an hour and a half out from Bang
Wan on a heading of west by northwest. The coast of Thailand
was still in sight but wouldn't be soon. At the same rate that it
was diminishing Grady was feeling better and better. Thinking
about how far he'd come. Not from Bang Wan but from a year
ago. A year ago he'd been all tangled up emotionally with Gayle
and her cheating, all tangled up ambitiously with Harold and his
duplicities. Ridiculous how a fellow as sharp as people said he was
could get into such a mess. One moment he'd been in the clear,
next he couldn't see the forest for the trees. Gayle and Harold.

The mark of them would always be on him. They'd happened to him. He'd allowed them to happen. He was ashamed of that. It certainly didn't recommend him. Julia had asked about them once, been told honestly and had never asked again.

Anyway, all that was behind him and he was wiser now, happier, had better prospects, what with the pending offer of the high-paying prestigious job with Kumura. After the Harold debacle he'd vowed never again to work for anyone in the gem trade, however he felt Kumura was an exception, not a hustler or business bully. On top of that, Kumura was exclusively in pearls and distanced from the hypocritical day-by-day milieu. It would take a lot not to make that job appealing, Grady thought. He pictured himself in San Francisco in that driven Bentley, in that elegant office, in that bracket. All that right there ahead of him, close enough to smell, almost close enough to bite a chunk of. Kumura wasn't leading him on, Grady assured himself. Kumura had no reason to lead him on.

The Thai coast was out of sight now.

The ketch's sleek fiberglass hull was easily cutting its way through the blue-black water, leaving a frivolous wake. Grady's hands on the wheel seemed to feel the boat's condescension, its taunt saying to the sea: *come on, pitch me, heel me, show me what you've got*. The Andaman was too vast to hear, just kept on being docile.

Next stop would be the island of Surin Tai fifty nautical miles ahead. Grady had studied the charts and decided Surin Tai and its sister island, Surin Nua, looked about right. They were remote enough and practically on the boundary of Burmese waters. Although they were comparatively large islands and inhabited, there were numerous smaller ones around them. There'd be plenty of places for good, solitary diving and possibly the finding of a pearl oyster or two and inside one possibly a perfect, creamy natural of, say, ten millimeters, or twelve, or maybe fourteen, Grady thought. He tried to convince himself that only the diving counted, but a pearl like that, of increasing size, persisted in his imagination.

Ko Surin Tai.

It came into view at early evening, changing from mauve to gray to green as the ketch proceeded to it. No reason to be satisfied with just having reached the vicinity; there was still light enough left to explore about, and as Grady had surmised, on the western end was a labyrinth of small islands, odd-shaped pieces of land that looked like they'd been negligently scattered. Thick green growth had jumped on them and so multiplied, it overhung their edges all around. There were no beaches, but many coves and narrow channels formed by the disarray.

Grady steered in among them, decided on a cove that appeared no better or worse than others he'd passed up, cut the engine and dropped anchor. Just in time. Daylight gave up suddenly and night pressed down.

They had a tossed salad and fried Bayonne ham supper on the fantail and turned in early. William could have taken the forward berth but chose instead to sleep out on the foredeck. Grady and Julia agreed that the quarter berths situated starboard and port aft of the companionway ladder looked invitingly snug. However, when they'd undressed and were in separate berths the in-between space got to them and they had to counter it by reading.

Julia had brought along her Alice A. Bailey and another book on spiritualism that she'd picked up in Bangkok. The part she was reading at the moment dealt with the premise that an earthly body with a forsaken soul could be taken over by a soul that would value it more and make better use of it. She wished she'd brought along something lighter.

Grady hadn't thought to bring reading material, but when he opened the locker above the berth he found plenty, including not only some recent nonfiction books and the last three editions of *Architectural Digest* but as well a five-volume set of *Jardins à la Mode et Jardins Anglo-Chinois*, reproduced sketches of gardens designed by the eighteenth-century landscaper Georges Louis le Rouge.

Kumura had, indeed, thought of everything.

Julia found in her identical locker several editions of the magazine *Contemporary Artist*, two modern gothic novels, an edition of *Suna No Onna* (*Woman in the Dunes*) by Abe Kobo and a Japanese erotic cartoon magazine depicting episodes of possible impossibilities. Julia got right into that. She credited her understanding to the drawings, gave nothing to the Japanese captions. This was, after all, the universal language. Every once in a while a physical exaggeration brought her to a giggle. How long it had been since she'd seen such a magazine, she thought. And then a second thought: hell, when had she ever seen one?

She didn't get all the way through the cartoons. They were too much of the same. She put the magazine back into the locker and resumed reading about the appropriating of the bodies of forsaken souls, in particular those of persons who'd given up on life and were contemplating suicide. It was contended that Albert Einstein had been one such.

She allowed the book to fall to her chest and glanced over at Grady. He was in the gardens. She wanted his opinion on forsaken souls but let him be. It was entirely unexpected when, without taking his eyes, only his mind, from the landscape sketches, he asked, "What was it that was going on between you and Paulette last night?"

"When last night?"

"When you were dancing by the pool."

"It was nothing."

"Didn't look like nothing."

"What could it have been?"

He didn't want to say. He hadn't even wanted to ask about it but like a little burp it had come out. "You want to talk about it?"

"Hell no."

"All it was was a couple of women dancing. In France and a lot of places women often dance with one another, right?"

"Hold on to that," Julia advised, clicked off her reading light and turned over to face starboard and sleep.

At first light they were up, and had strong coffee, cinnamon toast and jasmine honey. Grady activated the electronically controlled transom, that is, the freeboard of the stern. It unsealed and lowered outward so it was horizontal with the surface of the water and would serve as a platform from which they'd be able to dive more easily and come back aboard. To the platform Grady attached a four-step ladder with handrails that extended below the surface.

William meanwhile checked the air and valves of three of the tanks, bright yellow Dacor eighty-cubic-foot tanks.

They put on their skin suits. The water here was too warm for a full suit, even quite a few fathoms down it would still be too warm. A partial lightweight suit was enough, legless, armless, little more than a swimsuit really. Also, they wouldn't be wearing helmets or booties or gloves. It was, Grady thought, going to be an enjoyable dive, had the makings of his best dive ever.

He helped Julia get into her backpack with tank, attached her balanced regulator and digital instruments for depth, air, elapsed time, strapped a sheathed knife to the inside of her left calf, and while he was down there adjusted the heel straps of her fins. He even spat into the lens of her mask to prevent fogging.

All this she could have done for herself, however she let Grady have the pleasure of looking after her. She'd been diving twice. First time had been four years ago during a ten-day vacation in Cozumel. She'd taken the fundamental lessons then. Her second time had been a year later in Belize. Both times she'd rented the necessary gear. Her enthusiasm never reached a level that would make her want to buy.

She waddled onto the diving platform, turned her back to the water and flopped in. The fins propelled her downward and she reached the bottom at four fathoms, a plain grayish bottom. She looked up. Saw the white hull of the *Sea Cloud* and then at the stern of it a concussion of bubbles followed immediately by another. The plunging in of Grady and William.

They joined her on the bottom and the three swam along together, exploring. They soon found there wasn't too much to explore. The bottom was level and silty in spots, the underwater bases of the islands consisted of a molten-looking rock, smooth and uncolorful. No caves. Patches of green to dun-colored seaweed waved weakly and a few coral growths with well-defined arms like saguaro cacti contributed little to the eye. The only saving thing was the fish. Various kinds, mostly little ones in schools of many, an entire school changing direction simultaneously. Looking like a pack of identical dark dots when they were head on, becoming sudden flashings of silver and cerise as they angled off. They seemed to be performing or practicing, Julia thought, surely they didn't need the exercise.

She was trying her best to enjoy the dive. However, her reaction was taking her the opposite way. For some reason she was feeling increasingly uncomfortable. She was swimming and breathing easily but it seemed she had no compatibility with the water.

What was wrong? She'd never been claustrophobic. No, that wasn't it. The feeling didn't have any panic in it. It was more a mixture of self-consciousness and protest and...stifle and...now it was defining itself.

She felt encumbered.

She stopped, gestured to Grady that she was going to return to the boat.

Grady asked with a gesture was she all right?

She assured him with a nod and went up.

Grady and William continued on, around the point of the cove to another of the small islands. There they encountered three other divers. A short ways farther on they came within sight of two more, and as they went along they passed beneath the hulls of at least ten boats.

Before noon they'd had enough. Climbed back aboard the ketch and shed their gear. Julia had changed into white shorts and a T-shirt, was lying face up on a cushion on the cabin top.

She had lunch ready, what she called a "picky" lunch, a variety of delicacies such as cold smoked salmon, pâté de compagne and sliced tomatoes with basil, arugula and olive oil, but nothing solid. Grady and William were hungry. Julia wasn't because she'd munched considerably while preparing.

Grady asked why she'd quit the dive.

"I just wasn't in the mood," she told him

"You didn't miss anything," he said.

"The fish were pretty."

"Yeah, hooray for the fish," Grady remarked sardonically.

"What did you think, lover, you were going to come out here to an underwater paradise and pluck up a few pearl oysters?"

"Exactly."

"Well, blame yourself, you chose this place."

"I didn't even see a shell. Did you?" He turned to William.

"No," William said.

"The worst possible place. More divers than a public pool."

"Poor baby," Julia consoled. "You had your heart so set on better than this." She delivered a consoling peck to below his right sideburn, told his right ear, "We should go elsewhere."

"Where elsewhere?"

"You must have considered a backup."

"Yeah, but I don't want to be this wrong twice," Grady said and deferred to William. "You choose the next spot."

William thought a moment and deferred to Julia. "You," he said, "we'll let you choose."

After lunch, Julia and William went below to go over some nautical charts. Grady fixed a pitcher of lemonade and brought it to them, but he didn't butt in. He saw that Julia was taking the responsibility seriously, was using a magnifying glass to scan the charts, as though they were trying to hide something from her. He went up on deck with a powerful portable radio he'd found, relaxed in the cockpit while listening to a Sydney, Australia, cool jazz and hot topic station. For ten minutes a conservationist was alarmed about an endangered species and then for five Wynton Marsalis's trumpet cried.

Julia and William came on deck.

Julia told Grady she'd figured out where they should dive. She expected Grady would want to know where but he'd decided he wouldn't ask, would just go along with wherever it was, make a few points for his cooperative nature. Anyway, no matter what her choice, it couldn't be worse than here at Surin Tai.

With the press of buttons, Grady hoisted the anchor, started up the engine and hoisted the mainsail. He guided the ketch down the circuitous channel to the open sea. "What's the bearing?" he asked Julia.

"North by northwest," she replied with snap.

Grady recalled the chart he'd consulted to reach Surin Tai. A north by northwest course would in little more than an hour put them in Burmese waters. Should he call that to Julia's and William's attention? Surely they knew, had studied the charts. He wouldn't mention it, Grady decided. Hell, if they were game so was he.

The readout of the global positioning satellite receiver indicated where the ketch was at that moment. Having determined that, he set the course and wished for more wind so he could truly sail. Both the sea and the wind were the same as they'd been the day before.

The hour passed.

Nothing in sight, no islands, no other vessels. Nothing different about being in Burmese waters, Grady thought, but how far did

Julia have in mind? He still wouldn't ask, figured she or William would tell him soon enough. Probably what she'd chosen was an island just beyond the boundary, one that would allow them, if need be, to make a dash back to Thailand.

At eight o'clock Grady knew that was evidently not the case. They were well into Burmese waters by then and still running full on course.

"Way too deep to anchor out here," he told Julia when she brought him a hunk of Stilton, baguettes and a goblet of fine red.

"I know," she said.

"How do you know?" he tested.

"It said so on the chart."

"We're going to get to someplace where we'll be able to anchor, won't we?"

"Eventually, perhaps."

What kind of answer was that? Grady thought. "I assume you know where we're going."

"So do I." She took a sip from his goblet and licked the wine from her upper lip. "Why don't you let me relieve you?" she said, meaning at the helm but realizing the ambiguity, making the most of it.

"What's William doing?"

"He's in the galley drying some rose leaves."

"Drying rose leaves?"

"There was a bouquet of fresh roses in the main cabin, which, by the way, is where we're going to sleep and so forth tonight. It has an expediently firm double mattress, unless, of course, you're tired and would prefer last night's bunk."

"What do you think?"

"I think you're all horned up and you want to fuck me."

"You might say that." He kissed her a long, sloppy tongue-parrying one. Inhaled her neck. Her aggressive words were still in his ears. He liked that.

She knew he liked that and she was never going to hold back on him.

"No shit," he said, "William is drying rose leaves?"

"In the oven."

"Why?"

"It seems important to him."

Nearly night came and then entirely night. Julia and Grady observed the stars, more plentiful to the sight out there on the sea. They saw a lot of shooting ones.

William came up on deck and shared the sky with them for a while. Grady had a hug around Julia and she put a hug around William so he shouldn't feel left out. William would take over the helm.

"If you want, put it on autopilot. The radar doesn't show anything ahead for a hundred miles," Grady said. "You know how to set the auto?"

"No problem. I'll keep it on course."

"Wake me when we get to India," Grady quipped and followed Julia down the companionway ladder.

At four-thirty Grady came suddenly awake. He knew at once without having to reach with his legs that Julia wasn't in the bed. He got up. Nor was she in the head. He slipped on a pair of shorts and went topside.

There she was. At the helm with William. What they were having was more than a discussion, less than a disagreement. They went abruptly silent when they became aware of Grady there.

He noticed the heading was changed, now it was 275, close to due west, and William was changing it again to 250, west southwest, giving in to Julia, who'd been insisting on 250.

"Are we sailing around in circles or what?" Grady asked. He used the GPS receiver, determined their position and went below to look at the chart, returned and told them, "There's nothing out here."

No sooner were the words out of his mouth than a blip showed up on the radar screen. Another ship, a freighter or tanker probably, Grady thought watching it. He kept watching it and realized it wasn't moving. Could it be an island? If so, it wasn't on the chart. Nothing extraordinary about that though. There were uncharted islands all over the world, hunks of land not important enough to warrant a change by the chart makers.

Island or whatever it was, it was twenty miles ahead at Julia's bearing of 250.

They kept going right at it, and after a while the sun came orange over the horizon and struck their backs, rose higher and brought yellow. It was giving true color to everything when what had been a blip became definitely an island.

As they got closer, enough to it to make out its size and shape, Grady had the feeling that he'd seen it before. He chalked it up to déjà vu, however. If it was that it was stronger and of more duration than any he'd ever experienced.

Julia knew for certain what she was feeling wasn't déjà vu. There before her eyes was the island that had invaded her imagination when she'd painted the seascape for Grady's office. Its configuration, its hues, everything was identical with her rendering of it. Naturally, she'd painted it in her nonliteral style, underlaying, overlaying, dry brushing, overloading her brush and allowing runs. She'd made it up as she went along. Anyway, she thought she had until now.

William's memory knew the island well. As he guided the ketch around the high point of it near where twenty years ago he'd brought up that first blue pearl oyster and proceeded to circle the island, he saw it hadn't changed greatly. The reef had thickened quite a bit and grown higher in places but the lagoon and everything else looked just about the same. "Where do you want to dive?" he asked Grady.

"Makes no difference to me. How about off the reef?"

William brought the ketch close in to the reef so it was headed into the wind. Dropped anchor. Grady peered over the side to the water. "How deep do you think it is here?" he asked.

"Six to seven fathoms," was William's estimate.

"No more than thirty feet," Julia said with surprising conviction.

"You ought to know," Grady grinned, "it's your island."

She agreed.

"Are you going to dive today?" he asked her.

"I don't think so, maybe."

"How about you, William?"

"A little later."

"You ought to have some breakfast first," Julia told Grady.

His stomach agreed, but he was too anxious to get in the water. He converted the transom into a diving platform, put on his gear and flopped in. The sun was hitting the water at an easy glancing angle. He followed a diagonal shaft of it downward. Knew he was bound for beauty before he got to it, as he caught a glimpse of a sea whip, its scarlet tendrils beckoning him to come look.

The reef, particularly the base of it, was a dominion of unique life and vivid color. The less animate, the corals, were dominant. They got their sobriquets from their textures, such as the leather coral, the porcelain, the brain, the lettuce leaf. They were the composers of the reef, their accumulation and obdurate fatalities providing a beautiful irregular place for whatever chose to swim, crawl, dart or hide, especially hide.

Grady's presence sent all sorts of creatures into niches. Some, either dumb, fearless or too curious to heed their sense of survival, remained around him. An angelfish, a couple of clown fish. Perhaps they just knew they were better swimmers than he. A huge green sea turtle waited until the last moment of Grady's approach before scuttling off, stirring up a trail of the cobalt blue sand.

Grady hadn't ever seen sand that color. Like ground-up blue sapphires.

He swam along the bottom close to the reef, feeling good about where he was, taking in everything, telling himself to remember it. He lost track of time, wanted to. But after a while, decided he'd go up and persuade Julia and William to dive. This was something that Julia, with her appreciation for color, shouldn't miss.

He turned to go back, and it was in his turning that he spotted the oyster, the same sort of oyster being cultured by Kumura. About the size of a dinner plate, a *Pinctada maxima*, a silver lip. It was a solitary oyster, a stray, and it was in trouble. A red starfish had attached to its shell.

Grady tried to pull the starfish from the oyster, then tried to pry it off with his knife. Didn't want to hurt the starfish, so he just took it along as a passenger to the surface.

His find was heavier out of the water, weighed four to five pounds. He handed it up to William and climbed aboard. Julia came aft and they squatted around it as it lay there on the deck in the sun, the enormous oyster and its bright red, piggybacking deadly enemy.

"Were there any more?" Julia asked.

"This was all I saw but I didn't really look. There could be more," Grady replied. He was excited, on the verge of hyperventilating.

"There'll be more," Julia predicted.

The sun got to the starfish. The tips of all five of its arms curled up slightly, and after a couple of minutes it let go. Julia plucked it gently off the oyster and placed it in the sea, watched it revive and swim from sight.

The oyster was also feeling the heat, more so now without the starfish to shield it from the sun. There was a slight, nearly indiscernable opening between the oyster's meshing valves.

"Should we help it along?" Grady asked.

"Be patient," Julia told him.

The oyster responded slowly but surely and after ten minutes that seemed ten times longer to Grady it was open enough for Julia to slip a wine cork between its valves to keep it open. She picked up the oyster with both hands and held it up so Grady could look into it.

She enjoyed watching the expression on his face. His mouth went oval and his eyes went wide. Disbelief caused him to snap his head. He reached into the oyster with the first finger of each hand, pincering. Felt the slick, wet creature within, had difficulty because of its slickness, did not allow his overanxiousness to cause injury.

The size of the pearl he extracted was about eighteen millimeters.

It appeared to be perfectly round.

But most incredible, it was blue. A deep lively blue similar in shade to the natural pearl owned by Kumura. Rare nearly to the point of nonexistence and accordingly precious. Grady's gem dealer mind went right to the question of how much such a pearl was worth. A million? More. Several million? At least.

Julia and William each had a look at the pearl and shared Grady's excitement. Julia was happy for his happiness, gave him a tight, praising hug and shrieked jubilantly as she whirled him around. William beamed and congratulated, smacked Grady on the back. Grady had hit the long shot! Who said there were no more naturals to be found?

Julia looked after the benefactor, the oyster. She removed the cork from between its valves. Before placing the oyster back into the water she told it to be sure to steer clear of starfish.

"I'm going back down," Grady said.

"Not until you get something in your belly," Julia ruled.

"I noticed some chocolate bars. Just give me one of those."

"You ought to have something solid."

"I eat now I'll get indigestion," Grady said. "Come on, Julia, dive with me. It's beautiful down there. You too, William."

"Considering where we are someone should stay up top," William said.

"Go find another oyster," was Julia's pleasant way of declining. She went below and got two chocolate bars, unwrapped them for him. He stuffed his mouth with one whole bar, could barely chew, had to wait for the blob of chocolate to melt. It taxed his patience. He felt like spitting it out. He tossed the second bar back to Julia, went to the platform and, like a big, incorrigible kid, let out a whoop as he fell in.

He searched along the base of the reef, paying little or no attention now to the beauty of the underwater terrain. Not even a silvery, translucent jellyfish that looked like some extraterrestrial spaceship could distract him for more than a moment. He hunted back and forth, covering every foot of the sandy bottom there, knowing what he might overlook would be a fortune.

He came to a spot at the base where the coral pillars that formed the reef had broken way, leaving a hole more than adequate enough for him to pass through. A few undulations of his fins put him on the inner side of the reef and within the lagoon. The depth was the same there but the water was a lighter, more vibrant blue, and the bottom visibly sharper. Grady was immediately struck by how sparsely occupied this part of the lagoon was, as though it was forbidden territory. Only a few big-eyed blennies and sea horses swimming about, acting foolish. Even more pronounced was the quiet. He could barely hear the sea breaking against the outer side of the reef. Could clearly hear, louder than he could ever recall, the ascending bubbles of his exhales, the cool assuring boil of them.

He began his search within the lagoon. He was in its deepest part. From there its bottom inclined gradually to shallows. Oysters, even as fussy as they were, should love it here, Grady thought. Clean, quiet, secluded. A hell of a nice place to be a hermaphrodite. Christ, he was happy. It didn't matter if he found another oyster, another pearl. He had his.

Lime green streaked by him.

What was that? He hadn't gotten a look at it.

Shocking pink shot by on his other side!

And then came yellow, a citron yellow.

He didn't realize they were snakes until there were more of them, swimming slower, and closer. They were four to six feet long and big around as his forearm, had flat, paddlelike tails. He'd read about the species, how, unlike eels, sea snakes had to go to the surface to fill their neck-to-tail lungs with air, how venomous they were but gentle and friendly unless agitated. How the hell could anyone determine the disposition of a snake? And bet his life on that opinion? These seemed to Grady anything but amiable, the way they kept making ever closer passes at him, opening their jaws to display their fangs. How many were there? Twenty and growing in number. Others hurrying to get in on the kill. A green one and a pink one were treading in a coil only a foot above his head. He could make out the symmetry of their scales, their black eyes set mean in their heads. They hinged their mouths open and struck at the bubbles of his exhale, time and time again, lunged and disappointed their fangs. Evidently, that's what had them riled, the sound of his exhales. Perhaps, Grady thought, any kind of unusual sound turned on their anger, or was it just that the lagoon was theirs and this was the way they dealt with any intruder? That would explain the reason for the lack of sea creatures on this side of the reef. The creatures knew better, and, now, so did he.

He decided not to surface. That would be the fastest way out of the lagoon but it would also cause the most commotion. Did he dare move at all? He had to.

He turned slowly, extended his legs slowly, worked his fins slowly. The breech in the reef through which he'd entered the lagoon was about thirty feet away. It was like he was swimming in turquoise-colored gelatin. He put off exhaling his breath as long as possible. It was agonizing. Any instant he expected to feel fangs piercing his legs, venom being injected into him. If one, just one, started it, they'd probably all want to get in on him. They were swimming all around him now, at their top speed, weaving in and out of one another, keeping ahead of him, surrounding him. All the way to the hole in the reef.

Maintaining his slow motions he glided through the opening.

Thought they would follow after him, but they didn't. Were satisfied with having chased him out.

He needed safety, surfaced at the stern of the boat, raised his mask and clung to the platform with tremulous hands. "Fuck!" he uttered.

"What's wrong?" Julia asked. She saw how pale he was.

"In the lagoon, nothing but snakes. Real ugly fuckers."

"Maybe now you'll get out and have something to eat."

"Last thing I expected was snakes."

"Were you bitten?"

"No, just scared shitless. Good thing you didn't dive."

"You are getting out now, aren't you?"

He considered it, decided not yet. The best place for him to get his nerves back would be down there on the bottom. "I want to have a look around the point," he said, meaning the high end of the island about a hundred yards north. "Who knows, might be a bed full of beauties there."

"Bed full of beauties, huh?" Julia arched. "Just one won't do, you have to have a bed full?"

"Be nice," he teased and went under.

Julia found a pair of binoculars and went up on top of the cabin where she'd have a more elevated view. Powerful, wide-angle binoculars, they brought the various aspects of the lagoon to her, made her feel as though she could reach out and swish the water. She scanned the elliptical-shaped lagoon, swept the surface of it, and, finally, there they were in the shallows, pink, yellow, green, looking like water lilies not yet open for the day. Heads above the surface, catching a breath of air. Julia studied them, saw some heads sink from sight, others pop up. There were hundreds.

She went below, put the binoculars away and got a nylon net laundry bag from one of the lockers. Gathered up a length of soft woven half-inch line, her diving mask and knife and William's bowl of dried rose leaves, went to the foredeck.

William was there lying on a woven grass mat. He sat up, moved to one end of the mat so she could sit on the opposite end, facing him.

He noticed the laundry bag and the other things, searched her eyes for a long moment and believed he saw the reason for them.

"You shouldn't take too much sun," she said.

"Are you going to dive?" he asked.

"Yes." She handed him the mask and the dried rose leaves. He took up an ample pinch of the leaves and spat on them and formed them into a damp clump. Rubbed the lens of her mask with it.

She watched him at it, saw how thorough he was. That pleased her. "Do you want to swim with me?" she asked.

"I'll tend the line," he told her.

"But I know how much you enjoy swimming with me."

"Yes, very much."

"*Chi'sa-sakana,*" she said fondly.

William had heard but he wanted to hear it again. "What?"

"*Chi'sa-sakana.*" Little fish.

He looked away, had to. His eyes were moist. When he brought them around to her again she was standing, pulling the T-shirt over her head. No self-consciousness, and none when she removed her shorts and underpants. She took the mask from him, slipped it on, tried it over her eyes and, satisfied with its snugness, pushed it up to ready position on her forehead. Next she secured the sheathed knife to her calf.

William cut off a short piece of the soft, woven line and tied it loosely around her waist. To that he tied the laundry bag, using a special knot from long ago.

She followed him to the stern where from among the diving equipment he got a weighted belt. Fastened the belt to itself to make a loop and tied the soft woven line to it. An improvised descending weight, not an inverted cast-iron mushroom thing, but it would do.

She slid into the water. He lowered the weighted belt to her and she put her feet into its loop. She pulled her mask down over her eyes. Began taking the rapid, preparative breaths, deep as possible inhales, forceful, whistling exhales.

A long-ago sound for William.

Julia did a dozen of those to make reservoirs in her lungs, to oxygenate her bloodstream. With a final inhale she nodded to William and he fed out the line and the weights carried her under and down thirty feet to the bottom.

She swam along the base of the reef, her legs and bare feet working cadently. No, her feet were not as efficient without the fins but, she thought, it was much better to have them free. She'd disliked having all that equipment on her. She didn't need it. She swam easily, the back of her mind keeping track of the seconds. She had plenty of time left, air enough to enjoy the underwater sights. She spotted several awabi, told herself to remember to collect two or three on her way back. William loved abalone, as did she.

She came to where the coral of the reef had given way, swam through the hole there to be in the lagoon. The nearest shallows were off to her right. She headed in that direction, swimming effortlessly, quietly, a sea creature. She came up for air but hardly disturbed the surface.

She'd come about an eighth of a mile and thus far no snakes. Or oysters. She'd been on the lookout for both. The depth there was only about eight feet, and according to the incline would soon be shallow enough for her to stand.

She spotted the first oyster at almost the same moment as she spotted the first snake. The big silver lip oyster in clear sight on the bottom up ahead, the snake a shocking pink one doing wide, wary zigzags twenty feet off to the left.

She went for the oyster.

The snake went for her.

She picked up the oyster and deposited it into the laundry bag.

The snake veered away from her at the last moment, swam from sight.

Gone to tell the others, Julia thought. She was convinced that sea creatures spoke to one another or at the very least with their own. (Hadn't there been times when she'd thought she could hear them?) What at that moment was that pink snake saying to the others? *She's over there, let's get her.* Perhaps they were arguing about how to proceed, over who would get the first bite.

Not to think like that, she told herself, and continued searching for oysters.

Found another. And another. Put those in the laundry bag. And a bit farther on two more, making altogether five.

She stood upright on the bottom, her head now above the surface. Her mouth was dry as a result of her body's call on its adrenals. Her heart was doing at least a hundred and fifty. Deep breaths wouldn't calm. With so much zap in her system she surely wouldn't be able to sleep that night, she thought, that is if for her there was going to be a night.

For a moment she felt extremely out of place. What was she doing in this lagoon, up to her neck in danger? It was total fucking lunacy. The next moment her thinking was what a beautiful, unspoiled place, the turquoise-colored water, the soft blue sand conforming to her feet, the sun warming her soaked, matted hair. And over there on her left, a dark patch of what?

She submerged, swam to the patch and found it was what Grady had alluded to earlier. A bed full. The lagoon bottom there was covered with *Pinctada maximas*, one vast, contented congregation of big oysters.

She swam directly above them, practically skimming them, saw them clench their valves together as she neared. She wanted to assure the four more that she placed in the laundry bag that no more harm would come to them, in fact, quite possibly they were going to be made to feel more comfortable.

Now she had nine and, she decided, that would be the limit. The bag, heavy as it was and hung from her right hip, would impede her swimming.

She headed back to the boat by way of the reef, had gone only a short ways before the pink snake returned. Anyway it appeared to her to be the same pink. Julia was terrified but continued swimming, telling herself that each kick and stroke was taking her closer to safety.

The pink had brought five others with him, three yellows, a smaller pink and a green. They were extremely fast, came at her one after the other, bolted by and circled back to make passes at her from the opposite direction. It was like a competition for them, the object being to terrify her as they sped by, coming increasingly closer. At last there was contact. The length of one ran across the skin of her stomach, the length of another across her shoulders. Their scaly-looking skins were surprisingly smooth. Then they were gone and she saw no more of them all the way to the reef. She didn't negotiate the reef by the way of the underwater hole. Instead she searched the surface along it and found a place where the sea was washing into the lagoon, a channel of sorts barely wide enough for her to slip through.

William was waiting on the stern of the ketch. She saw concern leave him, but he didn't speak, nor did she. They were in routine, preoccupied with their separate responsibilities. She was familiar with the special traditional knot he'd used to tie the laundry bag to the line at her waist. She undid it and he reached down from the diving platform and hauled it up. He removed the oysters from the bag and didn't have to ask whether or not she was through. Knew she wasn't. He tossed the bag back to her.

She reattached it to her waist line and swam back to the reef and through the small channel to again be within the lagoon.

The snakes were right there, awaiting her. The same six—the pink, three yellows, a green and the smaller pink. They'd been merely treading, but now, as though expressing reaction to her return or hoping to dazzle her, they performed acrobatics. Coils and spirals, intertwined duets and trios. The smaller pink didn't participate, remained aside, apparently watching the others. Perhaps still learning, Julia thought.

She made for the oyster bed in the shallows. Swam alternately on the surface and beneath it with the coordination and endurance of an extraordinary swimmer, one who'd spent many hours of most of her days in the water.

The six snakes swam along with her like they were her escort. Protectors? She wondered if they were a little splintered-off gang of toughs, six that had chosen to hang out together. Or were they emissaries appointed by the mass to see that she wasn't there to stay and claim some territory?

Whatever, that was how it went for seven round trips. She didn't take a rest until after the seventh and then she didn't go aboard the ketch, rather, she found a flat protrusion of the reef and sat upon that.

Grady returned empty-handed from his dive around the high point of the island. He climbed aboard the ketch expecting Julia to be there, perhaps not just awaiting him but, as well, with a big, caring breakfast ready.

No sign of her on deck. There was William preoccupied with something on the bow but no sign of Julia. Probably down in the galley, Grady thought.

He was about to get out of his diving gear and go below to her when he spotted the many huge oysters arranged in a line on the deck along the starboard side, their rough, ridged, variegated black and gray shells going dry in the sun. Incredible! It was as though they'd decided to accommodate his highest hopes; had, like a collaborative legion, leaped aboard for his benefit. But how actually, had they gotten there?

He called out excitedly to William, who evidently didn't hear, remained turned away.

Then he spotted Julia. Or was it an apparition? Julia perched naked on an outcrop of the reef about a hundred feet away. What the hell was she doing there? She shouldn't be there. Just beyond her was the lagoon and those snakes. She was too close to danger for Grady's comfort.

He shouted to her, shouted that she should return to the ketch. She just turned an ear his way and perhaps his voice was lost in the wash of the sea against the reef.

He beckoned broadly, frantically, to convey that he wanted her back aboard.

She waved to him, adjusted her mask, turned and slipped into the lagoon.

Grady leaped off the stern and swam full out to the place on the reef where Julia had been. He climbed up with difficulty because of his fins, stood up and looked for her in the lagoon. Where was she? Not in sight. He quaked at the thought that the snakes had sunk their fangs into her, that she was helplessly dying or already dead somewhere on the bottom.

That fear was relieved by her head surfacing about a hundred yards away. She'd been swimming underwater and was now swimming on the surface. Shit, look at her go! She'd never told him she could swim like that, Grady thought. You'd think she'd have at least mentioned it. And what was that swimming along both sides of her, alternately above the surface and disappearing under. Yellow, pink, green. They could only be snakes. Christ! they were right there with her. She didn't have a chance, and it wouldn't do any good for him to try to get to her. Even if he made it in time, how could he rescue her? Grief was already loud within him: *Oh, Julia, I love you Julia, oh Julia, you, you crazy bitch, Julia. Life will be shit without you, Julia.*

She was plucking oysters from the bed. Ten went into the laundry bag this time. One extra for Grady, she thought. Perhaps in that one would be the best pearl of all.

Quite tired now, she headed back to the reef. The laundry bag felt more than heavier by one oyster as she towed it along. The six snakes accompanied her, swam circles around her, and as she approached the reef they must have sensed this would be her final trip for they whizzed by her full speed one at a time, and peeled off right and left as though saluting farewell.

Grady had anxiously watched her return progress, had pulled and prayed with her every stroke, seen her head change from a distant round thing with indistinguishable features to his Julia. She came out of the lagoon by way of the little channel. Grady swam to meet her, saw she was laboring and tried to relieve her of the laundry bag. He had trouble undoing that knot and it required more of her energy to tread and let him undo it, but she didn't want to deprive him of being helpful.

They climbed aboard the ketch. At once Grady got out of his diving gear. Julia let her mask drop anywhere. Her legs were wobbly. She walked somewhat lock-kneed to the foredeck. Stood there nude while William hosed her down with fresh water. Grady wondered about that. It was like something prearranged.

She let the air dry her. She let William massage her calves and thighs. Grady took the cue and massaged her arms and shoulders. She let them know with little inside sounds how good it felt.

They put off giving attention to the oysters until Grady had held her for a while and until she'd gone below and put on a fresh pair of shorts and a sheer shirt, guzzled a bottle of Kirin and chomped down a Brie sandwich.

Their catch totaled seventy-three oysters. Some were slightly larger than others, but on the whole they were about the same size and otherwise identical. They were in various stages of opening. The ones brought in earlier were gaping by now, and it seemed to Grady he could reach right in and easily divest them of their pearls.

Julia jerked his hand back, and he realized she'd saved him a hurt finger when he saw how fiercely the oyster clamped down on the cork she inserted between its valves.

They worked systematically with three corks, the one from before and two taken just then from bottles of 1985 vintage La Tache that anyway would be best after some breathing. William was in charge of inserting the corks, Grady removed the pearls, Julia returned the oysters to the sea.

From the seventy-three oysters came fifty-seven blue pearls. So, not just a remarkable color but a phenomenal yield. Twenty-seven of the fifty-seven were huge beauties, approximately eighteen millimeter in size. Eleven were just as beautiful though not as large, around fourteen millimeters. The remaining ten were various lesser sizes. What's more, all but twelve were spherical enough to qualify as rounds.

Grady had them spread out on a linen hand towel on the galley table. He and Julia and William sat at the table in an appreciating daze, poking at the pearls, rolling them to cause them to throw blue iridescence, picking up this one, then that one, trying to decide which was best, which was the favorite.

Grady had at one time or another seen extraordinary lots of Colombian emeralds, and exceptional lots of D-flawless diamonds, but he knew that nothing that his eyes had ever set upon were as precious as these pearls.

They weren't his. They belonged to Julia and William, he thought. He told them that.

"Three-way split," Julia said.

William agreed.

Grady didn't even consider refusing. He dropped the blue pearl from the oyster he'd found in with the others, making fifty-eight. He got three glasses from the cupboard and poured some of the '85 La Tache. They toasted their wealthy selves, toasted the overlooked island, the generous lagoon, the prolific oysters and even the obligingly dispositioned snakes.

They were well into the second bottle, feeling heady and happy, looking at the world through wine-colored pupils, when Julia said rather thick tongued, "Tomorrow I'll dive for more."

"No," Grady told her, "no more."

"There's a whole bed full more in the lagoon."

"Yeah, and maybe tomorrow'll be a down day for the snakes."

Julia shrugged resignedly.

Grady opened another bottle and toasted Harold.

CHAPTER
TWENTY-THREE

An hour before the next dawn's light, Grady got up for the head and decided he might as well stay up. He had too much of a hangover to bother with shaving, just brushed away his wine mouth, promised a more thorough brushing later and went up on deck.

There was a moderate breeze coming from the northeast. Moderate this early it would get stiffer later, Grady thought. He was anxious to be under way, to get back to where his and Julia's and William's new riches could be transformed into various other pleasant realities. It was, he decided, a normal attitude, not really such a venal one.

He turned on the global satellite receiver for a readout. Turned the receiver off and on again, double-checking the position. He repeated the position to himself several times, aloud several times. He'd never forget it. He thought it best not to write it down, one less concern if he didn't write it down.

Wait until dawn? No, no reason to. He pulled up anchor and hoisted the mainsail and within a few minutes was well clear of the island. He wouldn't need to rely on the engine today, not as long as the breeze kept up. He unfurled the headsail and set all the others. Christ, what a great boat, Grady thought as he adjusted to be on course, he'd get one just like it, keep it in a marina over in Tiburon where Harold would have to see it all the time. Better boat than Harold's. Julia had sure been right about this trip when on the plane coming over she'd predicted he was going to do well. He again wished that he'd been more of a believer. Maybe she'd make him one, she could. He'd been right too, though, right about her. Some woman. He deserved her, he told himself. Some woman. Would he ever be able to accept that she'd taken it on her own to go into the lagoon after those pearls? He tried to imagine what her thought processes had been at the time. She was more courageous than foolhardy, he believed. It was better to have a woman with such courage, self-sufficient, able to put all her potential to use. It was, he had to admit, also somewhat intimidating.

Julia came on deck then, with mugs of fresh-brewed coffee. "I really needed this and so, you benefit," she said, handing him his mug, handle first.

The mug was so hot it burned his knuckles and he nearly dropped it. And, yet, she'd carried it all the way up from the galley without so much as an ouch. He took a slurp and asked, "Do you still think we ought to get married?"

"Have I ever thought so?"

"Haven't you?"

"Not that you know. What an oblique, cowardly way to put the question."

"Was, wasn't it?"

"I suppose if we ever did get married that's how you'd ask for sex." She mimicked him, "Do you still feel like having sex tonight? Gawd."

"Would asking be necessary?"

"I should hope not. Maybe way down the road, but as things are now, maybe not even way down."

"An article I read said that a sexual fit is the strongest possible foundation for a marriage."

"Is that what we have, a sexual fit?" she smirked. "What's that mean, mine's tight enough, yours is big enough?"

"You're a mess."

"Want me another way?"

An emphatic uh-uh from Grady. After another slurp he asked, "Seriously, you see any reason we shouldn't get married?" He was fairly sure she'd say no quickly, but she gave it some thought. "Money, maybe," she said.

"Money's good for a marriage," Grady contended.

"Not always, possibly not most of the time. Maybe married people who have to dig in together and kick the crap out of not having stand a better shot in the long run."

"We should throw our pearls overboard?"

"Do what you want with yours," she said, "I'm for marriage with money from the word go."

Some woman, Grady thought, liking his future.

The ketch was making good time, running at a reach with all sails set, averaging fourteen knots. At that rate, Grady figured, they'd be out of Burmese waters by midafternoon and pulling into Bang Wan Bay before dark.

At eleven William spotted the helicopter gunship. On the horizon, low over the water. The helicopter came right at the ketch, passed directly over it, clearing the top of the main mast by only about ten feet. A noisy, yellowish-brown chopper with the scarlet and royal blue flag of Burma painted unmissably on its underside. It executed a banking turn and made another close pass over the ketch for a stem-to-stern look. It climbed sharply then and leveled off and kept going, its interest apparently satisfied. Soon it was in the distance, as small to the sight as it had been when William first spotted it. What a relief!

Grady kept the binoculars on the chopper. Watched it bank to the north. Followed it and saw it continuing around to be coming at the ketch again, this time from starboard.

At a range of seven hundred feet it launched one of its 2.75-inch rockets. An accurate warning that hit and exploded about fifty feet off the bow of the ketch.

No desirable choice for the ketch. Either stop or be sunk. Grady and William reluctantly furled the headsail and brought down the rest. Grady swung the ketch around ninety degrees so it was headed into the wind.

The chopper circled twice, then hovered off starboard. It had widespread pontoons, unusually fat, oversized ones, which the pilot managed to set down with only slight difficulty on the

334

334

water's unruly surface. The engine was cut, the single-blade rotor slowed and came to a stop in line with the chopper's body. Drift carried the chopper alongside the ketch. Before Grady and William could put out fenders one of the chopper's pontoons collided against the hull, but only with enough impact to cause a smudge.

The door of the chopper slid open. Two barefoot Burmese soldiers stepped out onto the nearest pontoon and climbed aboard the ketch. Typical Burmese, slightly built, grimly set expressions on their dark, burnished faces. They were armed with automatic rifles. One held his rifle cocked and at the ready on Grady, William and Julia, while the other secured a line to hold the chopper positioned.

A Burmese army captain stepped out onto the pontoon and came aboard. He was in lightweight dress uniform: shirt, tie, two rows of service ribbons and a .45 caliber sidearm in a highly polished brown leather holster. The incongruous thing about him was his black, wing-tipped shoes. He ran his disdainful look up and down Grady. Then William, then Julia. He didn't move his head, just his eyes.

Lethal-looking little fucker, Grady thought. Not the sort to tolerate much, would shoot them and toss them over the side if the situation got the least bit complicated. Or maybe not shoot, just toss.

The captain gibbered a few sentences in Burmese before abruptly shifting to English. He demanded identification. Passports were shown. He demanded the boat's papers. The papers were shown. He didn't express even a hint of satisfaction, snapped an order to his two men and they began searching the boat.

They searched methodically but carelessly, pulling things out of every locker and storage area, strewing clothes and equipment and supplies about. One of the first places they looked was in the main cabin, in the drawer of the cabinet next to the bed. The blue pearls had been kept there in one of Julia's white athletic socks. The sock was there now but not the pearls.

No pearls.

The captain climbed down onto the pontoon and reported that to someone, evidently a superior, who was remaining out of sight inside the chopper.

Grady thought this might be all there'd be to it. The captain would climb back into the chopper, would signal his men to do the same. The chopper would take off and good riddance.

However, the captain intently heeded what he was told by his superior. He came back aboard and reprimanded the two soldiers for not having searched thoroughly enough. They jumped to it, began going through everything again. A frantic, disorganized search during which they looked into some storage spaces and lockers as many as a half dozen times within a few minutes.

They gave special attention to the galley with all its cupboards and little bins, canisters, pots and cartons of foodstuff. The empty wine bottles in the trash receptacle would have been overlooked had not one of the soldiers brushed against a protruding neck. Causing the chinking sound of glass against glass and also a few telltale clicks.

The soldiers peered down the throats of the dark green bottles, held them up to the light, saw around the labels what was in two of them. They took those two to the captain.

The captain partially inverted one of the bottles.

Several of the blue pearls it contained rolled out and dropped into his palm, along with a dribble of La Tache.

Julia looked to Grady. He had his eyes closed to avoid witnessing the awful moment. Good thing, Julia thought, otherwise no telling what he'd do. Probably he'd go berserk and get himself riddled. She herself was close to that point. She'd almost pulled it off, though. Pearls in the empty wine bottles. When it became obvious that the ketch was going to be boarded she'd hidden the pearls there. Now the bottom line was the old L-L-L, all that swimming and risk yesterday, Love's Labor Lost. Oh well. She tried to prime up some optimism by telling herself this was a huge, expensive setback, but it didn't necessarily augur an unhappy ending. She also thought the wish that these Burmese miserables would be made to take a flying leap and a long, pink-yellow-green swim in that lagoon.

The captain commended the soldiers with a brief smile and one nod. Wine bottles in hand, he legged over the lifeline and got onto the pontoon. He had the bottles extended, handing them over to his yet unseen superior within the chopper when a swell caused the chopper to pitch.

One of the bottles was bobbled.

The superior grabbed for it, got it.

However, in so doing, his hands came into view. Just his hands. They were by no means the hands of a Burmese. Too pale to be that, and too large. Huge, coarse-looking hands. The sort of hands that would mark a Caucasian peasant.

Grady believed he recognized those hands.

So did William.

Grady's involuntary reflex was an aggressive step forward.

The soldiers alerted the aim of their rifles. Another step by Grady and they'd be firing.

William's shoulders slumped, his arms hung limp at his sides. He appeared to be giving up the situation. It was too much for him to bear. Spiritless, he lowered himself to his haunches. That lower position gave him what he'd hoped he'd get from his feigning. A different perspective of the inside of the chopper. The inside man was still keeping himself out of sight, however the glare from the sea was making the window opaque on the far side of the chopper's cabin, and from the angle William had of it the man's face was being reflected.

It was undoubtedly him.

Lesage. Bertin.

That meant the chopper wasn't really Burmese, just decorated to appear so. The captain and the soldiers also weren't what they were made out to be. They might be Burmese but they were hired, playing a role, probably Burmese army deserters. There were any number of those who'd jumped over the border. The real thing, though, were the weapons. There was no doubting those automatic rifles nor the threat that they'd be used.

The make-believe captain and soldiers got into the chopper. It drifted clear. Its door was slid shut, its rotor started. As it lifted and did a swooping side-slip away, the ketch and those aboard it were struck by a blast of insolent turbulence.

CHAPTER TWENTY-FOUR

Is that the lot?" Kumura asked.

"That's it," Lesage replied.

"You're not holding back a few or quite a few?"

"Why would I do that?"

"Possibly to strike a second, harder bargain after we've concluded this one."

"I wouldn't do that to a partner," Lesage said, wishing he'd thought of it. "Especially not to a partner who's also a close friend."

"Forgive me, Daniel. It's just that I know what a sharp dealmaker you are." Kumura hoped his flattery wasn't too thick. Evidently it wasn't. Lesage just soaked it up.

They were in the office-study on the ground floor of Kumura's house. On the surface of the desk between them lay the blue pearls. Kumura was trying his best to modulate his intense interest in the pearls, however each time he sat back and ignored them they soon enough drew him to them and had him on the edge of his chair and hunched. Meanwhile, Lesage was slouched in his chair as though for him the pearls, though blue and rare, held absolutely no fascination.

Lesage had assumed insouciance from the first word when he'd phoned Kumura a few hours ago and during a pause in their discussion regarding a trivial matter had dropped the fact that he (by the way) had acquired another batch of blue natural pearls. Was Kumura by any chance interested? Kumura had difficulty only saying he might be. Kumura let the subject go for a minute or two, then came back to it, suggested offhand that Lesage bring the blue pearls by so he could have a look at them. Lesage put him off until five with the fib that Paulette had a new pedicurist coming in from Phuket whom he also wanted to give a try.

That delay was intended to fuel Kumura's acquisitiveness, however what it did was give Kumura time to settle on how he'd handle the matter if indeed Lesage did have some blue naturals.

Thus, when Lesage showed up at five-thirty with a brown paper bag in hand, Kumura was prepared for him.

The pearls were removed from the bag and grouped upon a square of white velour. The bag was crumpled into a ball and tossed into the wastebasket. Kumura got a ten-power tripod loupe from one of the drawers of the collector's cabinet situated against the wall behind his desk. He chose pearls at random and examined them carefully, taking his time, making favorable comments. At times he got lost in the depths of their blue vibrancy, not seeing the pearls as pearls as much as he was seeing women. Women he would yet meet and fulfill, young, erotically greedy women whom he'd satiate with his virility, passionate sexual novices whom he'd initiate with such impressive technique and ardor that they'd go through life spoiled for all other men.

Finally, Kumura set the loupe aside. "So, how many do we have here?"

"Fifty-eight."

"Not fifty-seven or fifty-nine?"

Lesage shrugged indifferently. "To tell the truth," he said, "I didn't count them."

"You're jesting, of course."

"I played with them a bit and thought about counting them but then I saw no point in it. They're so obviously a large lot and I have no intention of selling them by the piece."

"I see. Still...I find it hard to believe you haven't counted them. Any other man would have done so a dozen times."

"You should know by now that I avoid doing the ordinary."

"That doesn't say much for me," Kumura smiled wryly. "Here I sit finding it hard to suppress the urge to know precisely how many there are."

"Go ahead, count."

It was crucial to Kumura that he know the exact number of pearls in the lot. Lesage had lied well and Kumura didn't know which to believe. Were there fifty-eight pearls as Lesage had first said or was it true that Lesage hadn't bothered to count?

Kumura used the flat edge of a silver letter opener to separate two pearls at a time from the rest—*thirty-two, thirty-four, thirty-six...*—and while counting asked, "Would you mind telling me where in the world you got these?"

"I'd mind."

"Somewhere in the Andaman no doubt."

"Somewhere."

Forty-two, forty-four... "I suppose you can get more whenever you wish."

"No, the source is depleted."

"You're certain of that?"

"It's cleaned out. There won't be more."

"What a shame. But, if that's the case you shouldn't mind my knowing where they came from." *Fifty-four, fifty-six, fifty-eight.*

Lesage remained silent.

Kumura abandoned that tack. He reached down into the waste-basket to retrieve the badly crushed brown paper bag. Pretending to have a second better thought he dropped the paper bag back into the basket. He stood and from one of the many higher drawers of his collector's cabinet brought out a tan, chamois drawstring sack. He put the pearls in the sack, had a slight problem with the drawstring. He paused for a long moment, seeming to be turning over in his mind the sack of pearls he had in his hand. Then, abruptly, as though having reached a decision, he drew open one of the high drawers of the cabinet and placed the sack of pearls into it. Slid the drawer shut sharply. "Okay," he said, turning to Lesage, "now, how much are you going to stick me?"

"This is twice as good a lot as the first."

"If you say."

"A hundred million," Lesage blurted.

Kumura smiled. "I knew you'd be reasonable."

"And..." Lesage continued, "controlling interest in the pearl farm here in Bang Wan. I thought what we might do is simply reverse our positions. I'd hold the majority share, you'd take over my limited standing."

"Is that all?" Kumura asked calmly.

"No. I want a quarter interest in Kumura Worldwide."

"What else?"

"Those are my terms," Lesage said firmly. He was quite sure Kumura would go for the hundred million and with owning a lesser share of the farm. He was just as sure Kumura wouldn't agree to a quarter interest in Kumura Worldwide. He'd included the latter in his demands only to have something to give up.

Kumura nodded thoughtfully to convey that he understood the terms. While evidently considering them, he began pacing back and forth in front of the cabinet. It was a huge piece of mahogany furniture. Over ten feet tall and six wide. Lacquered red as it was, with intricate gold-painted Oriental figures and motifs and hand-shaped brass pulls, escutcheons and hinges, it appeared to be authentically Chinese. However, in truth it was early nineteenth-century English, created by a maker in Bristol. Kumura had come across it one day in a shop on Curzon Street. The most appealing thing about it was its numerous drawers. Fifty-five in the upper section alone. Thirty-three more below. Not tiny drawers, either, but of useful size. For that reason it was called a collector's cabinet. It was Kumura's favorite. He regularly took advantage of its features and knew it well.

He stopped pacing, stopped equivocating. Faced the cabinet, pulled out one of its higher drawers. He was removing the tan chamois sack from that drawer when he again had trouble with its drawstring. The drawstring came loose. Several of the pearls escaped the sack and clacked against the mahogany bottom of the drawer.

"Damn!" Kumura exclaimed. He retrieved the pearls, fumbled them into the sack, tightened and tied the drawstring and placed the sack on the desk in front of Lesage.

"By nature," Kumura said as he resumed his seat behind the

desk, "I'm the impulsive sort. Too much so. Always have been. Lately I've been trying to check that shortcoming. My inclination is to make this deal, close it here and now and be done with it. This time, however, I'm going to listen to my more judicious self."

"Meaning?"

"I'm going to give it some thought."

"What's the problem? Are my terms too stiff?"

"You know very well I'd never part with any of Kumura Worldwide."

"So, I'm flexible when it comes to that. Exclude it from my deal entirely, just throw it out."

"And how about revealing to me the source of the pearls?"

It occurred to Lesage that inasmuch as he'd told Kumura that the source of the pearls had been picked clean he could indicate just about any remote island and say that was it. He acted reluctant, hemmed and hawed some before giving in. "I'll take you to it," he promised.

A grateful smile from Kumura.

Lesage believed he had him.

But Kumura was like a big fish that kept slipping off the hook. "You'll have my answer by tomorrow morning at the latest," Kumura said, "most likely sooner. Will you be turning in early tonight?"

"I'll be up," Lesage said, dejected. He undid the tan chamois sack, took a cursory look in at the pearls, retied the sack and departed.

Kumura stood by the window and watched Lesage's black Rolls out of sight. He felt like doing a dance around the room. He limited his glee to a single skip on his way to the collector's cabinet. From the drawer fourth from the top in the second vertical row from the left he removed the chamois sack containing the fifty-eight natural blue pearls.

It had taken some doing, he thought, as he opened the sack and poured a few of the precious blues into his cupped palm.

He'd prepared in advance of Lesage's arrival three sacks of pearls. One containing forty-five pearls, another containing fifty-five, and still another containing sixty-five. All were cultured pearls that he'd gathered and covertly dyed blue over the years, with the hope that each batch he dyed would somehow be as effective for him as were the natural blues.

He'd placed each of the three identical sacks in a separate drawer on the fifth row down. The sticky part had been the number of pearls. When it turned out that Lesage's natural blues totaled fifty-eight, Kumura had either to add three to the sack of fifty-five or subtract seven from the sack of sixty-five.

He'd decided it would be easier to take out rather than put in. Accordingly, the troublesome drawstring had been his spontaneous invention, allowing pearls to escape from the sack of sixty-five so that he could recover all but seven.

Thus, the sack he'd given back to Lesage held fifty-eight pearls and, in that regard, Lesage would be none the wiser.

It had been a perfect switch. All those identical drawers. Fifth row down or fourth row down, Lesage hadn't been alert enough to notice the difference. Also Lesage's affected air of insouciance had helped greatly. The bloody oaf, Kumura thought. He'd phone Lesage in the morning to tell him no deal.

Of course, Lesage would find out soon enough that his goods were cultured and dyed. As soon as he tried to sell elsewhere that would come out. Lesage would be insulted, perplexed and livid. In that order. When he mentally backtracked, he'd realize when the switch had most likely taken place. He'd rant and accuse, threaten all sorts of action.

Let him.

For Kumura it was a matter of *fellicific calculus*, the pleasures that would be forthcoming because of the switch far outweighed whatever else he'd have to put up with.

CHAPTER TWENTY-FIVE

The village of Na Yang.

Ten miles up the coast from Bang Wan.

Grady and William decided they'd put the ketch in there rather than sail directly to the docking shed.

Julia wasn't asked her opinion of the tactic, and, although she agreed that such stealth seemed a good idea, she resented not having been allowed a voice. Nor was she included in how Lesage should and would be dealt with. Grady and William could think or speak of little else, but when Julia tried to contribute, either her words got stepped on or it was like she was talking to herself. It had become a dangerous matter involving weapons and therefore a male matter.

Julia loathed that. She felt like punching them or at least kicking them (she only momentarily considered the balls) in the shins. Instead, she told herself to just bide her time. She stopped trying to make suggestions, sat there in the stern and silently approved on cue while they conspired.

When they had it worked out, her part in it was to hire a car in Na Yang to take them to Bang Wan and, when they got to Bang

Wan, she was to go to Kumura's and remain in the room well out
of the way until it was over. Typical shit, she thought as, apparently,
she accepted her role.

They arrived at Na Yang at dusk. Had it been any later they
probably wouldn't have been able to tie up because the dock there
wasn't much of a dock and most of it was occupied by small
overused commercial fishing boats. Grady just did manage to slip
the ketch in between two and attach a bowline.

While he and William tended to the sails and to making sure the
ketch was otherwise in order, Julia went ashore as she was
supposed to.

She found that Na Yang was much less of a village than she'd
expected. That was good, she thought. It consisted of one everything store, with a single weathered gas pump out front and no
more than a dozen congenially situated makeshift houses in the
tropical growth out back. Other than a couple of motorized
bicycles left outside the houses, the only vehicle seemed to be a
1967 Ford station wagon missing three fenders and one headlight.
It was parked on one side of the store. A tiny Thai woman was
loading slotted crates almost as large as herself into it, shoving the
last crate in when Julia, with a U.S. twenty in hand, approached
her.

A ride to Bang Wan? The woman snapped the twenty from
Julia's fingers. She said she was in a terrible hurry. The crabs in the
crates had already been out of the water too long. She was taking
them to the Coral Beach Hotel in Phuket. The more life there was
in the crabs when she got there the more she'd be paid for them.

The old, one-eyed station wagon started obediently, and within
a minute or two was the ultimate rattler on paved Highway 4
headed south. Another thing missing from the wagon was its
floorboards on the passenger side. Julia hunched down and placed
her feet up on the dashboard. The texture of the highway visibly
zipping by at close range beneath her and the frantic scuttling of
the crabs in the crates just behind her made it an even stranger
ride.

Julia expected she'd be let off at the private road, but the
woman asked her where to turn and took her all the way in to
Kumura's house.

Julia went in and up to her room. She took a quick shower,

shampooed and conditioned her hair. Did her makeup, her more natural version, included no real red but skillfully applied an artful, dark, wicked look bordering on evilness to her eyes. She'd already decided on what she'd wear. The pale yellow silk organza trousers she'd bought in Bangkok. Wide-legged, floaty trousers, precisely transparent enough so only her fanciest bikini panties would do. No blouse. Instead, a snug tank top of silk in a more chrome yellow. The combination was right, she thought, as she simultaneously slipped her feet into a pair of light scaled heels and appraised herself in the mirror: a susceptible show-off below, a bit tough above. She remembered to decide against perfume. (Hadn't it been said that her natural scent was provocative?) Neither would she wear any jewelry, not even ear clips. Bare eared would be better. She grabbed up an appropriate shoulder bag and, repressing another look at herself, hurried out.

William's red Porsche was parked off the drive. She borrowed it and within a few minutes was at the main entrance of Lesage's house. A servant answered the door. Julia was told to wait. The servant reappeared and showed her in and up to the second floor.

Lesage and Paulette were in the spacious study. Playing ennui, telling each other how bored they were there in Bang Wan and volleying with places they'd rather be. Lesage was sprawled on one of the sofas. He had on a white flannel, double-breasted suit with engraved mother-of-pearl buttons. No shirt or undershirt and no shoes or stockings. His feet were as knubby and ugly as his hands, Julia thought. Paulette was on the sofa opposite. All she had on was loose-legged, lace-edged silk panties and a matching camisole. Neither Lesage nor Paulette got up to greet Julia. Lesage did a minimal temporary smile around his hello. Paulette threw her a kiss. Rather than throw one back, Julia went directly to Paulette and from the back of the sofa tilted Paulette's head up and brought her lips down upon Paulette's for a kiss that was more than brief and obviously aggressive.

That didn't make Lesage sit up but it definitely got his attention. "*Brisant*," he remarked, but with restraint.

Paulette accepted the kiss as though it were expected. She patted the sofa cushion next to her as if Julia were an adoring pet to have come sit. Julia disobeyed, helped herself to some of the good *blanc de blancs* they were drinking. She noticed a round magnifying mirror and a pair of gold tweezers on the arm of the sofa. Evidently Paulette had been plucking her already perfectly shaped brows. From that Julia gathered that Paulette was truly bored, so the distraction she'd provide would be most welcome.

"Daniel and I were just agreeing that it's time to get away from here for a while," Paulette said. "I'm badly in need of some Paris."

"And some Côte d'Azure," Lesage said.

"*Pas moi*," Paulette said doing a moue. "I've had enough of seaside for the moment. I need some shopping. Alice Condolle must think I've died. I ordered two dozen panties and camisoles like this months ago and she hasn't heard a word from me. Look," she tugged at a single loose thread at a seam of the camisole, "I'm down to wearing tatters."

Now Julia sat beside Paulette, who, too lazy to reach for her own glass, took a sip from Julia's, leaving an unctuous pink lip print. From that spot on the glass exactly Julia took a sip.

Paulette was pleased. Her eyes let Julia know that. She was grateful for Julia, that Julia had been the sort that could be converted into a worshipper. Paulette had nearly everything she could want. Above the level of nearly was her need to corrupt, to test the effectiveness of her beauty in the most extreme and therefore more reassuring ways. Such as, in this case with Julia, foiling a romance.

"Where's Grady?" Paulette asked.

"Up the coast a ways, in a place called Na Yang," Julia replied indifferently. "He had a problem with the boat, the steering mechanism or something."

"You didn't stay out pearling long."

"No."

"The enjoyment is in the idea of it," Lesage said. "After a few unrewarding dives comes discouragement." Having submitted that fragment of wisdom, he rolled over onto his side, putting his back to them. No concern about how he was punishing the flannel suit.

"I sense that you and Grady had *une bisbille*, a little tiff," Paulette said.

"Not really," Julia told her. "I've just arrived at the point where I've had enough of him. As it turned out he's not rich enough for me nor does he have any prospects."

"Poor, poor darling," Paulette sided. "So you've come to us."

"Yes."

"Well, you're entirely right. Contrary to what's often said being rich is most important. Sometimes, when my imagination has it in for me, I envision myself without a sou. Believe me it's devastating, but also, believe me, if that were really the case, I wouldn't be poor for long."

Julia nodded soberly. She waited a beat, sat forward and said, "I saw you in the helicopter." Her words were intended, of course, for Lesage. It seemed she threw them at him and they went over the hump of his back and turned him over. "What did you say?" he asked.

"This morning you were aboard that helicopter. You were trying not to be seen, but I saw you."

"Are you telling me you were stopped by a Burmese patrol?" Lesage asked.

"Not an authentic Burmese patrol."

"I take it you were up in Burmese waters."

"Yes."

"You shouldn't have been up there. No telling ever what the Burmese are apt to do."

"I recognized your hands when you reached for the wine bottles," Julia told him levelly.

Lesage did a bewildered face followed by an amused scoff. "My hands? They couldn't have been mine." He held his hands up, as though they proved that.

"I also saw your face," Julia told him. "At least I saw the reflection of it in the window opposite from where you were seated."

"You're mistaken."

"No. It was definitely you."

"It was not," Lesage said firmly.

"You don't have to admit it. It's only important that you realize that I saw you."

"Saying that you did, why would it be important?"

"So you'd know where I stand," she replied.

"Which is where?"

"You have fifty-eight blue pearls. You could have ten times, twenty times that many."

At last Lesage was made to sit up.

Paulette had remained silent throughout, entertained by Julia's assertiveness and Lesage's wiggling denials. She placed her always appreciated legs upon the low glass-topped table, crossed them at the ankles and pointed her pampered toes ballerinalike. Gave Julia's back three encouraging pats as Julia told Lesage, "I know where that island is. I've been there. I know its exact position. I've seen the oysters in that lagoon. An incredible number just lying there waiting to give up their pearls. By comparison the fifty-eight you have now is a pittance."

Lesage lighted a cigar.

"What I have in mind is a three-way split," Julia said, "a third for each of us. We'd spread the pearls out and each take a pick in turn so there'd be no quibbling."

Lessage pictured it.

Julia could practically see his imagination working. She fed it. "A thousand, more likely two thousand natural blue pearls, hundreds of them eighteen-millimeter size, and we'd have our pick."

"*D'accord*," Lesage said, "you tell me the location of the island and I'll send some divers there."

"Sure you will," Julia said sarcastically. "And I'll be lucky to get one tiny pearl as a souvenir."

"I'd be fair," Lesage told her.

"Spare me," she told him.

"So, what do you propose?" he asked.

"For certain we shouldn't make a big thing out of it, involve a lot of divers and all. Once they know the island...well, you can imagine the consequences. I say we go there, just the three of us. The oysters are in the shallows, easy to get at. We could clean it out in practically no time."

What an audacious cunt, Lesage thought, and to think she now knew where the island was, that which had eluded him all these years. She knew all right. The fifty-eight blues he had in his possession attested to that. She wasn't all that smart, though greedy cunts like her never were, thought they were but weren't. Couldn't she see that she was asking for it? Sure, he'd let her take him to the island, but when they got there and he'd determined that the blue pearls were there, he'd kill her. Maybe he wouldn't also have to kill Paulette. That would depend. No, he decided, better, neater that he killed Paulette too. He'd almost had enough of her anyway. Only almost because a good time for him was being worked up between Paulette and this Julia. It would all come loose when they were out on the water.

He forced his mind back to the less ephemeral aspect. What would it be like to have such a huge cache of blue naturals, he wondered, to have the corner on a precious anomaly? Wouldn't he be famous? Wouldn't articles be written about him? His Lesage identity could stand up to such fame, he believed. Every now and then from his hoard he'd contribute a blue to a museum. His reputation would soar. He'd sleep in royal beds, deliver food to his mouth with royal forks, be able to thumb his ass at Kumura.

That was the clincher.

He brought out from behind one of the sofa cushions the tan chamois bag of blue pearls he'd brought home from Kumura's only a couple of hours ago. No word yet from Kumura. He'd been edgily waiting for the call and maybe could use the hundred million, but it didn't matter nearly as much now.

He opened the sack and allowed the pearls to roll across the glass top of the table. They collided with Paulette's feet, ran up the exquisite line of her calves. It was a cavalierish gesture by Lesage, intended to amuse and demonstrate his decision to go along with Julia's proposal.

Julia ignored the pearls.

"We'll set out first thing in the morning!" Lesage said enthusiastically.

"Tonight," Julia contradicted, "soon as possible."

"Why tonight?" Lesage asked.

"To get the jump on Grady and William. Remember, they also know where the island is. Had it not been for the problem with the boat they would have gone right back to it."

"Do they know I was in the chopper?"

"I kept that to myself. They swallowed the whole Burmese illusion."

"Then it must have shook them. I think you're wrong. It'll be a long time before they risk going back into Burmese waters."

"You don't know Grady," Julia said. "He'll be back there gathering up blues in no time."

Lesage retrieved the pearls from the table, some had rolled over the edge onto the carpet. He didn't count them, didn't know whether or not he'd found them all. From the heft of the chamois sack it felt as though he had. If he'd overlooked a few, to hell with them. "What do you think, Paulie?" he asked.

"I'm all for tonight," Paulette replied ambiguously.

"It's just that I don't like being at sea at night, never have."

A loud, intolerant sigh from Paulette.

"Once we're out of the bay you'll have nothing to be uneasy about," Julia assured. "We'll set the heading and let the boat sail itself on autopilot. Then, if you're still uneasy...well, you can shut your eyes if you want."

"Like hell," Lesage declared, with a lascivious grin.

He and Paulette went from the study to get whatever personal items they might need for a few days at sea.

Julia, left alone in this room that was so overbearingly Lesage, took stock of the circumstances she'd created. Ever since she'd gone ashore at Na Pang with the purpose of hiring a car she'd been only slightly herself. Most of her felt as though she were on a path between two walls, infinitely high, invisible walls that hemmed her in, refused her any other course. This same sense of being directed, steered, influenced, however it could be described, was something she'd experienced at various times during the past few months. To a lesser degree than what she was undergoing now but nonetheless the same. She'd traced it back to soon after the night when she'd decided against life and consumed those saved-up Nembutals. The first manifestation of it had been in her lawyer's office when she couldn't resist breaking her strand of pearls.

Initially she'd attributed that instance to her attraction to Grady. Hadn't it been nothing more than an assertive approach on her part? Wasn't it only that she'd wanted to meet him, broken the ice, so to speak, by breaking her pearls? Only much later on, when she reflected upon it, did she admit that she was compelled beyond herself to break the pearls. And she certainly didn't accept that it was merely a coincidence he happened to be a pearl dealer. No, that day in the lawyer's office had been like the obligatory opening scene in a melodrama.

Also along the line there'd been numerous other instances, little things, such as sudden contradictions in what she'd come to believe were her settled tastes, established dislikes, that for no apparent reason all at once became preferences.

And what about the more extreme, inexplicable occurrences? The way she'd temporarily lost the use of her arms on two occasions. Her knowing there was an island where nothing was indicated on the chart. Her swimming. She'd never been more than an average swimmer, but for that one afternoon she'd swam as though she'd been brought up in the water. And not just any water, the sea. Where had she gotten all that breath? All that courage and strength?

She couldn't chalk those things up to Grady's affect on her. She'd wanted to mention them to him but hadn't for the same reason she hadn't told him of her attempted suicide. For fear it would complicate their relationship, might even cause him to question her sanity. It was, she felt, absolutely essential that he love her, but why was it so essential? And what of her love for him? Was she genuinely capable of it or was that capability a transient accommodation like her swimming?

How confusing it was. She couldn't count on anything.

It seemed, she thought, she'd grasped a somewhat substantial thread of explanation from what William had divulged at one point during the sail back.

"My mother..." were the two words that got William started. "My mother was an ama. Her name was Setsu, Setsu Yoshida. She was a great ama. Given more of a chance she would have been an even more revered ama than my grandmother's grandmother, Amira, who is still to this day considered a legend."

"I take it that contrary to what you said, your mother knew how to swim."

"She more than merely knew how."

"What did you say her name was?"

"Setsu."

"Say it again."

William said it. Julia watched it come from his lips. The sibilant sound of it hung in the air between them for a long moment and then it seemed to go to Julia's eyes, causing them to tear. She blamed that on the wind. After a recovering moment she remarked: "Sometimes even the best swimmers drown."

"She didn't drown," William admitted.

"Oh?" Julia was aware that she had to pretend surprise.

"She was murdered. Both she and my Aunt Michiko were murdered."

Apparently William wanted to let it go at that, however Julia felt compelled to draw him out, and soon the awful truth came pouring from him. An account of the entire episode from the day when he and Setsu and Michiko first met the Frenchman named Bertin in Ban Pakbara to when they happened upon the uncharted island shaped like a shoe.

"Where *you* found the first blue pearl," Julia had to say as though it were a memory they shared. On swift second thought she added, "I assume."

William went on, got to the ghastly part, the murders by Bertin.

Julia shuddered, hugged herself. "Tell me more about this ugly fellow," she prompted.

"You know him," William said levelly. "Bertin is Lesage."

It puzzled Julia that she didn't even for a moment consider William might be mistaken. She merely accepted his contention, and continued to listen as William revealed how he'd recognized the *dah-she* knife in Lesage's study, kept by Lesage as a grisly memento—how from that certain incrimination he'd been able to undo Lesage's rearranged face and identify him as Bertin.

Throughout the telling William had frequently paused and looked to Julia as though she could verify his every word. Indeed, her involuntary nods were concurring testimony. She'd been especially stirred when William had boasted that Setsu was such a great ama. She'd been equally angered when he'd told her how on the murder day Bertin had struck him.

And now, here she was sitting alone in Lesage's house and being allowed a phase of objectivity. She should have gone along with Grady's and William's plan, just done her part, she thought. Why was it so crucial that she keep ahead of them in this matter? She had the urge to run away from the situation, to leave it all up to Grady and William. Run, she told herself, but when she stood up to run she merely went looking around the room.

"Let's go!" Paulette called in to her from the hall. And as they were hurrying down the stairs, Paulette told her, "I brought along some things more suitable for you to wear." A servant opened the main door to the courtyard with such perfect timing it seemed to Julia that he was an accomplice to their intentions.

Lesage drove. They sat three in the front of the black Corniche, Julia sharing the seat with Paulette. The top was down and the wind created by their speed whipped above and around them like a manic spirit. The docking shed was only a short ways up the bay, and they arrived there within a minute or two. Then it was hurry down the walk to beach level and into the shed.

Four of Lesage's people were there on the dock, evidently expecting him. They were young, look-alike Caucasians. Deeply tanned crewing types with streaked blond hair, dressed in white shorts and plain white T-shirts. Their body language conveyed impudence.

Lesage stopped to talk to them while Julia and Paulette went aboard the sloop. Julia glanced back and saw Lesage emphatically giving instructions to the men. The sloop's engines were already on and idling, riling the water of the slip, its exhaust causing gurgling and pops.

Lesage came aboard.

CHAPTER
TWENTY-SIX

G rady and William waited on the ketch for Julia a half hour before going ashore to look for her. They learned from a man in the everything store that she'd driven away with someone known only as the crab woman. Returning to the ketch, they got the two Glock semiautomatic pistols from the gun locker and put to pocket several full clips of eighteen rounds.

Ran the mile out to Highway 4.

Hitched a ride to the turnoff.

Ran the private road in to Lesage's house.

They wondered what would explain William's Porsche parked in the drive. Grady felt its hood. It was cool, had been there a while.

They entered the house, went right in by way of the main entrance. The downstairs hall was dark. One of the Thai servants appeared but when he realized their disposition and spotted the guns he dashed away. They paused there to listen for Lesage. The house was silent. It was decided Grady would search the downstairs, William went up.

William saw a light was on in Lesage's bedroom. It turned out to be just a light left on, but, according to the condition of the cigar in a bedside ashtray, he knew Lesage had been there only minutes ago.

The study was equally abandoned.

While crossing that room William stepped upon a pearl. In picking it up he spotted another beneath the sofa. Two of the larger blues. Why, he wondered, would Lesage be that careless? Then he noticed the *dah-she* knife was missing from its glass case, saw that someone had forced the case open.

The sounds of a scuffle downstairs, some strident, high-pitched swearing and screams.

William rushed down and found Grady had one of the Thai servants up in the air and pinned against the wall. The diminutive Thai was flailing with his feet, trying to kick Grady in the groin, but he suddenly ceased that, having come to his better senses, decided his well-being was worth more than his job. He was so eager to inform that his words were all run together and incomprehensible, but, finally, he got across that Lesage had gone sailing with Paulette and the other woman.

The other woman would be Julia, Grady knew. He and William hurried out the back way, down the terraced slope to the beach. From there they could see the huge, rectangular structure of the docking shed about two miles down the bay, light from a three-quarter moon glinting on its black glass exterior.

They ran for it, full out. The tide was up, so there was no helpful, hard-packed edge to the sand, just soft give; tougher going, and by the time they'd covered half the distance, they were panting loudly, grunting with practically every stride, their lungs complaining.

But there was no room in Grady's mind to admit the strain. His only thoughts were Lesage had Julia, at gun point, knife point, whatever, had her. Against her will. What had made her think she could confront Lesage on her own? Lesage was too much for her. Being courageous with snakes was one thing, murderer Lesage another. Lesage had her, Grady thought, she was in grave peril, he had to get to her in time.

He was soaked with sweat and his side had a stitch like an ice pick in it when he reached the docking shed. William had to struggle with him to force him to pause outside the shed—so they'd be in a condition to take on what they might encounter inside. Still, Grady couldn't allow himself more than thirty seconds.

The sweat had poured down his arms to his hands and the Glock pistol felt slippery in his grasp as he opened the door to the docking shed and rushed in.

The first thing he saw was Lesage's blue-hulled sloop. It was about a hundred yards down the dock. Its mooring lines were just then being freed and taken in.

The next thing Grady saw was the fair-haired young man in white coming at him. The black object in the young man's hands was a machine pistol. He wasn't coming in a crouch nor did he say anything, nor did he have any regard for the pistol in Grady's hand. He just kept coming straight up and when he got close enough to suit him started firing.

Grady dropped to the concrete surface of the dock. William darted behind an upright steel beam for cover.

The young man fired three raking bursts. Bullets lacerated the air above Grady, pinged off the concrete, caused sparks wherever they hit something that was steel. Another such burst was surely forthcoming. There'd already been an inordinate number of misses.

Grady extended his arms.

Gripped the Glock with both hands.

Squeezed off two shots.

At that same moment William also fired twice, so it was impossible to tell whose bullets struck the young man. Not that it mattered. His head snapped back and then forward, as though it were on a spring, and he seemed to be looking down at the wounds in his chest, as he stumbled backward and went down.

Grady had never killed anyone. Perhaps, he thought, he still hadn't.

Another young man, a counterpart of the first, came at a trot down the dock. He didn't appear to be armed. His only concern, apparently, was his fallen comrade. He went directly to the body, kneeled to it, seemed to hug it.

Grady, in his front-down position on the concrete dock, didn't have a good vantage. He saw the young man fumbling with something but he couldn't make out what it was. It was entirely possible the young man was about to ask not to be fired upon, was going to stand and let his grief show, apologize for his fierce-tempered friend.

William, however, had a somewhat better view. He wasn't sure but he believed the live young man was turning the dead one over on his side to use him for cover. Wasn't he digging into the dead one's rear pocket for a fresh clip?

Yes, that was it.

The young man released the depleted clip from the machine pistol and rammed the fresh one in. Began firing, kept well down, held the pistol up and fired over the dead body without taking aim. All that was momentarily visible to Grady was the hand and the machine pistol spurting. One burst, then another.

Fired from that low angle the nine-millimeter bullets glanced and skimmed along the concrete close by Grady. Belly down as he was and exposed head-on to the line of fire, he was extremely vulnerable. He fired back, but his shots just chunked into the flesh of the body that concealed the young man.

The young man was concentrating his fire on Grady, ignoring William for the time being. William realized that, realized how Grady was in peril, pinned down as he was and with no cover. It was only by chance Grady hadn't yet been hit and, William thought, only a matter of time before that happened.

William sidestepped out from behind the steel beam. Waited. There was the possibility that the next spray of fire from the young man would come in his direction. If so, he'd surely catch at least a bullet or two. Still, he kept his nerve, waited. And then, there it was, the black of the machine pistol in the young man's hand. Only in sight for a moment. No time for William to take good aim. He pulled off two shots.

The machine pistol flew from the young man's hand, landed beyond his reach.

The young man raised his bloodied hand and waved. Waved with both hands, signaling that he was giving up. He kneeled up with a pleading, thoroughly capitulating expression on his face. He stood up and turned away from Grady and William. He was counting on the possibility of their having the *good guy* compunction, that which he himself considered foolish and had never abided by. It was the reluctance to shoot someone in the back. He kept his back to them, took a couple of steps and then suddenly leaped into a sprint down the dock, where, no doubt, he'd find another weapon.

Grady was standing by now. He took careful aim, squeezed the slack from the trigger, felt his forefinger meet resistance, maintained the same pressure until the pistol discharged.

The bullet hit the young man where Grady had intended it to hit. The young man clutched at his right leg as it gave way, and he went into a spinning stumble, grabbing at the air as he went over the edge of the dock and dropped the seven feet into the water of the slip.

Two out of the way, how many more?

Grady saw Lesage's sloop was now well clear of the dock and under way down the slip, bound for the bay. He and William ran full out down the dock, although they knew it was futile. Even if they caught up with the sloop the jump to get aboard would be impossible.

When they'd gone about two-thirds of the length of the dock they again came under fire. Literally under it this time. Two more of Lesage's lethal young men had positioned themselves on the steel grate ramp overhung four stories above. They had a decided advantage and were making the most of it with their machine pistols, peppering shots down through the grating, causing lines of pocks on the concrete surface of the dock, near misses.

Grady and William quickly took to the wall, flattened against it. The overhang put them out of sight, but only barely.

Grady glanced to the open end of the huge boat shed. Just in time to catch a glimpse of the white-suited figure of Lesage at the helm in the stern of the sloop. Next the sloop was entirely beyond the docking shed and lost to the darker atmosphere of the bay.

CHAPTER TWENTY-SEVEN

Aboard the sloop.

While Lesage was at the helm, maneuvering the sixty-footer into the channel, Paulette and Julia were below in the main cabin.

Paulette hadn't declared discomfort or given any excuse for removing her clothes. She just proceeded immediately to take them off, did so in a way that distinguished her as a woman who knew best how to undress. There was nothing stripteasing about it, although it was done with regard to Julia's point of view from an upholstered chair across from the side of the bed. How little mind Paulette seemed to be giving to this performance. (What else could it be called? Certainly not a seduction, for as far as Paulette was concerned that part was a *fait accompli*.)

For contrapuntal accompaniment Paulette spoke of things only obliquely relevant. For no particular reason she got off on Agnes Sorel, mistress of Charles VII, claiming that in the fifteenth century the French were a drab, pious bunch until Agnes, who was the first to wear attractive underwear, pluck her brows and make something of her bare breasts.

It appeared that Paulette would go on about Agnes but she broke off the subject abruptly, hummed a few bars that sounded somewhat like Pachelbel's Canon and spoke of the wardrobe of man-tailored clothes she kept in her apartment in Paris. Everything made to measure, of course, and of the finest materials. Not that she wanted to obliterate her gender. It was just how amazingly secure she felt when mannishly dressed, and at the same time jaunty. For her the jauntiness was the most appealing thing, however when she had on trousers she felt handicapped with not being able to use the potent weapon that was her legs, Paulette said. Had Julia ever cross-dressed?

"Not entirely," Julia replied.

Then, from Paulette, came a string of non sequiturs. Such as a confession that she was extravagantly interested in herself—she wished she'd have a day added to her life for every time she'd promised an admirer, male or female, that she'd phone the following day and hadn't—why was it she was ashamed of being unhappy? Didn't she deserve her fair portion of desolation?

Meanwhile she was slipping out of, pulling down, unbuttoning, mistreating one button with haste, tenderly urging the next through its hole. She didn't take off her high heels, knew better than to divest herself of those helpers. Her rings were the last to go. They all cooperated except the large emerald on her second finger. "I always have trouble getting this one off," she said as she twisted and tugged it and momentarily gave up on it.

She pulled open the drawer of the bedside cabinet, carelessly dropped the other rings in and left the drawer open.

In the drawer, Julia noticed, was the black of a small-caliber automatic pistol and the tan of the chamois sack containing the pearls. Lesage had placed the sack in that drawer, had brought the pearls along for starters, he'd said, to throw into the yield before they'd even opened an oyster. Generous of him, he'd been told.

Paulette got two kimonos from the closet. They were identical, of pale lavender silk. Substantial, slippery silk, at least eighteen mommes weight. She put one on, casually tied its sash and tossed the other to Julia.

Julia didn't catch it, didn't try, allowed the kimono to slide to the floor and let it lie.

Paulette saw that as a sign that Julia was having misgivings.

Second or third thoughts about this escapade, perhaps even about her. The latter was unthinkable. "Don't be concerned about Daniel," she told Julia, "he only talks a good fuck."

Julia smiled a fraction.

Paulette believed she had Julia back on track. She returned her attention to the stubborn emerald ring, went into the adjacent head to soap up the finger.

At once Julia removed the sack of pearls from the drawer. Put them in her shoulder bag. Stepped noiselessly out of the main cabin and locked the door from the outside. She went aft, up the companionway ladder to be on deck. She joined Lesage there behind the wheel. He was preoccupied with reading the green strobing buoys that marked the channel of the bay, where it ran between the oyster-bearing rafts. There was about a forty-degree turn in the meandering channel just then and he took it easily. He had the sloop running on minimal power for slow but sure going.

"You're obviously quite a sailor," Julia said.

"I've done my share," Lesage said immodestly.

"It's reassuring to know I'm in such capable hands," Julia told him.

He concurred with a grunt, took out a pack of Gauloises from the breast pocket of his white flannel jacket and pulled one from the pack with his lips. Lighted it up. Usually when at the helm he was a no-hands smoker.

Julia pointed to a lever on the control panel. "What's that?"

Lesage told her it was the throttle.

She asked about other indicators and devices on the panel, appeared to be keenly interested, and he told her what each was, told her, "When we get out of the bay I'll let you take the wheel."

"Oh, no," she said brazenly, "we've better things to do." And with that she went and sat on the aft edge of the cabin trunk, facing him about ten feet away. She could faintly hear Paulette trying the main cabin door down below, rattling it and pounding on it. She imagined the fury in Paulette's eyes, that soft dark brown turned obdurate. She reached into her shoulder bag, kept the chamois sack hidden while she dilated its drawstring and got a fistful of the pearls.

"This is a much better boat," she said levelly.

"Huh?"

"Better than that old one you had, the one with the rotting sails."

"What the fuck are you talking about?" Lesage asked sourly.

Julia threw one of the pearls at him. It whizzed by his head, and went into the bay. He only barely saw it go by, had no idea what it was. Just something she'd thrown.

She threw two more, both missed him, and he decided she was being playful. Maybe she was on something, he thought. She had that detached, unpredictable look about her. He'd probably misheard that rotting sail remark.

Julia threw another. This one caught him high on the cheek. Lesage saw it was a blue pearl when it dropped to the slanted surface of the control console and rolled off.

"Crazy bitch!" he growled. He started toward her, momentarily forgetting he had to tend the wheel. The most difficult portion of the channel was coming up, where it was more winding and became narrower between sections of oyster rafts. The next buoy was a crucial one. He kept well clear of it.

Julia pelted him with more pearls, a fistful.

"*Con!*" Lessage shouted. "*Va te fair éculer!*" He was seething, and when she threw another fistful he reversed the engine and shut it down. The most that would happen was the sloop would give one of the rafts a little bump, he thought. Even if a bit more than a bump he had to deal with this woman. She'd already thrown away a fortune. Paulette was to blame. If it hadn't been for Paulette he would never have gotten into it. He'd make Paulette pay, and this Julia woman. He came around from the wheel and lunged at Julia.

She easily evaded him, was up on the cabin trunk, retreating along it.

He vowed to his anger that the first thing of hers he got hold of, arm, leg, neck, whatever, he'd break.

At that moment Grady and William were working their way toward the open end of the docking shed. The overhang of the steel ramp four stories above helped conceal them, however it was only a matter of time before their adversaries went around to the ramp on the opposite side of the shed to have a clear shot at them.

They sidled along, pressed against the wall, not swiftly enough to suit Grady. He knew that by now Lesage's sloop would be at least halfway out the channel. Once it was out of the bay there'd be no catching it.

He could only guess where the tender boats might be tied up. He believed they'd be somewhere near the end of the slip, which with all their daily coming and going to and from the bay was the logical place for them. The width of the dock and the distance from the edge of the dock to the water prevented him from seeing if they were there. He wouldn't know until he got to the edge.

They made a dash for it. Grady leading the way, William right behind, turning and firing up to the ramp.

Bursts of bullets pocked the concrete close around, ricocheted and stung their legs. When they reached the edge they found no tenders there, but two were tied up back about ten yards. They ran back along the edge like conveyed targets in a shooting gallery. Anyone who was a half-decent shot with a rifle could have easily picked them off, however strafing and spraying, not precision, were the special merits of machine pistols.

Grady and William dove into the tender. Grady scrambled to its outboard engine, dropped its drive shaft and propeller into the water and gave its starter rope a yank. And another. The engine nearly started on the third, desperate yank, definitely started on the fourth. Grady twisted the throttle on the steering arm. Wild shots were still being fired at them as they sped down the slip and out of the shed.

Lesage was now up on the cabin trunk, stalking Julia.

He was sure he'd eventually get her, corner her and have his way with her. He was going to enjoy killing her and, he suggested to himself, his pleasure shouldn't end there. After killing her he should fuck her. And make Paulette watch.

Julia jumped down from the forward edge of the cabin trunk to the foredeck.

Lesage kept coming.

She kept retreating in the direction of the bow. She didn't go all the way to the bowsprit, held her ground short of it and defied Lesage. "Your old fat boat couldn't handle rough weather, remember?" she said. "That old beat-up black boat with the rotting sails."

No doubt about what she'd said this time. It stopped Lesage, bewildered and distracted him so that when he lunged at her she ducked in under his grab and tauntingly proceeded up the portside deck access in the direction of the stern.

He continued to stalk her, hated her. How could she know about that old boat? he wondered. All the more reason to kill her.

She had no more pearls to throw.

She reached into her shoulder bag for something else.

At that moment she sensed physical changes taking place in herself. Sensed that the proportions of her body were being altered and that she was suddenly thinner, a little taller. Sensed that her hair was turning black and becoming more heavily textured. Her cheekbones more prominent, the shape of her eyes and the way they were set in their sockets, changed. Didn't she now have more forehead, less chin?

She sensed that she was undergoing mental changes as well. Somehow her memory was transformed, dilated so she could see inwards all the way to a small girl clutching her mother's long hair and the mother instructing her to take deep breaths and telling her to hold on as she took the child on an underwater ride.

Julia brought out the *dah-she* knife, held it up by its whalebone handle, allowed the moon to play upon its blade and disclose its razor-sharp cutting edge. "Buddha is generous," she said. However, as those words came through Julia's voice box she knew it wasn't her voice, rather one higher pitched and delicate. "Is that not true, Monsieur Bertin?" were words she couldn't restrain.

Lesage became Bertin. For nearly twenty years no one had called him by that name. Hearing the name said further impacted his sudden terror. He tried to steady himself, told himself it was an apparition, not really the Japanese ama, Setsu, poised there flashing the knife at him. However, his eyes told his brain to believe it and he felt the blood rush from his extremities, leaving him weak and hardly able to take a breath, incapable of stopping her as she went to the stern, to the control console.

She turned on the engine, pushed the throttle lever to full ahead, waited a few moments to attain speed before spinning the hydraulic helm.

The sloop veered so sharply to port it seemed it would overturn. It pitched up and slammed down on the side of its hull and hadn't recovered balance when it collided with a section of rafts from which pearl oysters were hung and sleeping. It raked those rafts, disturbed them, scraped along the uneven ends of the heavy bamboo poles that formed the rafts.

It didn't stop there, was hardly slowed. As though it was a drunk bent on causing destruction the sloop caromed diagonally across the channel to ram another section of rafts. Plowed bow first right into it, causing the fiberglass hull to scream as it was abraded and the cross-hatched bamboo poles of the rafts to splinter and snap apart.

The collision sent Bertin flying from the side deck access all the way forward to the bowsprit. He made a grab for the headstay, the line that ran from the bow up to the masthead, had it for an instant, but his momentum was too great for his grasp, and next he knew the lifeline cut across the small of his back to flip him overboard.

He caught a glimpse of one of the green strobing buoys before he struck the water and plunged past the shreds of bamboo afloat on it. Then all was dark, wet and he was completely disoriented. Which way to the surface? He could only guess, and even if he guessed right he couldn't get to it.

Because of his white flannel suit.

Saturated, it seemed to outweigh him and it wasn't something he could just simply let go of. It and its weight had him contained, buttoned and belted. He'd never be able to get out of it in time. What's more, one of the trouser legs was caught on something, caught on the wire mesh of one of the oyster cages.

Going to drown, Bertin thought.

Among the oysters.

Julia was also in the water. She spotted his white suit and swam to him. Swam around him like a predacious sea creature, observing his struggle, enjoying his plight. She still had the *dah-she* knife in hand, was slashing the water around him with it, coming closer and closer, taunting him with his death.

Before she got to use the knife on him, bubbles emerged from his nose and mouth and he began breathing water.

No matter that he was dead, the need to slash him still had its hold on her. He was hung there limply, the current of the bay slowly moving his free extremities, his head alternately floating chin down and chin up. When it was chin up there was the stretch

of his throat for her desire to open his flesh from earlobe to earlobe. She extended the moment, noticing with pleasure his eyes
were fixed corpse-wide, their whites an eerie bluish-white, a bit
fluorescent.

His head floated back.

His throat was presented.

However, Julia's hand that held the *dah-she* knife for some reason
refused to supply the force needed to make the slash. That which
had been providing it with the fuel of vengeance had all at once
departed, leaving Julia so that she was only Julia with the *dah-she* in
hand.

A vile thing, the knife. Julia released it abruptly and it spiraled,
whalebone handle first, down the dark steeps. Only moments ago
she'd had an ample reserve of breath but now her lungs were complaining. She kicked to the surface.

How grateful she was to see the night sky, the speckled heavens,
and then Grady and William coming in the tender to pull her
aboard.

CHAPTER TWENTY-EIGHT

The next morning.

Grady, Julia and William joined Kumura at his usual spot on the far end of the terrace. He was having a light breakfast, no Devonshire splits or any of that, just melon, toast and jam, coffee and tea.

When they'd taken places and were settled, Kumura commented on how rested they looked, how they must have slept soundly. "Except you, Grady," he said wryly. "You appear to be a bit...how shall I best put it?...depleted, yes, that's it exactly...depleted around the edges."

"Thank you," Julia arched.

"Pity about Lesage drowning like that," Kumura said to get that obligatory subject over and done with. "I've already made arrangements. In fact, at this very moment his body is on its way to France, presumably for a Foreign Legion funeral with all the military trappings. Lesage would have wanted that, don't you think?"

The irony provoked grins.

"As for Paulette, she departed sometime during the night.

Abandoned the Corniche at the airport and took off for who knows where."

To meet someone someplace whom she can say she'd met any number of other places, Julia thought.

"She certainly made a mess of the cabin door," Kumura said. "Shot the bloody hell out of it. Evidently in a panic trying to get out, although I still don't see how she could have possibly locked herself in."

"That's just one mystery," Grady said.

"What about these?" William asked. He placed two bright blue pearls on the pale blue tablecloth.

Kumura took them up, studied them briefly with intense interest. "Where did you get these?"

William told him.

"Are they naturals?" Kumura asked.

"You tell me," William said.

"No, I defer to an expert." Kumura handed the two pearls to Grady, who barely made a fist around them before pronouncing them cultured and dyed. (He'd had a look at them earlier with his loupe.)

"I trust your insight," Kumura said, "but I must say I've no idea how such blues should be in Lesage's possession."

"Then it remains a mystery," Julia put in conclusively. She'd been looking out at the bay and imagining how she'd paint it. She felt newly spirited, longing to face a fresh canvas, eager to get on with her life with Grady. So different a person than she'd been before. She loved him, no doubt about that. He would be the recipient of her time. She wasn't going to try to understand the various strange ways she'd behaved, no use chasing after such answers. Better that she accept what she'd experienced, benefit by it, know that from here on in she needn't give any energy to doubt or despair at being insular. "May I please have more coffee?" she said to one of the attending servants. Grady passed her the toast. She slathered a piece deservedly with damson preserves.

Kumura folded the *London Times* he'd been reading, placed it aside, revealing beneath it a legal document. "The agreement I had with Lesage now proves to be a provident one," he said. "It stipulates without the hindrance of fine print that upon his untimely or"—he said aside—"even his timely death, all rights to the pearl farm here shall revert to me. That includes as well the house down the way, its contents, cars, and so on, everything of Lesage's."

"Some deal," Grady commented.

"As it turns out," Kumura agreed phlegmatically, "the only distressing thing is how this farm could tie me down if I let it. Not that I'm not interested and proud of it and all that, but I'm at the point where I'd prefer to be able to come and go when I please. For example, this afternoon I leave for New York and then on to London and Milan. I have pressing appointments in those places, and I'd like to have the liberty of getting waylaid if I so choose. So, I desperately need someone to look after Bang Wan for me, someone who knows pearls, loves pearls."

"What would that person get in return?" Grady asked.

"Same as Lesage received," Kumura told him, "limited partnership, proportionate share of profits."

"Lesage's house?"

"Included."

"And contents."

"Of course. Will you do it?"

It was a sweet offer. Grady appeared to be turning it over in his mind. He pictured himself either here forever in Bang Wan or in San Francisco. No contest. "William's your man," Grady said.

William sat up.

"He told me just the other night that he was ready to fold the Lady So Remembered Gem-Cutting Factory," Grady said. "Didn't you, William?"

William managed a yes.

"I'd considered putting it to William," Kumura improvised. "It was just that I thought, considering the circumstances, you should have first shot."

"But you agree to William?"

"Offhand I can't think of any reason why I shouldn't," Kumura replied.

"Is that a yes?"

Kumura considered a moment and said it was.

"That's good," Grady said, "because I promised him we'd be doing a lot of business together."

Kumura was genuinely satisfied with this spontaneously revised arrangement. He extended his hand.

William shook it.

Done?

Done.

"Now," Grady said, "what about my San Francisco deal? I suppose now you want no part of me, or maybe that was just bullshit all the way."

Kumura was amused. "To the contrary, Grady," he said. "I've had your contract drawn up. In fact, I have it right here." He handed the legal document to Grady, who, in looking it over, skipped those parts that said what he had to do and read twice those parts that said what he'd get. Kumura, true to his nature, had been more generous than he'd initially proposed.

"Will you sign?" Kumura asked.

Grady had already given it enough advance thought, just in case. "On two conditions," he said. "First, I get time off to get married." He glanced to Julia. This still wasn't asking her properly, but she let it go.

"And your second condition?"

"I get to borrow your ketch for a week starting tomorrow."

AUTHOR'S NOTE

In 1989 the State Law and Order Restoration Council of Burma officially changed many well-established names. It was decreed that henceforth the Union of Burma would be referred to as the Union of Myanmar and the city of Rangoon would be called Yangon. For the sake of clarity the author has taken the license of using the old and more familiar designations.